terms & conditions

terms & conditions

a novel

JENSEN PARKER

Strangers Book Three

Made for More Publishing, LLC

Cover Design: Jensen Parker

Alpha'd: Ashley Vaccaro, Alexandra Cowell

Editing: Sophie B. Murphy, Eloquent Inkblot LLC.

ISBN (e-book) : 979-8-9879868-7-5

ISBN (printed) : 979-8-9879868-6-8

Published by Made for More Publishing, LLC.

https://www.jensenparker.com

For the ones who've lost something they never thought they would...
Me too.

This book is for the ones who like to deal with things in silence, but still need a little help now and then...

Author's Note

Terms & Conditions is the third book in the Strangers Series and can be read as a standalone. All books in the series will be interconnected standalone stories, however I suggest reading them in order for better enjoyment.

This book contains scenes with discussions of mature subject matter, including death, familicide, grief, anxiety, on-page sexual content, drinking, and explicit language, and is intended for mature audiences.

- *Jensen*

Strangers Series
Main Cast of Characters

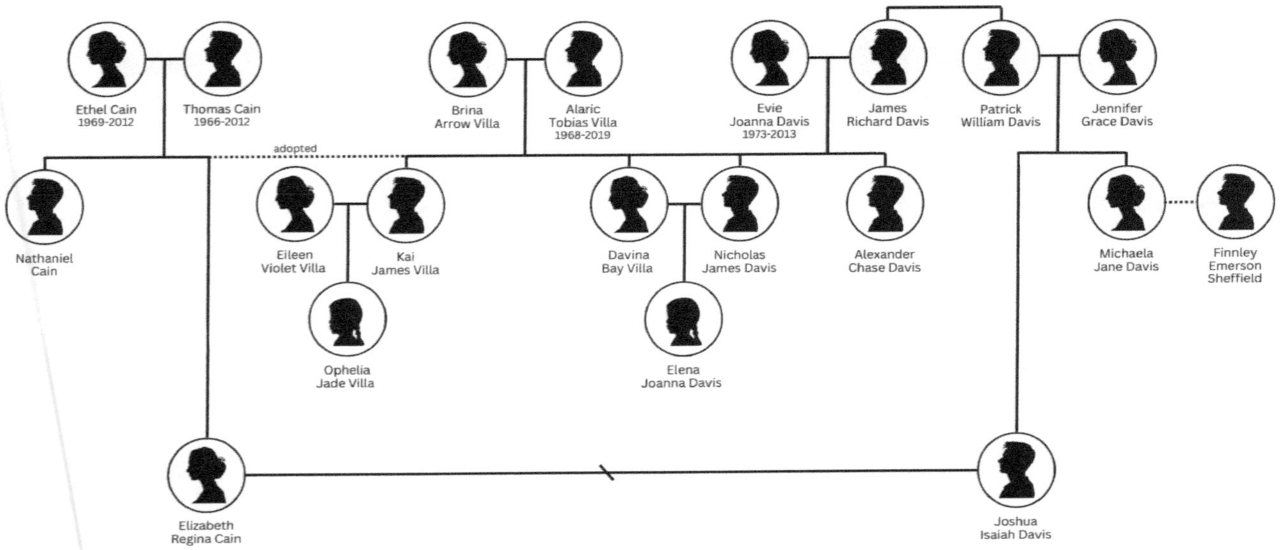

Characters are products of Jensen Parker's imagination or used fictitiously.

Before You Leave Me - Alex Warren
Forever After All - Luke Combs
Never Really Over - Katy Perry
Deeper Love - Nick Jonas
grave - Tate McRae
I Choose You - Forest Blakk
Kiss Me Goodnight - Alexandra Kay
Let Her Go - Passenger
Seasons - Thirty Seconds to Mars
loml - Taylor Swift
Strangers - Kameron Marlow & Ella Langley
We're Not Friends - Ingrid Andress
Save You a Seat - Alex Warren
Goodbye to You - Michelle Branch
I Remember - Forest Blakk
With Me - Underclass Hero
Don't Speak - Jonas Brothers
Message In A Bottle (Taylor's Version) [From The Vault] - Taylor Swift
High Road - Koe Wetzel & Jessie Murphy
Wine Into Whiskey - Tucker Wetmore
Half-Life - Duncan Sheik
Chainsaw - Nick Jonas
Have Yourself A Merry Little Christmas (feat. Jensen Ackles) - Jason Manns
The One That Got Away - Katy Perry
Hesitate - Jonas Brothers
Birds Still Sing - Taylor Acorn
That's So True - Gracie Abrams
Better Me For You (Brown Eyes) - Max McNown
Down Bad - Taylor Swift
It Was Me - Lauren Alania
Little Do You Know - Alex & Sierra
i almost do - Ashley Cooke
Sorry - Jonas Brothers
If I Knew - Bruno Mars
Breathe - Michelle Branch
Dammit - Alexandra Kay
Save Me - Forty Foot Echo
Burning Down (with Joe Jonas) - Alex Warren
Bigger Person - Lauren Spencer Smith
Chase Her - Bailey Zimmerman
Trouble With A Heartbreak - Jason Aldean

Apple Music

Spotify

CHARACTER CATCH UP

I write my books as interconnected standalone stories, but you will see characters from the other books involved in this book's events.
If this is the first time we're meeting, WELCOME! Here's a little guide to get you caught up...

Nick Davis and **Nina Villa** have their own book, ***Until Now***, which is the first book of the Strangers series. It is a fake dating, forced proximity, one bed romance. As you will see in all of the books, they are what brings all of these characters together, so they will be involved (a lot!). *Terms & Conditions* takes place almost seven years after the events of *Until Now.*

Michaela Davis and **Finn Sheffield** have their own book, ***Strictly Business***, which is the second book of the Strangers series. It is an enemies-to-lovers, brother's best friend romance. Michaela is Josh's little sister and Finn is his best friend. They couldn't stand each other up until a year <u>before</u> the events of *Terms & Conditions.*

Alex Davis is Nick's little brother, and Josh's cousin.

Kai Villa is Nina's older brother, married to **Eileen Villa**.

Elizabeth Cain-Davis is the adopted daughter of the Villa family, therefore is referred to sometimes as the third Villa child or sister to Nina and Kai.

Georgie Golding, **Lauren (Lola) Montgomery**, and **Selena Hart** went to college in Savannah with Elizabeth. The four of them go on an annual trip to Palm Valley during the holiday season, usually accompanied by their significant others. **Elijah Prince**, who dates Selena, went to university with Josh. **Noah Thompson** is married to Georgie. **Jeremy Vos** is dating Lola.

That's all I'm going to say about the characters for now! There will be plenty of breadcrumbs within these pages of what's to come...And if you want to see the full connection between everyone, please check out the family tree provided earlier a few pages ahead of this!

Happy reading.

TERMS AND CONDITIONS

A document governing the contractual relationship between the provider of a service and its user explaining how a product or service may be used, in a legally binding way.

terms (noun)
\ tərms \
1. provisions that determine the nature and scope of an agreement
2. a limited or definite extent of time
3. the whole period for which an estate is granted

conditions (noun)
\ kən-di-shən \
1. a premise upon which the fulfillment of an agreement depends
2. a provision making the effect of a legal instrument contingent upon an uncertain event
3. a restricting or modifying factor

marriage (noun)
\ mer-ij \
1. the state of being united as spouses in a consensual relationship recognized by law.
2. a formal agreement between two companies or enterprises to combine operations, resources, etc., for mutual benefit.

MARRIAGE CONTRACT

TERMS AND CONDITIONS

1. Joshua Isaiah Davis (Josh) will receive full immunity in the case of Henderson v. Theta Pi (Chadwick University Chapter). Josh will graduate from Chadwick University School of Business after completing the Spring 2016 Semester and receive a paid internship at the marketing firm of his choosing.

2. Elizabeth Regina Cain (Elizabeth) will receive the full inheritance from the Cain Estate following the execution of this contract. Elizabeth has the right to attend any school she wishes. Half the cost will be paid by the Villa family.

3. Josh and Elizabeth will make a minimum of ten public appearances every year.

> a) Appearances include but are not limited to: birthdays, anniversaries, Easter, Mother's Day, Father's Day, Thanksgiving, Christmas, and one vacation.

> b) The tenth event is up to their discretion.

4. Josh and Elizabeth are to marry following Elizabeth's graduation from the school of her choice or any day beforehand of their choosing.

> a) If they choose to wait until after her graduation, they will have six months to be wed.

5. Josh and Elizabeth are to remain married for a <u>minimum</u> of six and a half years.

> a) Should divorce occur before that time frame, the party who files agrees to pay a dissolution fee to the other party of an amount to be agreed upon.

6. Josh and Elizabeth must reside in the same house after the wedding until a legal separation has been filed.

> a) Consummation of the marriage and/or sleeping in the same

room is not a requirement.

b) A joint bank account will be opened and used for payment of household bills and expenses; each party will put in half the cost each month.

7.Josh and Elizabeth are not to tell anyone about the arrangement.

a) The only time either party may tell someone outside of the known parties (i.e. Joshua Davis, Elizabeth Cain, Brina Villa, Jennifer Davis, and Benjamin Campbell) is if they decide to date outside the arrangement. The decision must be agreed upon by both Josh and Elizabeth.

b) Dating outside of the arrangement is allowed. Other person(s) must be aware nothing long-term will come of their relationship while the arrangement is ongoing and extramarital relationships should not be instigated with anyone within the immediate area of Winchester, Bridgeport, or wherever they decide to reside.

8. If Josh and Elizabeth choose to dissolve the union, the year of separation under South Carolina law <u>will</u> count toward the final year.

a) Any debt accumulated during the arrangement will be split 50/50 between Josh and Elizabeth.

b) Josh will have no claim to any part of the Cain Estate in a separation.

c) Any property accumulated during the arrangement will be divided between Josh and Elizabeth. Property acquired before the arrangement will remain an asset of the sole proprietor.

9. In the event of death or great bodily harm before the end of the arrangement:

a) In the event of great bodily harm, the surviving party may decide how to proceed, whether to continue the marriage or end the arrangement. Upon separation, things will proceed as discussed in Term 8. Further, no dissolution fee will be required if separation occurs before the minimum period laid out in Term 5.

b) In the event of death, the surviving party (Survivor) will retain all assets of the deceased party (Deceased). Survivor will follow any and all terms laid out in Deceased's written will.

10. The Last Hoorah Clause

a) Either party may invoke this clause if a separation has been agreed upon.

b) The purpose of this clause is to afford the invoking party one final occasion or appearance in the relationship for whatever reason.

one

THEN

November 2015

"WHAT ARE WE DOING here?" I ask as we pull up to the massive wooden gate.

Behind those doors lies the lakefront estate of none other than the Villa family—the richest family this side of Appalachia. Correction: they're one of the wealthiest families in the world—think Walton and Rockefeller—and somehow, they decided to make the small town of Winchester, South Carolina, their home.

Before Mom can ring the call button, the doors swing open to reveal a winding red-brick driveway that veers to the right and disappears up a slope. As we drive through the gates, it feels like we've stepped into what I think the Tuscan countryside must feel like. Driving through an archway, we're greeted by the expansive estate. The house's exterior is made from the kind of stone you see on Tuscan villas in the movies. I wouldn't be surprised if they airlifted the thing all the way from Italy.

Kidding…kind of.

"You forgot to mention the part where the Villas were

involved."

"Just hold your horses, Josh," Mom says, driving around the circle and pulling into a small parking area off to the side. "Mrs. Villa has been gracious enough to invite us over to discuss a possible solution for your little *problem*, and you're not going to be rude."

Mrs. Villa—as in Brina Villa? My mother said we would find a solution to my problem, but she didn't say we were making a deal with the Devil. Brina is known for being a nightmare, especially when it comes to her daughter.

My sister, Michaela, introduced me to the daughter of the Villa family last year after they met at Rosecliffe University, and Nina shattered any preconceived notion I had about her. I got the sense there was more to her story than met the eye—and Brina Villa had a lot to do with it. Nina doesn't talk about it much, but that doesn't stop the rest of Winchester from sharing their opinions.

A grand, white-stone staircase leads up to a large, arched wooden door similar to those at the front gate. The door swings open before we even make it up the stairs. Brina stands there with a Cheshire smile. She's dressed in a hot pink suit with a black undershirt and black strappy heels—a bit overdressed for a day at home, if you ask me, but sure.

"Jen," Brina exclaims. "So glad you could make it!" She plants a kiss on each of my mother's cheeks and turns to me. "And you must be Joshua."

"Josh is fine," I say, earning a glare from Mom. "Nice to meet you, Mrs. Villa."

"Brina, please. I have a feeling we're going to get to know each other *very* well." The way she says it makes my stomach churn, and I have a feeling I'm not going to like what's about to happen. "Come, come, let's get out of this heat."

Brina ushers us inside a two-story rounded foyer, and my eyes are immediately drawn to the painted ceiling depicting ancient Romans lying about half-naked—interesting choice. Stepping through an archway, I decide the interior looks like it was pulled from a magazine, which, let's be real, it probably was. The open living area includes both a sitting and dining space with a fireplace overlooking a back wall made of windows. Double doors on both ends open to a large courtyard.

Brina leads us down the right side of a white stone hallway that goes in both directions. Two more arched wooden doors open to the kitchen, off of which a less (but still) formal living area is located down two steps. Two women I don't recognize cook in the kitchen, but they don't even acknowledge us when we pass through to the dining area. Just underneath a large window overlooking the backyard and the lake is a long, glass table where Elizabeth Cain, adopted daughter of the Villa family, sits with a steaming cup in front of her.

What is she doing here?

Our eyes meet, and hers narrow slightly. She's not happy, but I'm not sure if that's because I'm here or because of what is about to happen.

"Sit, sit, Anna will be finished with brunch soon," Brina instructs, falling into the chair at the head of the table. She turns to Elizabeth. "I'm glad you made it."

Elizabeth tears her gaze from mine, but she doesn't look any happier than when she looked at me.

"What did you tell Davina?" Brina asks, taking the cup of coffee one of the chefs offers her without looking up. Her bright, steely eyes don't match the smile she offers over the rim of the cup.

"Nothing, this doesn't concern her," Elizabeth quips.

Brina huffs. "And when she asks *why* you had to leave her company this morning?"

"I have other things to do besides be glued to her side day in and day out, despite what you may think, Brina."

I don't know about that. Elizabeth and Nina are inseparable, and while they may only be sisters in a legal sense, you'd never know the difference. I'm not sure where Michaela fits into the equation, but after meeting Nina in class last fall, she's been with them almost every day. That's how we met—Elizabeth and I—and it was obvious we were like two pieces of different puzzles. It was her attitude I disliked most. The holier-than-thou pretentiousness that made it seem like she was better than everyone else. While we've only met a handful of times, usually when Nina drags her along, it always ends the same: one of us pissed off and the other one satisfied.

"Can we get this over with? I'm driving to Savannah tonight," Elizabeth says, taking a sip of her tea.

"Don't get ahead of yourself." Brina smirks. "Nothing has been set in stone."

"Then, how about we get started."

"Soon," Brina says as the two chefs bring plates to the table. "There's no use rushing what you can't control."

The blonde chef, who Brina called Anna earlier, sets a fresh mug of coffee in front of Brina before stalking back to the kitchen to begin preparing yet another meal. I'm used to Mom making all of our meals; I never considered the fact that some people have private chefs to do it for them. The other chef—Janet, I think—left thirty minutes ago to get something from the store. I have a feeling she is taking her time because it doesn't seem like breaks are much of a thing around here.

Brunch was uneventful, the only conversation happening between Brina and Mom. It seemed like they were dancing around the real topic of conversation: why we're here. We've been sitting here for almost an hour and a half, and I still have no idea why that is.

"Now that we've had time to enjoy ourselves, it's time to get down to business," Brina finally says, taking a folder from a drawer in the antique hutch behind her. She sets it down on the table and looks my mother in the eye. "I've had my lawyer draw up an agreement, should the kids like what we are about to propose."

"And what is that exactly?" I ask.

"Well, Joshua, it seems you've gotten yourself into a bit of a situation. Correct?"

A wave of shame rolls through me, crescendoing with a thick coat of nausea stuck in my throat, but I force it back down. I glance at Mom, but she won't look at me. She hasn't said, but I know she's disappointed. Wondering where she went wrong. Wondering how her straight-A, straight-laced son could do something like this. If you asked my parents, they'd probably tell you I never drank or smoked or did anything wrong growing up. I was the model child everyone should strive to have. Little did they know that I wasn't as straight-laced as they thought. But I guess that's part of being a kid, isn't it?

"And Elizabeth here wants *all* of her inheritance and to attend her dream school," Brina says, looking at Elizabeth. "Isn't that correct?"

Elizabeth refuses to meet her gaze but meets mine briefly.

"What does that have to do with me?" I ask.

"There is a way to solve both of your predicaments." Brina opens the folder and lays it out in front of me.

Skimming over the first few lines, my stomach plummets at the words on the page. I look at my mom again. Surely this is a joke. She can't honestly think this is going to solve anything. "An arranged marriage? You're insane."

"Josh," Mom starts, but Brina lifts her hand, silencing her.

"I understand your confusion, Joshua, but it's really very simple. Elizabeth can't receive her full inheritance until she marries, per the will of her late parents, and she wants to attend the Savannah College of Art and Design, not Duke, for photography. Thomas and Ethel were adamant that Elizabeth attend her father's alma mater, another stipulation if she wants her college paid for. However, Duke doesn't have the program she wants. And you, Josh, need help making your situation disappear. I can make that happen, along with making sure you graduate *on time* and get a job."

Can she really do all of that?

That Cheshire smile creeps its way back onto her face. She knows she almost has me hooked. "In case you've forgotten, I'm Brina Villa. I may not be my husband, but that name still means something."

I swallow the lump building in my throat and meet Elizabeth's gaze across the table. She's hard to read, but she doesn't seem shocked by any of this, which means Brina has already proposed the idea to her, and the fact that she's sitting here tells me she's willing to accept it.

"We can't just...get married, everyone we know would be a little suspicious considering"—I motion between myself and Elizabeth—"we don't get along."

"Yes, that's all been laid out in the paperwork." Brina flips through the pages before landing on the one she wants. At the top of the page, in large, bold letters, it says: ***TERMS AND CONDITIONS.***

Beneath it, there are ten points. I skim them, each one detailing every aspect of our lives. The more I read, the more surreal this all becomes. Brina has thought of everything, and I can't help but wonder how long she's been planning this. Has she always wanted to rid the family of their adopted daughter?

"Six years of marriage is a long time considering it'll be four years of courting if we wait until she graduates," I say, looking up from the list and referring to term number five.

"Six and a half is the perfect number." Brina smiles. "Believable and random. Anything shorter would be suspicious."

"Nina will never believe this," I say. Not to mention, Elizabeth is dating William Cawthorn, son of a local congressman. Wouldn't it seem strange that she'd dump *him* for someone like me? We could probably fool everyone else, but Nina would see straight through it.

"She will if we sell it right," Elizabeth says, drawing everyone's attention.

two

NOW

I WANT A DIVORCE.

Those four words shouldn't have come as a surprise after spending most of the last year apart. They shouldn't have come as a surprise after spending our entire relationship lying. It was only a matter of time until one of us—more likely her—pulled the trigger. I figured there are plenty of people who have been put into arranged marriages that make it work, right? Some of them even end up falling in love. I guess that was never in the cards ~~for her~~ for us.

We kept our secret for over ten years. What started in December 2015 came crumbling down when I made a dumb mistake, and she realized our time, as required per the contract, was almost up. There was a division between us. One that had always existed but that we chose to ignore until we couldn't anymore. The longer we stayed together, the more we grew apart. She started coming home less and less until she didn't come home at all. I couldn't hold it in any longer. I told my best friend, Finn, last month. There were a lot of questions, but he took it well, I think. I'm not sure how you're supposed to take that kind of news. A few days later, I told Nick, my cousin and best friend, who didn't take it as well.

"I'm sorry," Nick said after a moment. He rubbed the tension growing between his eyebrows. "You're going to have to repeat yourself. I could almost swear you just said you're in an *arranged marriage.*"

"That is what I said."

He downed the whiskey in his glass, letting the words process before finally saying, "Josh, what the actual fuck?"

Nick stared at me across the desk of his home office like I had four heads. The same guilt I had felt over the years raged through me. I hated it—lying to him, to my sister, to everyone... Nick and I had been best friends our whole lives, even before my family moved back to Dad's hometown of Bridgeport, South Carolina. We were born just shy of two months apart, and despite the distance from Bridgeport to Gainesville, he always felt more like a sibling than a cousin. When we moved, it was the best belated birthday gift a four year old could ask for. We went from a seven-hour drive to ten minutes down the road. "You guys, you seemed so...*perfect.* So put together. So...in love."

"You'd know all about that, wouldn't you?" I swirled the whiskey in my glass.

On the outside, Nick and his wife appear to have a picture-perfect marriage, but don't be fooled; they've had their problems. What started as a simple favor to get Nina's mother off her back ended up being a can of worms no one ever expected to open. Despite everything that had happened between them (a fake relationship, blackmail, keeping secrets from each other, the death of her father—oh, and don't forget her mom fucking her ex-boyfriend), they are happy. Genuinely happy and in love. Watching them make it work despite everything...I guess I thought Elizabeth and I could do the same.

It felt good to tell the truth. This was a secret I'd been hiding for a long time, and as time passed, it got harder and harder to keep. Every time I thought we were getting somewhere... something would come along and tear us apart.

"What is it with this group of people and keeping secrets?" Nick scoffed.

"It's what the Villas are good at."

"Well, apparently, the Davises aren't far off." Nick shook his head and poured more whiskey into his glass and mine, even though I still had half of what he poured before. He mumbled something to himself before draining the glass again.

That was almost two months ago.

Since then, I've spent most of my time working. A recent promotion at work has kept me so busy that I wasn't even going to come today, but my sister threatened to kidnap me if I didn't show up. Considering who she's engaged to...I have no doubt Finn would make it happen. I get the distinct feeling they made the same threat to Elizabeth because she looked as annoyed as I felt when she walked in the door behind Nina.

Don't get me wrong, I'm happy to see my family, but this is the last place I want to be. Spending time with my soon-to-be ex-wife on Halloween isn't exactly the highlight of my day. Not to mention, her birthday is tomorrow, and I'm sure she's overjoyed to be here with me...

"Can you help Nick move those?" Nina asks, pointing to the oversized letters that spell out BOO and the balloon arch sitting off to the side of the dining room.

The whole place has been decorated top to bottom for the Halloween party my sister is throwing—the first of many in the new condo she and Finn have purchased together. I thought the décor was a little over the top when I walked in, but Michaela wants everything to be perfect. So, when Ophelia asked for a balloon arch and light bulb letters, she got them.

Ophelia is Nina's four year old niece and her father's pride and joy. She's had Nina's brother, Kai, wrapped around her little finger from the day she was born, and it didn't take long for her to do the same thing to my sister. They had become close even before Nick and Nina got married, which made them officially *my* family.

Our families have blended seamlessly, especially after Nick married Nina. I feel bad for Nina; she's trying to remain neutral in the battle between me and Liz, but I know it's hard on her. We didn't think about what would happen if or when we ever decided to end the arrangement. Or at least I didn't. Our lives had become too intertwined.

"Aye, aye, Captain." I salute Nina with a small smile. She's wearing a green neon shirt made to look like Mike Wazowski from Monsters, Inc.

In her arms is a tiny Boo in that cute purple monster costume with the googly eyes on top—you know the one. Inside is Elena Joanna Davis, Nick and Nina's two-month-old daughter. Just before their second "official" wedding last year, Nina was told there didn't seem to be much hope of her getting pregnant after none of the medical interventions had worked. Then, she woke up in mid-January sick as a dog and, thinking she had caught the flu, went to the doctor a week later only to find out she was five weeks pregnant. Elena came a few weeks early but is healthy as a horse and the sweetest baby ever. And that kid looks more and more like her mother every day (she has Nick's eyes, though). Just like Ophelia looks more like Nina's older brother, Kai, every time I see her. Those Villa genes are strong.

"Where are we moving these?" I ask Nick, who shrugs.

"She said anywhere but here," he says, throwing back the hood of his Sulley costume. "She told Michaela it was going to be in the way, but Mic said just wait and see. Now here we are…"

"Foyer?" I motion behind us through the doorway that

leads out of the living room and into the grand foyer.

"Works for me," he says, lifting his side of the balloon wall.

The penthouse Finn and Michaela purchased earlier this year is extravagant. The place has two floors, five bedrooms, six bathrooms, four terraces, a library, and an office. It's just shy of six thousand square feet. How do I know that? Because Michaela told me it's exactly forty-four square feet less, and it might be the only thing she has that's bigger than Nina's. Truthfully, I could see Nina buying a place like this more than my sister, or even Finn, but Nick and Nina settled for a simpler condo on the eighteenth floor of the Plaza.

The foyer overlooks the northwest side of the city with unobstructed views of the Woolworth Building and the One World Trade Center. There isn't room for the balloon arch near the stairs, but it will fit in the hallway that leads to the front door. There would be plenty of room for the letters by the piano in the sitting area to the right of the staircase. Everything would probably look better underneath the stairs, but I'd rather not try and find a new home for the thirteen-foot-tall Jack Skellington.

"How ya holding up?" Nick asks after we set the backdrop down.

I shrug. "How would you be?"

Being within feet of the person I've spent the last six years married to but trying not to make eye contact with or speak to has been much harder than I thought. I hoped we could at least be civil, but I guess not speaking is being civil in its own way.

"Well, my situation would be a bit different," Nick smirks. "I'm not in an *arranged* marriage."

There's a cheer from the terrace down the hall that leads through the kitchen and into the family room. My sister had Finn set up a beer pong table for the child-free adults. It's classy, I know, but it keeps them entertained.

Michaela pulls the orange wig from her head as she walks out of the kitchen. Then she pulls at the green scarf tied around her neck, loosening it, before straightening out her purple dress—she and Finn dressed as Fred Jones and Daphne Blake from Scooby-Doo. "What are we whispering about?" my sister asks. God, she's the nosiest person alive.

She was the third person I told the truth about my marriage; it was only a matter of time before she found out, considering both Finn and Nick knew. It was better she heard it from me than from one of them.

"Yeah, what are we whispering about?" Finn joins us. He kisses her temple before he plants another one on her lips. It's sweet—sickeningly sweet—and a tad gross, but I'm happy for them.

Their relationship came as a surprise to me but not to the rest of the family. Finn and I have been best friends since high school, but he and Michaela always seemed to hate each other until two years ago. At first, it was strange to think about— my best friend and little sister together—but after getting over the initial shock (and finding her half-dressed at his place one morning), with some help from Elizabeth, I got over it. Hard not to when you see how they are with one another. Finn says he didn't feel that way about her when we were younger, but I wonder if he's just kidding himself. Michaela, too.

"Are we telling secrets in here?" Alex, Nick's little brother, joins us from the dining room. He's dressed in an orange Garfield the Cat onesie.

"Nick and Josh were whispering about something," Michaela says.

"We weren't whispering about anything," I hiss.

"Sure sounded like it."

A knock at the front door echoes down the hallway, halting the conversation. We share glances, unsure who it could be. Anyone who was invited is already here. Finn goes to answer it.

"Sorry to bother you, Mr. Sheffield," a man says, and over Finn's shoulder, I see the head of the security for the building. "We have a small problem."

"What's going on, Scott?" Michaela asks, stepping up to Finn's side.

Scott huffs. "We got a noise complaint. Now look—"

"I bet it was that old woman, Glenda, down the hall," Michaela says with an eye roll.

"—I don't think you're being that loud, but I have to say something."

"Her name is Gladys," Finn corrects Michaela before turning back to Scott. "We'll do our best to keep it down."

"We're not even being loud," my sister exclaims and looks to me for support.

"You're being a little loud," I say with a simple shrug.

"Like I said, I think you're fine, but when a complaint is made, we gotta address it," Scott says. "Just tell your friends outside to turn it down a notch."

"You got it, Scott," Finn says before Michaela can get another word in.

"She is always on our case." Michaela groans. "She needs to give it a rest already."

"You need to give it a rest already, Shortcake," Finn quips, walking through the threshold with Michaela hot on his trail.

Nick turns to me when they're gone. "You want a beer?"

I consider it, but right now the only thing I want is a little peace and quiet. Maybe Gladys was onto something.

Walking into the guest room, I close the door behind me and fall back against it. Scrubbing a hand down my face, I rub my eyes and let a heavy sigh push past my lips as I walk down the small hallway further into the room my sister has designated as mine whenever I'm in town. Turning the corner, my steps falter.

Elizabeth sits on the ottoman against the floor-to-ceiling window overlooking the East side of Manhattan. She stuck out like a sore thumb among the other partygoers, dressed in her bright yellow plaid skirt and blazer set. White knee-high stockings and white Mary Jane pumps (are those what they're called?) rounded out her costume: Cher Horowitz from *Clueless*. It was a movie she had made me watch countless times.

"Cher, huh?" I offer a polite smile, but she doesn't do the same.

"It was the only thing I had, considering I wasn't even going to come." She stands from the ottoman, wiping her hands on the front of her skirt, straightening it.

"Michaela threaten you, too?"

"Nina."

A soft hum in agreement. I should've known Nina was the only reason she was here. Between my sister and my cousin's wife, there's no way either one of us would be able to avoid each other like normal divorced people. We're going to have to learn to put up with one another to get through the holidays for the rest of our lives.

"Sorry, I didn't know this was your room. I just picked one to get away from everything for a minute."

This is the first time we've been alone since she filed the papers a few months ago. I don't think it's ever been this awkward between us, not even the first time we were alone together. When she moves to leave, something in me forces me to try and stop her.

"Elizabeth, I'm sorry. I don't—We can't avoid each other like this. We're going to see each other, and I don't want it to be weird."

Her stare narrows. "A little late for that."

"It doesn't have to be. I know we couldn't make things work," I say, taking a small step toward her. I don't miss the slight twitch in her face. "But that doesn't mean we can't try and be friends again. For our family."

Her scoff is like a shot to the heart. "You still don't get it, do you?" Elizabeth shakes her head in disbelief, continuing, "Josh, we can't be friends…"

"Liz—"

"This was always the plan. Now, time's up, which means we don't have to pretend anymore. Make sure you tell Juliet I said hi."

Juliet? She can't be serious.

Elizabeth tries to push down the hallway, but I grip her hand, not letting her slip past. Warmth spreads down my fingers and through my veins at the touch, and when her eyes shoot to where our hands meet, I know she feels it too. Gently, I grip her chin and force her eyes up to meet mine. "I'm not seeing Juliet."

"Shocking. You were quick to run to her when that letter showed up."

"Elizabeth, she never showed."

"And if she had?"

My words falter. What *if* she had? I don't know. There was nothing in the letter she sent indicating what it was she wanted. She just said she wanted to talk. Fifteen years was a long time to send a letter out of the blue. I still don't know how she got my address, but regardless, there was something in me screaming to fly out to Wichita and find out what was so damn important. But then she never showed.

"I don't—I don't know!"

"Exactly. Goodbye, Josh."

"This isn't all my fault," I say, gripping her arm. "You didn't want this, Liz. You wanted out as soon as possible. You ended things well before that letter ever showed up. Don't act like you're innocent in all of this."

Elizabeth stares down the hall, avoiding any chance of eye contact.

"I loved you."

Her brown eyes blaze with fury when they finally meet mine. "You don't even know what that means."

"You left me, Elizabeth! You made the choice. You filed the papers. You—"

"We were never meant to stay together, Josh!"

"Then why do you act like I'm such an asshole?" It comes out louder than I meant it to, but this woman knows exactly what buttons to push to drive me up a damn wall. "What am I missing?"

A single scoff is her only response.

"For the love of God, tell me!"

"It wouldn't change anything."

Her gasp lingers between us when I push her up against the wall. My hands on her hips hold her in place, her jacket raises, and my thumb grazes a strip of bare skin on her side. Her skin is soft and velvety under my touch. Our faces are less than an inch apart. Her breath comes out in small gasps across my face, and the faintest smell of red wine still lingers.

The hum of anticipation of what could happen next buzzes between us. My lips barely brush against hers, but a crash from downstairs sends us jumping to opposite sides of the hallway.

Elizabeth lets out the last breath she has been holding, and I can see her boulding the walls back up piece by piece. She straightens her jacket and turns to leave. Before she walks out the door, she looks over her shoulder.

"Do you know what I realized, Josh?" A sad smile tugs on

her red-stained lips. "We were just biding our time, filling the void. But we don't have to do that anymore. We don't have to keep pretending. If we happen to be at the same place, I will be cordial to you, but make no mistake...We are not friends. We will never be friends."

three

NOW

FINN'S VOICE BOOMS DOWN the hallway. "There you are! What are you doing up here?"

An internal groan resonates. I should've stayed in my room. The party was starting to wind down anyway, so I could've disappeared until tomorrow morning without any real repercussions. I made my appearance, mingled, and had a couple of drinks, I even laughed a little. Michaela had nothing to complain about.

"Everything okay down there?"

"Fine." He waves it off. "Ophelia and her friends just had a little too much sugar. They went crashing into the BOO letters you moved."

I'm sure Kai's wife, Eileen, is ecstatic that her daughter is hyped up on pure sugar. Eileen had tried to manage some of the intake, but it didn't help that Mic was secretly giving Ophelia and her friends candy behind everyone's back. I'd walked into the kitchen earlier to find my sister shushing them as she handed them each another cookie. The girls stuffed their faces and ran past me in a chorus of giggles. Michaela's eyes widened when she saw me standing there, but I rolled my eyes and walked away. It wasn't my place to ruin the fun.

"Probably sounded worse than it was," Finn says, trying to cover a yawn.

"Guess we should've left them where they were, huh?"

"Don't say that too loud, your sister already started in on Nin about it."

Of course she did. Any opportunity to tell her best friend she was wrong.

"Y'alright? You snuck off during that last game of beer pong and—"

"Fine," I say with a tight-lipped smile. "Just needed some space."

Finn smirks. "And that space included your soon-to-be ex-wife?"

Shit.

"Look, I get it." His hands fly up in retreat. "One more for the road, but maybe not while we're all downstairs?"

"We didn't...I didn't...It's not like that!"

"Whatever you say, Joshy." Finn winks and heads down the hall toward the master suite. He pulls the orange ascot from his shirt with a relieved sigh before the door closes behind him.

When I walk downstairs, it's quiet, the quietest it's been all night. The majority of the guests have gone, and all that remains is the rest of the family. Eileen holds a zonked-out Ophelia in her arms, the young girl clutches her mother's neck as her mouth hangs open. Nick holds a car seat with a costume-free Elena inside, fast asleep. The two of them talk with Michaela at the front door, but the three Villa siblings are nowhere to be found.

"There you are," my sister shouts in a whisper, trying not to wake the sleeping girls. Nick and Eileen turn to see who she's talking to. "Where did you run off to?"

"Just needed a breather."

"Old man."

Nick starts to say something, probably about to add another insult to the pot, but is interrupted when Kai returns from the living room carrying Ophelia's witch hat.

"Got everything?" Eileen asks.

"Finally. It took forever to find this damn thing." Kai sighs, stuffing it in one of their open bags.

"We would've found it eventually, no biggie," Michaela interrupts like I'm sure she has a million times already.

"Better I find it now than deal with a potential meltdown later."

Eileen nods with a tired smile before trudging out the front door. She doesn't wait around for goodbyes. I'm sure she has probably already done her rounds and is ready to go. Kai thanks Michaela again for a fun evening and follows his wife.

"Nick, let's go. I want to get home before she wakes up to eat," Nina says when she and Elizabeth walk out of the kitchen less than a second later.

"Everything okay?" Nick asks, motioning toward Elizabeth, who hugs Michaela goodbye.

"We'll talk about it *later.*" Nina turns to me and asks, "Are you still coming for breakfast tomorrow?"

"You sure that's a good idea?"

But Nina's face is answer enough.

I had planned on having breakfast at their place until I learned Elizabeth would be staying with them. I don't think she wants to wake up on her birthday to find her ex-husband sitting at the breakfast table.

"Don't worry about it, Nin. I'm sure Mrs. Taylor will be up bright and early with breakfast and coffee waiting for us."

"You know it!" Finn says, rubbing his stomach as he takes the final step, now dressed in sweats and a plain white T-shirt. Mrs. Taylor was the mother of the high schooler who was

Finn's "little brother" in the Big Brothers, Big Sisters program. Knox and Finn hit it off pretty well, and when Mrs. Taylor was diagnosed with Parkinson's, he and Michaela insisted they move in. So, at the beginning of September, Finn bribed Nick, Alex, and me to help move the duo from East Harlem to the Financial District. Despite her diagnosis, Mrs. Taylor refused to quit cooking, and it seemed to be the one thing she could still do without difficulty. "That woman is a godsend."

"Well, if you change your mind—"

"Don't worry about me, Nin."

"You and Elizabeth should go out tomorrow," Nick says to his wife. "Elena and I can come over here."

"No, I don't want to leave Elena." Nina smiles down at the sleeping baby. Since giving birth in August, Nina hasn't gone anywhere without her daughter. She even turned down a few work events because she would have to leave Elena at home. "You can come over here, though. Elena can stay with us."

"We'll figure it out," Nick says. He kisses his wife's temple before thanking Finn again for hosting the party. I think he and Nina are just glad someone else did it for a change—the thought of hosting a party while dealing with a newborn sounds terrible.

"Never thought I'd see the day where we have kids at our parties," Finn says, motioning toward the car seat. "But here we are."

"Yeah, and you're next." Nick smirks, raising a brow at Finn.

"Oh God," I groan, earning a laugh from both of them. "I'm going to pretend I didn't just hear that."

The thought makes me sick, considering he's dating my little sister. Still laughing, Nick pulls me into a one-armed hug before doing the same to Finn. Nina hugs Finn but only offers me a tight smile. Our relationship has been strained since everything came out, that's for sure. Normally, she'd hug me and push a little harder for me to join them in the morning, but not anymore. And I'm sure Elizabeth told her what happened upstairs. "Bye, Short-stack."

"Bye, Bub."

Well, at least she still uses my nickname. That's a good sign, right?

Michaela walks them out the door with Elizabeth in tow. She had taken a step back from the conversation when I showed up. Was that how it was going to be from now on? When one of us was around, the other had to take a step back to make sure we didn't step on one another's toes? It feels unnatural. We've never been like that, not even when we were in the middle of a disagreement before. We had always been able to maintain a certain level of cordiality. But now, we don't *have* to do that. We don't have to get along in front of the others.

I find my way to the kitchen to make one final drink for the evening. As I walk in, Finn already has two beers on the counter and offers me one. "Figured you could use one of these."

"You figured correct," I say, taking the beer.

"You know," my sister says, walking into the kitchen. "If you and Elizabeth would just *talk*, I'm sure you'd both come to realize you actually do love each other."

"It's not that simple, Mic."

"Sure it is!"

I scoff bringing the beer bottle to my lips.

"You do love her, don't you?"

Yes.

"I don't know, Michaela."

"How do you not know if you love someone?"

"It's...complicated. Okay?"

"But—"

"Michaela!" I don't mean to yell, but right now, the last thing I want to do is deal with her meddling. "Just stop. Damn."

"Hey, chill," Finn warns. "Your sister doesn't mean any harm. We're all just trying to understand. Trying to get used to this new normal."

"It's not that hard to understand."

"Josh, you were in an arranged marriage." Michaela puts a large emphasis on the arranged part as if I'm not aware of what I've been going through for the past ten years. "That's not—it's not something that just happens!"

"How *did* it happen?" Finn takes a tug of his beer.

Now that's a long story.

four

A SOFT KNOCK ON the classroom door diverts my mom's attention from the paperwork in her hands, and a smile replaces her concentrated frown. She jumps from her chair and rushes to embrace me, squeezing me extra tight. I may only be three hours from home, but I haven't come back much since starting at Chadwick, embracing my newfound freedom in more ways than one. Each time I make it back to Bridgeport, I come with stories of my adventures, making sure to keep the stupid things out of them—you know how it is. But this time, I have no choice. I have to come clean about the stupid thing I did.

A very, very stupid thing, indeed.

"Joshua, what are you doing here? You're not on break, are you? Oh dear, did I miss something?" Mom shoots question after question before glancing at the calendar on the wall.

"No, Mom. No, I just missed you."

Her warm hand cradles the side of my face. "Oh, Josh, you're sweet." Her lips lift briefly in the corners before she drops her hand. "But I know that's not the real reason you're here."

I chew on my bottom lip, refusing to meet her stare. I find the painted cement wall much more interesting.

"Come on." She leads me toward her desk, making sure to shut the door behind us. She sits down and motions for me to sit in the wooden chair to the side of her desk—it's the same chair I used to sit in at the end of the day in middle school. I would do my homework while Mom finished grading papers or putting together the next day's presentation...It used to be a comfortable place, but now it makes me sick to my stomach knowing what I'm about to tell her. Mom leans back in her chair, twiddling with the pencil from her gradebook. When she speaks, her voice is calm. Whatever I'm about to tell her can't be *that* bad because her son could never do anything *that* bad. "Alright, spill. What's wrong?"

"What do you mean?"

"Joshua Isaiah Davis, it's a mother's job to know when something is bothering her children, and something is bothering you. So, you're going to sit there and tell me what it is."

I sigh. "I fucked up."

"Language, Josh."

"Well, I don't know any other way to describe it."

She laughs. "Oh come on, Josh. Surely, it can't be that bad."

"I'm about to be expelled."

Mom sits up a little straighter. Her smile falls. Her face stoic and unreadable. Honestly, the lack of a bigger reaction is worse than anything I imagined. "Expelled?"

"I got into some trouble and—"

"What kind of trouble, Josh?"

I take a deep breath. "The fraternity. Some of the guys got a little carried away with initiations and..." I tug at the ends of my hair. "I know it was wrong, but we all went through it. All of us. But this year...things got out of hand."

The disappointment in her eyes makes me sick. "I raised you better than this."

"Mom, I know..."

She narrows her eyes. "What did *you* do?"

"I wasn't part of the worst of it. I promise. I just had one of them as an errand boy; I couldn't bring myself to do what the others were doing. But when they did the paddling..." I can still hear the initiate's screams echo around me The first hits never seem that bad, and then you let your guard down. "I never did it."

"Josh, how could you do this?"

I squeeze my eyes shut, feeling the burning building in them. I swallow back the lump in my throat and blink away the tears. I didn't mean to do it. I didn't mean to screw up everything we've worked toward. "I'm sorry, Mom."

"How did the university find out?"

"One of the new guys went to the hospital. I-I dropped him off. One of the sophomores, a legacy, went too far, and—"

"You killed a boy?" I think she might pass out.

"No!" I reassure her quickly. "No, I didn't—He didn't die, he just got a little banged up."

Mom sighs heavily and tears brim her eyes. "What has the school said?"

"We're all suspended. Expulsion pending dependent upon their investigation."

"Why didn't they call us?"

I shrug. "I'm an adult. I don't think they're going to tattle to my parents when I do something wrong."

"We cannot tell your father." Her mood instantly shifts as she begins to plan how we're going to handle this. "He cannot deal with this. Business has been slow, and...Well, we cannot let something like this get out. It would ruin our reputation, absolutely ruin it. You know how people are around here, they talk and..."

"Mom, I'm sorry."

She raises her hand to silence me. "Let's just figure out what you're going to do to fix this."

"Dad is going to ask why I'm home," I say as Mom gathers her things and tosses them into her backpack.

"You're on fall break," she says nonchalantly. Her shoulders rise and fall with a shrug like it's no big deal. Like we aren't talking about my entire future being on the line. And, it reminds me of so many times in the past that I've watched her put up this wall to disassociate from whatever she's about to do. Whatever she has to do to protect the family—protect me.

"What about when I don't go back at the end of the week?"

"Let me worry about that." Mom heaves her backpack onto her shoulder, grabs her purse, and pushes me toward the door. "For now, you go about your business as usual."

That seems easier said than done.

five

NOW

MICHAELA'S MOUTH HANGS OPEN. Her blue eyes are blown wide. Utter shock is the only way to describe the expression on her face. I can see the wheels turning; she's trying to piece it all together. The when, the how, the why... none of it makes any sense to her. When I finally look at Finn, his expression is unreadable. His lips are pulled into a thin line, gaze narrowed as his thumb picks at the label on the beer bottle. I'm sure he's wondering why I never told him. He is my best friend, after all. That's something I could tell him, right? Should tell him. We told each other everything. Except that one time he was sleeping with my sister and didn't tell me... But who's counting?

"Josh." Michaela chuckles dryly. "You can't be serious. Please tell me you're joking." When I don't deny it, she shakes her head in disbelief. "You hazed someone? You? Joshua Isaiah Davis. You—"

"I didn't hurt anyone."

"But, you *hazed* someone."

"I-I guess...I mean, yeah, but—"

51

"Oh my God."

"Mic—"

"Who are you?" The shock is replaced with genuine hurt. "My brother would never do that. First, a sham of a marriage, now this? I feel like I don't even know you anymore."

If I'm honest, I hate to see her this hurt. I've always been protective of my sister, tried to be a good example for her, and tried to be there when she needed me. I hate that I've turned into someone she feels like she doesn't recognize.

"I didn't hurt anyone, Michaela. I wasn't the one beating the shit out of the kid. But I was the one who took the kid to the damn hospital while the others just stood there."

When I close my eyes, I can still see it. Him. His seemingly lifeless body in the middle of the frat house basement, with the rest of them just standing around staring down at him. The boy who had done it still clutched the handle of the paddle. I'll spare you the details of the rest of the scene, but the sight made my stomach churn and I was starting to get a taste of dinner for a second time that night.

Michaela chews on the corner of her mouth. Her fingers intertwine and she cracks her knuckles. When her eyes lift from the countertop to meet mine, she asks, "How does that lead to the marriage thing?"

I sigh. "I went to Mom when the school suspended us and she tried to find a way to make it all go away."

"And Brina could do that," Michaela says, and I nod. "Why would she go to Brina, of all people? She didn't even know her. Why wouldn't she and Dad just hire a lawyer and try to—"

"Dad didn't know anything. Mom told me not to tell him." I shake my head, swiping the bottle between my hands. "And the Villa name means something. Mom knows that as well as everyone else. I don't know specifics, Mom just said she knew someone who knew Brina. They were able to put her in touch with her."

As disappointed as she was, the whole ordeal had worked in Mom's favor. She had always admired Brina from afar. She heard the stories—we all did—and she had always wanted to get a taste of that world. Who wouldn't? And in the end, she didn't get just a taste, she got the whole meal.

"Why would you even agree to something like this?"

"I thought it was my only way out."

"But if you weren't involved—"

"We were all going to be investigated. Anyone who was there would be questioned and likely implicated. I knew it was going to get ugly and having something like that on my record…it would be hard to get a job at a decent firm."

It was something Mom and I had discussed a handful of times since that day in her classroom. Whether the paddle was in my hand or not, I was there. That meant I was just as guilty as the others because I didn't do anything to stop it. The only way I was going to be spared the investigation and whatever repercussions came with it would be to let Brina work her magic and make my name disappear from the record. The official story was that I was home that night helping my mom move some furniture.

"What about Elijah?" Finn asks. He means Elijah Prince, one of our mutual friends. "He was in your fraternity."

"He was at home that night."

"Unbelievable." My sister sighs.

"I got my name cleared, got to graduate on time, and had a job ready for me when I graduated."

"And what did Ellie get out of this?" Finn rests his hand on the back of Michaela's chair, and I imagine he's gently rubbing circles on her back through the purple dress she's still wearing. He's extremely attentive to her, more than her ex-husband, David, ever was when they were married.

"She got her full inheritance before turning thirty and before getting married, and she got to go to SCAD like she wanted. Her parents put a stipulation on her college money that she was supposed to go to Duke." It was asinine and seemed totally out of character for them, but Elizabeth said they were extremely proud of their alma mater and expected their children to follow in their footsteps if they were going to pay for school. "And she had to be married to get her full inheritance before thirty."

"All of this just to get out of trouble and get some money?" There it is, Finn can't hide his shock any longer.

"Seems a little extreme if you ask me." Michaela laughs darkly.

"Brina was looking for a way to get Liz out of her hair, and Mom was looking for a way to get me out of hers," I say.

When the Villas adopted Elizabeth, Brina put up a good front to the public, but in truth, she wasn't happy. Not only did she have one daughter she didn't want, but now she had two, and one of them wasn't even hers.

"But an arranged marriage—"

"People do it all the time in other cultures, hell sometimes in our own, and get *nothing* out of it. At least I got something."

"So, this is it, then? You're really going to just let her walk away," Michaela says.

"She's made her choice, MJ."

"And what about you?"

"It's complicated."

"What's so complicated about it?"

My head drops into my hands on the island between us. "It just is, okay?" Looking up at them, I say, "It's not always black and white. If anyone should understand that, it's you, MJ."

Last year was more than a complicated shit show for her. Not only did she hide the fact she had started dating one of my best friends, but she hid her divorce from the family. That's not even the worst part; after the truth finally came out, she stupidly broke up with Finn because he didn't tell her *why* he had started his foundation for foster kids, Sheffield House. Truth be told, Finn used to be a party animal, traveling the world, living off the money his parents put in his bank account weekly…He was a mess until his adoptive father had enough and told him to get his shit together. He had to prove himself to keep his inheritance. Michaela found out, and instead of looking on the bright side of things, she broke it off with Finn and went back to David. Their reunion lasted longer than anyone expected. Five months, I think? David was running for Congress, and in doing so, he tried to turn Michaela into a completely different person. She realized she couldn't be with him. Not only was he an obnoxious asshole, but she was in love with Finn. We all knew it, she just needed to figure it out for herself.

"I'm sorry for lying to you all these years, but legally, I didn't have a choice."

Legally, we weren't supposed to talk about the arrangement with anyone outside of it unless we agreed upon it, and we never did. Besides, I was scared of what might happen if someone found out the truth.

"You can't convince me this whole thing was for show. Trust me, Josh, I've seen you when you lie, and it's not pretty."

"Guess I'm better than you thought." The words hang between us. I hate that I'm still lying to her, but it's better than trying to explain the alternative. There's a lot that has led up to this moment, and it would be hard for anyone to understand. "Elizabeth was always going to walk away at the end. Anything between us was only to fill the void until she could be free. I've fulfilled my purpose in her life and now she's going to live her life the way she wants to."

That's what she said earlier, right?

Michaela wants to argue some more, but instead, she shares a glance with Finn before letting out a loud huff and walking out of the kitchen.

"She means well," Finn says a few beats later when he turns back to me after he's watched her disappear up the stairs.

"She's nosy."

He chuckles. "She's Michaela. Of course, she's nosy." He pulls two more beers from the fridge and passes one to me. "Now that she's gone, you wanna tell me how you *really* feel?"

six

THEN

December 2015

THE ANNUAL CHRISTMAS BALL in Winchester was hosted by local Congressman Harvey Cawthorn and his wife at their home. The plantation house sat back off the road a good half mile or so, down a dirt drive that was filled in with gravel until you got closer to the house, where they had poured concrete (and repoured it every other year to keep up appearances).

The white house had a large veranda with four classic columns and four windows—two on each story on either side—each of which was currently decorated with evergreen wreaths sporting red bows. Small porches extended from the side of the house and the driveway formed a circle around a large fountain just below the ten steps that led up to the front door with a carved tympanum (at least that's what Michaela called it when she saw it).

The opulence of the Cawthorn Mansion made it the obvious choice for the location of the Christmas Ball. The Christmas Ball was an event that only the most prominent families in the area were invited to attend. The "official" purpose was to raise money for families in need during the holiday season, but it was really just an excuse for some of the richest people in town to have a party.

The Davis family had never been invited until this year. Scratch that; the *whole* of the Davis family had never been invited until this year. I have been invited a few times over the years after I became ~~friends~~ acquaintances with Harvey's son. I rarely chose to attend. This kind of thing isn't my scene, but I don't have a choice this year (or for the foreseeable future).

Walking inside, I notice the house is full of people dressed to impress. Women wear ball gowns and men are dressed in five-piece suits. Servers pass through the crowd with trays of champagne, sparkling juice, and cocktails. It looks like Christmas threw up. I feel like there should be a rule against two Christmas trees in one room. I don't remember there being this many decorations when I visited during Christmas before.

Across the room, I make brief eye contact with Nina before a large mass steps into view—William Cawthorn, son of our host and Elizabeth's current boyfriend. Michaela saunters off to meet Nina and Elizabeth, leaving me alone with him, and that's the last place I want to be right now. I am about to steal his girlfriend, after all.

The paperwork has been signed. Elizabeth has been registered at SCAD, starting the winter quarter in January. My name was scrubbed from everything to do with the hazing incident, which has been made public and the police are heavily involved. The kid's parents are going after the school and fraternity because of the injuries he sustained; luckily, he did live. Had I not taken him to the hospital…I don't even want to think about it, but my name got scrubbed from that, too. I'm set to graduate this spring and start a job at QC Marketing, a firm in Charlotte. Brina was gracious enough to throw in a year's lease on any condo of my choosing.

The "relationship" won't make a public debut until after the new year, though. One of Elizabeth's last-minute stipulations was that she wanted to spend the holidays with the Cawthorns, and I wasn't going to protest getting to spend one final holiday with my family.

Elizabeth's idea of "selling" this whole arrangement was contingent on my reputation as one of the town's golden boys. She would stage a break-up with William at a time and place that we'd set later and then I'd swoop in to help pick up the pieces of her broken heart.

"Josh, dude, what the hell is going on up at Chadwick?" William asks.

"Crazy, right?" I try not to wince at the mention of it.

"Did you know about—What am I saying? Of course you did! You went through it too, I imagine?"

"It wasn't this bad, but the guy who supposedly did it was newer—a sophomore."

"Shit," he breathes. "The kid is supposed to make it, though, right?"

"Far as I know."

Something over my shoulder catches William's eye, and I turn to see Elizabeth laughing at something Michaela whispers behind her hand. Elizabeth takes a sip of champagne, her lips gracefully enclosed around the rim of the glass, letting the golden liquid slide down her throat before she pulls away without leaving a stain.

When I turn back to William, he is still staring at her.

"Everything okay?" I ask.

"I don't know." He sighs. "Elizabeth has been acting weird lately. I think the distance is getting the best of us."

William has been at Duke while Elizabeth has still been in Winchester, not to mention she has been traveling a lot since she graduated high school last spring. At least, that's what I hear from Michaela.

"If she would just go to Duke like we planned—"

"She's not?" I feign ignorance.

William sighs. "She enrolled at Savannah starting next month."

"I mean, Savannah isn't *that* far."

"Dude, it may as well be on the other side of the country. Not to mention, do you know she's making me wait?" I'm not quite sure what he means. "She won't sleep with me! Something about not being ready. We've been together for two years, Josh! *Two.* I could have anyone I wanted up there. The girls are just there for the picking, but I—"

"Will, you can't be serious."

"I haven't done anything!" He's getting defensive, and I can't tell if it's because he's worried I'll say something or because he's just *that* frustrated. Honestly, I almost feel bad for what's about to happen. He seems to want to make things work with her and has no idea what's coming.

"But, if she's going to SCAD, I think I need to end things after the holidays."

Scratch that. This asshole can kick rocks. Who talks about their girlfriend like that?

I've always known he was somewhat of a prick, but this... this is on another level. And as much as I want to tell him to go fuck himself, tell him he doesn't deserve someone like Elizabeth...I bite my tongue. "Kind of a dick move there, Will."

"No one wants to spend the holidays alone." He shrugs so nonchalantly it pisses me off. Will takes the glass of whiskey from a waiter who appears out of thin air. He takes a long sip of the amber liquid, his gaze returns to Elizabeth once again before turning back to me. "Besides, Mom would murder me if I did it beforehand. She feels so bad for Elizabeth because of her parents and all that. It's been three years, like give me a break."

"Dude."

"What? You're suddenly Team Elizabeth or something?"

"Don't be such an ass."

"Well, she uses them as an excuse to—"

I don't hear the rest of *his* excuses because I walk away from the conversation. Suddenly, I don't feel so bad about what's coming. I'm happy to help Elizabeth get away from that asshole. William calls after me, but I ignore him, continuing through the house until I find Finn conversing with Oliver and some of his business associates. Not exactly the conversation I was looking for, but anything is better than William.

My sister blabbers on about...something. It started with how incredible it was to be invited this year, but I lost track around the time she started talking about the food. I have only been throwing in the occasional *Mhmm* and *Sounds interesting* so she thinks I'm still listening, but I couldn't tell you the last thing she said.

Stepping out of the house, I spot Elizabeth talking with Harvey further in the backyard.

"That's great, Mic. Look, I'll be right back." Pushing past her, I ignore my sister when she calls out to me. My gaze is locked on my target as she laughs politely at something the older man says. She takes another sip of her champagne. When I approach them, Harvey offers a polite smile.

"Joshua, it's so good to see you!"

Harvey extends his hand, and I return the gesture. William may be an asshole, but his dad is far from. Even on the congressional floor, he remains poised, even-tempered, diplomatic, and assertive but polite. I don't think I've ever heard a story of him losing his temper with his constituents.

He gets the point across without being the loudest one in the room.

"Thanks for the invite, Mr. Cawthorn."

"It's Harvey, you know that."

I met the Cawthorns when Finn introduced Nick and me to William a few years ago. Even though Nick couldn't stand him, I didn't think he was so bad. That being said, being introduced to a congressman for the first time was one of the most nerve-wracking things I'd ever done. I had no idea what to expect. The nerves only grew bigger as we pulled into the driveway the first time William invited us over, but they faded as soon as we walked in. Nick and I were welcomed with open arms and a homemade meal prepared by Mrs. Cawthorn.

"Well, the family is happy to be here," I say. "Really enjoying it."

"It's been a pleasure to meet them. I'll be sure they get an invite from now on."

Whether or not that's true, the sentiment behind it is nice enough.

Glancing at Elizabeth, I ask Harvey if I can steal her away from their conversation. "Nina is looking for her," I explain.

"Be my guest. I wouldn't want to keep Miss Villa waiting."

Harvey nods toward Elizabeth and leaves, but it's not long before he's pulled into another conversation with a different group of partygoers. I imagine that's how he spends most of his night at a shindig like this.

"We need to talk," I say in a low voice.

"Rain check." She hands me her empty glass with a tight smile. "I need to see what Nina wants."

This girl is more oblivious than I thought. Isn't it obvious that I was only saying that to get her away from Harvey? Elizabeth should know better. If Nina was looking for her she'd have no problem finding her.

"She doesn't want anything, but it was the only way not

to look suspicious asking to talk to you alone." I set her empty glass on one of the high-top tables. "Now, walk with me like we're heading to find Nina."

"And why should I?" Elizabeth protests when I press my hand to her lower back to guide her through the crowd.

"Just do it," I hiss with a tight smile.

Elizabeth rolls her eyes but does as she's told. When we're finally away from the crowd, she pulls away from me. "What is so damn important—"

"William is going to break up with you."

"What?"

"I said—"

"I heard you," she snaps. She steps forward, pressing one of her manicured nails into my chest. Up close, it's easy to tell the nail has been meticulously dripped with the perfect Christmas red and little Christmas figures hand-painted on each one. "And how would you know that?"

"Does it matter?" It shouldn't matter. What should matter is the fact that it's going to happen.

"Of course, it matters!" Her slight outburst catches the attention of two bystanders.

I smile at them before taking her by the hand and dragging her inside.

While the downstairs is bustling with guests, the upstairs is off-limits during these types of events. Her hand tightens around mine as we swim through a dense group, breaking through on the other side to reach the hallway to the kitchen. Inside, at least five chefs work at various stations to ensure the food is ready for dinner, which is supposed to take place in the next thirty minutes. We'll have dinner followed by the debuts of the girls "coming out" in society (whatever that means) and then the crowning of the next Miss Winchester. Not a single chef seems to notice as we pass through to the back staircase. Up the stairs and down the hall, my pace finally begins to slow, reaching one of the alcoves inside of a dormer window.

"Would you let go?" Elizabeth pulls her hand from mine and takes a step back. "Now answer my question! How do you know he's going to break up with me?"

"He says you've been acting weird."

She scoffs, leaning back against the banister. "Like he'd know."

"I guess, the distance isn't helping."

"Yeah, no shit." Elizabeth crosses her arms, staring down the empty hallway. It's pretty obvious her thoughts have moved far away from this conversation. If she's anything like me, she's thinking about our impending union. How this conversation goes doesn't really matter, how William wants to break up with her doesn't really matter, because the fate of their relationship was sealed last month.

"He wants you to go to Duke," I say, stuffing my hands into my pockets. I lean back against the wall directly across from her.

"Well, that's not happening."

Obviously, or I wouldn't have to be making a trip to Savannah in the next few months, per the contract.

Elizabeth's eyes raise to meet mine. The light from the sconce nearby brings out a warmth in them that I've never seen before.

"How do you know all of this?" she asks, breaking the trance.

"He uh...He told me about it earlier. Said he wanted to wait until after the holidays.—."

"That asshole!"

"—because he doesn't want you to be alone."

Her mouth opens a handful of times, trying to find the right response, but nothing seems like the right thing to say.

"Look, I just thought you'd want to know."

"Oh, *that* was very considerate of you, Josh. Thanks a ton."

"Don't shoot the messenger, okay?" My hands raise. "Just because you've been freezing out your boyfriend—"

"I have not!"

"Might want to tell him that. Seems to me his resolve is dwindling with all the girls *throwing* themselves at him up north." Way to go, Josh. You were supposed to keep this subtle. You were just supposed to warn her, not tell her everything. "Look, I just wanted you to know. Figured you might want to beat him to it."

I turn on my heel and head back the way we came, but I don't expect her to follow me.

Elizabeth grabs hold of my sleeve, turning me back to face her. "Why do *you* care if William is going to break up with me, huh? It's none of your business. Just because there's a piece of paper saying I'm going to eventually be your wife doesn't make my life any of your business." She shoves that red nail into my chest again. "Do us both a favor and—"

I clasp my hand around her fingers and we step back simultaneously until her back hits the blue-and-white striped wall. "Let's get one thing straight. The day we signed that paper, anything to do with you and your life *did* become my business. You may not like it—hell, I may not like it—but we're stuck together for the foreseeable future."

I watch her throat swell as she swallows whatever she was going to say moments ago. Her eyes drop down between us where our hands are trapped between our bodies, with no space to breathe between us. When her eyes return to mine, they're darker than they were seconds ago, and I don't hide the fact that my gaze flickers between her eyes and her lips.

Fuck.

Fuck, fuck, fuck, fuck, fuck.

Don't, Josh. Don't do it. This is not how you want to start this. She's still with William and she doesn't even want you. You're not the one she wants. It's just the heat of the moment.

End the conversation right now.

Her voice is barely above a whisper. "Josh—"

"Do us both a favor and don't make this any harder than it has to be." Taking a step back, I drop her hand and my body instantly lacks the warmth of hers.

Her pupils are blown wide, the realization of what just happened crosses her face, and I turn on my heel to get the hell out of dodge. "You're such an asshole!"

"Whatever helps you sleep better at night, Sugar."

seven

THEN

December 2015

"HAVE YOU SEEN ELIZABETH?" Nina asks, appearing from behind me. Why is she asking me? Shouldn't she know where Elizabeth is?

"Not for a while." I shake my head and answer without looking away from the dance floor. Guests float across the waxed and polished wooden floors to the tune of a Christmas song from the piano in the corner. There's an oversized tree next to the piano fit with oversized ornaments and ribbons. There's a stage in the middle of the room along the back wall where they will present the girls shortly and crown the next Miss Winchester. I motion toward the dance floor. "Shouldn't you be out there with Lee?"

"I have better things to do," Nina says with a tight smile.

Why she stays with that guy, I'll never know. Lee Madigan is the son of another prominent family in town and a grade-A asshole. Nina could do so much better, but for some reason, she stays with him. It's not like she needs his money, and he treats her more like a toy than a girlfriend. Maybe there's something I'm missing. Don't know what it could be, but maybe.

"What's up, Nin?" Finn asks.

Nina seems to debate whether or not to say something. She looks around the room once more before turning back to us. "She and Will have kind of been at odds lately. I think her decision to go ahead and go to SCAD isn't helping. I have a sneaky suspicion things might blow up sooner than later."

Nina's eyes bore into mine, and it feels like she *knows*. Like she knows everything about the deal we made. Except she can't possibly know the truth. We aren't supposed to tell anyone. But this is Nina, and if there is one thing I've learned, it's that Nina Villa always finds the truth.

"Any luck?" Lee suddenly appears at her side. Where did he come from? I don't remember seeing him before.

"So, you haven't seen her?" Nina ignores him, asking us again.

"Nope." Finn pops his lips to emphasize the word. "Sorry."

"Don't worry about it, Dove. Elizabeth is a big girl. She can handle herself," Lee says, earning an eye roll from his girlfriend.

Nina starts to take off in search of Elizabeth again, but the music dies, and Harvey takes the microphone to begin the Miss Winchester portion of the evening. Not before he thanks everyone for joining them this evening, of course. "We've done it again," he states proudly, holding up a piece of paper that a woman passes him. "We've beat our previous record! This year, we raised over sixty-thousand dollars for the families in our area."

The crowd roars with excitement before he quiets them down again. He thanks a few more people by name for their hard work to make this all happen and then hands the stage over to his wife.

A few paces behind Mrs. Cawthorn, Elizabeth steps on stage wearing the Miss Winchester crown and sash—she was crowned the winner last year. The smile on her ruby lips doesn't quite reach her eyes as she stands poised and ready while each girl is announced alongside their suitor. I lose track of who is who and what each girl's short biography reads. Why does all of this matter again? It's not like this is going to actually matter when they go off into the real world, it only matters while they're still safe inside their little Winchester bubble. This entire ordeal is simply to give these people a reason to get dolled up and throw a party.

When the final girl is announced, I count them—sixteen total—but I don't recognize most of them.

"And the next Miss Winchester is…" Mrs. Cawthorn pulls a small card from the envelope in her hands. "Wren James!"

Wren James does her best pageant queen, faux surprise face. Her eyes shine under the lights as she approaches the stage to receive her crown. The crown Elizabeth wears is swapped for a much smaller one and placed on Wren's head. I notice Elizabeth's eyes sweeping over the ballroom, searching…but for what? I start to do the same, but I can't quite figure out what she's looking for.

Mrs. Cawthorrn motions toward the band to begin playing a tune, and each couple gets into formation to share their first official dance in society. Elizabeth steps off stage, her eyes still sweeping around the room. *William.* She's looking for William because they're supposed to dance alongside the girls.

"You're fucking joking," Nina whispers to herself, noticing the same thing.

As the dance begins, William still hasn't shown his face and has left Elizabeth alone on the dance floor. I can only imagine the ass-chewing he's going to get from his mom tonight for causing such a scene, but right now, I'm more worried about the girl he's left stranded. I can't stand the image in front of me. There's a tug on my heart. An invisible string pulls me forward and I start to take a step but pause, sharing a look with Nina. She doesn't hesitate to urge me forward.

Elizabeth looks shocked when I approach her. Without

a word, I bow. When I stand, I lift my palm to face hers, as the other suitors had done moments ago. She doesn't hesitate placing her hand next to mine, centimeters apart, and we join the others in the dance. Finally, I pull her close, one hand holds hers and the other rests on the small of her back. I'm transported back to that moment in the hallway. The way we had been so close, too close for people who weren't in an intimate relationship. The smell of her perfume—a mixture of sweet florals and sandalwood—filled my space and it was intoxicating.

She clears her throat, bringing me back to the present moment. "What are you doing here?" she whispers, her brown eyes staring up at me under thick lashes.

"Saving your ass. Now, smile, and let's get through the next three minutes."

I can feel the weight of every eye in the room on us. I catch a glance of Nina, whose lips curl into a smirk like she knows something. Finn, too. My sister looks shocked from her spot next to our parents. Mom's brow is raised in surprise, while Dad wears a proud smile. And in another turn, I catch sight of Brina, her expression unreadable. Turning back to the woman in my arms, I see she looks sad, but she does her best to hide it.

"It's his loss, Sugar," I whisper, and that earns a small smile—a real one. One that softly tugs the corners of her ruby-red lips upward.

As the song ends, we take a step back in line with the others. The men bow again while the young women curtsey. Elizabeth and I share a deep sigh; it looks like our arrangement is going public a lot earlier than anticipated.

"That's not good," Finn says as we walk onto the back deck, and I follow his gaze to see William and Elizabeth arguing. Shit, this is not good. Not the time or place for this. We pick up the pace down the steps, trying not to draw too much attention to ourselves from the few partygoers outside, but the lover's quarrel seems to be getting more heated with each passing moment.

William says something, and Elizabeth gasps, taking a step back. He takes the opportunity to walk away, but when she recovers, she follows, hot on his heels.

Dammit, Elizabeth. Just let it go.

"You are nothing more than a manchild, William Cawthorn!" I can hear her as we get closer. "You think just because your daddy is—"

"Look who's talking, Lizzie!"

"We are not the same."

"You think just because your parents are dead, it gives you a pass to say and do whatever you want. To treat people however you want. But it doesn't! You're nothing more than a spoiled little bitch."

"Hey, now!" The words tumble out of me before I can stop them. Bringing up her parents in the middle of an argument like this isn't fair. "C'mon man, there's no need for all that."

"Oh, look who it is." William scoffs. When he speaks again, his voice has raised at least two decibels. "Come to save the day again?"

"There's no need to cause a scene, Will," I urge him, trying to keep my voice down. "Why don't you guys take it upstairs? Settle this like adults."

"You're one to talk, huh, Josh?"

"Will, stop it," Elizabeth interjects, but it doesn't do any good.

"Running off with *my* girl, telling her I'm gonna break up with her, telling her she doesn't matter because all the girls are *throwing* themselves at me?" He steps closer to me and for some reason (Stupidity? Pride?) I don't back down.

"William," Elizabeth hisses.

"And for what? To cause problems? To start a fight? So you could make me look like the asshole, and you could swoop in and play hero?"

"Doing a pretty good job of that yourself," Finn mumbles. William glares at him, but Finn simply shrugs in response. Finn is used to William; used to his tantrums. They've known each other for a long time. And even though he has always rubbed Finn the wrong way, sometimes you put up with people like William because they're the only ones around.

"Stay the fuck out of this, Sheffield." The fist at William's side clenches. This is going to get a lot uglier if we don't do something to defuse the situation.

"You're the one who left *your* girl stranded in front of the entire guest list. So, if you're looking for someone to blame for your problems, take a look in the mirror."

William starts to lunge.

I step between, trying to keep them apart, and the blow lands on my cheek.

Fuck.

The thought enters my mind, but I don't register it at first, the hit dazing me for a moment. I can hear distant yelling from Elizabeth, but I don't know what she's saying. When my senses finally return, I take a deep breath and glare at William. He's in the process of rolling up his sleeves, readying himself for the fight sure to come. My gaze is ripped from his, and I'm met with concerned brown orbs. Elizabeth. She gingerly touches my cheek, examining it before offering me a tentative smile. She's apologizing.

"Can't take a hit, Joshy boy?" William taunts when the last of his shirt sleeve is tucked away in the fold at his elbow.

I scoff. "Will, unless you want to get laid out in the middle of your own party, I suggest you go back inside. I've given you your one hit, now it's my turn."

William starts to lunge at me again, but Finn steps between us, managing to avoid the right hook William throws.

"Stop it," Finn hisses. "Do either one of you really want to cause a scene on a night like this?"

"Get the fuck out of my house!" William shouts. "I never want to see either of you again. If you ever so much as—"

"Oh, for once in your life, shut the fuck up, Will," Elizabeth interrupts him.

Will's burning gaze turns on her and my feet move on their own to put myself between the two of them. I watch the wheels of his mind turning, mulling over what she just said. I don't know if I've ever heard Elizabeth talk to him that way.

Despite his unwavering gaze, she stands tall, until finally his eyes narrow. William opens his mouth, ready to spew whatever vile line he's spent the last two minutes coming up with, but his gaze flickers to me and the words escape him. Looking between us, he tries to think of something else to say, but the best he can come up with is: "You deserve each other!" before he runs back to the house like a little kid who didn't get the toy he wanted.

Has he always been so dramatic?

A few guests who had just stepped out onto the back porch watched him stomp inside before they turned in our direction. I turn toward Elizabeth, whose narrowed gaze has yet to leave the backdoor.

Damn, I really made a mess of things. I should've just kept my mouth shut.

As if she can hear my thoughts, Elizabeth looks at me, gaze still narrowed. I ready myself for her fury to unleash, but it never comes.

"It's his loss, Sugar," I say, repeating the same words I said to her on the dance floor.

The corners of her red lips lift briefly. With a deep breath, she mentally prepares herself for her next task: distracting party guests. She leaves us to join them on the balcony, greeting them with a polite smile and starting a conversation to clean up the mess we've made.

eight

NOW

IT'S BEEN A WEEK since Halloween, and it's been radio silence from my sister since I left New York on Sunday morning. Normally, we talk a few times a week—whether by text, phone call, or the occasional FaceTime because she just *has* to show me something—and I would never admit it to anyone else, but I've missed our conversations. At least the group chat between Finn, Nick, Alex, and myself has been moving at a pretty normal pace. Finn and I had a conversation two days ago about the fantasy football league we're in. Things seem fine on that front, but I don't want to ask him. I know what the problem is…Michaela is still trying to digest everything, and I get it. I've had ten years to process all this information, but they're just figuring it out.

Falling back into my desk chair, I stretch and pull my glasses down onto my nose. I begin digging into the presentation my team sent over earlier. We've been trying to acquire a new client with quite a reputation, a client that the firm has been trying to acquire since I started working here nine years ago. This presentation has to be perfect.

I flip through the slides and make note of small things here and there, but overall it looks fine—though, I can't be too sure because I can't stop thinking back to Halloween. Finding Elizabeth in my room. Being so close to her after all this time. The smell of her perfume mixed with a twinge of red wine…It was intoxicating. Had the girls not knocked over those letters, I can only imagine what might have happened.

Checking the clock, I see I have three hours until the end of the work week, and then I'm supposed to meet Nick and Alex at the house for a guys' night. Nina is kicking Nick out of their house for the night so she can get some peace and quiet. I'm not sure how much peace and quiet she's getting with a newborn around the house, but Nick said not to question it when I asked.

As much as I could use a night with the guys, the only thing I can think of is the amount of time it takes to get from here to Jupiter Beach, a small town on the coast about thirty minutes outside of Charleston. The small town Elizabeth moved to after she officially moved out of our shared home in Winchester. And if I leave now, I'll be there just after five o'clock. Surely, she'd be home by then, right?

"Fuck it," I whisper and log off. I haphazardly throw my stuff into my bag and close the office door behind me. My assistant, Sienna, sits at her desk, and her bright blue eyes meet mine when I walk out. "Cece, I'm leaving a little early. Anyone needs anything, just forward it to my email, but you can leave if you want."

"You got it, boss." She offers me a small salute before I leave without a second glance.

As I pull into the brick driveway, the robotic voice of my GPS notifies me that I have arrived at my destination. The house sits a few hundred feet off the street, with giant magnolia trees planted along the front of the property for added privacy. It's a three-story house with a large front porch extending the length of the front. A semi-circle segmented window is nestled inside of a gable that extends off the roof—possibly a window looking into the attic or maybe a loft.

I park in front of the detached three-car garage but don't turn the car off. She hasn't seen me yet. I still have time to back out of this if I want to. Do I want to? Kind of.

No, I need to do this. We need to talk this out. We owe it to ourselves. We shouldn't leave things the way they have been for the past sixteen months.

Turning off the car, I pull the keys from the ignition and climb out before I can talk myself out of it. The last time I was here, the house was decorated for the fall season, but now her white house has been thoroughly decorated for Christmas. It's Elizabeth's favorite holiday, and she does not play around when it comes to décor. Evergreen garlands with white lights outline both the house and garage. Oversized wreaths hang from the light fixtures on the front of the garage with red bows. White lights have been wrapped around the trees that line the driveway and front yard. Two poinsettias sit on each step leading up to the front porch, one on each side.

The front porch is wide, bigger than it looks from the road. More evergreen garland hangs from the rafters of the roof, and another large, pre-lit garland drapes over the door frame. Two wreaths with red bows hang on each mahogany door, the stain matching the color of the wood beneath my feet. Different-sized evergreens with artificial snow in rattan baskets and wrought iron lanterns with a candle inside sit on either side of the threshold. A wooden sign leaning against the wall spells out NOEL with a golden Christmas star above it.

The plain doormat reads *Merry Christmas* in ruby red letters, resting on top of a red plaid accent rug. Another evergreen sits next to the bench at the far end of the porch. A string of unlit garland runs along the top of the backrest, waterfalling down the ends to the floor. The olive-green pillows from before have been swapped with pillows specific to the holiday.

There are paneled windows on either side, and I know I shouldn't, but I look through them. I don't see much, just a straight shot off the staircase, stained to match the color of the dark brown wood floors, and down the hallway to the living room. There's no movement inside, and it makes me wonder if she's even home.

Fuck it.

When I knock, it's quiet for a moment, and then I hear it. A voice from deep in the house, but it's not the voice I was expecting. The door swings open a moment later to reveal Nina. Her eyes widen when she realizes it's me, and she steps outside, closing the door behind her. "Josh, what are you doing here?"

"I came to talk to Elizabeth. What are *you* doing here?"

"Elizabeth needed help with…something."

That's not suspicious. Wait, I thought she was kicking Nick out of the house tonight.

"Where's the baby?"

"Not that it's any of your business," she says, slightly offended. "But, if you must know, she's with her father." Well, that would explain the lack of response from Nick when I texted him, canceling our plans. Nina glances inside before repeating, "Why are you here, Josh?"

The door swings open again, and this time, it's the woman I was expecting moments earlier. She's dressed in what can only be described as a date night outfit: high-waisted denim jeans, a black belt with the signature double-G's, and a long-sleeve corset-type top with a deep V-neck.

She looks good, damn good.

When I meet her brown eyes, she looks annoyed—more than annoyed. She looks on edge. Before Elizabeth can ask me what I'm doing here, the sound of someone pulling into the driveway catches our attention.

"Shit," Nina says under her breath.

The truck pulls to a stop next to the steps leading up to the front porch. A blond-haired man steps out, straightens his outfit, and reaches inside the cab before walking around the front carrying a bouquet of roses. What an idiot! Elizabeth hates roses—she prefers carnations.

"Oh, am I interrupting something?" he asks, reaching the steps and finally looking up to see the three of us.

Yes.

"No, Ryan," Elizabeth answers. "I'm about finished. Give me two minutes." Elizabeth steps forward to take the bouquet from him. She rushes back inside, leaving the door open in the process.

"Nina, good to see you." Ryan nods towards her, but she doesn't respond—her gaze remains locked on me. Ryan turns to me, extending his hand. "I don't think we've met. I'm Ryan Dickson."

I glance down at his hand before meeting his big green eyes, swallowing the lump growing in my throat. I extend my hand to him. "Josh."

"Nice to meet you, Josh. You a friend of Lizzie's?"

Lizzie? You've got to be kidding me. Does this guy know *nothing?* Elizabeth cannot stand to be called Lizzie, not after what happened with her brother. She isn't even a big fan of Liz, but she always let me get away with it, though she preferred Sugar. She rarely accepted new nicknames and much preferred to be called Elizabeth. The only other one she would allow was Ellie, and only Finn could call her that. In the beginning, I didn't get it. I thought she was just being pretentious and stubborn, and then I learned the reason why.

"Josh is my husband's cousin," Nina says before I can introduce myself. She meets Ryan's gaze and loops her arm through mine with a small pat on my forearm. A warning not to say anything. "He was just coming to take me to dinner since we both happened to be in town."

Elizabeth steps out of the house and throws me a glance before walking straight into Ryan's arms. Even in heels, she still has to stand on her tiptoes to plant a kiss on his cheek.

"Have fun, but not too much fun," Nina says, ushering them down the stairs. She waves as the truck begins to back out of the driveway, and her smile doesn't fall until we are hidden behind the magnolia wall. When she turns to me, she shakes her head with a small sigh. "I'll be right back; I meant it when I said you're taking me to dinner. I'm starving."

When we get back to Elizabeth's after dinner, the house is dark. She is still on her date, and from the way Nina doesn't seem phased by it, this was to be expected. I can't help but wonder how long Elizabeth has been seeing this guy.

"Can I ask you something?" I ask, following Nina up the steps to the front porch.

I shove my hands into the pockets of my dress pants and lean back against the railing. I hadn't brought this up the entire evening; I didn't want to make it any more awkward than it already was. We danced around the topic in an attempt to make a normal conversation, but not bringing it up only made the elephant in the room grow bigger. It was strange.

I'm used to a more upfront Nina. She's never been one to hold back, and I wish that's who I went to dinner with instead of this reserved version.

Nina pulls her cardigan tighter against the November breeze. A few loose pieces of her hair blow in the wind, but she doesn't even seem to notice. "Josh—"

"I'm not trying to make this worse, Nin. I just want to—"

"Just stop." Nina closes her eyes, chewing on her bottom lip. She's doing her best to remain neutral, but I know it's getting harder to stay that way. With a final sigh, her burning green eyes meet my own, and her gaze is sad, knowing. "What did you think was going to happen?"

Before I can get a word in, she continues, "What am I saying? You didn't. You didn't think, neither of you did!"

"I'm sorry, Nin."

"I believe that, but that doesn't change what's happened."

My stomach flips when a set of headlights pulls into the driveway. Fuck, I didn't want to be here when they got back. When they retreat and drive away, I let out a breath I didn't realize I'd been holding. I have to get out of here. Next time I won't be so lucky. "I should go."

"Yeah, you probably should." Nina's voice returns to its neutral tone as she wrangles back in her emotions from moments ago.

nine

NOW

ELIZABETH IS SPENDING THANKSGIVING Day alone and it's my fault.

She's not alone; she's probably with Ryan, that little voice in the back of my mind reminds me.

The thought makes me sick. Pulling down the magnolia-lined driveway, the Villa-Davis house comes into view. The house sits a good half mile from the gated entrance inside the already gated community, but that isn't uncommon for this side of our subdivision. The side where people like the Villas, the Cains, and the Madigans own homes. The house Elizabeth and I own sits on the other side of the community, in the less gaudy subsection where the houses are a little more humble. It was my one request when it came time to buy something. But it didn't matter what side you lived on, if you lived in Meridian Hills, the rest of the town put you on a pedestal.

Nick and Nina's house is a magnificent structure made of stone, stucco, and wood that sits on two acres of land with an unobstructed view of the lake. Nina had built the house years ago—maybe nine at this point—and Nick moved in after their courthouse wedding in New York three years ago. It sits back from the water for added privacy from the immediate shoreline down the hillside while maintaining the incredible views. The best part is they're able to have a backyard, a pool, and a waterfront—a win-win-win in my book. Elizabeth and I don't have a lake view, but we have a backyard and a pool, and that's enough most days.

The driveway comes to a fork—the left leads to a three-car garage, and the right leads to an uncovered parking area where six cars are already parked. Six? That's odd. There should only be five. Maybe Nina invited her assistant to join us. Eddie is a cool guy, a little quiet, but his timing for jokes is always spot on. I shrug it off and pull into an open spot next to the black Range Rover I don't recognize.

Stalking toward the front door, I carry a handle of bourbon in one hand and a pecan pie in the other—I couldn't come empty-handed. Especially not when Nina was having to spend the holiday without her sister because of me. The front door is solid black, with two large paneled windows on either side. On my left leading up to the door is a wall of windows blacked out by privacy screens; to the right, along the face of the house, more blacked-out windows behind a bench that appears like it's more for decoration than actual use. I'm shocked the house isn't more decorated for the holidays, usually Nina decorates the first week of November.

Before I can knock, a blonde blur races past the front door. *Elizabeth.* No, there's no way, it had to have been Michaela or Eileen. Elizabeth isn't supposed to be here.

Moments later, she returns, and I catch her attention through the side window. It is Elizabeth. She hesitates, looking toward the living area where I assume everyone else is. Wondering if she should let one of them open it. Instead, she rolls her eyes and opens the door.

"Thought you weren't coming," I say, wiping my feet on the

rug outside and stepping across the threshold. I slip my feet out of my shoes and leave them near the others collected by the front door.

"I wasn't." Her response isn't exactly rude, but it's not very inviting, either.

"And yet, here you are."

Dark-painted lips pull into a thin line in response to my smile. I wonder if something happened. Last I heard, she wasn't going to be here. She didn't have to anymore—neither of us did—our contractual obligation to be at family holidays together was now null and void.

A few days after my spontaneous drive down to Jupiter Beach, I got the first call from my sister since I left New York. She didn't waste any time informing me that Elizabeth wouldn't be at Thanksgiving this year and then informed me that she thought Elizabeth was seeing someone.

"Why would you think that?" I asked when she said it, muting the television.

"I just get this feeling," Michaela said with the sounds of the city in the background. It was two o'clock on a Sunday afternoon, and since Finn was in California, I imagined she decided to go for a walk to think about things. Especially after receiving whatever news she was about to tell me.

"Did she say something?"

"No, but Nina—I don't know. I just get this feeling."

"What about Nina?"

"She just said something the other day, and it made it sound like Elizabeth was seeing someone." She sighed on the other end of the line. "And, I guess, it made me realize this is really happening."

"It's been happening, MJ."

"I know, but you know how it is…It's not real until it's *real*."

You have no idea. I sighed, letting my head fall back against the couch.

"I'm sorry, Josh," Michaela said quietly.

"Yeah, me too," I said. We sat in a comfortable silence for a few moments until she delved into a story from the previous week. Something she had been dying to tell me, but the week was crazy, and she barely had a chance to breathe until that day. Truth be told, I don't think she knew how to start the conversation. Was she supposed to say something about what I told her? Or was she supposed to act like everything was fine?

"Josh, finally!" Alex shouts, bringing me back to my current situation and breaking the tension between Elizabeth and me. He strolls past the double-sided stone fireplace into the foyer with a plate of random pieces of meat and cheese from the charcuterie board. "Hey, answer something for me...Would you rather—"

"No," I interrupt him before he can even finish. I am not falling for one of his stupid scenarios where I lose either way.

"But I didn't—"

"I don't even want to know what you were about to say."

Elizabeth stifles a laugh, and when I look over my shoulder, she offers a small smile. "You really don't."

Nina's voice echoes from the kitchen, "Alexander Chase Davis, you better not be doing what I think you're doing."

Alex heaves a sigh with an exaggerated eye roll. He whispers, "She's such a mom."

Moments later, Nina appears around the fireplace, wiping her hands on a dish towel. A white and blue striped apron is tied around her waist. "Help your brother with the firewood, would you?" It's less of a question and more of a command, and Alex knows it. He lets out an annoyed huff and stalks off to help Nick.

"I brought pie," I say, raising the pie in the air when she turns back to us.

Nina offers a polite smile in return and immediately I

notice she seems more tense than usual. Taking a deep breath, she says, "You can put it in the pantry with the rest of the desserts."

She holds that polite smile and motions behind her toward the kitchen. When I don't move, she motions with her eyes again, and I finally take the hint. She wants to have a conversation with her sister without me sticking around.

Elizabeth fiddles with one of the leaves of the fern on the entry table, avoiding my gaze.

"I'll just go put this away then," I say and glance back at Elizabeth one more time before stepping between them to join the others. I can feel Nina's stare on my back the whole way to the kitchen.

"Finally," Nick says, clapping me on the back and taking my party contributions from my hands.

"You get lost on the five-minute drive over here?" Finn asks from behind his whiskey glass.

"Or something." I try to catch a glimpse of the women in the foyer, but the fireplace hides them from view. What I wouldn't give to be a fly on the wall for *that* conversation.

"Whiskey or beer?" Nick asks, coming back from the pantry.

"Something strong," I say, finally pulling my attention away from the fireplace. "I have a feeling I'm going to need it."

ten

THEN

June 2016

"WHAT THE HELL DO you have in here? Bricks?" I drop the box on the bed with a huff. I don't care what she says, there are definitely bricks in there. What in the hell could be that heavy?

Elizabeth vaguely looks over her shoulder and smirks. "Books."

She turns back to the shoes that she's been organizing for the last twenty minutes on the shelving unit in her closet. I've never seen one person with so many shoes, not even Michaela, and when I commented on it with the last box I brought up, she told me I should see Nina's closet.

We've been "dating" for the last six months, going public in January, a few weeks after the Christmas Ball incident. It happened sooner than either of us expected, but I don't think it's been as bad as we expected either. We haven't seen much of each other because she's been busy with school and I've been busy at work. I graduated from Chadwick in early May on a Friday afternoon and started work at QC Marketing the next Monday. She started at SCAD in January and has been taking extra classes so she can graduate early—within the next three years instead of four.

Classes ended two days ago, so this entire weekend has been dedicated to helping her move into her new townhome. The tan-colored stone home has black shutters, a black door with a worn gold metal doorknob, and a single step with worn black paint from years of entry. After living in on-campus housing for two quarters, she was ready to have her own space that wasn't shared with other students. One where she could go to the bathroom with a respectable amount of privacy that just doesn't come with living in the dorms.

When she brought up the idea of buying something, I was on board immediately. Not that my opinion really mattered, it was her money and her name going on the house. But I hated dealing with the living situation in the dorms the few times I had come down. In the comfort of her home, we'd be able to get a real break instead of being on guard twenty-four-seven. At least, that was my hope. Little did I know she'd be inviting two of her friends to live with her. It's not that I don't like Lola and Selena, I just thought we'd have a little more privacy, but the more I thought about it, the happier I was she wouldn't be completely alone.

"Just put it by the shelves right here." Elizabeth motions to the bookshelf outside of the closet. With a sigh, I do as I'm told, lifting the box of bricks and gently setting it in front of the shelves that sit between the closet and bathroom doors.

The bedrooms are smaller than what she's used to, but for an older house (built in the late 1800s, she said), they were bigger than I thought they'd be. Her king-sized bed is pushed back into an alcove to the right of the door with a three-drawer nightstand on either side. Brass vintage swing-arm wall lamps hang above the nightstands. A storage ottoman sits at the foot of the bed filled with her blankets and sheets. Her desk is loaded with boxes of schoolbooks and desk supplies on the other side of a door that leads to a small deck overlooking the backyard. Another bookshelf sits next to her desk. A tall dresser stands across the room from the bed, and above it, I still need to mount her TV to the wall. The closet is nothing more than a large box, but somehow, she has (as of now) managed to put all of her stuff inside it. At least, what she's brought with her. I know there's still a lot left in her room at the Villa Estate.

The bathroom is twice the size of the closet, maybe triple. When you walk in, there's a fireplace—yes, a fireplace—and a linen closet to the left, and to the right, a single vanity and a closed-in toilet room. Along the back wall, an updated marbled walk-in shower. The other bathroom that Selena and Lola will share is a smaller version of the same, sans the fireplace, and with a dual vanity.

Leaning against the doorframe of the closet, I can't help but enjoy the view, following the curves of her body as my mind wanders down a dangerous path. Her shirt rides up, exposing a sliver of tanned skin. There's a jagged red line on her side, and it reminds me why we're here—two very different people forced together in what would normally be considered an unlikely relationship.

In the past few months, I've seen just how self-conscious she is about the scars she bears from that night almost four years ago. She rarely wears anything without sleeves, and she always checks to make sure her shirt is tucked in. If she does wear a shorter sleeve, she wears something to cover the scars on her arms. Only recently did she stop covering her scars around me all the time.

Elizabeth reaches for a pair of shoes on the very top shelf, but she can't quite reach it, not even on her tiptoes. I take another minute to appreciate the curves of her body before stepping forward. My front flush against her back, my arm brushes against hers when I reach for the pair of purple heels she can't reach. She turns in my arms, gazing up at me with her chest now flush against mine. A deep inhale fills my senses with a warm floral mixture; it's intoxicating. My hand grips the shelf, leaning down just a little closer, and when I do, her eyes move from my eyes to my lips and back.

"W-was there something else?" she stammers.

I smirk, enjoying how flustered this makes her. "Only thing left in the truck is your couch, armchairs, and desk for downstairs."

"W-what are you d-doing there, then?" Elizabeth tries to hide the continued stammer in her words, but nothing can hide the rapid beating of her heart against her chest. I can feel it hammering between us like it's trying to break free from its cage.

I bring down the shoes and hand them to her before leaving, heading down to the truck to wait for her to catch her breath before we move the rest of the furniture inside. Truth be told, I could use a minute for myself.

Over the past six months, Elizabeth and I have spent a lot of time together, getting to know each other better. And we've had a few close calls—losing ourselves in the moment. The line between what is real and what is a result of acting certain ways because of that damn contract have become blurred.

When I arrived in Savannah on Friday morning, she wasted no time running into my arms the moment she saw me on the street. The force knocked me back a few steps as she clutched onto me, her arms wrapped tightly around my shoulders, legs around my waist, and her face buried in my neck. I kissed her temple and carried her back to the dorm entrance where her friends stood.

"Thank God. Now we won't have to listen to her complain about when you're going to get here," Georgie said with an eye roll.

"Don't listen to her," Selena said. "She's just upset because Aaron hasn't called her back."

Georgie shot her a death glare and Selena returned it with her own sweet smile.

"I missed you too, Sugar," I whispered against Elizabeth's hair.

When she pulled back, her gaze moved from my eyes to my lips and back. That pull was back, drawing us closer together, but the thought of this being the first time we kissed didn't sit right with me.

I cleared my throat and slowly lowered her from my arms. She looked confused and dare I say a little hurt as I set her on her own two feet. "C'mon Sug, let's get you packed up," I said and kissed her forehead before taking her hand and going inside to finish cleaning out her dorm.

That moment has been replaying in my mind since. I wondered what her reaction would have been if we *had* kissed. If we had crossed that line for the first time. It didn't feel right letting the first time we had a real connection be in front of her friends like that. But now, I'm wondering if I made the wrong choice. Maybe I should've let it happen, said fuck it, and kissed her right there on the sidewalk in front of the whole world.

Finishing off my water bottle, I crumple the plastic and toss it through the open window of the front passenger seat. This is going to be a long fucking day.

"When do the girls get back?" I ask, lugging the final grocery bags into the kitchen. The previous owner had painted the kitchen a neutral green color that I would have never picked seeing it on one of those sample cards in the hardware store, but it actually kind of works. The color is almost a lighter olive green, and it looks great against the white marble countertops, white subway tile backsplash, and red tile floor.

"Tomorrow," Elizabeth says, putting the yogurts in the fridge. She will never admit it, but I can tell she's getting nervous. I'm supposed to leave shortly because I have to work in the morning, but I'm starting to think I need to spend the night. The first night in a brand-new place is always kind of nerve-wracking, especially alone. I can live on a few less hours of sleep if it means she feels better on her first night here.

"You'll be okay by yourself?"

"I'm not a child, Josh," she snaps before mumbling to herself. "I can spend a night by myself."

She begins arranging the fruit in the bowl on the counter next to the sink.

Taking her hand, I remove the banana and set it in the bowl. This close, she's practically cornered in the "L" of the peninsula island. "I can stay tonight if it will make you feel better," I say.

Elizabeth shakes her head but her eyes are glued to the countertop. I bend down to try and meet her stare.

"It's not that far. I can manage the drive in the morning." I don't even know when it happened, but we're suddenly much closer than we were moments ago. Faces centimeters apart. I'm starting to get the strangest sense of déjà vu. "I can stay with you tonight. Keep you company so you're not all alone tonight."

I can audibly hear her swallow at the suggestion. It's not the first time we've spent the night together, but it would be the first time we were *alone* together. Her gaze falls to my lips before she leans in a little further, and our lips brush. I pull back slightly.

"It's a four-hour drive," Elizabeth whispers.

Four hours here and back every couple of weeks to keep up

this charade. Normally, I dread the thought, but right now, the only thing on my mind is how close her lips are to mine. How every time we've accidentally brushed against each other—hands, arms, anything—there's a spark that rushes through me. A small crackle of electricity beneath the surface, I've never felt anything like it before.

"I'll manage," I say softly, and our lips brush again, but we still don't close the gap.

"Josh…"

My name on her lips is sweeter than honey, and it's enough for me to finally jump across the line with both feet. I press my lips to hers, swallowing the gasp that escapes her. Lifting her off her feet, I plant her on the counter and step between her legs. Elizabeth wraps herself around me, pulling me closer as her hands explore my body—down my shoulders, arms, and chest. Her fingers play with the hem of my shirt, slowly lifting it, and the air is cool against my skin, breaking the trance. Pulling away from her, I lick my lips, tasting her still: a cherry tang on my lips from her chapstick. Separated, our chests rise and fall, trying to catch our breath.

We can't go any further, no matter how badly I want to. Fuck, I want to, but we shouldn't. Not yet.

Her gaze is fiery, longing…She wants this, maybe even as badly as I do, but it's only because she's lost in the moment. She'd wake up in the morning and hate me for it. We haven't truly gotten to know each other. I'm not even sure I'd call us friends yet, but we're getting there. We still have some work to do before we can go any further.

Brushing my nose against hers, I press another longing kiss to her lips. "I'll see you in two weeks, Sugar," I whisper against them and turn on my heel. I leave her there, sitting on the counter, and walk out the door because if I don't do it now, I won't do it at all.

eleven

NOW

"YOU KNOW," ALEX STARTS but takes a sip of his beer, and I have a feeling I'm not going to like what follows. "For someone in an arranged marriage, you don't seem too happy about getting out of it."

"Alex." Nick pinches the bridge of his nose.

"Look, someone had to say it!"

"He's not wrong," Finn adds.

The four of us found our way outside not long after we finished stuffing our faces with various pies and desserts. Nina was putting Elena to bed. Dad and Uncle Jim were watching the football game while Michaela, Mom, and Uncle Jim's girlfriend, Tessa finished cleaning up the kitchen. Tessa is the owner of a local cafe in Winchester. Nina had introduced them two years ago, and they started dating a few months later. Just before I walked outside to meet the rest of the guys, Kai snuck off to take a phone call (because, apparently, business truly never stops) while Eileen played with Ophelia. And Elizabeth…Well, I'm not sure where she snuck off to.

"I know he's not wrong," Nick says. "But—"

"No, he's right." I sigh. "I'm not happy about it." Shit, this is the first time I've admitted that out loud. What good would it do anyway? It's not like she's coming back. "I care about her—"

"Not enough to fight for your marriage," Alex protests, earning a warning glare from his brother. Alex rolls his eyes and leans forward to say, "What? It's not like you haven't thought the same thing."

Nick doesn't respond though, he just stares into the distance, taking a sip of his beer.

"It was never going to last." I sigh. "Elizabeth didn't want this. If it had been up to her, she would have married William."

"Yeah, okay." Finn scoffs.

Finn forgets that Elizabeth and William were headed for the aisle in the next few years had she not been forced to end things because of this arrangement. Not only a Cain, but an adopted Villa child, marrying the son of the local congressman was a match made in heaven. It was everything Ethel Cain could have wanted for her daughter, everything Brina could have wanted for her, too. But then I had to come along and mess up those plans.

"Despite his shortcomings, Will was a good match for her, in terms of lifestyle and—"

"You're leaving out the part where him leaving her high and dry on the dance floor wasn't part of this ruse," Finn says. "That was just him being an asshole. Oh, and let's not forget, he planned on breaking up with her at the beginning of the year anyway. So no, William was *not* a good match for her."

"Well, I think you should fight for it," Alex says, taking another sip. "You guys are good together. I don't care what you say, that wasn't all for show."

"It doesn't matter," I say, scratching at the wood arm of the chair. Elizabeth doesn't need me anymore, she has Ryan, and she seems…happy. Despite how I feel, I won't ruin her opportunity to be happy. I clear my throat and readjust my glasses, adding, "She's already moved on."

It's Nick's turn to scoff.

"Something you want to share with the class?" Finn asks.

Come to think of it, Nick has been awfully quiet this whole time. Does he know something?

Nick swirls his beer around the bottle and chews on the inside of his cheek. I can tell he isn't sure telling us this is the right choice. Whatever he knows, I get the feeling his wife won't be very happy if he decides to tell us. Thinking about it a second longer, he decides to do it anyway. "Ryan is a fucking douche. Nina hates him."

"Funny, she seemed friendly enough with him," I say, earning a confused glance from the others.

"What do you mean?"

Nina didn't tell him about my trip down south? That's surprising. I would have figured Nick would be her first call as soon as I left.

"When I went down to Charleston...Jupiter Beach...Wait, Nina didn't tell you any of this?"

The confusion on his face confirms she did not tell him.

A humorless chuckle escapes me. "I went to Elizabeth's house. I was going to...Well, I'm not sure what I was going to do, but I just knew I had to see her. When I got there, Nin answered the door, and then this guy showed up."

"You met him?" Alex practically jumps out of his seat.

"Remind me why we don't call Jerry Springer?" Finn asks.

I think he's joking, but I also think he's partially serious. Truthfully, we could probably get some good ratings with all the shit that goes down around here.

"Nina kept the interaction brief and ensured no one could ask too many questions, but she seemed happy to see Elizabeth moving on."

"Nick," Nina interrupts the conversation and all heads turn toward her. Her gaze is narrowed like she knows what we've been talking about. And she probably does. Who knows how long she's been standing there? "Your dad is leaving. Pat and Jenny, too."

"Right." Nick sighs, rubbing his palms on his thighs before he stretches into a stand. "Probably best to call it a night, anyway."

We walk back into the house, where Ophelia sleeps soundly on her father's shoulder as he follows Eileen out of the house, careful not to wake her up. Michaela is telling Mom and Dad bye, since she and Finn are staying here until Sunday, along with Elizabeth. I offered them a room at my house, but Michaela preferred Nina's guest bed. And I can't lie, they are pretty nice.

Mom pulls me into a tight hug, tighter than the one I reciprocate. Sometimes, I barely recognize the woman in front of me and I've started to wonder if the woman I grew up with ever existed. She blended into the world of the Winchester elite without pause, while Dad still struggled sometimes. He was a simple man and didn't require the glitz and glamor this world had to offer, but I know he wouldn't trade it either. He loved his family, loved the life he'd been blessed with since Elizabeth and I were thrown together. But not Mom, she relished in her new status and all that came with it.

Dad only offers me a handshake. He and I haven't talked much since the news broke about the separation. I don't know if he knows—about the arrangement—but from the little interaction we've had since May, I think it's safe to say he knows something. I haven't brought it up because if he doesn't know, I'm not sure I want to have that discussion. I've already disappointed one parent, I'm not sure I can handle disappointing him, too. Mom wasn't thrilled about the separation, but she said she wasn't all that surprised, either. I was out of my league with Elizabeth and I was lucky she'd stuck around as long as she had, even with the agreement in place.

Uncle Jim grips my shoulder and squeezes, and it's a little comforting before he and Tessa follow my parents outside. Like Dad, I'm not sure if he knows the truth, and I haven't asked. If they don't ever know the *whole* story, I just might be okay with that. Nick and Alex join them to say their final goodbyes, leaving me and Nina for one of the awkward goodbyes that we've become accustomed to.

"Thanks for dinner, Nin." She doesn't respond, only offers a small smile, and I pull her into a hug. "I know this isn't easy for you, and I'm sorry, but I just want you to know that I love you."

She tightens her embrace a little before taking a step back. "We'll get through it."

Her words are so simple, but they mean a lot, and for the first time, I feel like maybe we will. Dinner was okay tonight; nothing eventful happened, and Elizabeth and I kept our distance for the most part. If things stayed this way, maybe we could do this after all. It will take some time for the awkward tension to subside, especially when she brings Ryan, but we can do it...I think.

Nina squeezes my arm one last time before heading back toward her bedroom to check on Elena.

"You off tomorrow?" Michaela asks, coming out of the guest room at the top of the stairs.

"Depends."

"Lunch?"

"Only if you're paying." I smirk, earning an eye roll from my sister.

"Fine." She nods and pulls me into a hug before sauntering off to the kitchen. From the sounds of it, she's pouring herself another glass of wine.

Elizabeth is the only one that remains. Before I can say anything, she glances around the fireplace toward the kitchen. Satisfied that Michaela and Nina are preoccupied, she grips my hand and pulls me down the hallway off the foyer. "We need to talk."

Talk?

"Sunday, meet me at Millers All Day."

"In Charleston?"

Why the hell does she want me to drive all the way to Charleston to talk? The last time that happened…

"Shh! The last thing I need is your sister or Nina hearing."

"Why can't we just talk now?"

"Because," she snaps. "I don't need any of them poking their nose in my business."

Fair point.

"Sunday, eleven-thirty."

What in the hell could be so important that I have to drive all the way down to Charleston again to talk about it? I want to say no, but from the look on her face, I know that I can't say no.

"Fine, but make it one o'clock."

twelve

NOW

I WADE THROUGH THE line of hungry patrons trying to get their name on the list to dine at Millers All Day, a favorite in downtown Charleston. Breaking through the line, I'm met with the gracious but tired smile of the young hostesses. The restaurant's interior gives the vibes of a modern-retro diner with a coffee bar on the right, a bar along the back wall with an old-fashioned PRESCRIPTION sign above, large inviting booths along the far left wall, and—

Is that a living room area?

Servers move to and fro with haste that lacks the typical frantic look in the eyes of servers in a place as busy as this. They wear warm smiles and welcome their guests as though they're family they haven't seen in a while.

"How many?" One of the hostesses asks, and I give her the name before the other leads me further into the diner. Around the bend, there are even more tables, and in the far corner, I see her planted at a two-top. She sips on what looks like a mimosa that lacks the typical yellow color of orange juice. Instead, it's a faded purple color—lavender, maybe? There are two plates on the table bearing a cinnamon roll as big as my head mounted with icing and a puff pastry that resembles a strawberry pop tart.

"Enjoy your meal," the hostess says with a warm smile before two-stepping back to the front door.

"This place is hopping," I say, sitting in the chair across from Elizabeth.

"There's *always* a line, but it's worth it." She nods towards the plates between us. "Try the cinnamon roll; the cream cheese is to die for."

I dig the fork into the crust, and when I take the first bite, I'm reminded almost of a cinnamon biscuit. The cream cheese icing melts across my tongue. It's the perfect balance of sweet and savory.

The server appears with a steaming cup of coffee—black—with exactly two sugars. "Do you need a few more minutes on lunch?" she asks, looking between me and Elizabeth.

"Just a few. Thanks, Holly," Elizabeth says, dismissing her with another sip of her mimosa. She nods toward the steaming mug between us. "I assumed you still drank your coffee the same."

"You assumed correct," I say, ripping open the sugar packets and letting the crystals dissolve in the warm liquid. Flipping over the menu, I have no idea what to choose. The hot honey chicken sounds kind of interesting, though. "What do you recommend for food?"

"You'd like the honey chicken donut sandwich. Unless they have the lobster roll. Then the lobster roll." Her words make the corner of my mouth tick upward. She knew exactly what I would want, not to mention she ordered my coffee (exactly how I take it) so it would arrive when I did. Maybe we aren't so hopeless after all.

Elizabeth rolls her eyes when she sees my smile. "What?"

"Oh, nothing," I say, looking back down at the menu. The

server returns a moment later, and I order the hot honey chicken without hesitation. Elizabeth orders the biscuits and gravy with a side of pimento cheese and a hot honey chicken breast of her own.

The silence between us is filled with the background noise of the restaurant. However, this silence isn't as comfortable as it used to be. Silence wasn't a problem for us. We were used to it, spending most of our time together in the quiet, but this... this is torturous. Elizabeth finishes the mimosa. Before she can place the glass on the table, another one appears.

"How is—"

"What are—"

We both stop, waiting for the other to continue, but neither of us does until she finally releases a deep sigh and says, "I'm invoking the *Last Hoorah Clause.*"

The sip of coffee gets stuck in my throat. I cough to clear my throat, and the liquid burns my chest the whole way down. "Excuse me?"

"The final term in our arrangement," she says. "Line Ten of the—"

"I know what it is, Elizabeth." Line Ten, Subsection B. I could never forget the ten lines that have outlined my life for the last ten years. "Why are you bringing it up?"

"Well, I was supposed to take Ryan with me, but..."

She scratches at something invisible on the table, avoiding eye contact. So, whatever this event is, it must be pretty damn important to invoke this clause. I thought the whole thing was stupid when I read it the first time ten years ago. In what world would one of us need to have a contractual agreement to force the other to join them at some event, regardless of our relationship status, up until we are divorced?

"...but we're not exactly speaking right now."

"Shocker," I say over the rim of my coffee mug. Is it wrong that I feel a smidge of satisfaction hearing that they aren't getting along? Though I have to admit, I'm not all that surprised. I mean, the guy doesn't even know her favorite flower or respect the fact she doesn't like to be called Lizzie. Or maybe he did those things because she didn't correct him— and what does that say about their relationship?

Elizabeth shoots me a glare. "It's the annual Palm Valley trip with the girls next weekend and—"

"If you were taking your new boyfriend, wouldn't it be a little weird for *me* to show up?"

"They don't know I was bringing him," she says, her attention turning back to the invisible mark on the table. "They don't know about the separation."

I lower the mug to the table and scrub my hand down my face. What does she mean they don't know about our separation? She tells those girls everything. We've been legally separated since May, almost...seven months at this point. Why wouldn't she tell them?

My hand covers my mouth and I sigh. "Elizabeth—"

"I was going to tell them this weekend, I swear. Introduce them to Ryan and tell them about us getting a divorce, but it looks like that won't be necessary."

"You still can, without me."

"Josh, I can't show up alone."

"Elizabeth."

"Josh." Her lips pull into a straight line. "You can't say no."

She says it so matter-of-factly. It's like she knows she has me backed into a corner...because she does. She's right; I can't say no. It's part of the contract. But I'm not sure I can handle spending another moment pretending to be the loving, doting husband when I know at the end of the weekend, I'll be left alone...again.

"C'mon, it'll be fun. One last hoorah before we sign the papers."

I scrub a hand down my face. I'm going to regret this, I

know it. "Fine. When do we leave?"

The Winchester Times
September 19, 2012
8:00 A.M.

Written by: Zach Williams

Prominent Winchester Family Attacked: Parents Killed, and Teenager Fighting for Life as Search Continues for Suspect

Nearly a week after prominent Winchester residents Thomas and Ethel Cain were found dead at their home in the affluent Meridian Hills neighborhood, those close to them are still looking for answers. The Winchester Police (WPD) and Hamilton County Sheriff's Department continue to investigate the incident, which was reported around 10:30 p.m. On September 14 at the private residence just off Cove Road.

According to WPD, officers were called to the home after receiving a report of a house fire and an unconscious, impaired female. Upon arrival, paramedics located the teenager outside of the home, which was already engulfed in flames. The teenager, whose name has not been released, was taken to a nearby hospital, where she remains in critical condition.

After battling the house fire for more than four hours, authorities were able to investigate the interior of the home, where they discovered two bodies. On Saturday, September 15, the Hamilton County Coroner's Office identified the remains as 46-year-old Thomas Cain and 43-year-old Ethel Cain. Their deaths have been ruled homicides.

Police are currently searching for the victim's son, 19-year-old Nathanial Cain, who is believed to have been at the home earlier in the day. Residents with any knowledge of his whereabouts are encouraged to contact WPD or the Hamilton County Sheriff's Department.

earlier in the day. Residents with any knowledge of his whereabouts are encouraged to contact WPD or the Hamilton County Sheriff's Department.

thirteen

THEN

September 2016

WE HAVEN'T TALKED IN almost two weeks. Correction: *she* hasn't talked to me in two weeks. I have occasionally sent a text to check on her, but it's been radio silence on her end since she left to head back to Savannah after Labor Day. Why haven't we talked in two weeks? I'm glad you asked. It's because I got jealous. That little green monster reared its ugly head and I couldn't reign it in.

Brody Cox. Some aspiring starving artist from SCAD decided to try and make a move on Elizabeth last month while we were at a coffee shop. She had picked a spot at a table near the window while I waited for our drinks, and he took the opportunity to swoop in. After some stupid pickup line, she giggled. She fucking giggled. He had "seen her around campus" and wondered if she wanted to get coffee sometime. He handed her a scrap of paper with his phone number and winked before he left.

"It's not a big deal, Josh," she said, stuffing the phone number in her pocket.

"Elizabeth—"

"It's not like I'm ever going to see him again." She rolled her eyes and promptly walked out of the coffee shop. The heavy door slammed behind her, catching the attention of the other shop patrons.

That was two weeks before she came home for the holiday weekend, and we spent most of it ignoring each other. She went straight to Nina's house, sent me a text letting me know she had arrived, and turned off her phone—at least, that's what I thought. Going radio silent while she was with Nina wasn't completely out of the norm, especially if she wanted a little extra girl time, so I didn't think anything of it. But when I arrived at the Villa Estate Sunday morning for a day on the lake, it was pretty obvious something wasn't right. She spent most of the day with her face in her phone. Occasionally, a smile or a laugh that she'd try to hide would creep its way onto her face. It wasn't until Nina chastised me later that afternoon for blowing up her phone the past two days that I realized what was going on. A pit formed in my stomach as I apologized to Nina, assured her I would never mean to interrupt their time together, and promised her I would be more mindful next time. She seemed happy enough, but I was left with the knowledge that my girlfriend was talking to someone else.

"How's Brody?" I asked that night, walking into my condo. She would be staying at my place for the rest of the weekend, which meant she'd get the guest room to herself because there wasn't anyone else around to find that odd. We'd go to the Davis Labor Day party tomorrow, and then she'd wake up early Tuesday to go back to Savannah for class in the afternoon.

"I don't know—"

"Don't you dare finish that sentence." I stopped her.

Her mouth opened and closed a few times before she settled on saying nothing.

"Are you fucking kidding me, Elizabeth? You've spent the last two days texting *him* and I get a fucking lecture from Nina because she thinks it's me? Did you even spend time with her or were you too preoccupied talking to your latest conquest?"

"Grow up, Josh," Elizabeth hissed. The pointed end of her black nail glared at me across the kitchen island. "It's none of your business who I talk to. We aren't married. We aren't together. You have no right—"

"I have a fucking piece of paper that says otherwise."

"And I have a piece of paper that says I'm allowed to date outside of this fucking arrangement."

Line 7, Item B.

I know.

At the time of signing the papers, it seemed like an okay idea, but now...

The thought of someone else anywhere near her makes the adrenaline course through my veins at rapid speed. My hands clenched at my sides at the thought of her sneaking him into the townhouse, taking him upstairs, and letting him touch her in the same bed we've shared countless times. The same I've only ever slept next to her in, both of us tiptoeing up to the line of something more, but never stepping over it.

"So, fuck you, Josh. Take your unfair jealousy and shove it straight up your ass."

"Unfair? You're my—"

"I don't care, Josh. We are not together. We are not in love and we are not going to live happily ever after. We are only together on paper and only because we both needed a way to get what we wanted. You have no right to be upset if I'm talking to someone else, someone who is there."

"Someone who is there?" I scoff. "Elizabeth, I—"

"Yes! Someone who isn't going to run the second things start to get real. Someone who—"

"Who's running, Liz? Because it sure as hell isn't me! You're the one talking to some other guy. I haven't so much as looked at another woman since this whole thing started. You're the one running, not me."

Her nails clicked against the countertop in a uniform rhythm and I awaited the fury behind her next words, but it never came. She plucked her purse from the island and walked to the door without a second glance. "I'm staying at Nina's."

The door slammed behind her, and my feet carried me to the threshold, ready to follow her, but no matter how tight I gripped the doorknob, my hand wouldn't turn it.

When I went a week without any sort of communication, I called the only person I could discuss the situation with: my mom. I called her before school started on Monday morning, but after I knew she would be on at least her second cup of coffee. She answered the phone with surprise. "Joshua?"

"Mom—"

"Is everything okay? I'm at work and—"

"Elizabeth and I had a fight." The words were met with silence, but I knew she was there. I could hear the sounds of a copier and a distant conversation in the background. She was probably in the teacher's lounge getting ready for the school day, which was set to start in an hour. "We got into an argument after the party at the Villas and—"

"Well, that's to be expected," she said with a slight chuckle. "Couples have arguments sometimes."

"But, we haven't talked in—"

"Joshua." Her tone cut me off immediately. With a sigh, she excused herself from the others on her side of the line. "Josh, you cannot mess this up. Do you understand me? If you screw this up, you're not just losing this amazing opportunity that you have been given, but you could be implicated in what happened to that boy. You should be grateful for whatever Elizabeth gives you considering that without this arrangement, you would've never ended up with someone like her."

"But she's been talking to some—"

"Let her," Mom snapped. "If she wants to talk to a hundred

other guys, you let her. Why do you care who Elizabeth decides to spend her time with? Falling in love was never part of the agreement."

Mom was right. Elizabeth falling in love with me wasn't a requirement of the contract. She could talk to or date anyone she wanted, as long as they didn't interfere with our agreement.

"Right." I sighed. "Yeah, I guess that's true."

"Don't mess this up, Josh. You can't afford to lose her," Mom said. "Now, get ready for work or you're going to be late."

Without saying goodbye, I dropped the phone on the counter and my head fell in my hands. Why can't I just let Elizabeth do what she wants? Why do I have to get that pit in my stomach at the thought of her being with someone else? This was never about falling in love, it was about getting what we both wanted. What we both needed. And I needed to be grateful for what I had.

After the past two weeks, I considered not coming tonight. I know she probably doesn't want to see me, but I couldn't do it. I couldn't let *this* go by without at least checking on her. Tomorrow is the fourth anniversary of her parents' murder, the night she almost died. I don't know much about what happened that night, but a double homicide (almost triple) isn't exactly common in our neck of the woods.

News traveled fast about the Cain boy who sought revenge on his family for being cut off.

I told myself I wouldn't bother her. I'd give her some space. She was probably finding solace in Brody anyway. But the more I thought about it, the more it ate away at me, and I couldn't bring myself to just sit at home. I had the rest of the week off work anyway, so I packed a bag and drove to Savannah, surprised to find the house dark and quiet since it was only ten o'clock at night.

Now, I'm not sure if she's even home. Or maybe she's just in the kitchen; you can't see the light on with the front blinds closed.

Using my key, I open the door to find the house dark and still, but then I see a sliver of light pouring down from the upstairs hallway. I close the door loud enough that if she's awake she'll hear it before I climb the stairs.

From the door, I can see that the TV is off and the bathroom door is closed, which means she's probably in bed. God, I hope I'm not about to walk in on her and Brody doing something. Shaking the thoughts from my mind, I turn the corner and find her in bed...alone. She's sound asleep in the warm light from the lamp above her, a book at her side and her glasses still on her face. Her eyes are slightly red and puffy like maybe she had been crying earlier.

I slide the book from her hands, resting it upside down on the nightstand, the portrait of a pale-faced woman with dark brown hair in a white dress staring back at me. *Pride and Prejudice.* How many copies of this book does she have? I swear I've seen a hardcover copy with an intricate design before. Who needs more than one copy of the same book?

It's not important right now, Josh.

Gently slipping the glasses from the end of her nose, I fold them and place them next to the book, just as her eyes flutter open. Brown eyes stare up at me in confusion, and when I offer her a soft smile, her eyes begin to well with tears. I don't even think about it, I crawl into the bed and pull her close. Tears soak the front of my shirt as sobs rack through her.

Despite what she said that night in my condo, despite the radio silence since she walked out, I know I made the right choice.

Waking up the next morning, I'm surprised to find the bed next to me empty. A cool breeze creeps its way into the room, rattling the blinds on the back of the balcony door, bringing a mixture of fall air and the faint scent of fresh coffee that wafts in from the hallway. The clock on the nightstand tells me it's past eight in the morning, and with a groan, I drag myself into the bathroom. A quick search of both rooms comes up empty for the T-shirt I had been wearing last night, but the mystery is solved when I walk into the kitchen. It hangs low on her hips, covering the pair of pajama shorts she wears. Her hair has been pulled into a messy bun, but a few pieces have fallen out, falling in her face as she drops chocolate chips in the perfect circles of pancake batter. I wrap my arms around her waist and rest my chin on her shoulder. "You sleep okay?"

She doesn't offer a verbal response. Instead, she leans back further into my embrace and flips over the pancakes.

"I'm sorry, Liz." I sigh. "I hate that you left with things that way, and I'm sorry for showing up when you told me not to, but—"

"I'm glad you came."

Well, that was easier than expected. But why? I expected her to put up a much bigger fight after how things went that night in my condo.

Elizabeth pulls the pancakes from the griddle and turns in my arms. "Thank you for coming, it...it means a lot."

I don't know what to say, everything I think of doesn't sound good enough.

"You were right, Josh. Talking to Brody...I know, technically, we're allowed to, but it doesn't feel right. I'm sorry for acting the way I did. I hope you can forgive me."

Her words light a strange spark of hope in my gut.

"I mean, if I found out you were doing the same thing with some other girl, I would've reacted the same way. Regardless of if this thing between us is *real* or not, whether we stay together in the end or not, I don't want to share. I won't expect you to, either. I'm—"

Her words stop short when I kiss her. I don't know what comes over me, but it's the only way I can think to respond. Elizabeth melts into me, wrapping her arms around my neck, and she whimpers when I press her against the cabinets. We haven't kissed since the day I moved her into this townhouse, and fuck, I'm really starting to regret that. The feeling of her body against mine is addicting. I can't help but think of what it would feel like to be even closer.

"Josh," she whispers, parting from me. "I really am sorry—"

"You're mine," I say the words without a second thought. "Until we sign the papers at the end of it all, you're mine, and I'm yours. Completely."

fourteen

HER FINGERS INTERTWINE WITH mine over her shoulder as we walk through Forsyth Park, a huge green space smack dab in the middle of Savannah. After eating breakfast, Elizabeth dragged me out of the house to explore the city she loved so much. Every time I visit, we usually stick around the house, but I think she's trying to keep her mind off the looming reminder of today. We spent most of the day on a hop-on-and-off trolley tour before eating lunch at The Olde Pink House—a literal pink house that has been around since the 1700s and is said to be haunted. Sadly, I didn't run into any ghosts. I even went to the basement bathroom, but I walked out of the stall unscathed. Kind of wish something did happen, because I'd love to have a ghost story up my sleeve. Elizabeth hasn't talked much today, locking herself in her head, but I can't even begin to imagine what she's been through.

"I've always wanted to get married here," Elizabeth says, leading me down the main drag of the park toward the fountain. Local artists have set up periodically along the pathway, and there's even a trumpeter playing a classic tune as locals enjoy the beautiful fall day. Some read books, others play with their dogs, a few people sketch, and even a handful doze in the September sun.

"Let's do it."

"We don't—"

"Why not?" I don't have anywhere I've ever dreamed of walking down the aisle. The least we can do is give her the opportunity to do this where she's always wanted to. "Where else would we do it?"

"It's where my parents met," she says softly. "They spent their whole lives in Winchester, but they never knew each other." We reach the fountain, and a small smile tugs on the corner of her red lips. "It wasn't until my father came to Savannah to visit his grandmother that he met my momma, who just happened to be in town for her aunt's wedding."

I squeeze her hand gently, reassuringly, because I don't know how else to respond. There's nothing that seems appropriate in this moment. While I want her to feel comfortable enough to share the details of her parents with me, I don't want to push her. She doesn't have to talk about it if she doesn't want to, but something tells me the more I learn about them, the more I'm going to learn about her.

"It doesn't get any easier." She sighs. "The scars may fade a little more every year, but it never gets any easier."

"Do you want to talk about it?"

Elizabeth stares into the water of the fountain, contemplating, and I'm about to apologize for pushing when she says, "It was her birthday weekend. They were supposed to leave that afternoon to go to San Diego…"

But that didn't happen. As she recounted the events from that night for the first time, my insides wove themselves into a tangled mess. I had never heard anything so horrific.

Elizabeth had come home four years ago from a football game to a seemingly normal house. The lights were off, and the doors were locked, nothing out of the ordinary, especially since her father had recently told Nate to pack his shit and leave. She dropped her keys in the basket on the counter and started the search for a snack, settling on a few spoonfuls of peanut butter. Her parents weren't home; they'd never know. Her mother used to raise her brow and ask "Were you raised in a barn?" when she would eat straight from the jar. But what Momma didn't know wouldn't hurt her.

On the way to her bedroom with her peanut butter jar, Elizabeth noticed the light on in her father's office.

She called for him but got no response. As she pushed open the door everything looked normal, she thought maybe he just forgot to turn the light off, but then she saw it…The crimson pool leaked from underneath her father's oak desk. Behind the desk, she found her father lying in a pool of blood. She didn't register her own scream until the jar of peanut butter landed on her foot, breaking the trance. She screamed for him, for help, but no one came.

Then she thought about her mother. Was she okay? Was she hiding somewhere? She rushed to her parents' bedroom. Opening the door, she silently prayed her mother was just hiding in the closet or bathroom, but her knees gave out at the sight.

Her mother had been stabbed, the knife still sticking out of her abdomen, a pool of blood surrounding her. Elizabeth clung to her mother's body, searching for any sign of life, but there was none. She tried to dial 9-1-1, the blood smearing across her phone screen with each attempt.

Then she heard a voice shouting, "Hello?" in the distance. The voice sounded a lot like her brother. What was her brother doing there? She thought their father had taken his key when he kicked Nate out last month. Scrambling to her feet, she ran down the hallway to the kitchen and found her brother rummaging through a cookie jar on the counter. "Nate, what are you—"

"Lizzie!" Nate practically jumped five feet in the air. "What the fuck?" His eyes widened at the sight of her—blood covered her arms and legs, soaking into the fabric of her cheer uniform.

"Nate, they're dead," she cried. Crossing the kitchen, she fell into his arms. "Momma and Papa, they're dead."

"It's gonna be okay," he said, but his tone turned cold, distant.

"We need to—we need to call the police," she stammered and started to redial 9-1-1. She was so focused on trying to dial the emergency number that she didn't notice her brother reaching for something on the counter.

"Don't," her brother commanded. When she continued, he swatted the phone from her hands sending it flying across the room. "Lizzie, do not call the police."

When Elizabeth looked up from her empty hands, she saw a knife in his hand. When did he get that? Nate chuckled darkly, "You just *had* to fucking come home, didn't you? You couldn't stay at Nina's like planned."

"I wasn't—"

"Shut up!"

Elizabeth's feet cemented to the floor as he inched closer. Her mind yelled at her to run, but her body betrayed her. She begged her brother not to do something he would regret, but he wasn't going to regret it because no one would know it was him. He didn't want to hurt her, but he had planned on her being gone, and now...Now she was home, and she'd seen too much. He didn't have a choice. And if she was gone, he wouldn't have to share with her. He'd get everything to himself.

Finally, her feet freed themselves from the paralyzing feeling, and she ran, but her brother was faster. Nate grabbed her ponytail and used it to smash her face into the front door, stunning her, and then did it two more times before tossing her onto the ground like she was nothing more than a rag doll. He straddled her and sank the knife deep into her stomach. Once, twice, three times…and then again and again and again. She lost count as the number climbed. A new fire ripped through her as he took the knife along her wrists multiple times.

Barely clinging to consciousness, she heard him sigh before the knife clattered to the floor next to her head. He moved around the house before she heard the garage door open and then his footsteps and a splash. Constant splashing. The sound disappeared before returning, and then a metallic *tink* before a loud *whoosh* and the roar of flames. Nate retreated through the foyer, stepping over her before leaving the front door open behind him.

"If Nina hadn't gotten into a fight with Brina that night, I don't think I'd be here," Elizabeth says, jarring me back to the present. She plays with her fingers in her lap as we sit on a bench on the outskirts of the fountain under a giant magnolia tree. "I don't even remember dragging myself out of the house, but somehow I made it to the front steps where she found me." She absentmindedly rubs her arm through the sleeve of her sweater, and I reach over to stop the movement. I tug her into my arms and squeeze. Her shoulders rise and fall with a shuddered breath before she relaxes into my embrace, and I kiss the top of her head.

What can I say that will make it any better? What can I say that will take the pain of that memory away? No words seem right at this moment. Instead, I just hold her and let her go through the motions for as long as she needs. Finally, when she pulls away, she wipes her eyes and offers me a grateful smile.

Walking home, I make a vow to myself and a silent one to her: no matter where we are, no matter if we're getting along or not if we've fallen in love, are just friends, or nothing…I will always find my way to her on the anniversary.

fifteen

NOW

THE NEXT WEEK AND a half goes by too quickly. I feel like I blinked, and it's already the tenth of December. I've been holed up in my office most of this week, preparing for my departure tomorrow morning. I'm supposed to meet Elizabeth at her house before we drive down to Palm Valley to spend the long weekend with her college friends. The one saving grace is my old college friend, Elijah, will be there with Selena, along with Lola's boyfriend, Jeremy. Her friend Georgie's husband, Noah, is nice enough, but sometimes I just wish he'd shut up about his job.

There's a knock on my office door, and when I look away from my email, I see none other than my cousin standing there.

"A mid-week visit from *the* Nick Davis. To what do I owe the honor?" I ask, leaning back in my chair.

Though he's not one to boast, Nick has become one of the best architects in this part of the country. Since taking over the architecture side of things for Villa Inc. last year, he's been even busier, traveling a lot more and taking on a much wider load. But, like his wife, he handles it with the kind of grace only certain people possess: natural-born leaders. However, I don't think he enjoys it as much as Nina does.

"Shut up." He falls into the chair across from my desk with an exaggerated eye roll. "I had a meeting downtown, so I figured I'd pop in."

"Nick, you don't just 'pop in.' What are you really doing here?"

My cousin sighs and leans forward, elbows resting on his thighs. "I just wanted to give you a heads up."

Interesting. Okay, I'll bite.

"About?"

"Dee was talking to Elizabeth last night. I think things with that guy are getting serious with Elizabeth's boyfriend. The one you met down in Jupiter," Nick explains.

My stomach sinks at his words, and I do my best not to react, not to reach for my phone and see if she sent a text canceling our weekend trip.

"I overheard Nina giving her a once over about it. Guess Elizabeth is going on some trip this weekend with her college friends—that annual trip you guys used to do. She said she was taking someone with her. Taking him there must mean they're pretty serious, right?"

"Did she say she was taking *him?*"

"I don't know, but who else would it be?"

"Me."

The word hangs between us, and after a moment, Nick starts laughing. His face falls when I don't join him. "Wait, you're serious? Josh, what the fuck?"

"She asked me to go with her right after Thanksgiving."

"You're getting a *divorce*—or did you forget that?"

"Well, unless she sent me a message canceling..." I finally pull my phone out of the desk drawer to find no message. "...I'm still the one going."

"You realize how fucked that is, right?"

"I don't have a choice."

"What do you mean you don't have a choice? Of course you have a choice!"

"Contractually, I have to go. She invoked the *Last Hoorah Clause*." I watch as his mouth falls open, and he looks at me like I have three heads. "Don't worry about it, okay?"

"Josh…this isn't normal."

You can say that again.

Nick continues, "None of this is *normal*. How am I not supposed to worry? I'm extremely worried!"

"Because you and Nina are so much better?"

"My marriage, my love for her, wasn't because of a fucking piece of paper!"

Basically. What else do you call pretending to be someone's boyfriend for money? The only difference is they didn't have a piece of paper detailing everything for their trip to Haven six years ago, and we didn't get paid to be with each other. Well, technically, I guess she did, but that's beside the point.

"You can be such a judgmental asshole sometimes, y'know that?" I roll my eyes.

"Do you love her?" Nick asks, and I scoff. "I'm serious, Josh. Do you love her? Because I'm not convinced this whole thing was just for show between the two of you. You can't be with someone that long and not develop some kind of feelings for them."

"I don't—"

"Because if you do…why aren't you fighting harder for her?"

"She doesn't want me, Nick." I sigh.

"Sure about that?"

"She's moved on."

"If she's moved on, why isn't *he* going this weekend?"

The rest of my rebuttal gets stuck in my throat. That's

a good point. What was it she said at Millers? They're "not exactly speaking right now," whatever that means.

"Wanna know what I think?" Nick asks.

No, but he's going to tell me anyway.

"I think she wants you to fight for her."

"She's the one who ended things, not me."

"I hear it was 25-75, you."

What does that mean?

Nick gently raps his knuckles on my desk and stands up. "Well, I'm gonna go. I think I've caused enough trouble." Before he goes, he pauses at the door and points at me. "Just think about it, hmm?"

I don't reply, only nod absentmindedly because I'm too busy doing exactly what he said.

It's unseasonably cold for the Charleston area, even more so because her house sits on the coast, only a few blocks from the beach. The drive to Palm Valley is only about an hour from here, situated perfectly between Jupiter and Savannah, but I have a feeling it's going to feel more like ten.

Walking up to the front door, I can't help but think about what Nick said yesterday in my office.

I think she wants you to fight for her.

Is he right? Surely, he can't be. Elizabeth is the one who left. She's the one who admitted this was how things were always going to end. While she might be the one who pulled the trigger, I can't deny that I probably pushed her closer to the edge with my trip to Wichita last year. I was just preparing myself for the inevitable and seeing if something else was out there waiting for me...

Before I can knock, the door swings open, and a blur of black and tan charges me.

"Bear!" Elizabeth shouts from inside.

The blur is a dog, a German Shepherd to be exact. The dog sizes me up, a soft growl deep in its chest, sniffing the air in my direction. I hold my ground, slowly raising the back of my hand toward it, and after a few more sniffs, its tail begins to wag, and it licks my hand.

"That's...odd," she huffs, standing in the doorway with confusion written all over her face. "He normally doesn't like men."

I scratch behind the dog's ear, and then he falls to the ground with a loud *plop*, offering me his belly.

"He hates Ryan."

I bite my tongue, probably not the best time to comment on how dogs can usually tell the difference between a good guy and a douchebag. "When did you get him?"

"My birthday."

I don't remember seeing a dog when I was here last time, and that was...almost five weeks ago, the week after Halloween. Then again, Nina didn't invite me in for a look around, either.

"C'mon, Bear, I gotta go," she calls him, and his ears perk up at the g-word. "No, not you. I have to go." Elizabeth rubs his ear affectionately when he deflates, and leads him back inside.

Her bags sit on the bottom stairs, and I take the first step into the house. Despite my curiosity, I grab her suitcase and duffle bag and walk back outside.

"Is he going to be okay?" I ask when she follows behind a moment later.

"I have someone stopping by a few times a day...He'll be fine." Elizabeth locks the door and saunters down the steps to my waiting Bronco. Tossing her bags in the back with mine, I wonder *who* is stopping by a few times a day. Is it Ryan? Surely not, she just said Bear doesn't even like him. And if things had improved to that point, I wouldn't be the one going with her this weekend…Right?

sixteen

NOW

"WHOSE HOUSE IS THIS?" I ask, unloading our bags. I was surprised when Elizabeth gave me the address of a different house than the normal one we reside in. Normally, we stay at the Thompson beach house, owned by Noah's parents. The girls had been coming to Palm Valley almost every year for the last eight years, and when Georgie started dating Noah Thompson, we invaded his parents' home instead of renting out another one. The house was a gorgeous, three-story mansion with direct beach access. Blue-gray ("It's called Faded Flaxflower," Noah's mother once doted) vinyl siding with white accents met with a mix of gold metal roofing and "Desert Tan" shingles. If you think the Villas are pretentious, you haven't met Noah's parents. Luckily, they rarely showed up when we were here.

The new house was located in a more private, secluded area of the Palm Valley community, nestled in a neighborhood at the tip of the island. Pulling into the driveway, there are only two cars: a gray Jeep Wrangler and a white Toyota Highlander. That means we're second to last to arrive. Maybe the Thompsons moved. Doubtful, I can't imagine Noah's mother getting rid of that house, but maybe. Seems weird that Noah is joining us, but we aren't staying at his family house.

"Not sure," Elizabeth says, looking up at the home that towers over us, sizing it up as if it's a monster to conquer.

The house is different than the normal vibe. I'm not denying it's gorgeous...but it's different. The exterior is made of white stucco with a red Spanish-tiled roof. An abundance of foliage and landscape surrounds it, a tropical paradise. It's the opposite of the Thompson home: an oversized, overpriced house that sits a few hundred feet back from the dunes and ocean waves.

"All Gigi said was that the Thompsons couldn't accommodate us this year."

Couldn't accommodate us? That doesn't make sense. Georgie is married to their son. How could they not accommodate him?

Elizabeth chews on the inside of her lip and pulls her cardigan tighter against the ocean breeze. Nervous. Anxious. Overthinking.

Welcome to the party, I've been here all week.

"You sure you wanna do this?" I ask.

"Do we have a choice?"

"There's always a choice."

Her brown eyes raise to meet mine for the first time since we left her house. The drive down had been quiet and a little awkward. She kept to herself and her phone for the most part while I listened to an audiobook.

"Elizabeth!" A chorus of squeals echo around us. Georgie Golding and Selena Hart tramp down the stairs before pulling Elizabeth into a bone-crushing hug. Elizabeth, Selena, and Georgie went to SCAD together, along with Lola Montgomery. Elizabeth attended for photography, Selena for fashion, and Georgie and Lola were in theater, with Lola double majoring in media.

A few steps behind them is Selena's boyfriend, Elijah Prince—he is also one of my former fraternity brothers from Chadwick and he and Selena met at our wedding. He wasn't involved in the hazing incident and still doesn't know I was there. I've never told him that I was the one who took the kid to the hospital. Elijah had a hard enough time digesting what happened that I didn't want to add fuel to the fire. Sure, we went through the same initiation, but it was nothing like what happened that night.

"Thank God, another man in the house." Elijah sighs.

"Noah isn't here?"

"Wasn't here when we got here." He shrugs. "Georgie said he's coming later. Had a few things to do first."

That's odd. First, we're staying at a different house, and now Noah isn't even here? Surely, if something is going on, Elizabeth would have warned me, right?

Georgie and Noah got married two years ago after dating for three years. This is the second longest relationship she's been in since I met her when Elizabeth started school in Savannah. She was normally a serial monogamist—always jumping from one relationship to another, never leaving much room in between. And before Noah, there was Jonah. They dated on and off for a year before he proposed but he left her a week before the wedding because he found his "true love" and someone "less demanding" at the office. That was two years before she met Noah, and how he managed to win her over was still a mystery to most. While Georgie didn't like to be alone, she didn't want to be tied down either.

"Lola is running behind, too," Elijah continues, picking up one of our suitcases because the girls have run back inside. "She's bringing her new boyfriend."

"I met him at New Year's. He's pretty chill. Didn't you meet him at Christmas last year?" I ask.

"Nope." He pops the "p" at the end of the word as we climb the front steps. "They were supposed to come to the Monroes but never made it."

Christmas at the Monroes. Our friend Dean's family had a cabin in the Blue Ridge Mountains of North Carolina near the Alderidge Estate where Nick and Nina got married last year. Most years a large group of us spent time there during the Christmas season. I met Dean through Nick; they went to Boston University together when Nick went back to school. Dean, Nick, Elijah, and our other college buddy, Daniel, all studied architecture. I was the odd man out studying marketing and economics. They liked to call me the "brains" of the group, but I think their jobs are harder than mine. I've picked up on a few things over the years—it's hard not to when you're around them and Nina and my sister—but I could never do what they do.

"Guess some shit went down, and they are just now starting to get back to normal," Elijah says.

"What do you mean? They seemed fine at New Year's."

"Elizabeth didn't tell you?"

Skeptically, I shake my head.

"Lola's old assistant went like batshit, turned into some stalker."

Yeah, no, she didn't tell me that. What the fuck?

"I don't know much, but Sel said it was bad."

"When was this?"

"Not long after the new year."

Holy shit. I can't remember noticing any tension between them while I was in Los Angeles with Dean and Finn, or maybe they were just pretending. That doesn't explain why they wouldn't go to Christmas, though. "Is she okay?"

"Guess so. She got a little banged up but is getting back to normal...whatever that means. I guess we'll find out this weekend, huh?" Elijah goes inside, leaving me on the porch to figure out exactly what this weekend has in store for me.

From the sound of it, we aren't the only ones going through shit right now. Stepping across the threshold, I get a feeling deep in my gut that tells me the terms of our contract could never prepare us for what this weekend holds.

The bedroom we're staying in is bigger than the one I'm used to at the Thompsons. There's a large bed centered against the back wall with a big, fluffy white duvet, baby blue decorative pillows, and a throw blanket. Various beach and ocean paintings in white frames hang above it. The furniture is all rattan—a rattan nightstand on the right side with a rattan drum table on the other. A rattan dresser opposite the bed with a circular rattan mirror above it. A rattan chair with white cushions occupies the corner next to the sliding door that leads out to a deck overlooking the property and ocean. They thought of everything except a TV...at the Thompson's, they put a TV in each room, providing an escape when you need one.

"Don't let Mrs. Thompson see this," I whistle, peeking into the bathroom. It's almost as big as the bedroom. This might be the biggest bathroom I've ever seen. Holy shit. It has a small sitting area leading into the closet and behind a dividing wall, a glass walk-in shower, a soaking tub, and a dual vanity.

"You can say that again," a voice says behind me. Elizabeth's fingers tap against the screen of her phone as she sends what looks to be a long message. A brief thought of wondering if it's Ryan crosses my mind, but I stop myself. It's none of my business.

"You didn't tell me about Lola."

"What?" She finally looks up from her phone.

"The stalker incident."

"Oh."

That's it? That's all she has to say? We are literally about to spend four days with this girl, what if I had said something to trigger some kind of PTSD without even knowing…and all Elizabeth can say is *Oh?*

Elizabeth shrugs. "Well, I didn't think it was any of your business."

"Might have been helpful to know considering I'm spending the weekend with her."

Elizabeth starts to argue, but her mouth closes with a resigned sigh. I'm right; she knows I'm right. She falls on the edge of the bed, fingering the fringe of the throw blanket.

"I don't know much," she says, but I don't believe her. She knows everything that happened, I know that Lola wouldn't keep it from her. "She's kept it pretty tight-lipped. Her assistant—Jenna, you remember? Well, she went a little crazy. It just started with keeping her away from some of her other friends. Then, trying to keep her from spending time with Jeremy and Gabby. I guess Jenna didn't like Jeremy—"

"Something we should be worried about?"

"I don't know." Elizabeth shrugs. "I haven't met him. You're the only one here who knows anything about him. Anyway, Lola left him, fired Jenna, and went back to Australia." Lola was born in the States, but her father was from Australia. She spent a good amount of time growing up there and considered it just as much home as she did San Diego. "Jenna followed her, and it got pretty ugly."

What does that mean, *It got pretty ugly.* How ugly?

"But she's okay now?" I ask.

"They're coming this weekend, aren't they?"

The whole thing sounds off. She knows more than she's saying, but I guess the nitty-gritty details aren't any of my business.

"Anyway," Elizabeth says and stands from the bed, straightening her sweater. "Can you run into town with Elijah? Pick up the groceries and some wine." Without waiting for an answer, she returns to her phone and leaves.

seventeen

NOW

GEORGIE COMBS THROUGH HER hair before pulling it into a short ponytail on top of her head, and not thirty seconds later, she lets it back down again. She's been restless most of the evening, moving between making circles on the rim of her glass and playing with her hair since we sat down. She's been unusually quiet, too. On top of the fact that she chose water instead of wine—when I made sure to grab a bottle of her favorite at the store. Her gaze is zeroed in on the plate in front of her. Her husband, Noah, finally arrived with the take-out Georgie had called in for dinner not long after Elijah and I got back from the grocery. I was shocked to see Noah with scruff on his face and hair long enough to pull it into a small man bun—I've never seen him without a clean-shaven face and (at most) a modest length on top. Something told me the reason for this new look wasn't just out of curiosity.

There is palpable tension between Georgie and Noah, that much was obvious from the moment he arrived. He walked into the kitchen with the food, and she leaned in to kiss him, but he turned so her lips fell on his cheek. He didn't return the favor. Throughout dinner, there were a few times she had reached for his hand or his arm, and he would draw away from her, only to return to her hold a second later.

Lola and Jeremy arrived before Elijah and I got back, and for someone who had just gone through a crazy stalker situation, she seemed to be doing just fine, except for changing her hair...Drastic hair changes seem to be the theme of our group this year. First, Georgie chopped her long, black waves up to her shoulders, then Noah grew his out; Elizabeth cut her hair last year, maintaining the shorter length; and Lola dyed her hair strawberry-blonde, adding extensions to reach down to her waist. Otherwise, she seems...normal. Can't say I'd be the same, but hey, good for her. And Jeremy...Jeremy is still just as nice as he was when I first met him.

Jeremy Vos—actor and musician turned philanthropist. Being a former TV producer, Lola knows a lot of people in the industry, and they met when a mutual friend set them up on a blind date. The only difference I've noticed is the way he keeps a close eye on her, not in a bad way, not in an overbearing way, just in a protective way. Attentive. What is there to dislike about the guy? Her assistant *had* to be crazy to hate him.

"So, Elijah," Georgie starts from across the table. Oh boy, this oughta be good. I'm surprised she's targeting Elijah first instead of Jeremy, but the weekend is still young...There's plenty of time.

Georgie is anything but subtle. When she sets her sights on someone, there's no escape. I'll never forget the first time she decided to question me. It was the second weekend I had gone to visit Elizabeth at SCAD. It was like twenty questions, except it didn't stop at twenty. By the end of her interrogation, Georgie seemed satisfied with my answers, giving Elizabeth a small nod and smile as if her opinion of me meant something. Little did she know, it didn't matter what she thought, or anyone else. We were stuck together for the next ten years.

Elijah looks to me for help, but there isn't a single thing I can do to stop what's about to happen. Settling in, I rest my arm on the back of Elizabeth's chair, my fingers gently grazing her arm, and take a sip of my whiskey. Elizabeth lets her left hand rest in my lap, resting her chin on the other, interest peaked. To everyone else, I'm sure we look like the picture of peace and tranquility, but my entire being feels like it's in a constant state of fight or flight right now.

"Georgie." Selena tries to play interference, but Georgie hushes her.

"What are your intentions with Selena?" Georgie asks.

"I don't—What do you mean?" Elijah chuckles.

"Well, you broke up with her last year, didn't you? So, what are you doing here?"

Elijah swallows the lump in his throat loudly. He did, in fact, break up with her last year. Elijah and Selena met at our wedding six years ago, but he had just gotten out of a long-term relationship. Sure, they flirted, and I'm ninety-nine-point-nine percent sure they hooked up, but nothing more came of it until they reconnected at Nina's holiday party three years ago. Even though they'd been together for a while, he'd never met this group of Selena's friends outside of Elizabeth. The trip to Palm Valley had been canceled for the past two years due to schedule conflicts among the group, but I'm starting to think there's more to it than that.

"Actually," Elijah starts adjusting in his seat. Oh boy. Here we go. "Selena is the one who broke up with me..."

"Not helping your case," I whisper, and Elizabeth squeezes my leg.

"I got a promotion back home in Dallas, and she didn't want to do the long-distance thing. I respected that."

"Gigi, c'mon," Selena whines.

Georgie shoots her a glare. "I just want to make sure he doesn't plan on doing it again. It's not fair to lead you on like that."

"No one is leading anyone on," Elijah hisses. "She didn't want to move across the country, and I couldn't say no to the job. I respected her decision not to want a long-distance relationship. Even if every day was shit without her."

Selena offers him a sad smile and squeezes his hand.

"Two months ago, I couldn't take it anymore. I booked a flight to Tampa to beg her to take me back, even if it meant leaving my job and starting all over."

"If you were so in love with her, why have you never come around before now?" Georgie pushes.

"Not like I had much opportunity." Elijah scoffs. "You've canceled every trip planned the past few years, and we don't all have the luxury of being able to take off work on a whim."

"He sounds like you, Joshua," Georgie throws my way. I roll my eyes at her smirk; she knows I fucking hate it when she calls me *Joshua.*

"We can't all be rich heiresses, Georgina." Her face falls flat when I use her legal name, and I match the smirk she had moments ago.

"No, but you made sure to marry one, huh?"

"Georgie," Elizabeth warns.

"Enough!" Selena interrupts. "Before one of you breaks out the rulers to see whose is bigger."

"Oh, don't worry, we all know Georgie's is bigger," I taunt. "That's why Jonah didn't stick around."

"Oh, fuck you, Josh," Georgie hisses, pushing up from the table.

"Josh." Elizabeth sighs and follows her friend.

Was it a low blow? Sure, but that's what Georgie and I do. We taunt each other and go back and forth, eventually ending in a good laugh. It's never supposed to be taken to heart. But I guess bringing up Jonah was crossing some kind of line.

Elijah and Jeremy share a look, both confused about what

in the hell just happened. "Who's Jonah?" Elijah asks, and Selena rolls her eyes.

"Welcome to Couples Weekend," Lola says to no one in particular, and downs the wine in her glass.

eighteen

NOW

I'D LIKE TO HAVE a word with Mother Nature about this cold weather. We live in the South for godsake. I know it's mid-December, but why is it thirty-six degrees? The breeze cuts through my hoodie and sweats as I slow my pace a few hundred yards from the boardwalk that leads back up to the house. My heart beats against my chest, and now that I'm not running, the sweat has started to form along my hairline. It doesn't get very far with the cold breeze that blows in from the water.

Last night was the opposite of what this weekend was supposed to be about, and I still feel kind of bad about what I said to Georgie. At the same time, it's been six years, and she's married to someone else, should it matter that much? But with the tension between her and Noah maybe it was making her a little extra sensitive.

Not long after she stormed off, I ventured out to the back patio to find her and apologize. I didn't want there to be animosity when this might be the last weekend I had with everyone.

Georgie sat with Elizabeth in the pool house at the far end of the patio. When Elizabeth noticed me walking toward them, she glared over her shoulder. Georgie looked calmer, but she glared when she saw me, too. I raised my hands in surrender.

"I come in peace. I just wanted to apologize. What I said was out of line."

Georgie's gaze remained narrowed.

"You and I have always done this—given each other shit. It's what we do, but...I took it too far tonight, and for that, I'm sorry, Gigi."

With a sigh, her face finally relaxed. "It's not your fault, Josh. I just...There is a lot going on."

"Anything we can help with?"

Georgie offered a small smile, glanced at Elizabeth, and then back to me. "No, thank you." She reached over and squeezed Elizabeth's knee before standing. "I'll see you both inside."

When she was gone, Elizabeth shot up from her chair. "What the fuck, Josh?" Her stare was deadly. "Just because you don't want to be here this weekend doesn't give you the right to be an asshole!"

"I know."

"That was so uncalled for. Georgie was just asking—Wait, what did you just say?"

"I said, *I know*," I said simply. She looked taken aback by the words. "You're right, Liz. It was uncalled for. I'm sorry."

"Why are you agreeing with me?"

"Because you're right."

"No!" Elizabeth shouted. "No...You don't do this. You don't just *agree* with me."

Okay, now it was my turn to be confused. What does she want me to do?

"You never do that."

"I mean, I guess, in the past, I've not been quick to

apologize…But I was wrong this time. It was a low blow."

Since then, I've been trying to think of our other arguments. Did I really never say sorry or agree with her? Surely not. Surely, I had apologized and admitted I was wrong before. And there were times I had agreed with her. The only time I can think of is the fight right before she left—because I wasn't wrong. I was looking out for myself like she had been doing for months, even years, before that, but she didn't want to hear that explanation.

Elizabeth was already in bed when I retired to our room last night. Everyone had gone to bed, but Elijah and I had one more drink, catching up on life—minus one major detail. She slept as close to the edge as possible without falling over, and part of me wondered if I should just make a pallet on the floor, but my back couldn't take sleeping on the hardwood. I'd never be able to move in the morning. Instead, I crawled into bed and cuddled up to my edge.

When I woke up this morning, the sun had just started to peak over the horizon, and it became quite apparent I was not in the same position I had fallen asleep in. My left arm draped over something. Not just something, someone. My hand splayed across her stomach underneath the long sleeve she had worn to bed.

Shit. If she wakes up, I'm a dead man, was the second thought that popped into my mind. The first was how good it felt to be this close to her again. I took a deep breath, inhaling the scent that had become so familiar to me—hints of florals and sandalwood mixed with her coconut shampoo.

She began to stir, and my body tensed.

Fuck. Fuck. Fuck.

But she only settled further into me before falling back asleep. I took one more moment to enjoy this, being so close to her, feeling her body against mine, because I wasn't sure I'd ever get this opportunity again.

One part of me is happy she didn't wake up. I didn't want to fight the whole weekend. It would only make this whole thing that much more difficult. This entire trip was all for show. We weren't really together (or back together, I guess?). I'd spent the past ten years pretending to be her husband; I could do it for three more days, right? Besides, by the end of the weekend, she'd tell them about the separation, and it would all be over with.

A different part of me wishes she had woken up. Maybe it wouldn't have been a fight. I mean, she *did* snuggle closer to me, right?

Trekking through the sand, I climb the wood steps leading to the boardwalk, winding through the dunes to the house. It empties out into the side yard, where another set of stairs leads up to the back patio.

"Finally!" Elijah says when I walk through the sliding door into the dining room. "I was about to send out a search party." He and Jeremy sit at the table with empty coffee mugs in front of them.

"Dramatic, much?" I roll my eyes.

"Georgie and Elizabeth went into town already."

I check the time on my watch: 8:48 a.m. They left already? It's not even nine o'clock. That's strange. Not to mention they went without Selena and Lola. That's even weirder.

"We're meeting them at Teddy's whenever you're ready," Jeremy says.

Normally, we don't leave for breakfast before nine-thirty, maybe even ten.

"Let me go shower real quick, then we can go," I say.

nineteen

THEN

December 2016

WHY I LET HER talk me into this I'll never understand. After what happened last year, I thought we would be officially uninvited for the rest of our lives. When the invitation showed up in my mailbox, I sent her a picture with a quick "lol," but she told me to shove that "lol" up my ass because we were going. Truth be told, we both knew we couldn't refuse. It would look far worse than showing up.

With my hand on her lower back, I guide her through the double doors of Cawthorn Manor with Finn and Michaela in tow. They had been going at it the entire ride here, and pulling into the driveway, I warned them to be on their best behavior, or they'd be walking home in the rain.

I spot Nina in the foyer at the same time Elizabeth does, but our line of sight is blocked when none other than Harvey Cawthorn steps in front of us.

"Josh! So good to see you. We've missed you around here."

"It's good to see you, sir," I say with a tight-lipped smile.

"Miss Cain." He nods toward her.

Elizabeth is trying not to show her nerve, but it's hard not

142

to. I gently squeeze her hip, and she stands a little taller. "Mr. Cawthorn."

"How is SCAD treating you?"

"It's been wonderful."

Harvey offers her a genuine smile. "I'm happy to hear that. You've always been very talented with a camera in your hands. I look forward to seeing your work."

Elizabeth's eyes well, genuine appreciation in her smile. "Thank you, Harvey. That means a lot."

"And I hear you're doing well at QC." He turns back to me.

"Yes, sir. I was offered a full-time position a few months ago."

"Good man." Harvey looks around the room like he's making sure no one is paying particular attention to our conversation. "Look, kids." He sighs. "I don't know what happened last year, and probably don't want to…Surprisingly, William has kept mum on the whole thing."

That *is* surprising.

"But, on the record, let's keep the drama to a minimum, okay? Mrs. Cawthorn likes these things to go off without a hitch. When she's happy, I'm happy. Right? And your little incident caused quite the stir in her circle."

Despite there being less than a handful of guests outside last year, one person is enough to get the rumor mill churning.

"And off the record?" Finn asks.

Harvey smirks at him. "Off the record, I'm glad to see you two finally pulled your heads out of your asses."

What the hell is that supposed to mean?

Michaela and Finn share a laugh before covering it with a cough when we look back at them.

"Have a good time, kids." Harvey winks at us before he's pulled away into another conversation.

"What is that supposed to mean?" Elizabeth hisses.

"They're so dense," my sister whispers to Finn.

"Look who's talking, Shortcake," he retorts. My sister huffs in reply before stalking off, only for him to follow, further annoying her.

twenty

NOW

BREAKFAST AT TEDDY'S ON the first morning in town has become a tradition since the girls discovered the diner during their second year here. The restaurant sits on the end of the main drag in Palm Valley, a block away from the water. The inside looks like a vintage diner, with red faux leather booths and yellow lights included. The exterior is reminiscent of a train car—long, rectangular—with blue paint and stainless steel siding. Large picture windows give you a glimpse of the inside. A large sign above the door reads *Teddy's Diner.* Typically, we'd walk along the beach until we reach the access point running along the side of the restaurant, but the new house is too far, and it's too cold to even consider it.

"Is he always so friendly?" Elijah motions toward Noah, who lags a few steps behind on his phone. Selena and Lola have gone ahead inside to look for Elizabeth and Georgie.

"He's usually more talkative, but it's kind of nice without his constant yammering about stocks and bonds," I say, earning a chuckle from Elijah and Jeremy.

Noah is a decent guy, but when I say he *loves* to talk about his job, he loves to talk about his job. He followed in his dad's footsteps, getting involved in the finance world, and last I heard, he was promoted to director of private equity at his firm. I still don't know what that means; I just know he's good with money and makes a lot of it.

Walking into the restaurant, I hold the door, but Noah motions for me to go ahead and answers a phone call. Selena waves us over to the middle of the restaurant, where they've secured a long table. The spot left open for me is at the end of the table, next to Elizabeth. The only other empty spot sits across from me, next to Georgie, like an elephant in the room. The waitress—*BETTY*, her name tag reads—appears with a tray full of drinks, including a black coffee with two sugars for me. A smile tugs on the corner of my lips when she sets it in front of me. I turn to offer my wife a smile of thanks, but she's too engrossed in the conversation with Selena. Instead, I rest my arm on the back of her chair and squeeze her shoulder gently. And it seems as if, on instinct, she reaches over and rests her hand on my thigh under the table.

Georgie's nose has been in her phone since we sat down. Odd. Usually, she's yelling at everyone else to stay off their phone. She types furiously before letting out a huff and tossing her phone back into her purse. Her fingers, painted Christmas red, play with the tag of her tea bag—that's also odd. She *never* drinks tea; she's a huge coffee snob. First, water with dinner, now tea at breakfast…What's going on?

"Hey, Lola," I ask, catching her attention on the other side of Jeremy. "Do you want to trade places? I'm sure you guys want to have some girl talk." She doesn't think twice, jumping up from her seat to take mine, putting me now between Elizabeth and Jeremy, across from Elijah.

"Is it always this…tense?" Jeremy asks when the girls return to their hushed conversation, even Georgie seems to have joined in again.

"Not usually." I sip my coffee, glancing out the window where Noah is still talking on the phone.

"I feel like there's something we're missing." Elijah chuckles.

"Probably." I shrug. Isn't that always the case? "Welcome to the club, boys. Where we're always two steps behind."

The rest of breakfast is uneventful unless you count the awkwardness between Noah and Georgie. Something is seriously wrong there. Not that it's any of my business, but they could at least try to hide it a little better if they're going to fake it. Every once in a while, she'll reach over and try to touch him—his hand, the back of his neck, his arm—and he pulls away. Albeit, only a little, and to someone not paying attention, they probably wouldn't notice, but I am paying attention.

"What's the plan for today?" Elijah asks as he stuffs a piece of pancake in his mouth.

"Well, after breakfast, we go to the Christmas market," Selena says and pushes her empty plate away from her. She stirs creamer into her fresh cup of coffee.

"It's super tiny and cute," Lola adds. "A lot of local vendors and artists."

"And donuts! Don't forget the donuts."

"Yes, the donuts are to die for."

"Noah, will your parents be joining us?" Selena asks, sipping her coffee. Typically, the Thompsons join us for a stroll through the market before they run off to one of the many holiday soirees they get invited to.

"N-no," he stammers. Clearing his throat, he answers more soundly. "No, they're actually in the Caymans right now."

The Caymans? I shoot Elizabeth a confused look, but she keeps her gaze fixed on Georgie. If his parents are in the Caymans, why couldn't they accommodate the group at their beach house? That doesn't make sense. Looking around the table, no one else seems to pay any mind to the fact that he just admitted we were uninvited from the place we usually call

home in Palm Valley.
Am I the only one who finds all of this strange?

twenty-one

THEN

December 2017

"JOSH, WHERE'S ELLIE?" FINN asks, stuffing a few barbecue meatballs in his mouth.

He showed up at Uncle Jim's around the time I did. His parents didn't exactly have your typical holiday traditions with family. Instead, they would host a dinner or luncheon of some sort a few days before and spend the actual holiday on some tropical island or at some fancy resort. Finn used to join them until we became friends after he was kicked out of The Hills Academy and transferred to Bridgeport High. When my parents heard about his family traditions, they invited him to join us if his parents would allow him, and he's been with us every holiday since. This year, he had spent his obligated time at home a few days ago during the Sheffield Christmas party before his parents jetted off to the Caribbean.

"Oh." I swallow a drink of beer. "She and Nina are having a girl's day since the Villas are gone."

I don't miss the way Alex perks up hearing Nina's name— that kid has had the biggest crush on her for as long as I can remember. Nick rolls his eyes at his little brother; he thinks

Alex is ridiculous. *You don't even know her,* Nick would often say. Maybe not, but we all knew the stories. Nina was known around town for being much more than just the daughter of the Villa family. If you looked up how to have fun in your early years, you'd find a photo of her next to it.

And after his brother was done chastising him about his dream girl, Alex would chime in with something like: *Neither do you, but that doesn't stop you from being a judgey-judgerson.*

Alex always claimed there was more to Nina than being a spoiled heiress, but was never able to persuade his brother. That's never stopped him from trying, especially when he found out that I was dating Elizabeth. Alex made sure to remind his brother who Elizabeth's adoptive sister was. Truth be told, I was concerned Nick wouldn't like Elizabeth since she and Nina are so closely related, but they took a liking to each other pretty quickly. Alex thought I'd be able to convince Nick to give Nina a chance, but I knew better. Nick was going to have to figure it out for himself.

"Nina could've come along," Mom says, walking in from the kitchen.

"I told her." I shrug. "But she's going through a pretty bad breakup, so I think she just wanted some time."

"Oh, that poor thing," Mom coos.

"No one should be alone on Christmas," Uncle Jim agrees.

"She's not alone; she has Elizabeth," I say. "I'll go check on 'em a little later."

Elizabeth is probably grateful I'm not there, anyway. She was more than happy to stay back, even though Nina was practically pushing her out the door. Elizabeth wouldn't budge.

We started dating (like *dating* dating, giving-it-a-real-shot dating) last October, the weekend of Nina's twenty-second birthday. Elizabeth had come home on Friday after class for the birthday party on Saturday evening and instead of going straight to Nina's, she came to my condo. We hadn't seen each other since I had gone down to Savannah for the anniversary the month before. After I left that time, we started talking on the phone more often, and I could tell there had been a shift in our relationship. We spent time getting to know one another and becoming friends—real friends.

I was nervous to see her. I spent most of the day wondering how things would be once we were together in person. But the moment I saw her, the nerves disappeared. I walked out of the elevator lobby to my condo building's garage and spotted her unloading the bags from her car. She had two suitcases—who needs two suitcases for a weekend trip?—and one large gift bag that read *Happy Birthday* in fancy script.

"What, are you moving in?" I called down to her, catching her attention.

She slammed the back of her Jeep. "I was thinking about it. You have room for one more?"

"Suppose I could get rid of the guest room, not like I get many guests anyway."

"I was thinking the master," Elizabeth said with a smirk as she approached me. Before I had a chance to respond, she stepped up, and without hesitation, kissed me.

"What was that for?" I asked, eyes still closed, when she pulled back.

"I missed you."

"I missed you too, Sugar." I kissed her forehead, taking the bags from her. "C'mon, let's get upstairs."

"Wait, Josh," Elizabeth said, her hand covering mine when I tried to take hold of her bags. "I have something I want to say."

"You don't want to do that upstairs where it's a bit, I don't know, warmer?" I chuckled.

"No, because if I don't say it now, I don't know if I will."

Hearing the nerves woven into her words, I dropped my hold on the bag handle and brought my hand up to cradle her cheek. "What's going on, Liz?"

Elizabeth rolled her shoulders back, standing a little straighter, before she looked up to meet my stare. "I want to do this. Us. I want to try…for real. And I know that may sound silly because now that I'm hearing myself say it, it does. But I want to know if there is something—"

I kissed her and she melted into my embrace. "Thank God," I whispered against her. "You took the words right out of my mouth."

She smiled against me and I pecked her lips once…twice… three times before pulling away.

I opened the door to the lobby for her, following behind with her bags. "Let's take this stuff upstairs and we can go get food."

"Thank God, I'm starving. What's for dinner?"

"Whatever you want, Sugar," I said and scanned my resident card.

Things went well, really well, until about two months ago. We were one week out from our first anniversary and we had a small argument that turned into a big one that turned into a breakup. The difference is when we break up, we can't *break up*. We're still stuck with each other. Guess we didn't think that one through. To this day, I still don't understand what started the whole thing. I showed up in Savannah on Saturday morning and she was in a bad mood the moment she opened the door. Everything just seemed to escalate from there.

Now I get to spend time with my ex-girlfriend, pretending to be happy-go-lucky while wishing to be anywhere else… it's not exactly my idea of a good time. The fact it happened around the holidays makes it that much harder. Any other time of year, we could've lived more separate lives, minus a few appearances here and there. But that's not the only reason it's been hard. The hardest part is wanting to touch her, hold her, and kiss her when she's near, even though I know she wants me as far from her as possible.

Later came a lot sooner than I expected. Mom and Uncle Jim packed an entire smorgasbord of food to take back to Nina's, despite my protests that we didn't need that much food. Finn offered to join me, but I declined the offer. I'm sure it would be nice to have the company, but I don't think Nina is in the mood to entertain any more than she already is with us.

Securing the to-go container in the backseat, I jump a little, not expecting someone to be there when I turn around. "Give a guy a heart attack, why don't you?" I mumble.

Mom stands with her arms crossed, lips pulled into a thin line, and I can already tell I'm in for it. What about? I have no idea, but I'm sure I did or said something that was out of line. And she wasn't about to let me have it in front of the rest of the family. She probably guised her disappearance as making sure I had everything for the girls before I came back in to tell the family goodbye. "Why didn't Elizabeth come with you today?"

"I already told you."

"You shouldn't be leaving your soon-to-be bride alone on the holidays."

"Can you not say that so loud?" I snap. She isn't exactly the quietest person on the planet and our family is known for being nosy, especially one person in particular. The last thing I need is my sister overhearing this conversation.

"You better get your act together, Joshua. Fix whatever you've broken. We can't afford for Elizabeth to decide to walk out on you before time is up."

What she really means is *she* can't afford for Elizabeth to walk away. If anyone has reaped the benefits of this relationship more than me, it would be my mother. Since Elizabeth and I started dating, Mom has been invited to more social gatherings in the elite society—the whole family has. And while the rest of us didn't seem to care, to Mom it was everything.

"Josh," she says with a gentle tone, reaching out to touch my cheek. "You're a good boy, right? You don't want to mess this up for yourself. You don't want to lose everything you've worked so hard for, do you?"

I try to look away from her prying eyes, but she refuses to let me.

"I don't care what happened between the two of you, fix it. Elizabeth doesn't have to love you, but the two of you better start *acting* like it before the rest of the family gets suspicious."

She's right, just like always. Elizabeth and I don't have to fall in love, we don't even have to date, but I can't let our petty argument get in the way of our contractual agreement. I should've pushed harder for her to come today, then the family wouldn't have been asking so many questions.

"Clean this up, Josh. You can't afford to lose her," Mom says. "And get inside to tell everyone bye, you need to get back to Elizabeth." She offers me her hand and a polite smile before tugging me to her side. She guides me inside without another word, pushing me in the direction of the rest of the family to say goodbye.

When I finally make it back outside after a goodbye that takes thirty minutes longer than it should, I close the door behind me, taking a long, deep breath. Things are only going to get more complicated from here…I can feel it.

The door opens again and I jump two feet ahead as Nick pops outside, closing the door behind him. "You, uh, want me to come along so you're not outnumbered?"

My brow quirks so high I'm sure it's almost in my hairline. Nick Davis is offering to come and spend time with Nina Villa willingly…that's new. Of everyone here, he's the last person I expected to offer. "*You* want to go with me to Nina's?"

"I mean…We can all go. Make a thing of it." Nick crosses his arms over his chest, trying to act nonchalant about this entire conversation. Trying to act like he didn't just suggest doing the one thing he's been avoiding since Elizabeth and I got together.

Gut feeling tells me that I'm missing something.

"What is—"

He interrupts me. "No one should be alone on Christmas."

"You know, it's weird when you get all sappy." I try to hide my smirk but fail miserably, even chuckling a little.

Nick rolls his eyes.

"Thanks for the offer, but I don't think Nin is in the mood for a lot of company right now," I say. "I'll send your condolences though."

"What is that?" Nina asks when she opens the front door. She is still dressed in her pajamas, and her hair sits in a messy bun on top of her head, the same way I left her this morning. She watches in amusement as I haul the armload of leftovers before dropping them on the kitchen island.

"Thanks for the help," I say, pulling off my jacket and earning a playful eye roll from her. She falls back on the couch next to Elizabeth, and they watch as I sort out the food across the marble countertop. Ham, prime rib, green bean casserole, yams, mac'n'cheese, mashed potatoes, homemade stuffing, cranberries, Brussels sprouts, carrots, asparagus, remnants of a fruit platter, rolls, Christmas tree-shaped pizzas, and a whole pumpkin pie. Honestly, there's so much, we could probably eat off these for the next few days. "My family refused to let either of you go hungry or feel left out on this holiday."

Nina jumps up from the couch, finally coming to inspect the spread. "Is that a Christmas tree pizza?" she asks, picking up one of the mini pepperoni pizzas.

"Michaela and my cousin, Alex, have been making those every year since we were kids. It's not Christmas at the Davis house without them."

"That's sweet."

"Everyone was sad you guys didn't come, so they said sending food was the next best thing."

"They would be right." Nina pops a grape into her mouth and pulls plates from the cabinet. Setting them down, she rushes back down the hallway toward her bedroom, mumbling something that sounds like "be right back."

"This was sweet," Elizabeth says, joining me at the island.

"Yeah, well, you know how they are."

She nods and offers a small smile. "Still, thank you. She's been...Well, she's trying to act okay, but this has been hard on her, and I just—I couldn't leave her."

"She could've come. You both could have."

"But we both know she wouldn't." Elizabeth steps closer, placing her hands gently on my arm and standing on her tiptoes to kiss my cheek. "Thank you."

Being this close to her, I don't waste the opportunity. I wrap my arms around her waist and pull her close, burying my face in her neck. With a deep breath, I inhale the sweet scent of her, before pressing a light kiss to her skin. My lips linger against her skin and I whisper, "I can think of a way you can thank me."

"Joshua Davis." Elizabeth puts her hand to her chest in fake shock. "Are you trying to seduce me?"

"Is it working?"

She laughs and pushes me away. "No."

The sound of someone clearing their throat catches our attention as we separate. Nina stands at the end of the hallway but hasn't quite stepped into the kitchen. She looks between us. "Do you guys need a moment or..."

Elizabeth rolls her eyes and picks up a plate without saying a word.

twenty-two

NOW

THE PALM VALLEY CHRISTMAS Market is nestled in the large courtyard in front of City Hall in Town Square. There are more and more vendors every time we come, and after being gone for the past two years, it seems like it has tripled in size from the last time we were here. If they keep growing at this pace, they'll have to find a new location for it. The market is made up of food and small item stalls with a stage and dance floor at the far left end and a skating rink carved out in the middle. Every year, they have a different souvenir mug. One year, it was a snowman, and another was Santa's boot. All I know is I can't wait to get my hands on some roasted peanuts and spiced wine, two food staples of the market. Getting closer to the market, the air begins to smell like Christmas: nutmeg, cinnamon, freshly baked donuts, and cider. My mouth begins to water just thinking about it.

I drape my arm around Elizabeth's shoulders, pulling her close, and her arm hangs loose around my waist as we fall in step with each other. Walking down Main Street from Teddy's toward Town Square, Georgie and Noah walk side-by-side, holding hands—and this time, Noah doesn't pull away when his wife reaches for him. I'm beginning to think I've been imagining the whole thing. Maybe I haven't been, maybe I'm just reading too far into it. Maybe they're trying to come down from the stress of everyday life. Georgie has always said Noah's job stresses him out a lot. You know, it's none of my business anyway.

Lola pulls Jeremy through the crowd once we get close enough, and he laughs at her enthusiasm. I like him; he seems nice enough, and he seems to really like Lola. He's protective of her—I can tell by the way he's in tune with her every move—and she seems…different. Not in a bad way, but in a "she's been through some shit" kind of way. Then again, who wouldn't be different after going through a traumatic stalker situation?

Walking through the rows of stalls, our group begins to break off one couple at a time until it's just me and Elizabeth strolling down the main drag. It reminds me of the first time the girls invited their significant others to join on their third trip to Palm Valley. It was the same year we got married, just a few months after the wedding. That year, I bought Elizabeth a set of Santa Claus stacking dolls from one of the vendors. Her mother collected stacking dolls, and Elizabeth had always been fascinated by them, but she lost her mother's collection in the fire.

Elizabeth had been eyeing the Santa Claus dolls, even went up and inspected them, but didn't buy them. She complimented the shop owner on his craftsmanship and considered buying them, but put them down with a heavy sigh and walked away. When she was preoccupied skating with the girls, I went back to the vendor and bought the dolls, saving them for her to open on Christmas morning. I'll never forget her face when she opened the box to find them, the tears that welled in her eyes before she kissed me wordlessly and set them up on the mantle.

"What's going on with Georgie?" I ask, but Elizabeth doesn't answer. She doesn't even flinch or show any sign of hearing what I just said. "I know you know something."

"Just leave it alone, Josh." She sighs.

"Liz—"

"I said leave it alone." Elizabeth tears herself away from me and storms off.

Oh, she definitely knows something.

I stand in the same place, watching as she swims through the sea of people. Should I follow? Yeah, I should. Right? If I don't, it could look bad to the others, and I'm supposed to be keeping up appearances. We're supposed to be getting along. We just have to get through this weekend, that's it. Then we don't have to do this ever again...

It takes only a few minutes to find her, and when I do, my heart sinks. Her blonde hair blows in the breeze standing in front of the same vendor from six years ago—the one I bought the nesting dolls from. Cautiously, I approach her, stepping up beside her as she fingers a set of dolls—a nativity set.

"My mother had a set like this," she whispers. Her fingers run over the face of the Mary doll. "She loved getting it out every year, and did it in place of a normal nativity."

Picking up the set next to the display, I hand it to the shop owner ready to purchase it. The whole ordeal takes barely two minutes, and the entire exchange is silent, aside from the owner telling me the total. I hand him a hundred-dollar bill, and he hands over the now wrapped-up doll set.

It's not until we're a few steps away that she says, "You didn't have to do that."

I wrap my arm around her shoulders again, pulling her into my side, and plant a kiss on her temple.

The souvenir mug this year is a penguin dressed in a suit with a teal-colored bowtie. The warmth of the spiced wine and the sun breaking through the clouds fend off the breeze that blows through the market. At least the sun came out to play.

Elizabeth sips on her cider, walking close by. Since the exchange at the doll vendor, she's kept minimal distance between us. When we come to the skating rink, I see Elijah struggling on the ice, being led by Selena, who can't keep a straight face no matter how hard she tries. Jeremy and Lola skate circles around him, either offering him words of encouragement or heckling him, I can't tell. Elizabeth giggles as Elijah attempts to let go of Selena, only to desperately grab for her moments later when he starts to go down.

"Do we need to get the push bar for you, Eli?" I ask.

"No, you ass," he retorts with a sour face, earning another giggle from Elizabeth.

"We all had to start somewhere, no need to be embarrassed."

"Yeah," Elizabeth calls to him, trying not to laugh. "Pay no mind to the little kids skating circles around you."

We both laugh when he shoots us another glare. Even Selena can barely hide her laugh.

"I don't understand how anyone thinks this is fun!"

Lola and Jeremy skate over, meeting us on the side of the rink, and in sync, we tilt our heads, watching as Elijah's feet slip from underneath him. Lucky for him, Selena catches him before he goes down. Lola finally says, "You're trying too hard, Elijah. You can't think so much. It's just like rollerblading."

"So much harder than rollerblading," Elijah huffs. "At least with rollerblading the ground isn't wet and slippery!"

"He's not very good at that either," Selena adds sheepishly.

"Oh, Elijah, you're doing it all wrong!" Georgie appears beside Elizabeth with a pretzel. "You're supposed to put your weight forward."

Selena sighs. "That's what I—"

"I'll fall on my face!" Elijah interrupts Selena.

"Just try it," Georgie encourages him.

"C'mon babe, just try." Selena tugs on his arms to pull him forward a smidge more. Elijah groans in protest, and Lola urges Jeremy to demonstrate for him. "See, watch Jeremy!"

Jeremy bends his knees slightly, then pushes off and lengthens his right leg, gliding forward before shifting his weight gradually to the other foot as he lengthens his left leg, alternating his strides. He uses his arms to steer and control, keeping his posture as straight as possible. He makes it look easy. Too easy.

"Think of it like a scooter," Georgie adds. "You stand on one foot and use the other to propel you forward!"

Elijah hesitates before he slowly pushes his right leg forward. "A scooter," I hear him mumble to himself as Selena lets go, and his left leg moves forward wobbling. The next thing I know, he's faceplanted in front of us.

"I don't think that's how it's done," Noah says, taking a sip of his beer. He appears next to Georgie, watching the scene unfold. When the hell did he get here?

Everyone laughs as Elijah crawls to the edge of the rink, pulling himself up from the ice. With a death grip on the wall, he inches his way toward the exit, absolutely *over it*. Selena calls after him, following him out of the rink and onto one of the benches, where he rips the skates from his feet. Jeremy and Lola follow, still chuckling, as they exit.

"What's that?" Georgie asks, motioning to the bag in Elizabeth's hand.

"Hm?" Elizabeth questions before realizing she is talking about the doll. "It's just a nesting doll set. It reminded me of one Mom used to put out at Christmas time."

She opens the bag gingerly, pulling out the set. As Georgie turns it over in her hands, Elizabeth meets my gaze and smiles softly. There's a soft tug on my heart seeing her like this. A genuine smile on her pink lips, a smile I was able to put there for the first time in a long time.

"It'll look great on the mantle of the new place," Elizabeth says, taking it back from her friend and rewrapping it to put it away.

"New place?" Georgie asks.

Elizabeth's brown eyes widen at the realization of what she just said. *Shit.*

"You didn't tell me you moved." Georgie looks between the two of us, and I'm just as tongue-tied as Elizabeth.

Shit, shit, shit. Of course she didn't tell them she had a new place. She hasn't told them about the separation yet.

"Hey Noah, you're makin' burgers tonight?" I ask him, trying to steer the conversation, but the question goes unanswered as the others finally join us.

"What's going on?" Lola asks.

"Did you know they moved?" Georgie demands.

"Who?" Selena asks.

"These two." She points at us. "Mr. and Mrs. Perfect."

Elizabeth rolls her eyes at the nickname. She has always hated that Georgie calls us that—so do I—and it's only because we've been together the longest and always stayed together no matter what. I can only imagine the shit-talking that will ensue if Elizabeth chooses to tell them about the arrangement. I doubt she will because they'll never let her live it down— Georgie won't anyway.

"Where did you move to?" Lola seems shocked, they all do. "You guys were so happy there!"

"I'm surprised you'd leave Nina," Selena adds. "I mean, you loved being so close to her."

"Yeah, what's Nina think about you leaving?" Georgie asks, her gaze narrowed.

In my opinion, Georgie has always seemed somewhat threatened by the relationship between Elizabeth and Nina. I don't know why. Elizabeth loves Georgie, and they are close, but Elizabeth will never be as close to someone as she is to Nina. That's her sister. That's a different kind of bond.

Their voices start to blend together as everyone continues to throw out question after question. Elizabeth tries to answer what's tossed at her but can never quite get a word in. I can't stop myself. I cut in, putting a stop to their interrogation.

"She just meant the beach house." Looking down to meet the panicked gaze of my brown-eyed girl, I try to offer her a reassuring smile, but it doesn't quite reach as far as I'd like. "Where we'll be spending Christmas this year."

The words are like a stab to the heart because we both know they're not true. When we leave here, we won't be going home to prepare for Christmas together. We won't be finishing some last-minute shopping and wrapping gifts to bring to the Villas. I won't be helping her make her Christmas cookies for Mom's classroom holiday party. She won't be surprising me at work with lunch plans before going to Nina's to help her with last-minute Christmas prep…We won't be doing any of that anymore and I don't know that I truly, *truly*, realized it until this moment.

"I—We bought a house in Jupiter Beach," Elizabeth adds, her eyes never leaving mine.

"Charleston?" Georgie scoffs. "Why Charleston?"

"I'm not in Charleston proper." Elizabeth rolls her eyes. "Besides, Jupiter is more private; the tourists stick around the other beaches, like Folly and IOP."

"Well, I won't be visiting."

"No one was inviting you, Georgie," I quip. I hate the way she criticizes Elizabeth's choice of beach home. So what if

Georgie doesn't like Charleston? Elizabeth does.

The raven-haired woman whips toward me with a death glare, but before she can get out whatever snarky response she's formulating, her husband places his hands between her shoulder blades, grazing the back of her neck in a slight hold. "Who's hungry? I'm making burgers!"

twenty-three

THEN

November 2018

I'VE REREAD THE SAME damn sentence forty fucking times now. Every time I try to focus on this damn book, my mind wanders to the woman standing on the other side of the wall with a toothbrush hanging out of her mouth. The water gushes from the faucet as she finishes brushing her teeth and begins her nighttime face routine. It's the same thing every night—brush teeth, remove makeup, wash face, apply lotion and serums (don't ask me which ones, but I know there's a particular order), apply Chapstick, and change. Same thing. Every night. How do I know this? Because we have been "together" for almost three years. Sometimes, it feels like it's been much longer than that. Others it feels like just yesterday we were signing on the dotted line.

We've had our ups and downs, like everyone else, but despite it all, we've managed to become friends. *Real* friends. And right now, I wouldn't say we're "dating," but we aren't on bad terms either, and that's okay. After our breakup last October, we never got back together. Christmas helped us ease back into friendly terms, though. Slowly but surely, we found our footing, and we have been able to open up again little by little. I'd rather be friends than nothing at all. It's better than being stuck together when all you want is space from the other person. And two months ago, when I came down for the sixth anniversary of her parents' death, we had the conversation we'd been dreading since the beginning of all this: the engagement. Elizabeth was graduating in the spring, which meant the clock on our impending nuptials was ticking. We had six months after May 31st to say *I Do*, per the contract. That meant we had to be married before the end of November, which was only one year from now.

Elizabeth moves to the closet to finish her routine and change out of her jeans and black floral blouse into her nightgown, but I interrupt her.

"Can we talk?" The words tumble out and she steps out of the closet—one foot in and one foot out—about to undo the buttons of her blouse. She throws a suspicious glance my way. "I just, I want to...do something."

I clamber out of bed and meet her on the other side.

"Okay." She draws out the word. "Is something wrong?"

"No!" I clear my throat. "No, I just...Liz, I—"

Okay, Josh. Relax. Take a deep breath. You can do this. It's just Elizabeth. Your friend. Your partner. The other half of your equation for the next seven-ish years.

Taking her hands, I take another breath and drop to one knee. Her brown eyes widen—bigger than I have ever seen before. Normally, the scene would be quite romantic. Cozy night at home, a fire in the faux fireplace across the room, the only other light coming from the Christmas tree in the corner. I had come down two weeks ago to help her decorate for Christmas because Elizabeth did not play when it came to decorating for her favorite holiday. "Elizabeth Regina Cain, I—"

"Josh, what are you doing?" She interrupts me. "We said

we'd do this at—"

"I know." I stop her. "I know we said we'd do this at Thanksgiving with the family, and that's fine. We can. But I wanted to do this here, just us. Without all the fanfare and glamour that Brina and Nina forced upon me as soon as I told them what I was planning to do."

Her features soften, and she squeezes my hand slightly.

"When I met you four years ago, I never imagined we'd be where we are today. But from the moment I met you, I knew you'd be an important piece of my life. You were beautiful and kind, funny...and you never took any of my shit. I liked that, even if I didn't want to admit it. And now...Now, I can't imagine my life without you in it. Whether we come out of this as friends or lovers, I just know that I don't want to do life without you."

Tears begin to brim her eyes and mine. Fuck, I didn't think I'd be this emotional.

Swallowing back the tears, I say, "I know this isn't perfect. It's not the life you imagined, and I'm not the husband you imagined but just know that I'll do everything I can to make the next seven-ish years as painless as possible for you. So, Elizabeth Regina Cain...Will you be my wife?"

A tear slips down her cheek as she takes a shaky breath and nods. I don't hesitate. I stand and capture her lips in a kiss that catches us both off guard. We haven't been intimate in over a year unless you count the PDA we have to display in front of others. Every time, it leaves me wanting more. But this kiss...There's something different. Something real and raw. My mouth moves against hers; our tongues dance in a desperate embrace. Elizabeth wraps her arms around my neck, pulling me impossibly closer, and I delve deeper into her, earning a soft moan against my lips.

"Elizabeth," I whisper against her.

She presses a chaste kiss to my lips as her fingers move to

undo the buttons of her blouse. I take her hands, stopping her. I don't want her to feel pressured into something she doesn't want.

Just because I proposed doesn't mean she *has* to offer herself to me, even if I'm desperate for her. We haven't slept together in the three years we've been together. It was a conversation we had on my second trip down to Savannah after I kissed her and left to drive back home on her first night in the townhouse. Elizabeth said she wanted to wait until marriage. She wanted her first time to be with someone who she knew truly loved her.

After she told me, William's eagerness to jump ship and screw around with the girls at Duke made more sense. He didn't want to wait around when he had plenty of fish right in front of him. Elizabeth told me she would consider compromising since we were going to get married eventually, but I refused. I wasn't going to compromise something she believed in, regardless of if we were going to get married. I wouldn't push her. And while a man has *needs*, it hasn't been that bad. There are other...ways to keep the needs at bay.

"Liz—"

"Josh."

"We don't have to do this." I tuck a strand of honey-blonde hair behind her ear. "You said—"

"Not like I can change my mind now."

"Elizabeth, if you aren't one hundred percent sure—"

"I am."

I swallow hard. I don't want to push her into something. I don't want her to compromise herself because she thinks she has to. I've waited this long; I can wait a little longer. I can wait as long as she needs. "Elizabeth, I don't want you to give up something you've held onto and held sacred just because—"

"You're my husband, Josh." The words send a shock wave through my system. "You became my husband the second we signed that damn paper three years ago."

"I'd rather it happen when you want it to. Not just because I proposed. You said—"

"And I want this," she says.

Fuck, I want this too. So bad. But I'm scared she will wake up in the morning and regret it.

In my moment of hesitation, she steps closer, her hands wrapping around the back of my neck, pulling me down to meet her lips. "I want you."

"Elizabeth," I whisper, her breath skating across my face. My fingers brush against her flushed cheek before I kiss her. There's a different spark that erupts between us. This one is different than anything I've felt in the past. The burn in my veins tells me we're crossing into new territory.

The line of no return.

She whimpers when I bite down on her bottom lip, plying open her mouth and stroking her tongue. I tighten my grip on her hips and push further against her, her back scraping against the doorframe of her closet, but she doesn't seem to mind. Her arms wrap tighter around my neck, a vice grip, and I lift her feet off the ground, wrapping her legs around my waist. I moan against her mouth when she grinds against me. She tastes like the butterscotch she was eating earlier—a mix of sweet and savory. I would be perfectly fine if we stopped right now. If we parted ways and went to bed, but fuck, I don't want to. I want all of her.

I carry her to the bed and gently lay her back before leaving a trail of kisses down her jaw to her neck. She gasps when I bite softly on the skin of her collarbone. Her shirt opens with a pop of each button, and I leave a trail of open-mouthed kisses to her chest and down to her stomach. Thirteen jagged scars span across her torso that have slightly faded over the years. She tries to cover her stomach, but I push her hand away and hold her gaze, pressing a light kiss against the discolored skin.

Tears cloud her eyes when I do the same to each one before I bring her left wrist to my lips and do the same to the right, never taking my eyes off hers. I crawl back up her body and stop just before our lips meet. "You're beautiful."

A shaky inhale against my lips.

"And strong." I kiss her neck.

"Courageous." The valley between her breasts.

"Stubborn," I say against her stomach, and she laughs.

"Caring," I mumble against the skin just above her jeans.

Slowly, I unzip the denim, and she helps me shimmy them down her legs. My fingers trace her center over the underwear, and she gasps. "Already so wet for me, huh, Sugar?"

"Josh," she groans.

"Patience." I blow on her center through the damp cloth, and she squirms under my hold. Lying beside her, I pull her body close to mine, propping my head on my left hand to look down at her. "Can you stay still?"

My other hand traces a line down the center of her body, and I can feel her vibrate with anticipation. I stop at the edge of the white cotton.

"I've waited three years to know what you taste like. I can wait a few more minutes. I want to watch first, watch as you come undone with just my fingers, and then my mouth, and then my dick. I want to know what makes you tick…so I'm going to take my time with you, Sugar. Going to enjoy every moment of this."

Her chest rises and falls with heavy breaths, and I haven't even touched her yet.

I say her name, catching her attention. "Can you do that for me?"

She nods, and I slip my hand inside her underwear. A finger ghosts over her entrance, and she bucks against my hand greedily.

"Fuck, you're so wet." I slip one finger inside her and then another. Her fingers clutch the white duvet covering the bed, trying not to move. Her walls tighten around my fingers, and I slip one more inside her, using the heel of my palm to rub her clit. She gasps, eyes screwed shut. She's trying so hard not to move, her fingers white against the sheet. "Look at you, Sugar. Fuck, you look so good like this."

"Josh," she whimpers.

She's close, I can feel it. Feel the way her body winds up around my fingers, milking them; feel the way her body vibrates with each stroke of my palm on the bundle of nerves between her legs. Without warning, I pull my hand from her and bring my fingers to my mouth. Her eyes meet mine as I stick my index and middle finger in my mouth.

Fuck.

I moan, she tastes so good. I smile when I pull my fingers from my mouth and kiss her, plying her mouth open and stroking her tongue so she can taste herself. "You taste better than I thought, baby."

She whines against my lips.

"Soon, Sugar." I nip her bottom lip and slip my fingers back inside her. I crook my fingers to find the spot that will make her come and let my palm rub against her clit to create the perfect storm.

I push the fabric of her bra to the side and take one of her hardened nipples into my mouth. She practically jumps off the bed when my teeth graze the sensitive bud. Her body vibrates, and my name falls from her lips, she's so close to the edge…I hum against the soft flesh of her breast and suckle on her nipple.

"Come for me, Sugar," I whisper against her chest before biting her nipple, and she does. She tries to pull away from my assault on the sensitive bud between her legs, but I don't give in just yet. Her voice wavers under the pressure when she cries out my name. Without hesitation, I pull her underwear down her legs before tossing the cloth aside. I kiss her stomach and settle between her legs, resting them over my shoulders.

She gasps when I blow a small puff of air against her entrance before I lick one stripe up her center. Manicured fingers dig into my hair, twisting and pulling with each lick that follows. When she tries to pull away from me, I wrap my arms around her thighs and hold her still. A string of expletives and moans of pleasure fill the air around us, and when I push one finger inside her alongside my tongue, the sound she makes is heavenly.

Our eyes meet briefly before I push another finger inside, and my teeth scrape across her clit. Her head falls back, her mouth agape, and her hips buck against me.

"Baby," she moans. I can barely hear her, but the word sends a jolt to my dick.

Never has she used a term of endearment, not even when we gave dating a real try. Nothing outside of the occasional "hun" that's required in front of the family because calling me Josh or Joshua twenty-four-seven might raise a red flag or two.

"Baby, please," she gasps. She bucks against my mouth again, and I curl my fingers to reach the spot that will send her spiraling. My left hand reaches to massage her breast, teasing her nipple. One more suckle on the small bud of nerves, and she comes on my tongue. I moan against her, the taste of her sweet as she tugs harder on the ends of my hair.

Her chest continues to rise and fall with each breath. I push my shorts down my legs, lining myself up with her entrance.

"Look at me, Sugar," I command, and when her dazed eyes meet mine, she smiles. "You sure 'bout this?"

She nods, and I push inside of her slowly, letting her adjust the whole way until I'm seated fully inside her. "Fuck," I hiss. "You feel so fucking good."

"Shit," she gasps.

Fuck, she's tight. Between coming twice already and being

a virgin, her walls clench my dick with no remorse.

I pull out almost all the way and push back in slowly, starting to build a good pace. Fuck, she's so wet, so tight, and she takes me so good. If she keeps making noises like that, I'm not going to fucking last.

She reaches between us to play with her clit, and if she was close to the edge, she's one foot off now. Her right hand rakes down my bicep, nails digging into my skin when I lift her left leg over my shoulder, and with each thrust, I'm starting to lose control.

"Baby," she whimpers, eyes screwed shut.

"You wanna come on this dick, Sugar?"

She nods.

"Hold it," I command, and she cries. "Hold it, Sugar."

I slow my movements, pulling all the way out and pushing back in, maintaining an excruciatingly slow pace. Once, twice, three times. "Feel good?"

She whimpers. I pull out once more and wait a moment before I say, "Come."

As I push back in, her body spasms beneath me, her muscles clenching my cock, milking it as I continue to fuck her. I lift her hips and begin to drive harder into her until I come.

twenty-four

THEN
November 2018

SO, THINGS DIDN'T EXACTLY go as planned. I was supposed to propose on Thanksgiving with the entire family there, but the universe had other plans. Michaela and Dad came down with a nasty stomach bug, Nick wasn't in the mood to spend the holiday with the Villa family, and Alex got stuck in Boston. Brina told me to do it anyway; everyone would understand, but I refused. I wanted everyone to be there when I popped the question…again.

That was a week ago, so we're going for round two, and almost everyone is here. Uncle Jim had a doctor's appointment, and Alex had class. Nick had to run the garage. At least, that was his excuse. Could he take off? Yeah, probably. But I knew he wouldn't show without his dad or brother, not if it meant having to deal with the Villas. When I called to inform him of the new date, he declined, and I reminded him he wouldn't be able to avoid the Villas forever. For example, at the wedding. "I'm not avoiding them, I'm just busy," he said, but we both knew that was (mostly) a lie.

Everyone else is here, except Nina and Elizabeth. Since

the weather was nice and considerably warm for the end of November, the ruse was the girls were coming to meet Michaela for wine and sunset-watching on Jupiter Beach. Poor Nina. She is so excited to surprise Elizabeth that I can only hope Elizabeth is able to play along to spare Nin's feelings. My parents, Michaela, and the Villas hide, trying to stay out of sight but still get a view of the action.

In the distance, I can see Nina lead Elizabeth down the boardwalk and over the dunes, ending at the beach. They slow their approach, reaching the candles that have been buried in the white sand to create a pathway leading her to me. I stand on a white sheet laid out in the middle of a large square formed by roses—their stems stuck down in the sand to stand at attention.

Seeing her walk toward me, that feeling I got while I helped her decorate the house for Christmas a few weeks ago forms in the pit of my stomach. The same one I felt when I proposed two weeks ago in her bedroom. It's hard to explain, the feeling, but I think it's...love.

Yeah, it's love.

I've fallen in love with the woman in front of me, but I don't know how to tell her.

You became my husband the second we signed that damn paper three years ago.

Her words have echoed in my mind ever since, and even if she's never said it, those words told me she feels the same way I do. There isn't anyone else I'd want to do this with. How sick and twisted is that? I mean, what a fucked up way to find the woman you want to spend the rest of your life with, right?

Nina hangs back a few steps and Elizabeth's steps falter when our eyes meet just outside of the box of roses.

Wow, she mouths, and I laugh.

Wow, indeed.

This isn't how I would have chosen to propose. The simple

ask in her bedroom is more my style, but the Villas would never allow it—well, Ric maybe, but not Nina or Brina. Especially not Brina.

Elizabeth takes a final look around and takes a deep breath. "Nina?" she asks, implicating her friend in the choice of décor.

"More Brina and Michaela, but she had some input."

She laughs, and it's a sweet melody that puts my nerves at ease. Taking a deep breath, I whisper, "You ready?"

"No turning back."

I drop to one knee, this time digging a small velvet box from my pocket, and Elizabeth covers her mouth in a shocked expression, really selling the moment. "Maybe a little less dramatic." I chuckle.

I was proud of myself. I had picked the ring out without help (unless you count Nick). Nina had offered to set me up with a jeweler in Charlotte—it was Tiffany & Co., shocker, I know—but I told her I already had one in mind. There was a local jeweler in Winchester that Finn introduced me to years ago and I wanted to see what they had before I went running off to endure my first *Pretty Woman* moment.

It only took five minutes from walking in the door to finding the ring I wanted. The diamond was cut into the perfect oval shape—not too thick, but not too slender either—and it sparkled like the stars in the sky on a cloudless night. It rested in a white gold diamond-studded band. It was on display with a wedding band full of diamonds slightly larger than the ones embedded in the engagement band. The two rings looked beautiful together and they were exactly the kind of thing Elizabeth would want. I wasn't nervous about my choice until I brought Nina along to pick them up, but my worries faded the moment she opened the box. She didn't stop smiling even after we walked out of the jeweler, telling me over and over that Elizabeth was going to "be over the moon about them."

"You know they're eating it up," Elizabeth says.

With another calming breath, I open the box to reveal the ring and her eyes widen. "I meant what I said the other night in your bedroom, Sugar."

Her smile falters slightly when she realizes I'm no longer playing around. She looks between me and the ring three times before finally landing on me. And this time, she covers her mouth in true shock, as real tears cloud her vision. "Josh," she whispers.

"I can't imagine life without you. Regardless of how this ends for us...I don't want a life without you in it. I know this isn't how you imagined your life would turn out or how you'd find your husband, but I don't regret it. And I promise to make this whole thing as painless as possible. So, I'm going to ask one more time...Elizabeth Regina Cain, will you be my wife?"

twenty-five

NOW

AFTER THE WAY THINGS turned out at the market, I'm thankful the rest of the day was uneventful. Georgie even spared Jeremy one of her grilling sessions. I'm still confused about that. No one has ever been spared, so why now? Is it because he's an actor? Maybe Lola introduced them before, or maybe Lola warned Georgie not to after everything that just happened. That seems more likely. Lola is one of the few people in the world Georgie actually listens to. I've never heard the full story, but from the little bit I've heard over the years, something went down their freshman year at SCAD, and Lola had no problem putting Georgie in her place.

Elizabeth's legs rest across my lap underneath the fleece blanket Selena had tossed our way when we sat down. She sips on a glass of red wine—Pinot Noir, her favorite—and I swirl the last sip of whiskey in my glass, committing the scene to memory. On the way back from town, I decided if this was going to be my last year here, if this was truly our last hoorah, I was going to make the most of it.

Somewhere in between Selena telling us she'd be moving

to Dallas at the beginning of the year and Lola announcing she decided to get back into producing for a special project with one of her old Hollywood friends Elizabeth had closed the gap between us. Her arms draped around my chest, still clutching her wine glass, as she laughed along to a story one of her friends told. A little while later, she moved to lay back against the couch, with her legs across my lap and her perfectly manicured left hand resting on my shoulder, occasionally playing with the hair at the base of my neck.

The other couples lounge in similar positions, minus Georgie and Noah. They had kept a small gap between them as they sipped on their hot apple cider—keeping up with Georgie's no-alcohol stance this weekend. She slipped away quietly about ten minutes ago and has yet to surface to help the other girls reminisce not just about their times at Palm Valley but their years of friendship in general.

"Oh no," Selena groans when Lola asks if she remembers *that* guy. How in the hell is she supposed to remember him by calling him "that guy?"

"You brought him in…2020, maybe? Yeah, it had to be! But he said he used to live here, so he kept trying to get in the way of our plans. And then"—Lola snickers—"he got sloppy drunk and told you he loved you."

Selena tries to hide her cringe. "He wasn't that bad."

"He was pretty bad."

"Tried to make a move on the bartender when you were in the bathroom, right after he told you he loved you," Elizabeth adds.

"And when she rejected him, he started trying to sweet talk me even though Andrew was right there," Lola says. Andrew was Lola's ex-boyfriend, the man she had assumed she would settle down with, but in the end, he said he didn't see a future with her (after three years of dating). "I think he said he loved all of us that night."

"Me, included," I say.

"Yep, same." Noah chuckles.

Selena covers her face, trying to hide her giggle.

"Where did you meet this guy?" Elijah asks.

"We reconnected from school."

"Oh! So, an *arteest*." He gives the word extra emphasis.

"She was always a sucker for a painter," Elizabeth says.

"It's romantic," the girls say in unison. Elizabeth and Lola imitate Selena at the same moment she defends herself.

"It is!" Selena demands.

"Are we talking about Selena's infatuation with painters again?" Georgie asks when she returns to the pool house.

Elizabeth smirks behind her wine glass. "Lola was just recounting that one guy Sel brought who got sloppy drunk and started hitting on everyone."

"Derek! From school, I remember him. Didn't he used to call his mom 'mommy?'"

Yes, yes, he did, and you want to know something? I could have gone the rest of my life without being reminded about that. We had been sitting around the fire out back at the Thompson house, just like this, when Derek's phone rang. He was about to ignore the call until he saw who it was. "Hi, Mommy!" he answered enthusiastically and tromped off to find a quiet place to talk to her.

"He sounds like a real winner." Jeremy snickers when Selena covers her face in embarrassment.

"That's one way to put it," I whisper, earning a playful glare from Elizabeth before we share a laugh.

"What an odd place to tell someone you love them," Noah says. He crosses his arms and leans back onto the couch. "There were a lot of red flags, but that should've been the biggest."

"Didn't you date him for like two more months after that?" Lola asks, finishing the wine in her glass.

"Unfortunately." It comes out mumbled, and Lola begs

Selena to repeat it, much to Selena's dismay. "Unfortunately, I didn't see the red flags until it was too late."

Part of me is curious; the other part doesn't think I want to know what that means. When I glance at Elizabeth, she shakes her head, and that's all the answer I need.

"Didn't he break up with you before—"

"No!" Selena yells, interrupting Georgie. She points a tawny finger at her friend for extra emphasis. "No. I broke up with him."

"Oh, right. That was Kyle, the one after."

"And then we got together," Elijah says. It's simple and soft, but it's sweet, especially the way he leans over, gripping her chin to kiss her.

"You didn't tell her you loved her in a bar, right, Elijah?" Noah asks, earning a laugh from his wife.

"And then turn around and tell the bartender the same thing?" Jeremy adds, this time earning a laugh from all the guys, and Elijah's face turns into a beet.

"Never," Selena swoons, her dark brown hair falling over her shoulder as she smiles up at him. "It was completely out of nowhere, though." Elijah protests, but she pushes back. "I walked into your apartment, and you just…blurted it out. Out of nowhere!"

"There's more to it than that," Elijah says and rolls his eyes, taking the final sip of his beer, and Selena quirks her thick brow in a manner that says she still doesn't believe him. "It was a Saturday morning. You had just walked in from your yoga session and you brought back donuts from our favorite bakery by the studio. When you walked in, it put everything in place… You had turned my apartment into a home—our home—and seeing you in there felt right. I knew I had fallen in love with you. So yeah, maybe I just blurted it out, but I didn't want to wait to tell you. I wanted you to know right then and there."

Elijah pulls her to him again, pressing a soft kiss to her lips and then her temple before she settles back into his side.

I'm happy for them. Happy they were able to make it work. Selena isn't the only one who has dealt with some bad relationships in the past. Elijah has had his fair share too. The girl he had just broken up with before our wedding had more than one screw loose if you know what I mean. Let's just say there was a car involved when he broke up with her—do with that information what you will.

"Remember when you told me you loved me?" Georgie bats her eyelashes up at her husband, snuggling a little closer to him.

"I do," he says with a small smile, but that's his only reaction.

"Trust me, we all do." Elizabeth shudders at the thought.

Yes, we do, unfortunately. Noah had never said he loved Georgie until the day he proposed. He popped the question on the beach outside his parents' house, and needless to say, they spent the day locked away in their bedroom. The rest of us did our best to steer clear of that part of the house, including Selena, who ended up sleeping on the couch downstairs that night instead of in her room next to them.

"You guys are so dramatic." Georgie scoffs.

"Tell that to my trauma," Lola argues.

"Oh, Noah! Noah! Yes!" Selena imitates just some of what we heard that day if we dared enter the house.

"Right thereeeeee!" Lola and Elizabeth add before they fall into a fit of giggles. Georgie rolls her eyes before smiling at her husband, who stares off into the darkness of the sideyard.

"What about you two?" Elijah asks Jeremy. "Have you said it yet?"

"He said it pretty quick, actually," Lola says, taking a sip of wine.

"Hey, when you know, you know." Jeremy shrugs and pushes a strand of strawberry-blonde hair to the side so he can rub her back. "I won't say it was love at first sight, but pretty damn close. And when I saw her with my daughter… that sealed the deal."

"Don't let her fool you, Jeremy. She called us not long after meeting you and said she was head over heels for you," Selena says, earning a *what the fuck* look from Lola. "What was it you said, Lo? Oh right, 'I'm going to spend the rest of my life with that man.'" She adds a swoon-worthy sigh for extra dramatics.

"Oh really?" Jeremy's brow arches, smirking at his girlfriend.

"When you know, you know, right?" Lola shrugs and smiles when he kisses her.

It makes me even more curious about what could have driven such a wedge between them amid the chaos of the stalker situation.

"How old is your daughter?" Elizabeth asks.

"Gabby is six. Her mother and I realized pretty quickly after we got married that we weren't meant to be together. We're far better as friends," Jeremy says as Lola absentmindedly plays with his fingers, eventually lacing their hands together.

"Shay is a great mom, though," she adds. "It's nice to have a good co-parenting situation instead of the alternative."

"You're one of those super secret romantics, aren't you, Jeremy?" Elijah says, pointing his finger toward the actor. "I can see it."

Jeremy laughs in return. "I may have rented out her favorite restaurant with a violinist and a shit ton of roses for the occasion."

"I knew it! You just have that vibe."

"What about you two?" Jeremy asks me. "Surely, Mr. and Mrs. Perfect have a great story of how you knew you were in love."

Elizabeth and I share a sheepish glance before Georgie answers for us. "Everyone knows their story. Well, I guess everyone but you, Jeremy."

Lola rolls her eyes. "Josh and Liz have been together longer than all of us put together, and they'll be together until the end of time."

"Oh, we have not." Elizabeth scoffs.

"Have so! You've been together for what, ten years at this point?"

"Ten years since I rescued her on the dance floor," I say, smiling at Elizabeth—a real, genuine smile thinking of the memory. When she meets my stare, she offers nothing in return, her gaze unreadable.

"And seeing her standing there, in that light, you knew you'd just found the woman you'd marry one day," Georgie quotes, and Elizabeth finally smiles, hearing the rehearsed story I've told many times over the years. "Yes, we *know*."

"That's not when I knew," I say, but I never take my eyes off Elizabeth, whose face scrunches in confusion. "No, I mean, yeah, I think deep down maybe...but that wasn't when I realized I was in love with her."

Elizabeth rips her gaze from mine, staring into the fire, and takes a sip of her wine.

I take the opportunity to re-memorize everything about her—the two freckles on her left cheek; the way her cheeks flush from a combination of the wine and heat from the fire; the small scar (almost unnoticeable to anyone who wouldn't know it's there) on her neck just below her jaw from that time she begged Nina to pierce her ears because her parents wouldn't let her; the soft, natural wave in her hair now that she keeps it short, tucked behind her ear; the reflection of the flame dancing in her eyes, still refusing to look at me; the way she clutches the ends of her long-sleeve in her left hand covering the scars of her past, and the right dangles her glass from the edge of the couch, swirling the red liquid absentmindedly. She's beautiful. She is the most beautiful woman I've ever known, with a heart of gold and a soul to match—but sometimes, it gets buried deep to protect herself from any potential hurt.

"It was her birthday. We were at the house in Savannah, decorating for Christmas. She was supposed to be studying for finals, but she called and begged me to come down and help her decorate because you girls wanted to study first and decorate later. I told her she should be doing the same, but got in the car and drove down anyway. Got there around one in the morning, but it was worth it when the door swung open, and she had the biggest smile plastered on her face."

I notice a slight tick upwards in the left corner of her mouth.

"I begged her to please let me get some sleep, and I promised we'd get up early and get started…Well, she held me to that, woke up at eight on the dot."

My laugh is joined by the others.

"But, that night…She was finishing up the tree, singing along to 'Have Yourself a Merry Little Christmas,' and I walked back from the kitchen and the sight…It took my breath away. This feeling came over me. It's hard to explain, really, but when she turned and looked at me with that smile…I knew I'd never be able to go on without her. I didn't want to. It'd be unbearable."

I watch as her lips curl inward, chewing on my words, turning them over and over again in her mind.

"Part of me thinks, maybe, I fall in love with her every day. There's something new every day that reminds me of why I want this. I'm blessed to have this beautiful, amazing woman by my side…And I can't imagine the day I have to go on without her."

The others are too busy swooning over my words to realize *what* I just said, but not her. Not Elizabeth. She heard me loud and clear. Even though she still refuses to look at me, I can see the tears brimming in her eyes and the way she bites her lip to hide the small quiver.

I clear my throat and the tears that have started to form in my own eyes. "I need another drink."

twenty-six

NOW

"WHAT THE FUCK WAS *that?"* Elizabeth storms into the bedroom at the same time I come out of the bathroom. I can feel my eyes widen as she all but slams the door closed and crosses the room to jab her finger into my chest. "'I knew I'd never be able to go on without her…I can't imagine the day I have to.'" She scoffs. "Are you fucking kidding me? We are getting *divorced* in a few months, or did you forget that?"

Why is she so mad? She's the one who wanted me to play along this weekend because she didn't want her friends to suspect anything was wrong. I was only doing what she wanted, right?

Wrong. I had crossed the line. Maybe it was that last glass of whiskey or maybe it was because I was feeling a little too sentimental, but my admission out by the firepit was not what she wanted from me this weekend. I had let my guard down a little too far and now I was facing the consequences. Now it was time to clean up that mess…

"I was just…playing along," I say as my shoulders raise with a shrug.

"Playing along?"

"Yeah, that's what you wanted, right? You don't want them to suspect anything, so I was just doing what you asked."

Elizabeth narrows her gaze before throwing her hands up with an exasperated sigh and walking into the bathroom.

"I could've told them the truth. Would you have preferred that?" I ask, leaning against the doorframe, meeting her glaring gaze in the mirror. "You don't want me to act like the doting husband—"

"Because you're not the doting husband!"

"Because you didn't want me to be!"

"Didn't want—" She scoffs, shaking her head. She looks up to the ceiling as if asking God the Creator for help. "Didn't *want* you to be?" Elizabeth finally turns from the mirror and storms to meet me. "You're the one who stopped caring, Josh. You're the one—"

"Don't feed me that bullshit. I never stopped caring about you. You're the one who walked out, Liz, not me."

Elizabeth takes a step back; her tongue wets her lips before she pulls them between her teeth. Another scoff. "Sure, okay. If that's what you need to tell yourself to feel better about this… be my guest. But I'm *done*. I'm done waiting for you to wake the fuck up and realize everything you could've had and lost. I can't do it anymore, Josh."

"What's that supposed to mean?"

"Get out." She tries to close the door, but I won't budge.

What the fuck does that mean? *Could've had and lost.* We had been broken up for months before she finally decided to leave, so what does that even mean?

"I said, get out!" She tries to push me from the bathroom, but I grab her wrists and hold her in place, bending to meet her gaze.

"Everything I could've had? You never planned on staying, Elizabeth!"

And she doesn't deny it. From day one, I told myself not to fall in love with her because, at the end of the day, she was going to leave. That was always the plan. Her plan. But it didn't matter because no matter how hard I tried, I did fall in love with her. Through the years, we walked a fine line between what was real and what was a result of circumstance, constantly teetering from one side to the other. Despite my best efforts, I couldn't stop myself. I fell completely, hopelessly in love with Elizabeth Regina Cain, even though I knew it was going to crush me when our time was up.

And when it did…when things came to an end that final time, she made it clear there was no going back. We would live out the rest of the arrangement separately unless it was something we had to do.

The ache in my heart was worse than anything I could've imagined. Knowing it was the end—that despite my best efforts, she wasn't coming back, she was leaving—I had to do something to try and dull the pain, even in the slightest. So, when Wichita happened, I thought it might be the universe allowing me to move on.

Elizabeth's phone rings in the bedroom, and I feel her body jump from the sudden burst of noise, but she doesn't move. She stands there a moment longer before she takes a deep breath and says, "You're right, Josh. This was always the plan."

Slipping from my grasp like butter, she walks into the bedroom and pulls her phone out of the nightstand drawer. There's a slight hesitation when she looks at the screen. She starts to swipe to answer but then decides against it. She stuffs it back into the nightstand and slams the drawer shut before huffing back into the bathroom.

twenty-seven

"THANK YOU FOR DROPPING those pies off to your mom earlier," Elizabeth says from the doorway.

Warm light with an orange hue streams through the windows of my home office, signaling that it's way past time to be working, but I had taken a little extra time off this afternoon to help my sister put her plan in motion. Elizabeth looks radiant standing there, and I lean back in my chair, admiring the woman who is about to become my wife. We have four months until we're supposed to say *I Do*, and wedding planning has been nonstop since January. Who knew there was so much shit to do before walking down the aisle? I didn't. Luckily, she has been taking care of most of it with Nina's help.

"They were a hit at the PTA meeting, or so your mom says."

"They always are."

Elizabeth had picked up baking after her parents died. It gave her something to do, something to take her mind off things. Recovery was a long road, and baking gave her a sense of purpose again. There was a great sense of accomplishment in transforming simple ingredients into a delectable treat. Not only was it her escape, but it offered new challenges, bringing a sense of pride every time she was able to conquer a tough recipe.

"Why did you drag Nick with you to Nina's office today?" she asks, raising her brow as she sits in the chair across from me. She crosses her legs before folding her hands on top of her knee.

"He needed to grab a part from the store. I was already going into town, so I offered him a ride, and thought we could grab a bite."

"*And* stop by Nina's with the pies for your mom when you could easily drop them off at school?" Elizabeth laughs when I shrug. "I'm assuming MJ told you about Brina threatening to set Nina up with the neighbor."

"She may have mentioned something about it."

"Let me guess." She lightly taps her chin before turning to me with a smirk. "She told you about it, and then you both decided *Nick* was the answer?"

The plan was simple. I'd call Nick and invite him to lunch. It just so happened that fate was on my side, and Nick needed to go into town anyway. When Michaela mentioned Nina was in a predicament and wondered if Nick would go for it, I told her absolutely not, but it was worth a shot. Our cousin was in desperate need of a vacation. The past six years had been anything but kind to him. Why not give him a shove in the right direction? I never anticipated the two of them already knowing each other. Nick had always avoided any interaction with her that I was aware of; I should've known something was up when his mood instantly changed the second we pulled up to DV Designs on the square. I just assumed it was because of whatever his previous presumptions were. Until...

"What are *you* doing here?" Nina had asked, genuinely surprised when Nick turned away from her older designs displayed on the wall.

"You know each other?" Michaela asked, sharing a confused glance with me.

"He's the guy who spilled coffee on me."

"You're coffee boy?" My sister all but shouted.

"Coffee boy?" I asked, confused by the entire interaction.

"Nick ran into Nina two weeks ago and spilled coffee all over her."

"Correction, she ran into me," Nick interjected, a smirk spreading across his lips as he stared down the woman I brought him to meet. After a quick re-introduction, Nick had no interest in sticking around to get to know her, ready to get back to work at the garage. He didn't say much on the way back from town, but then again, I didn't expect him to.

"I know my cousin," I say to Elizabeth. "He needs a break. It's been six years since Aunt Evie died and…I don't think he's come up for air since."

Elizabeth sucks in her bottom lip, chewing on the thought. If anyone should understand something like that, it's her. Standing from the chair, she sighs and shakes her head, done with the conversation.

"You love Nick. Why do you care if he's the person Nina decides to ask?"

"She already decided to ask him."

I wonder if MJ knows. Who am I kidding? Of course she knows.

"Isn't it better for her to take someone we all know instead of some random guy off the street?"

"Joshua Davis, are you a secret romantic?"

"It's not a secret, Sugar," I say with a wink, and she rolls her eyes, but I can see the blush rising in her cheeks.

"You're pretty confident Nick will say yes." Elizabeth shrugs, leaning back into the chair a little further. "Maybe you don't know your cousin as well as you think."

"What's that supposed to mean?"

"You and I both know Nick would never go along with something like this. Lying to the family, betraying that trust… You know how much family means to him. That's why you never told him about *our* little arrangement."

"Legally, I'm not allowed to."

"Well, you could if you wanted to. I wouldn't mind. Out of anyone, Nick would be the only person I'd trust to keep his mouth shut. But we can't risk anyone screwing this up for either of us. Then again, you have a lot more to lose than I do." The smirk on her red lips makes my stomach churn. It's true, I do have a lot more to lose, and I cannot let anyone screw this up. If the truth comes out, I risk losing everything. I risk losing Elizabeth.

twenty-eight

July 2019

THE COFFEE TABLE IS littered with various invitation sets, and we (she) *must* pick one today, per the wedding planner, for the printer to get them done on time. We have a little over nine weeks until the big day. Truth be told, I thought Elizabeth had already done this and the invitations had been sent, but apparently, that was only the Save the Dates. Occasionally, she would hold up a set and ask my opinion, but she would only sigh and put it back on the table. The whole thing had become tiresome, but I don't want to be one of those men who doesn't support their bride-to-be in their planning endeavors, even if she doesn't want my opinions. So, I was here to help…until I got a call from Nick.

I kiss the top of Elizabeth's head, jumping off the couch at the opportunity to look at something, anything, that isn't a wedding invitation.

"Thank God. I was starting to go cross-eyed staring at all those invitations," I say, rubbing my eyes and walking out of the living room. "Not that I'm not glad to hear from you, but why are you calling me? I thought you were in Denver."

"We are." He sighs. Oh good, this sounds promising.

"Why are you calling me? Isn't it like 9 a.m. There? You should still be in bed with your *girlfriend*. Liz said you guys are actually dating now."

"Josh, listen—"

"How did that happen?"

"Josh!" Nick huffs on the other end of the line, mumbling a *fuck*. "Josh, I-I think I fucked up."

"What does that mean?" I practically trip over my feet, hearing the next words that come out of his mouth: *We slept together.* "I'm sorry, you what? You've only been dating for what, five minutes?"

"You're one to talk."

"I'm not judging. I'm just surprised. Really surprised, actually. First, you start dating for real, and now this...You always seemed so anti-Nina." I scrub a hand down my face, trying to process this information. And then he tells me there's more. "What do you mean *more?*"

"Brina is sleeping with Lee."

What the actual fuck?

"I beg your pardon. You're going to have to repeat yourself. I swear you just said Brina is sleeping with Lee."

"I caught them hooking up back at the house."

"You *saw* them?"

"Not the first time, but then—"

"There was a second time?" I practically yell. "Nick, what in the hell is going on out there?" Elizabeth and I have joined the Villas out in Haven plenty of times, but it has never been this action-packed.

"Honestly, I have no idea." Nick sighs, and I hear the sounds of a busy room behind him. "Brina, she—she's blackmailing me. She knows I saw them, and now she's threatening Pop, and the garage, and Alex if I say anything to Nina or her dad."

"Fuck," I breathe. Fuck, this is bad. This is worse than bad.

"And then, she sent me this text last night." He fumbles around with his phone, pulling up the message. "'It will serve you well to remember our discussion about your family. I've been told there's more to you than meets the eye. I'd hate for things to take a turn for the worse.' And that wasn't even the first one. She's sent multiple, reminding me what will happen if I step out of line."

"Dude, you have to tell Nina."

"I can't! If I tell her, Brina will—"

"Nina can handle her mom, that much I know. Do you have any proof of what you saw? You can always go straight to Ric about it." His sigh is answer enough. "Look, I can't make the decision for you, but I can tell you that it will be much easier if you're honest about what's going on. Nina might not like it but she can handle the truth over a lie."

"I don't know, Josh. I'm in way over my head here."

"Whatever you decide to do, you have to be prepared for the consequences that come with it, including the truth about who you are and—"

"I gotta go." His sudden change in tone catches me off guard.

"What are you gonna do?"

"Fuck if I know." His words don't inspire much confidence, and I get the distinct feeling I'm not going to like what is about to happen. "She's going to be up shortly. I gotta go. And Josh, don't tell Elizabeth."

Without another word, Nick hangs up, leaving me with a ticking time bomb and only a red wire. And now I have to go back into the other room where the woman who could get secrets out of a spy if she wanted to, and somehow I'm not supposed to tell her that her adoptive mom is fucking her sister's ex-boyfriend. Is he serious?

"I can do this." I hype myself up because Lord knows I'm gonna need all the help I can get.

"What did Nick want?" Elizabeth asks when I finally walk back into the living room. She doesn't look up from the invitations in front of her, but I look over her shoulder at the current one she's holding. It's nice. The actual invitation is some type of frosted acrylic, and the words printed on it are white. The envelope is olive green to match the accent color I'll be wearing, along with my groomsmen.

"They uh…they slept together."

The invitation clatters down on the table.

"They slept together?" Elizabeth repeats, finally looking at me, and I nod. "Holy shit."

I fight the urge to tell her the other thing Nick called about, but I know she will run and tell Nina. I can't let that happen. I can't be the reason *that* bomb implodes the Villa family any sooner than it has to.

"That's the only reason he called?"

"Yep!"

It comes out a little too quick, a little too peppy, I can tell by the way she narrows her gaze. After what feels like an hour, she rolls her eyes. "God, you're such guys."

She turns back to the invitations in front of her and my smile slips when she's no longer looking.

twenty-nine

NOW

ELIZABETH LIES IN BED with a book I've never seen before. Its cover is reminiscent of one of those cutesy cartoon romances I've seen walking through the store. Blue-gray tortoiseshell reading glasses sit on the end of her nose, and her eyes roam across the page. I climb into my side of the bed with my copy of *Atlas Shrugged*, opening to where I left off about halfway through the book. I can't even comprehend the growing chaos and economic collapse of the country due to Galt's strike because I'm too damn focused on the woman next to me. If my brain was run by little workers, then they're jumping ship just like the individuals who have joined the strike, leaving me behind to function without their contributions.

I'm done waiting for you to wake the fuck up and realize everything you could've had and lost.

Her words still bouncing around my mind, and I analyze every bit of them. What does she mean?

Closing my book, I turn toward her and wait for her to acknowledge me, but she doesn't. Her eyes continue to flick across the pages but never look too far to the right so she doesn't accidentally catch a glimpse of me.

"Are we doing the right thing?" I ask, and she scoffs but still doesn't look at me. "I'm serious. I don't—"

"Of course we're doing the right thing." Elizabeth cuts me off, finally turning to look at me. She pushes her glasses to the top of her head and rubs her eyes with the heels of her palms. "Soon enough, you'll be free to go to Wichita as much as you want. Hell, you could move there if you wanted."

"Would you just forget Wichita for one fucking second?" I take one of her hands in mine. Her eyes drop to them and I'm almost certain she feels that same warmth bloom under her skin that I do. I reach up to cradle the side of her face, letting my thumb graze the delicate skin of her cheek, and her eyes flutter closed. "I just want you to be happy, Sugar. Whatever that means. If that means signing the papers in May…Fine. I'll do it. But only if you can tell me with one hundred percent certainty that *this* is what you want."

She doesn't say anything, swallowing the words she had mentally prepared to throw my way. And when her eyes flutter open to meet mine, I can see the questions swimming through her mind.

"Elizabeth, I'm sorry for lying to you. There is no excuse, but I had to. You were so adamant that you didn't want me to go out there. There's obviously a reason Juliet reached out after all of this time."

"It doesn't matter, Josh."

"Of course it matters! How you feel matters to me. You're hurt that I didn't tell you and I'm sorry. But Elizabeth,"—I pull her gaze to mine—"please believe me when I say that nothing happened. Juliet never even showed up."

"Well, I'm sure you can find a way to get ahold of her if you really want to."

"I don't want to," I say. "You're the one who ended things the last time, Elizabeth. Why did you care so much if I went to Wichita or not? Weren't you even the least bit curious what she wanted to tell me?"

"It's not hard to guess if you read that damn letter."

Without another word, Elizabeth turns back to her book. She can't focus on it; I can see it in the way her eyes gloss over the same sentence over and over and over again. She sighs. "Josh, just do what you came here to do, okay? We're not here to try and fix things."

"I'm just trying to—"

Elizabeth slams her book and glares at me. "Is that what you thought this weekend was about? I'm in a relationship, Josh!"

"Right, how could I forget." I scoff. "You know something I'm curious about…When did you and Ryan start dating?"

She doesn't answer, but that's answer enough.

"Where'd you meet?"

Her eyes narrow behind her glasses. "That's none of your concern."

"It is my concern when you're still *my wife*, Elizabeth. In case you've forgotten, we are still legally married until we sign those papers on May 22nd. You are still m—"

"Ryan wants to work things out," she cuts me off.

"He wants to fix things? If he wants to 'fix' things, why isn't he here with you this weekend?"

If Ryan wanted to work things out, why didn't he come with her this weekend? I guess the better question is, why didn't she invite him? Why am I still here instead?

"You know what I think?" I try to catch her gaze. "I think you're scared."

"Scared?" She scoffs. "Scared of what?"

"Moving on."

"You can't move on from something that was never there to begin with." Her words are like a punch to the gut. Why though? It's the truth. Everything we had was just a way to pass the time we were required to spend together. This was just part of the plan.

"Spew your bullshit to them." Elizabeth motions toward the door, toward her friends. "But we both know your 'feelings' for me weren't real. They were a product of being forced to spend time together. That's not real, Josh. It's not genuine. Anything we felt was artificial."

Maybe that's what we've been telling ourselves, but the longing in my bones is anything but artificial.

"Let's just get through the rest of this weekend, okay? Then we can move on with our lives."

"Why do you care so much about what your friends think? It's not like any of them are living picture-perfect lives. Yet, you can't even be honest with them about your own issues."

"It's none of their business."

"None of their business?" I scrub my hand down my face. She cannot be serious. These are supposed to be some of her closest friends. Why wouldn't she want to go to them for support? "Elizabeth, what happens when you show up next year with some guy who isn't me? There isn't a post-divorce *Last Hoorah Clause*. You're going to have to tell them."

Without giving me a response, she reaches over to shut off the lamp before turning her back to me.

thirty

NOW

ELIZABETH IS ALREADY GONE when I wake up the next morning. Her nightgown and robe hang from the hook next to the sink; the shower is still wet from where she got ready. There's a lipstick-stained mug still sitting on the vanity, half full. Glancing out the window over the tub, I can see it's overcast. The sun tries to peek through, but the clouds refuse to let it. The waves seem a little rougher today, the tide a little higher. Let's just hope this isn't some kind of omen.

When I walk downstairs, Jeremy is making breakfast—pancakes, and from the looks of it, he's attempting to make them into Christmas shapes. *Attempting* being the keyword. Selena and Elijah cuddle on the couch in the TV room just off the kitchen, and Georgie has curled herself up in the armchair. She looks a little paler than normal, still dressed in her pajamas, clutching one of the pillows to her abdomen. From the sounds of it, they're watching your basic Hallmark Christmas movie—Selena's favorite. Lola and Elizabeth try to offer Jeremy guidance from the kitchen island, telling him how to make his pancakes a little more Christmasy and a little less blobby. I don't think about it, I walk straight up to my wife and kiss her temple, pulling her into my side. Elizabeth sinks further into me. I'm almost certain she lets out a small sigh of contentment, but it's probably just my imagination. After our conversation last night, I know it's nothing more than that.

Everyone is accounted for except Noah. I take a second look around and, this time, notice him sitting outside by a small fire. Pouring two cups of coffee, I shoot a wink at Elizabeth, who watches with careful observation before I walk out. This seems like the perfect opportunity to figure out what in the hell is going on between him and Georgie. Call me nosy, but I'd consider myself more of a concerned acquaintance. Noah and I have never been super close, but he's a good guy. He might love talking about stocks, bonds, and his most recent investment a little too much, but he can be a lot of fun if you get him away from his normal topic of conversation. And he's pretty funny.

It's bitterly cold as soon as I step outside, and the breeze has picked up, whipping around me, pushing and pulling me slightly as I make my way around the pool toward the cabana. Noah has dropped three of the plastic enclosures, offering some shelter from the wind, but the fire still whips back and forth in the pit, refusing to give in. Despite the front wall remaining open, it's much warmer inside the shelter than I anticipated. There's a mug in his hand, resting on the top of his knee as he reads through the newspaper, but he hasn't taken a drink since I stepped outside. "You looked like you needed another," I say, offering one of the coffees.

Noah glances up. Setting the old mug down and folding his newspaper, he takes the new mug with a slight laugh. "That obvious?"

"You've been a little quieter than normal." I take a sip, feeling the liquid warm my insides as it works its way through my system. "Everything okay?"

Noah sighs. He traces the edges of the mug, staring into the dark liquid. Finally, he looks up. "How do you do it?"

"Do what?"

"You and Elizabeth. You've been through so much together. Ups and downs, highs and lows, good times and bad, but you always come out on the other side…stronger."

My stomach drops.

"I've always admired that about you guys. You've been together for so long. That feels rare nowadays."

"It's not always easy."

"No, I imagine not, but you still make it work." He shakes his head slightly, chewing on his bottom lip. "Gi and I have only been together maybe half the time you have, and I've never felt more distant."

"Something happen?" I watch his head bob subconsciously, but he doesn't say anything aloud. "Noah?"

"Georgie had an affair." Noah's words shock me and I almost drop my coffee. Georgie may be a lot of things, but a cheater? I would have never seen that coming. He runs a hand over his hair before tightening the bun that hangs at the base of his neck. "I've been traveling a lot, trying to secure a deal out in Washington, and before that, it was Europe…It's always been this way. She knew that. It never bothered her before; it meant she had the freedom to do what she wanted, when she wanted, and the money to do it with. When I was home, we'd spend it all together…but I guess it became too much, and she…she started an affair with someone at her father's company."

"Christ." I sigh, raking a hand over my face.

"She's pregnant."

This time, the mug does fall from my hands, falling to the cement and chipping the rim. "Fuck, Noah. I'm so sorry."

He chews on the inside of his cheek, shaking his head in disbelief like he's still trying to process the words himself. "We can't all get it right the first time, can we? Or, in my case, the second time."

"Third time's a charm?" I joke because it's better than the alternative, and he laughs. Noah doesn't talk about his previous marriage much, and Georgie only mentioned in the past that they were college sweethearts who eloped against his parents' wishes before they decided to go their separate ways. She never explained why, but I had a feeling it had to do with Noah's mother.

"I'm sorry, I didn't mean to dump this on you."

"Don't worry about it." I shrug. "We all have shit going on."

"I've decided to file for divorce," Noah says, looking up from his hands. Shit, he's really dropping the bombs this morning. "We've been trying to make it work, but—"

"You don't have to explain yourself. I get it. That's a hard line to come back from." Elizabeth and I may be in our own fucked up situation, but at least I know she didn't cheat on me—even if she's convinced herself that I cheated on her. "That's why we're not at your parents' this weekend?"

Noah nods. "I tried to keep it from them, but you know my mom. She has a way of getting things out of you, and when I told them…At first, they tried to say I should make it work, but when Mom found out Gi is pregnant." A heavy sigh. "It was the final straw."

"They never seemed that fond of her to begin with." I take a sip of my coffee making sure to avoid the chipped section of the rim.

"Mom has always been skeptical of anyone I bring home. Once people find out you have that kind of money it changes things. You get it, being related to the Villas."

Being related to Elizabeth alone is enough to make someone understand.

"Georgie doesn't know it yet. So, I would appreciate your discretion about it."

"You haven't told her? Shit, Noah!"

"No." He groans. "I hadn't decided until a few days ago. I've been trying to make it work, but I can't get past it. And I didn't want to ruin her weekend with you guys. What a downer to the party, y'know?"

Oh, trust me, I know all about that.

"When we get home, we'll have that conversation. Truthfully, I think she knows it's coming."

"There you are!" Elijah shouts as he and Jeremy get closer to us. I didn't even notice them come outside. "What are you guys doing out here? Breakfast is ready."

"That was fast," I say to Jeremy. When I left, he was still struggling. "Give up on the shapes?"

"The girls took over. Their shapes put mine to shame."

"I need a refill anyway," Noah says, standing from his chair. "Thanks again, Josh." Patting my shoulder gently, he walks back to the house, and his words from moments ago strike a chord in me.

Was Ryan's choice to want to work things out with Elizabeth because of her relation to the Villas? Because of her own wealth? It wouldn't be hard to do a little digging and figure out that kind of information.

The thought of him only wanting to fix things between them because of this sudden revelation leaves a sour taste in my mouth.

There's something about this guy I don't like, and it's not just because he's dating my wife. Not to mention, Nina doesn't like him. That's what Nick says anyway. So, why is Elizabeth so adamant about pursuing this relationship with him? I doubt she'd tell me anything if I asked...

"What was that about?" Elijah asks, looking back from Noah's retreating figure.

"Oh, nothing," I lie with a tight-lipped smile. "He was just asking me a quick marketing question. C'mon, let's go before they steal all the good pancakes."

thirty-one

I WAS GOING TO skip my run today, but after the news that Noah just dropped, I need one. I need time to think—time to process—time away from the others. Before I can pull my sweater on, Elizabeth walks into the room without warning, and her eyes are immediately drawn to my bare chest. When she finally looks up, her cheeks turn bright red, caught. "G-going somewhere?"

Finally pulling my sweater over my head, I nod. "Gonna head down to the beach for a run."

"How about a walk and some company, instead?" She bites down on her lip before offering a shy smile. I want to say no. I need this alone time—it's the little bit of peace I get away from the craziness—but somewhere deep inside, there's a voice screaming *yes*. Telling me I shouldn't miss out on this chance, the one I've been hoping for. The chance to smooth things over between us before we end up making family events awkward for the rest of eternity.

"Sure." The word is a little skeptical, a little colder than I meant for it to be, but I'm still not set on letting her come.

Elizabeth runs into the closet and returns, pulling an oversized sweater over her head, and whether she realizes it or not, it's one of mine. The Chadwick University design has faded substantially over the years, but it's still unmistakable. She adjusts her ponytail, slips her feet into her sandals, and grabs her camera from its bag. This is the first time I've seen her with it all weekend; normally, it's hanging around her neck like another appendage as she snaps photo after photo to preserve the memories. When she's finished adjusting herself, she stands at attention. "Ready!"

I can't help but chuckle, opening the door to let her go first.

We've been walking for almost an hour and it has been mostly silent, aside from the occasional snap of her camera shutter and the beating of the waves against the cold, wet sand. She left her sandals back at the house, letting her toes sink into the sand with a sharp intake of breath, and I laughed as she did a small dance, trying to get adjusted to the cool grains. Thankfully, the sun had finally managed about twenty minutes into our stroll, winning the fight against the clouds and fighting off a bit of the chill in the air.

There's a lot we need to talk about, but I don't know where to start.

The snap of the camera captures my attention, and looking over, I see the lens pointed straight at me.

"Sorry." Her voice is soft like the smile on her lips. "It was the perfect shot. I couldn't resist."

My tongue pokes out to wet my lips, and I swallow my reply. I can't remember the last time she took a photo of me that wasn't forced—family photos at the holidays and such. It had been well over a year. Shit, maybe even closer to two. Instead of offering a response, I put one foot in front of the other and keep moving. Hands shoved deeper in my pockets, I try to think of the best way to start *any* conversation, but I don't know what that is. I just don't want this to turn into another argument. I don't want to spend the rest of our lives fighting. We're going to have to figure this out. Eventually, we'll have no choice.

"Josh, I'm sorry."

Her words catch me off guard. I guess that's one way to start it.

I clear my throat, which suddenly feels extremely dry. "For what?"

Elizabeth sighs. "Everything." She covers her eyes with sleeve-covered hands. "This isn't easy on either of us, and I know that I haven't made it any easier on you. I feel bad about that, but sometimes…sometimes, I get so…so wrapped up in my head, and…" Her sudden pause begs me to say something, but I wait. "And it's not fair to you. I went about all of this the wrong way. I know that. But—"

"You did what you thought was best."

A slight tug in the corner of her mouth.

"I don't fault you, Elizabeth. I just wish…" The words get stuck in my throat. Do I really admit it? Right here, right now. Will it change anything?

"You wish what?" She pushes.

Meeting her gaze, I make the decision to push the boundaries. What can it hurt? She's already divorcing me. I say, "I wish we could've ended on better terms."

Elizabeth deflates a little at my admission. Was she hoping for something else?

C'mon, Josh, be a fucking man. Just tell her the truth.

"We don't have to end on bad terms," she says quietly.

"No?"

Elizabeth lifts her camera, pointing it toward a small house that sits at the edge of the dunes up ahead. When she's satisfied with the shot, she drops the camera from her face, but her hands still grip the sides. Her fingers absentmindedly tinker with the buttons.

"Elizabeth," I say gently, and her eyes lift to meet mine.

"Well, I just mean...We're stuck together, considering we're bound by marriage outside of this...us."

"Avoiding each other would be futile," I say. Her sudden change of heart is somewhat shocking. We've had this conversation before, barely two months ago on Halloween—hell, just last night—and she seemed set on the idea that we couldn't be friends. There was no chance of it happening despite our bond through Nick and Nina. "You seemed pretty set on not being friends on Halloween. What made you change your mind?"

She shrugs, chewing on her bottom lip and looking out toward the water. Tears brim in her eyes, and the sight chips away at my heart. I hate seeing her cry. I hate knowing I'm part of the reason for her tears. I pull her into a tight embrace and without pause her arms wind around my torso. Her hands clutch the fabric of my sweater as she buries her face into my chest. Resting my chin on the top of her head, I close my eyes, relishing the feeling of her in my arms because I know I'll never get to experience this again. The sweet, floral scent of her mixed with the sea air fills my lungs, and it's enough to soothe my racing mind, if only for a moment.

I don't know how long we stand there, wrapped in each other, but after a while, I kiss the top of her head, and she untangles herself from me. She wipes under her eyes with a small sniffle before readjusting herself.

"It's okay, Sugar," I say. "We'll figure it out. May not be today or tomorrow, but we'll figure it out."

"We're in this together?" Elizabeth asks and her words tug at my heartstrings. She pulls the sleeves of her sweater down over her hands and tucks them into the crooks of her arms against the breeze.

I shrug, tucking my hands in my pockets. "How's Ryan going to feel about us being friends?"

"Ryan is...He and I are...I don't know. It's complicated." Elizabeth sighs.

"Want to talk about it?"

Her brow cocks. "You, my soon-to-be ex-husband, want to talk about my relationship problems with my current on-again, off-again boyfriend?"

"That's what friends do, right?"

Elizabeth laughs, shaking her head. "You act like Nick hasn't told you everything already."

"Nick hasn't told me anything." Actually, Nick has told me next to nothing about her and Ryan. "Is there something he should've told me?"

Elizabeth's lips pull into a thin line and her gaze narrows. "We should probably head back," she says, catching me off guard.

Glancing at my watch, I realize we've been gone longer than I thought. The others have probably already had lunch at this rate. I nod, but neither of us makes the first move. I don't want to go back, not yet. I want to keep going. To find out the real reason she changed her mind about the future of our relationship, to find out what she thinks I already know...but I can already see some of her walls being rebuilt before my eyes. Fuck, I'd do anything to stop that from happening. To get a little more time as Josh and Elizabeth, not Josh *and* Elizabeth, before this weekend comes to an end.

"C'mon, Sugar," I say and I wrap my arm around her

shoulders, pulling her close again. I kiss her temple before beginning our walk back. If this weekend is truly our last hoorah, I'm going to make the most of the time left and enjoy these final moments while I can.

thirty-two

"WHAT'S THE DEAL WITH them?" Elijah asks, motioning to the front window of Savoy, the bar Elizabeth demanded we come to before everyone heads to bed. Tomorrow is the big day. I think she's trying to put it off for as long as she can. The sooner we go to bed, the sooner tomorrow comes, and the sooner we solidify this thing more than we already have. Through the front of the bar, I can see what Elijah is talking about: Nick and Nina. They look more comfortable in each other's presence than during the earlier rehearsal. There is zero space between them, their hands intertwined standing on the other side of the street.

"It's...complicated."

"Obviously." Elijah laughs. "He's been watching her like a damn hawk, but she says nothing is going on. If that's nothing, I must have been doing it wrong with some of my exes."

I chuckle and roll my eyes.

"Are you talking about Nick and Nina?" Selena asks, stepping into the conversation. "Please tell me they're gonna fuck this weekend. I mean, I would—"

"Sel, enough," I cut her off.

"I'm just saying! Everyone can see it."

"Don't tell me you didn't notice the tension between them when they were walking down the aisle earlier," Elijah adds. He means earlier when Elizabeth had forced them to walk down the aisle together because Lola hadn't arrived yet, and Nick needed "practice" so he could show Lola what to do tomorrow. Her true intentions were obvious, and if they weren't, they became obvious when Nina grumbled something in Italian to go along with the tight smile on her face.

Nick and Nina approach the bar, and he brings the back of her hand to his lips, drawing her even closer. She says something when they stop a few feet from the door, the tension so thick between them, you could cut it with a knife. I wish they could just figure their shit out, but I'm not one to get involved in other people's business. Especially not when it concerns Brina Villa. You couldn't pay me enough money to get on her bad side and Nick did it for free. Besides, I have my own shit to figure out.

"I invited her to join us at Monroe's for Christmas," Elijah says. "Said she should bring Nick with her."

"Dean's place?" I ask.

He nods. "More the merrier. You know Dean's mom loves having everyone there."

"Can I come?" Selena asks, batting her long eyelashes at Elijah.

A wide grin spreads across his lips, giving her a once-over. I could see the mental drool forming in the corner of his mouth at the sight of the burgundy dress against her warm, cinnamon skin. "Especially you."

I roll my eyes and notice Nina swimming through the crowd without Nick. Elizabeth greets her with a glass of champagne when she emerges in our little corner. Something happened, I can see it in Nina's expression as she talks to Elizabeth before they both turn to look at Nick. He paces the front of the bar, his hand tugging at the end of his hair, talking to someone on the phone. Whoever it is has changed his demeanor, and I have one guess as to who it could be...

Nick stares inside the bar—stares straight at Nina, finds her in the crowd with ease—and sighs. A silent agreement with the person on the other end of the line. A moment later, he shoves the phone into his back pocket and takes a deep breath, entering the bar. I notice Nina starts to make her way to him.

Shit, that's a bad idea.

I can't let her get to him. She's going to confront him. Demand to know what's going on. She's not stupid. She knows something is wrong. Knows there is a reason for the way he left things in Haven. The way he flipped like a switch so suddenly after he called me two months ago to tell me about Brina and Lee sleeping together. Do you know how hard it's been to keep my mouth shut when I've seen Brina recently? I still can't believe Nick just left Haven in the middle of the night, coming home and convincing Uncle Jim to fly to Boston on a whim. I understand that Nina may want answers, and she deserves them, but this isn't the time or place to confront it.

"Everything okay?" I ask, reaching Nick before she can.

"Fine."

"That was convincing." I chuckle. "Was that who I think it was?"

"Just wanted to make sure I wasn't getting any ideas while I'm here."

"Dude, just tell Nina. She can take care of it."

Nick sighs and stares past me. There's a longing in his eyes, but as long as he refuses to come clean about Brina and Lee, it will always be there. I guess it's not as simple as it seems. I know he wants to tell Nina....He wants to be honest, but what about his brother? What about his dad and the garage? Brina has made it very clear she will do everything to ruin their reputation and get Alex kicked out of college, blacklisting him from any other school. And Nina, all it would take is a few well-placed "clients" to tarnish her reputation. I have no doubt Brina would do every bit of it to keep her secret.

"I can't, Josh. You know I can't. I've already caused enough issues between her and her family. You said she's barely speaking to Ric, why would I want to risk making things worse?"

There's that too. Nina and Ric have not been the same since Haven. It's not entirely Nick's fault. Nina knew the risks of lying to her dad about her new relationship, but she did it anyway.

"Besides"—he glares at me—"you're the one who told me not to tell her—"

"No." I stop him. "I told you to be ready for the consequences when you *do* tell her. To be ready for everything to come out, and you weren't. You made a decision—the wrong one, in my opinion—and that's on you."

"I'm just trying to protect her."

"And look how that turned out." I grip his shoulder when he lets out a heavy sigh. "C'mon, let's get a beer." I try to guide him towards the bar, but he pulls away.

"I'm just gonna go."

"Nick—"

"I'll see you tomorrow." He turns away, swimming back through the crowd to reach the exit.

"What the fuck is going on?" I turn to find Elizabeth staring up at me. "You know something."

"I don't know anything." The lie flows easier than it should. I hate lying to her, but I know that I can't tell her this. She would never be able to keep this from Nina, or Ric for that matter. Hell, I don't want to keep it from them, but it's not my place to inform them about Brina's extracurricular activities—

that's Nick's job. And I can't betray Nick's trust because, at the end of the day, he's the one who is going to be there when this all comes to an end. I can't risk blowing up the Villa family—the only family she has left. Despite how screwed up their family is, it's still family.

Not to mention, we're already on thin ice after Ric found out about me and Elizabeth. I don't know how, but he found out the truth about our upcoming nuptials and now he and Brina aren't coming to the wedding.

Alaric Villa has always been a kind and gentle man, but sitting across from his desk two weeks ago after he found the truth was a place I never wanted to be again. I was sure this was going to be over before it even started.

"Can either one of you give me one reason I should allow this to continue?" he asked, his hands folded neatly on top of his desk.

Brina rolled her eyes from the corner of the room. "Dear, I've already told you—"

"I didn't ask *you*, Bri," Ric said, cutting his wife short. "I might have expected this from my other two children, but never from you, Elizabeth. What in God's name could have possessed either of you to enter into an arranged marriage? I can only assume you have a good reason for going along with this nonsense."

"Yes, sir," Elizabeth said, adjusting in her seat.

"And that is?"

"Well, my parents put certain stipulations on—"

Ric scoffed. "I see. So, this was all about your inheritance?"

"And being able to choose my own future. They had my whole life planned out for me. This was my chance to do what I wanted."

"By entering into a contractual marriage? Doesn't sound very *freeing* to me."

"With all due respect, sir," I jump in before Elizabeth can

respond. "This relationship has given us both an opportunity that we wouldn't have had without it."

"Oh, I'm well aware of your situation, Joshua." Ric's fury turned on me. "I just never took you for an opportunist."

There was no way he was going to keep it a secret. If it wasn't for the contract we signed four years ago, I'm sure he would've canceled the whole thing. After we left, Elizabeth and I waited all night for a phone call from Nina, but it never came. I guess that was one benefit of the aftermath from Haven. The truth about Nick and Nina's relationship was far worse than the truth about ours—"hiring" someone to be her boyfriend wasn't exactly *Villa* behavior. I suppose this anger towards Nina was justified to some degree, but it put a huge rift between them, something that had never happened before. Thankfully, Ric's focus was on what he did wrong there, instead of what he did wrong *here*.

Elizabeth stands before me with her hands on her hips, glaring at me. "Josh."

"Elizabeth," I say in a warning. "Let it go."

"If we're going to be stuck together the next six and a half years, we might as well get used to sharing secrets," she pushes.

"You first."

Her eyes narrow, and her lips pull into a firm line.

"Now." I wrap my arm around her hips and lean down. "Give me a laugh and kiss because everyone is watching." After a brief moment of consideration, her face falls, and she takes a breath. She laughs (it's not as good as it could be) and she grips my chin to pull my lips to hers. "Good girl," I mumble against her lips.

"Normally, that would be a turn-on," she says when I pull away. There's a hint of mischief in her eyes, biting down on the corner of her lip.

"I didn't know you had a praise kink."

"There are things you don't know about me, Joshua Isaiah

Davis," Elizabeth whispers against my ear. "And you never will." She gives me the sweetest smile when she pulls away, placing another peck on my lips and skipping back to where Nina and Michaela are waiting for her.

I stand there a moment longer, admiring the woman I'm about to marry. Her head is thrown back in laughter as Selena tells an animated story. The longer I stand there, the more I wonder how much more we can take before the dam of lies and hidden truths begins to break.

thirty-three

THEN

September 2019

AS I STEP UP to the altar staged in front of the fountain, the adrenaline works double time, coursing through my system. I wonder if this is how everyone feels when they're about to get married or if it's just me…I think it's just me. Elizabeth has been so calm and collected throughout this entire weekend. I don't know how she does it. Years of training, I guess?

From what she told me of her mother, Ethel Cain was kind and loving, but could be just as cold as Brina when she deemed necessary. She liked things a certain way. And she liked Elizabeth a certain way, but it was rare for her to show that side. I suppose going from her mother to Brina wasn't too big of a jump, except living with Brina, she was missing the love and support she was used to. Instead, the Villa children were expected to be a certain way regardless of anything else.

Through the trees of Forsyth Park, I can see Nina talking to someone on the pathway leading to the main stretch—Elizabeth—and my heart beats faster, if that's even possible. One more turn, and I'll be face-to-face with my soon-to-be wife. *Wife.* That sounds weird to say.

The wedding march starts, and my heart lurches out of my chest. This is it. It's happening...

My breath hitches when they turn the corner. Elizabeth looks breathtaking. Warm, honey curls flow down her back and shoulders; a veil rests gently on top of them. Long sheer sleeves cover her arms, and the V-neck is classy but gives the dress a certain edge. The white material hugs her curves in all the right places, leading into a small train flowing behind her with each step. I meet her brown eyes, and there's a small uptick in the corner of her mouth.

Holy shit, we're going to do this...

A hand squeezes my shoulder, but when I glance back at Nick, he's staring ahead...at Nina. His gaze never leaves her, not even when she and Elizabeth reach the altar, and she gives me a stern glance.

"I know where you live, Joshua," Nina warns, earning a laugh from the crowd.

"Love you too, Nin," I say and kiss her cheek, taking Elizabeth's hand.

I know I'm not supposed to, but I kiss her temple and she takes a centering breath.

"You look beautiful," I whisper and meet her gaze. The fire I'm used to isn't there, replaced by a level of uncertainty I've only seen twice since we started this whole arrangement. "You ready?"

The real question is, does she *want* to do this? If she told me no, I'd happily walk back down that aisle and help her escape. Help us both escape. Fuck the repercussions.

When I snuck down the hallway to her room this morning, Elizabeth opened the door with a weary smile and said, "Bad luck to see the bride before the wedding, y'know."

"Something tells me you can't get rid of me that easily," I joked.

I expected some kind of smart-ass remark in return but

got nothing. Stepping inside her room, I bent down to look her in the eye. "What's wrong?"

"Nothing," she quipped and tried to pull away, but my grip on her arms held steady. She refused to look at me. "Josh—"

"What is it, Sugar?" When I said it, she tried to hide the small tug on her lips at the nickname. Gripping her chin, I forced her to look at me. "Baby, what's going on?"

Elizabeth took a shaky breath and closed her eyes. When she reopened them, they were glassy. "They're not here."

Her parents.

I sigh, I should've known this was coming. Despite *why* we're here, it would be normal for anyone to be upset that their parents couldn't be around for their wedding day.

"I always dreamed of this day." Elizabeth sniffled and wiped her cheek. "And it's everything I always wanted, but they're not here." It didn't help that her adoptive parents weren't here either. Ric had stuck to his guns and refused to show up. Everyone else thought he got stuck at work, and I'm sure part of that excuse was true, but it wasn't the whole reason.

Her bottom lip quivered as she tried to hold back tears. I did the only thing I could and pulled her into my arms. I kissed the top of her head and felt the warm tears soak into my T-shirt, her fingers clutching the same fabric.

"It's okay, Sugar," I whispered against her hair, tightening my hold around her. We stayed locked in a tight embrace even after her quiet sobs had subsided. A knock on her door broke the trance. Nina's voice on the other side of the door called out to Elizabeth. They had to leave for breakfast before Elizabeth's hair and makeup team arrived.

"We're in this together," I said and kissed her forehead.

Elizabeth didn't say anything; she grabbed her purse and left to join the girls. I waited a few beats before leaving to find Nick and Finn.

Despite it all, standing here at the altar, if Elizabeth tells me no right now, I will happily walk right back down the aisle and find a way out of this mess.

Elizabeth takes a deep breath and there's a new level of certainty when she says, "Yes." She nods like she's trying to reassure herself and me. I take my own deep breath and intertwine our hands, leading her to the final step toward the beginning of our new lives.

thirty-four

NOW

THE CREDITS FOR CHRISTMAS *Vacation* roll up the television screen as Chevy Chase's character stands out on his snowy front lawn wearing a Santa Claus hat, his home covered in bright white lights behind him. Per tradition, the third night of the weekend is PGM (Pizza-Game-Movie Night), as it was so eloquently named by Selena a few years ago. We make Christmas-shaped pizzas for dinner, play a large game of Uno, and then watch a Christmas classic. PGM is my favorite tradition because we spend the night eating—pizza, popcorn, garlic knots, cheese bread...the list goes on.

When Elizabeth and I returned from the beach earlier, Lola and Selena were preparing the dough for pizzas while Georgie paced the back porch on a frantic phone call. Normally, I would say it's safe to assume she was calling her husband, but now I can't help but wonder if it's the guy she was seeing. Everything was fine, she promised when she came back inside. Noah had disappeared again, having to do something for his parents, and it should only take a minute, but that minute turned into an hour and then two. Everything made so much sense now that I knew the truth, but being one of the only two people to know made it that much more awkward. I'm certain that Elizabeth knows the truth, but it almost seems stupid to ask her. Of course she knows. It's the only thing to explain the secrecy earlier this weekend.

After dinner and a round of Uno, everyone meandered down to the beach at Georgie's request. Actually, she only asked the girls to join her, but Elijah, Jeremy, and I decided to tag along anyway. Elijah chased Selena down the beach, catching her by the waist and hoisting her into the air. Laughter turned into screams of horror when they tumbled into the water.

"Don't even think about it," Lola warned Jeremy.

"Well, I wasn't, but now..."

"Should we join them?" I asked Elizabeth when Jeremy took off after Lola.

"Don't miss out on my behalf," Georgie said.

"Absolutely not," Elizabeth warned. I laughed, pulling her to my side and kissing the top of her head. She snuggled a little deeper into me, tightening her grip on my torso.

Selena kicked water at Elijah before running back up the beach. I didn't have time to register what was happening before Elizabeth was ripped from my arms and sandwiched between Selena and Lola—both soaked and covered in sand.

"I hate you guys!" Elizabeth squealed, and I laughed. Finally slipping from their grasp, she glared at me. "You think this is funny, Davis? Let me show you how funny it is!"

I tried to take a few steps back, but she had already wrapped her arms around me. The cool night air seeped into my clothes the same way her laughter seeped into my soul. When she pulled away, our eyes met, and it felt like there was a string between the two of us being pulled taut, bringing us closer together. My hand grazed her cheek, bending down to—

"Unless y'all want to catch a cold, I suggest we go in and change," Georgie said, cutting the string between us. Elizabeth jumped about a foot away before she hustled up the boardwalk.

Now, the clock on the wall reads eleven o'clock, and the only ones who didn't knock out during the movie were Jeremy, Noah, and me. Selena and Elijah were the first ones to pass out, cuddled together on the floor below me and Elizabeth on the couch. Lola was next; she was always a lightweight when it came to movie night, but at least she can say she lasted longer than Eli. Georgie wasn't long after, falling asleep with her head in Noah's lap. He arrived back at the house just before we started the ultimate debate of which movie to watch, and Georgie's whole mood shifted when he walked through the door. She offered him the pizza she had made for him, but he declined—not hungry because he had eaten while he was out. Normally, that wouldn't bother her, but I saw the tears she tried to hide that welled in her eyes. Pregnancy hormones, I guess?

Noah disappeared into their room after that and returned a few minutes later; it was like he had realized how tense things seemed because he tried to be a little less standoffish. Georgie doted on him, eventually snuggling up to him and falling asleep.

Elizabeth was last to fall asleep. Somehow, we had managed to secure the couch. I expected her to sit on the floor, but she laid down next to me, her backside pressed right up against me. With my arm thrown over her waist, she eventually fell asleep, turning over to snuggle further into my side.

I begin to rouse her. "C'mon, Sugar. Time for bed."

She groans in response and snuggles closer.

Jeremy does the same with Lola, who yawns but does as she's told.

I nudge Elijah with my foot, stepping off the couch, and he jerks awake instantly. His brown eyes are wide and alert, searching for the source of his rude awakening. When he realizes the movie is over and there isn't a murderer standing over him, he groans and begins to wake Selena.

I gently shake Elizabeth's shoulder, and she swats me away. After a little more prodding, she finally mustered the strength to get up. Yawning into a stretch, she rubs her eyes...

Noah peels himself from Georgie and the movement jolts her awake. She reaches for him, but he doesn't seem to notice, or he doesn't care. "Ready for bed, baby?" Georgie asks, her words dripping with sugar-coated honey.

"Yeah, let's go, Gi," Noah says, stalking out of the TV room without looking back.

Georgie notices my stare and offers a quick smile. "See y'all in the morning." Without another glance, she hastens her steps to follow Noah down the hall.

"That is so awkward," I say, following Elizabeth into the bedroom.

"What?" She yawns.

"Georgie pretending everything is fine with her and Noah when it's very obvious it's *not* fine."

"What are you talking about? Everything is fine. Why would you—"

"I know, Liz. About the affair and the baby."

Elizabeth starts to question how, but I interrupt her.

"Noah mentioned it earlier when we were having coffee."

Elizabeth sighs, rubbing her eyes. "Gi is trying her damndest to fix it, but I don't think it's working."

Should I tell her the truth? Tell her she's right, that all of Georgie's "efforts" aren't working? No, I can't betray Noah's trust like that. And if I do tell her, she's going to tell Georgie.

That's where her loyalty lies, not with Noah. But is that where my loyalty lies? This feels like Nick and Nina all over again, except at the end of the day I don't have stakes in what happens to either Georgie or Noah.

"It's not." Those two words slip past my lips without my realizing it. Shit, I shouldn't have done that. Noah really wanted to wait until the end of this weekend, and it's not my place to upend his plans. Looking up from my feet, I meet the burning gaze of my wife.

"What?" Elizabeth stands in the threshold of the bathroom, gripping the doorframe. "What did he say to you?"

"I shouldn't have said anything."

"Josh, what did he tell you?"

Chewing on the inside of my lip, I know I've already crossed the line. She knows too much and whether I tell her everything or stop right now, she's going to tell Georgie. "He's already contacted a lawyer."

Elizabeth sighs. "This is going to crush her."

"Then maybe she shouldn't have cheated on him."

"Oh, that's rich coming from you."

Her words make my stomach sink. Does she still think I cheated on her? Does she forget the promise I made to her?

Elizabeth shakes her head and starts to walk back into the bathroom, but I follow. My hand reaches out to grab hers, stopping her. "I never cheated on you, Elizabeth. Juliet never showed up that day. Why won't you believe me when I say *nothing* happened in Wichita?"

She won't answer me; hell, she won't even look at me.

"Listen, Sugar, if this *friendship* is going to work, we have to be honest with each other." She still refuses, and when I grip her chin to pull her gaze to mine, I find a new level of hurt in her brown eyes. "Never. I would never do that to you. Do you remember what I said to you in the kitchen that morning all those years ago?"

There's a small tug on her lips, bringing a smile to my own.

"Let me remind you…until we sign those damn papers in five months, I am *yours*. Whether you and Ryan are together—"

"We're not."

"You're not?" There's a sudden flutter in my stomach.

"I mean, I don't know. We've kind of talked, but…I don't think—I don't think he's the one."

My heart picks up speed hearing those words—he's not the one. How did we go from wanting to work things out to saying he's not the one? I don't know, but right now I don't really care.

Stepping closer, I tilt her chin, holding her stare. "Until we sign those papers, you are mine."

A shuddering breath escapes her lips.

I glance from her eyes to her lips before meeting her gaze again. Pupils blown wide. She sticks her tongue out to wet her lips, and she doesn't wait, she pulls me to her as I stoop down to capture her lips in a hard kiss. My body vibrates with anticipation but also awareness. This could make things so much worse, but with her body pressed against mine, I can't bring myself to care. All I can think about is the feel of her lips against mine. The way her body fits against mine like we were made for each other. Like we've always been meant for each other.

I ease her backward until the bed presses against the backs of her thighs, and a soft squeal falls from her lips when I lift her onto the white duvet without an ounce of difficulty. The sound squeezes my heart and makes me smile. She sits on her knees at the edge of her bed, pulling me to her by the hem of my T-shirt before lifting it over my head and letting it fall. Her perfectly manicured fingers run up the grooves of my chest, her lips following close behind. Each kiss against my skin sends another shock straight to my dick. She sits back on her thighs and meets my gaze as she slowly grips the hem of her sweatshirt and lifts it above her head.

Elizabeth clutches the cloth to her chest for a brief moment before letting it fall.

Fuck, she's beautiful.

I bring her mouth back to mine, tasting her as I slide my hands up the sides of her body. She laces her fingers on my nape, bringing me down with her.

My left hand caresses her breast, pinching and squeezing until her nipple stands to attention through the black lace before I bend down to bite the raised bud through the fabric. She gasps, and I reach behind her to unhook her bra, tossing it to the side. I rub one nipple with the pad of my thumb, licking the other, and my tongue swirls around the straining peak. She writhes beneath me, getting more antsy as the pleasure rolls through her, and we're only just getting started.

I run my tongue down her stomach until I reach the waistband of her shorts, her body tensing as I lift my gaze to look up at her. Her hands reach to cover the scars on her stomach. They've faded more over the years, but they'll never fully be gone. I push her hands away.

"Don't ever cover yourself in front of me."

Tears well in her eyes, and she looks away briefly, but the pull is too strong and she meets my gaze again.

"You are so *fucking* beautiful. These don't take anything away from you. They make you who you are, and I love who you are. I love everything about you, including every single one of these little jagged lines." My finger traces across them, and my lips follow until I've traced every single one. Leaving a final kiss just below her navel, I tug the pajama shorts and panties down her legs and push her thighs apart. A soft gasp escapes her lips as the cool air touches her swollen folds.

She's so fucking wet already.

And she's all mine.

As much as I want to feel her come on my tongue, I'm not

feeling patient tonight. I want to feel her wrapped around me the first time she comes; I want to watch her come undone beneath me, with nothing but my name on her lips.

She tries to close her legs, but I hold them still before sliding my hand up her thigh and pushing my pointer finger inside her. She practically jumps off the bed, throwing her head back with a moan. I rub my finger inside her and nip at the skin on her hip before lapping it with my tongue. I lick up her side and between the valley of her breasts, slipping another finger into her, silencing her moan with a firm, hard kiss.

"I can't wait to be inside you," I mumble against her lips. Her hips begin to rock against my hand when I rub small circles over her clit. It doesn't take much for her to reach the edge, but I pull my fingers out of her without warning.

"Josh!" Elizabeth groans, at the end of her patience.

Another hard kiss before I reach for my sweats, pulling them down my thighs, and her eyes darken at the sight. Her tongue pokes out to wet her lips, eyes running up my length to the swollen head where a drop of semen glistens at the tip. Grasping my erection, I give it a few pumps before settling between her thighs.

Pinning her hips down, I tease her entrance, and she rocks her hips greedily, trying to get more.

"Stop being such a damn tease," she says.

A smile curves my lips, and I push forward inch by inch, enjoying the feel of her enveloping me, pulling me deeper.

"Baby," she moans when I plunge myself the rest of the way until I'm seated completely inside her. Angling myself, I flex my hips so I can move my cock in deeper, and I can feel her walls clenching around me. She reaches up, tangling her fingers in my hair and yanking me down into a demanding kiss. She locks her ankles at the small of my back and lifts her hips.

Fuck, this woman will be the death of me. She feels so good

wrapped around me. No matter how much of her I get, it will never be enough.

Planting my hands on either side of her head, I pull out and thrust back in. A sound rumbles in my chest, low and deep. With each breath, a soft moan spills from her lips, and it only deepens the hunger I feel for her. The aching need for her. There's nothing else that matters. This connection, this closeness, is what I've been missing for so long.

With each thrust, her back arches, and her nails dig into the taut skin of my shoulders.

"Tell me what you need, Sugar," I grit out. "What do you need?"

"You," she breathes.

The answer is so simple, but it shoots straight to my heart.

"You, Josh," she repeats herself, and I kiss her to hide the emotion I know is displayed on my face. Hide the tears that brim my eyes and the pressure building in my chest. My tongue plies open her mouth, tasting every inch of her. Everything we've been through, all the lies, the games, the fights, the hurt…it has all led to this moment.

To the here and now. Our inability to stay away from each other, like moths to a flame. We couldn't resist the burn anymore.

Her brown-eyed gaze is fixed on me when we part, the glow of her arousal like morning dew on her skin. I speed up my thrusts, and her walls flutter around me. I can feel the start of her orgasm. Her walls squeeze so tight it initiates my own.

"Baby, please," she moans.

Reaching between us, I rub her clit with the pad of my thumb, and her eyes screwed shut in bliss.

"Look at me," I command, but she doesn't. "Look at me when you come, Sugar."

When her eyes meet mine, her nails dig deeper into my skin, and the rush is like nothing I've felt before. We've had great sex before, we always did, but this…this is different. Pure fire and adrenaline course through my veins. I lose every sense as I continue to dive into her over and over again. She clutches at me as I come, but even when I'm done, I continue to fuck her. I don't want to let this feeling go.

Her fingers interlock at my nape, her nails gently grazing the skin, sending flames across my already burning flesh. I kiss her temple but don't move so I can remain inside her. She snuggles into me, and with half-lidded eyes, I take a deep breath, letting the mix of scents fill my lungs: the smell of her shampoo, her perfume, the smell of sex and sweat, and a hint of my body wash.

"Josh," she whispers into my neck, but I don't pull away to look at her.

"Yeah, baby?" A kiss on her temple.

"What—what does this mean?"

I'm sure she can hear the thick swallow as it slides down my throat. Staring up at the ceiling, my fingers twirl a piece of blonde hair around them. What does this mean? I have no idea. There is still so much we need to talk about, so much we need to work through…

Doesn't this cross a line way past being just *friends?*

"What do you want it to mean?" I ask.

Elizabeth pushes up from my chest and I look up to meet her gaze. "I want you to be honest with me for once in your life. I want you to tell me what this—us—means to you."

Everything. This means everything to me. *She* means everything to me. But, I'm still me, and I don't deserve this woman. The only reason we've been together this long is because of that fucking contract. She deserves so much better than me.

"That's not my call, Liz. I don't even deserve to be here. If it weren't—"

"What are you talking about?" Elizabeth scoffs.

"I'm only here because of that damn clause." Pulling her mouth to mine, I kiss her gently once…twice…three times.

Elizabeth plants her palm on my chest, putting a small distance between us. "You're here because I want you here, Josh."

"You deserve better than this, Sug. Better than me."

"I deserve what I want, and that's you, Josh." Her hand reaches to cradle the side of my face and I can't help it, I lean into her touch. Her thumb grazes my cheek before she swoops down to kiss me.

thirty-five

THEN

May 2022

SOMEHOW, I LET NICK talk me into coming with him to New York for an interview. It's a Tuesday afternoon in the middle of May, and instead of being at work, I'm sitting on the patio at Raised Bistro—a restaurant on the outskirts of Central Park and Columbus Circle. His interview isn't until tomorrow, but we got here a day early to meet with Dean Monroe, Nick's friend from Boston University. Dean is textbook tall, dark, and handsome, as cliché as that sounds. Piercing green eyes and dusty brown hair matched with perfectly tanned skin. The kind of tan that isn't too tan, but just the right amount. Since I met him two years ago, I've always wondered if it's natural or if he goes to a tanning salon. His right arm, covered in black ink, rests comfortably behind his best friend of almost twenty years: Raeanne DeLuca.

His missing puzzle piece, he said when he introduced us an hour or so ago, but I have yet to determine if that means she is actually his girlfriend. I can't remember him mentioning her in the past, or maybe I just assumed he didn't have a steady girlfriend considering how many other girls he has always chased after.

Rae has natural sun-kissed skin that most girls pay hundreds of dollars for. She doesn't wear a lot of makeup, and her dark hair falls down her shoulders in easy waves. She's part Columbian, at least I think that's what Nick said, and she reminds me a lot of Nina.

Dean's hand grazes her bare shoulder while her hand rests in his lap, and she laughs along to the story Nick just finished telling about a drunken night with Dean. I think it's the lost-in-a-Boston-suburb story, but I haven't been listening, my mind wandering to the woman I've been missing for the past week. We haven't talked much. She's been busy being upset with me because I refused to drop everything and run off to California with her.

Rae excuses herself from the table, Nick waits for the door to close before he turns to Dean. "So, when are you gonna lock it down?"

"What?" Dean laughs.

"Don't be stupid."

"Rae?" Dean seems shocked, and we both give him a look as if it's the most obvious thing in the world. "Me and Rae? I told you, it's not like that. She's my best friend!"

"Who you sleep with," Nick says.

So, not his girlfriend, but they sleep together. Friends with benefits kind of deal. Got it.

"I mean…" Dean draws out the last syllable, trying to think of an excuse, but it doesn't seem like he can find one good enough. "Yeah, so? Friends with benefits is a thing."

"Dean." I scoff.

"It's not that serious."

"That's not what you said before," Nick counters, turning to me to add, "Mr. it's-not-that-serious here got drunk a few years ago and told me he's always wanted *more* with Rae. That was before they ever slept together."

"That was never supposed to happen!" Dean defends himself.

"You were the idiot who suggested being friends with benefits when you could've just told her how you felt."

Dean sighs. "I just don't want her to settle. She could do much better than me. You should have seen the last guy she was with; he was some hot shot at a consulting firm. He made killer money. He was always taking her on fancy vacations and buying her nice stuff."

"You think that matters?"

"Of course it does. Women like that shit." Dean rolls his eyes.

"You're a dumbass," Nick laughs, shaking his head.

"Well, if I am, what does that make you?"

And the point goes to…Dean.

Damn, that was a good one. They are still locked in a glaring contest when Rae rejoins us. She looks at me, confused, and asks, "What did I miss?"

"Not much." Dean finally breaks the stare and squeezes her thigh reassuringly. "I was just telling Nick that he should come to the cabin for Memorial Day."

"Yes! Nick, you have to. Everyone would love to have you."

I didn't think Nick's face could fall any further, but I was wrong. His mouth falls into a straight line, and his gaze narrows. "You're not gonna try and set me up again, are you?"

"Dean, you didn't." Rae turns to her best friend.

"I didn't know he had a girlfriend!" Dean throws his hands up in defense.

Before I can say anything, Nick doesn't even turn to look at me. He just holds up his finger in my direction and says, "Shut up." Then he points it at Dean. "Not my girlfriend."

"May as well be," Dean says, earning an eye roll from my cousin. "Nick admitted his feelings for this girl and then ran off to Boston."

"That is *not* what happened."

"Pretty much," I say, laughing when Nick shoots me a look that says *Shut up.*

"You spent the summer at her family house, slept together, and then you ran," Dean counters.

"Sounds a lot like someone else I know," Nick smirks.

Point Nick.

And now we're tied.

Raeanne looks between them. "So you were dating or…I'm confused."

"It's a complicated story, but in the end, we agreed it was best if we spent some time apart…to find ourselves."

"And I had no idea he had a girlfriend, so I tried to set him up with this girl's roommate because they were a package deal," Dean says.

"I wasn't looking to be set up."

"Because you still have feelings for this girl?" Raeanne says it as if it were the simplest thing in the world. And it could be if he and Nina weren't two of the most stubborn people on the damn planet.

"Why don't you bring her with you to the cabin for the holiday weekend?" Dean suggests when Nick doesn't answer. Raeanne agrees with him, but I can tell Nick is leaning towards no. It's been almost three years since he and Nina have seen each other. I thought things would have been cleared up by now, but they've held up their "agreement." Somehow they have even managed to successfully avoid one another at family events.

"We haven't talked or seen each other in…a long time. Don't you think it would be a little weird to call out of the blue and invite her on a trip?" Nick asks as if he could hear my thoughts.

"How long is a long time?" Raeanne asks.

Nick's lack of response catches my attention. He weighs

the answer in his mind before finally saying, "A while."

What does that mean? Have they been talking? I know he's sent her flowers in the past, but that was on the first anniversary of Ric's death. Unless they have been talking and keeping it a secret...Does Elizabeth know that? Why didn't she tell me? Why didn't Nick tell me? God, I'm so tired of our lives being filled with so many secrets.

"We talk in our own way."

"What does that mean?" Raeanne asks for all of us.

"He sends her flowers," Dean smirks behind his water glass.

Raeanne swoons. "That's so romantic!"

"Isn't it?" Dean adds to her swoon. "Roses and peonies. Occasionally throws in something else, but *always* roses and peonies."

"It's weird you know that," Nick huffs.

"You know those are both flowers of romance and love, right?" Raeanne swoons.

"I'm a secret romantic, sue me." Nick shrugs, sipping his coffee.

"Just call her, then! It's been long enough, don't you think?"

"I'd say," I whisper, earning a glare from Nick, but Dean smirks behind his water. He didn't say it, but he sure was thinking it.

"What does she do?"

"She's an interior designer and decorator but has been helping her brother run their family company for a while now."

You can tell by the way Nick talks about it he's extremely proud of Nina. We all are. She has stepped into her own the past two and a half years, opening three new DV offices, and stepping into a bigger role at Villa Inc. to help Kai shoulder some of the weight so he can enjoy being a first-time dad. She's given a few seminars and guest lectures, all in the hopes of helping others learn how to be successful. I don't know how she manages to do it all. It makes me tired just thinking about it.

"So, she likes to stay busy."

"Very."

But as proud as we are, we all know Nina tends to overwork herself. There have been a handful of times I've seen her break down from exhaustion and stress, only to pull herself back together almost immediately and keep going.

"Wasn't she named Designer of the Year or something?" Dean asks.

"Wait." Raeanne's eyes light up, the realization crossing her features. "Are you talking about Davina Villa?" When no one answers, she gasps. "Oh my gosh, you're in love with *Davina Villa?* My sister is obsessed with her! Dean, I can't believe you didn't tell me."

"Not my business." He shrugs.

"Why are you applying in New York? You could just work with her!"

"I don't want to use her for that," Nick says and sinks a little further into his chair.

"I'm sure she—"

"Rae," Dean cuts her off. "He doesn't want to."

"It's okay." Nick offers her a small smile when Raeanne sinks back into her chair. "I don't want to ask something like that of her. She's given me a lot, more than I could ever repay her for. And I guess I want to do it on my own. Prove something to myself."

When Nick first told me about their agreement to spend time apart and, quote, "get their lives together," I called bullshit. They could have made it work, or maybe I just hoped they would. Watching them live apart over the past few years, it was glaringly obvious neither of them was searching for anyone else. They were biding their time until they could find their way back to each other. And anytime someone (ahem, Alex) would bring it up, Nick would tell him the same thing.

He wanted to do this on his own; he had to work on himself so he could be who Nina needed him to be.

Every time he said it, I felt like I was listening to myself. I had never said it to Nick before, but I think he knew how I felt about the difference between me and Elizabeth, and now he was going through the same thing with Nina. Maybe it was a Davis man thing…grasping for the women outside of our league. And no matter what we did, we felt like we had to work twice as hard to belong in their world.

It was sweet, though. Watching him and Nina try to make it work despite it all gave me hope that Elizabeth and I could do the same. Nick and I were cut from the same cloth. If he and Nina could find a way to work through those differences…

Except Nick had earned the right to this life the right way, unlike me.

"So, off the topic of Ms. Villa," Dean changes the subject. "Are you gonna come to the cabin or what? I promise not to try and set you up."

Nick rolls his eyes but agrees.

When Dean looks at me, I say, "My wife will never leave Nina on a holiday."

"Won't have to if Nicky boy over here gets his act together," Dean says.

Nick walks out of the three-story walk-up and greets me with a shake of his head. Not this one. Not the one before, or the one before that, either.

"How'd it go?" I ask, meeting him at the bottom of the

steps.

He shrugs. "Okay, I guess."

"You guess?"

"I don't know if it's the right fit."

"You've said that about every single one so far."

"And every single one just hasn't felt like *the one*."

"Because you're avoiding 'the one.'"

Every firm he had interviewed with, from Boston to New York to California to Texas, had yet to feel like the right choice. He said he couldn't figure out why. He said it was *just a feeling*.

It was bullshit. We knew why, but I never pushed the issue because I knew he'd give me the same answer he gave Raeanne yesterday.

"Oh, you may want to check your phone." I try to hide my smirk when I hand it to him. "It was blowing up the whole time you were in there."

"What in the world?" Nick scrolls through the multitude of notifications on the lock screen. Over five missed calls from Alex, at least fifteen texts, and one missed call from Michaela. "Didn't they call you?"

"Who?"

Nick narrows his gaze but calls one of them back. Barely after the first ring, I can hear Alex yell, "Dude!" through the other end of the phone. "You'll never guess—"

"Yes, my interview went fine, thanks," Nick quips, putting the phone on speaker.

"Okay, cool. Nick, listen."

"Spit it out."

"You'll never guess who is in New York!"

"I don't know, Alex. The queen? I thought something was wrong. You called me *five* times and sent me a million texts."

"No." Alex scoffs. "Why would the queen come to New York?"

"Alex, I don't know." Nick groans, rubbing the crease

between his brows.

"Nina."

Nick almost drops his phone. Wide eyes meet mine, and I can't hide my smirk anymore.

"She showed up to my graduation after you left."

"That was nice." Nick's voice betrays him. He's probably wondering what would have happened if he had stayed just a little longer at his brother's graduation ceremony instead of rushing off to New York. "Alex, you better not be fucking with me."

"I'm not! Mic and Elizabeth are with her. They're checking out offices. Call MJ. I'm sure she can tell you—"

Nick doesn't wait for Alex to finish, hanging up the phone and looking at me. "Did you know?"

"I may have heard something."

"And you didn't want to share that information?"

"Elizabeth just told me when I called her while you were in there."

That part was true; she *had* told me she landed in New York a little bit ago, and they would be going to look at another office shortly. A space that just came up on the market, and Nina was sure it was the one. But I don't have to tell him I knew they'd be coming to town last week, do I? I didn't even know we'd be here until a few days ago.

"Nina found a new office at the last minute and wanted to check it out."

Nick doesn't wait. He dials another number. "Mic?" I can only imagine the struggle my sister is facing to keep a straight face while she stands next to Nina right now. That loudmouth is probably ready to shout from the rooftops that Nick is on the line. "I hear you're in the city."

Walking down Fifth Avenue toward the park, I can feel the nerves radiating off my cousin. It's making *me* nervous. Michaela called back about an hour ago to tell Nick that one, Nina had offered her the opportunity to take over the New York office, and two, Nina would be going for a run before dinner. And, according to Nick, the only place she'd go for a run in the city was Central Park. How he knew where to find her was beyond me, but he said he had a feeling he knew where she'd be.

"The fountain is about fifteen minutes through the park," I say, standing on the corner of Fifth Ave and 59th. "You're sure that's where she'll be?"

"Positive." Nick takes a deep breath, staring into the green space before us. "I'm doing the right thing, right?"

"You're doing what you should've done years ago."

He stonewalls me.

"Yes." I laugh. "You're doing the right thing."

"I'm gonna ask her to marry me." It comes out in a quick breath, and at first, I think he must be joking.

"Wait. You're serious?" I ask when he finally rips his gaze from the park to meet mine.

"Why not? I love her."

It's simple, but it's honest and the only thing that matters. And it makes my heart ache at the thought.

I smile and clamp my hand down on his shoulder. "Go get her."

Nick takes another breath before heading through the park. When he's gone, I pull out my phone to call my wife. She answers, "Yes?"

Just like earlier, her answers are short and quick. Our relationship has been a little...strained recently. Work has been stressful and I've been spending more time in the office than at home. We've fallen into a bad routine. Being so busy at work, I've missed a few date nights, a few game nights, and a few spontaneous trips; leading to one big fight that we haven't completely gotten over yet. That she hasn't completely gotten over.

My job is one of the biggest (if not the biggest) issues in our relationship. I put in a lot of time at the office, not only because I enjoy my job, but because it proves I can be successful on my own. I was given this job because of my connection to the Villas—to my wife—and because of that connection, I've felt an even bigger need to prove myself worthy from the first day I started at QC Marketing.

Elizabeth doesn't get it. How could she? She's never had to work for what she has, not really.

It's quiet for a brief moment before she tries to get off the phone.

"Liz," I interrupt her. "I love you. I know I may not say it often or do the right things all the time...But I love you, Sugar. And I'm sorry."

There's a deep breath on the other end before, "Manhatta, eight o'clock. The reservation is under Nina."

The line goes dead.

While it may not be exactly the response I wanted, it's a start.

thirty-six

NOW

"OKAY, I'M JUST GOING to ask," Elijah says, both hands lifting his coffee cup to his lips. "What's the story with you and Lola?"

When I woke up this morning, I had left Elizabeth in bed to try and get a quick run in before the chaos of packing to leave erupted. As I pulled a sweater over my head, I met her hooded gaze from under the covers. A lazy, sleepy smile graced her lips in the morning light, and a wave of emotion flooded through me. The same one I felt years ago, watching her sing along to her favorite Christmas song as she decorated for her favorite holiday. Then, the overwhelming dread of returning to a life without her hit me. Being away from her. Our actions last night made the pit in my stomach even deeper, like a black fucking hole ready to swallow me whole. *I deserve what I want,* she said. But I still had no idea what it all meant and what would happen when we went back home. Was it even possible to go back to normal? What was normal? I don't think either of us truly knew. Her voice broke through the million questions swimming around my brain. "You alright, baby?"

"Oh, y-yeah. Still just a little tired, I guess," I lied.

"You can always come back to bed."

I shook my head and mustered up a smile, leaning down to kiss her forehead.

As I walked out of the bedroom, the house was quiet until I reached the kitchen. Lola sat at the island trying to get some work done, but Elijah and Jeremy were too busy discussing the latest fantasy football picks to notice. She looked like she was about to murder both of them and her annoyance only grew when she saw me. Without a second thought, I invited the guys to breakfast down at Teddy's, and Lola's blue eyes lit up. I shot her a wink as I followed them out of the kitchen and she waved over her cup of coffee, returning to her work without a second glance.

"I should've seen this coming," Jeremy chuckles, digging his fork through the leftover potatoes on his plate.

"We don't mean to pry," I say.

Elijah doesn't waste time adding, "But can you blame us?"

Jeremy sighs. "No, I guess not. Honestly, I thought Elizabeth and Selena would've just told you."

I *knew* Elizabeth knew more than she let on.

Jeremy chews on the thought for a moment. I can only imagine the thoughts running through his mind, but I can't imagine it's easy to relive it either. "Did either of you know Jenna?"

"Was she at New Year's at your house last year?"

"Unfortunately. Tall, skinny thing, with short blond hair."

"So, everyone there," I joke.

Jeremy laughs, nodding. "Nothing that would make her stand out in a crowd, so you probably saw her and didn't even notice." Slowly, his smile begins to fall, and he sips his water. "Jenna was...obsessed. That's the only word I can use to describe it. She met Lola on a set where she was an extra before Lo decided to take a break, and because Lo was nice to her—"

"She took it a little too far."

Jeremy nods. "Even though she took a step back from producing and show running, Lola was still involved with some projects on the creative front. She needed help, needed someone who could handle the mundane things while she took care of the big stuff...Enter Jenna."

Jenna had sold herself well enough in the interview that Lola hired her almost immediately, but from the beginning, Jeremy was skeptical. She almost seemed too perfect. And he wasn't the only one. Lola's best friend, Stephanie, voiced her concern after meeting Jenna for the first time. But Lola brushed them off. Jenna was nice and had been able to help Lola get back on track, so maybe she had gotten a little attached. Lola didn't mind having someone else to talk to.

Slowly, Jeremy noticed Lola growing more and more distant. First, Lola became emotionally distant—fewer hugs, kisses, and physical closeness overall. Then they stopped talking as much, even though they lived in the same house. Jeremy tried to put more effort into fixing the distance that had grown between them, but she didn't put in the same effort. All of her effort and attention was being put into work. And the more time she spent at work, the more time she spent with Jenna. Lola and Jeremy had multiple fights over the four months that Jenna had been working for her, but the final one happened two days before Lola's birthday in mid-January. Lola packed a bag and left without any indication as to where she was going or whether she was coming back home. A week later, he and his daughter came home and found Lola packing more of her things in the house. Gabby tried to ask questions, but Jeremy put a stop to it. He didn't want Gabby to to worry about what was going on between him and Lola. When the time was right, he'd explain it to her...

A month later, Jeremy found out Lola had fired Jenna

that same day. She decided to leave Hollywood for good and Jenna's services were no longer required. She could handle the rest of her business on her own.

"How did you find out?" Elijah asks, interrupting Jeremy's story.

Jeremy scoffs, shaking his head. "I found the letter from Lola in Jenna's apartment."

Elijah and I share a confused glance before I ask what we're both thinking. "Why were you in Jenna's apartment?"

"I hired an investigator to look into Jenna," Jeremy says, taking the final sip of his coffee. "I was *that* boyfriend." He traces the rim of his now-empty coffee mug, his gaze narrowing in on the table. "And I thought maybe if I went there, I'd find something that could lead me to Lo. I got way more than I bargained for."

What does that mean?

"I got inside and there was this room…" He bites down on his bottom lip. "The walls were covered, *covered,* in photos of Lola. Press events Premieres. Pap photos. Airport photos. Selfies. Social media posts. Any photo ever taken hung on those walls. There was one that stuck out to me, it was a picture she had taken on our first date, except I was no longer in the photo. Jenna had cut me out of the photo, out of every photo. I found the cutouts on her desk with big red Xs through my face."

"This sounds like a movie," Elijah says.

"I wish it was," Jeremy retorts. "I've never seen anything like it in real life. But, neither of them was there. So, I called Steph and eventually, she told me where I could find Lola."

Stephanie told him that Lola had been hiding out at a family home in Australia. After alerting the authorities about Jenna's shrine he jumped on the first flight. But what he found was truly like something out of a horror movie.

"The door was wide open, it looked like someone had taken

a battering to it. Lights were on throughout the whole house. Shit was in disarray—furniture turned over, drawers emptied, broken glass everywhere, pictures off the walls." Jeremy closes his eyes and his jaw flexes involuntarily as he recounts the image from memory. "Blood, everywhere." He takes a deep breath before opening his eyes. "I heard someone walking down the hallway and I prayed it was Lola, but I prepared for it to be Jenna…That's when I saw her, Lola. She was pale and covered in blood. She had this gash on her cheek—"

"I haven't seen a scar," Elijah interrupts with the same thought I had.

"She covers it, but if you look hard enough you'd probably see it. She's still pretty self-conscious about the whole thing." Jeremy gnaws on the inside of his cheek. "Jenna got her good on the leg. Just barely missed the artery."

"Fuck," I breathe.

"It was…" Jeremy sighs. "It was bad. Jenna had followed her and when Lola told her to fuck off, Jenna lost it."

Silence follows for at least two whole minutes as Elijah and I try to let it all sink in. When Elijah told me about this when we first arrived in Palm Valley, I never imagined it would be something like this. This was truly like something you see in a movie…Except it wasn't. It was real life.

Learning the truth about Lola made it seem like all the problems Elizabeth and I had faced were so trivial compared to this. If Lola and Jeremy could make it past a crazy, stalker, killer assistant…Why couldn't Elizabeth and I make it past a few misunderstandings?

No amount of coffee or even the cool morning breeze could wake me up enough to prepare for the warzone I just walked into. Opening the front door was like lifting a veil and breaking the sound barrier. Shouting echoes from deeper inside the house, mixed with crying. What in the hell happened while we were gone that turned a peaceful morning into utter chaos? Elijah and Jeremy had gone in ahead of me when I got a work call, and I figured it had to be pretty important since it was a Sunday. It wasn't, in case you were wondering. It was a fire that couldn't be put out until tomorrow when the rest of the world was open for regular business hours.

Walking into the kitchen, I find Elijah pouring a fresh cup of coffee. A loud bang echoes from down the hall, but I don't see anyone, only hear the muffled sounds of an argument coming from the direction of Georgie and Noah's room.

Shit. I get the feeling this is all my fault.

"What the fuck is going on?" I ask, following Elijah out of the kitchen into the dining room.

"Noah wants a divorce." Elijah sips his coffee, and my stomach drops.

Jeremy stands in the far corner, huddled over something. Not something, *someone.* Lola. He cradles her face in his hands, speaking to her in soft words, and she takes slow, calming breaths.

"Should we go outside?" I ask, catching their attention.

"N-no," Lola stammers. "I'm okay." She looks between me and Jeremy before removing his hold on her. "I'm okay, I promise. I should go check on Selena."

Jeremy watches her walk down the hallway and only when she's no longer in sight does he turn to me and Elijah. "Did you guys know Georgie had an affair and got pregnant?" Jeremy asks.

"Yeah." I sigh, there's no use lying about it.

"You knew?" Elijah practically shouts, and we shush him.

"What the hell, dude! You didn't tell me."

"Noah told me yesterday, but he said he was going to wait until after this weekend to tell her."

"Damn," Jeremy breathes. "That's rough."

"How'd she find out?" I ask.

They shrug in response.

Shit, I hope Elizabeth didn't tell Georgie.

Loud footsteps echo down the hall, and I give you one guess as to who it is. We all take a few steps forward to get a better vantage point of what's going on and see Noah in the foyer with his bag hanging from his shoulder. Georgie follows a few seconds later, black, curly hair pulled into a messy bun on top of her tear-stained face. She's begging him, pleading with him not to do this. They can make it work.

"No, Gi, we can't," Noah says, pinching the bridge of his nose.

"I can't believe you're doing this, and on this weekend!"

"I wanted to wait until after, but you wouldn't let it go. You kept pushing!"

Georgie's bottom lip wavers.

"I'm sorry, Gi, but I can't do this." Without looking back, Noah storms out of the house, Georgie hot on his trail. Selena follows a few steps behind, trying to pull Georgie back inside—because we wouldn't want to cause a scene with the neighbors.

Is this my fault? Did Elizabeth tell Georgie? There can't be any other explanation. How else would she find out the morning after I told Liz? Noah had held out the entire weekend, why drop the bomb now? That doesn't make sense.

Lola returns to the dining room with a solemn face, she rubs her eyes and leans into Jeremy's side.

"Where's Elizabeth?" I ask.

"I think she's still upstairs," Lola says.

I don't waste any more time, taking the steps two at a time. Elizabeth is stepping out of the room just as I'm about to open the door. Her brown eyes widen seeing me standing there. She opens her mouth to ask me what's wrong, but I beat her to it. "Did you tell her?"

"Tell who?"

"Georgie. Did you tell her about Noah wanting a divorce?"

"No!" She looks genuinely offended. "Why would I tell her? You asked me not to."

"Why wouldn't you?"

"Josh, I didn't tell her."

"Then how did she find out?"

"I don't know." Elizabeth scoffs. "Maybe Noah went ahead and told her."

"Noah was waiting until after this weekend!"

"Well, obviously not." She tries to keep her voice down since we're still in the hallway, and I guarantee the others are waiting downstairs to see where this goes. "I didn't tell her."

"I knew I shouldn't have trusted you. This is why I never told you about Nick and Brina. You would've told Nina."

Elizabeth scoffs. "So, you *did* know."

"Of course I knew! That's why he called me in Denver."

"You've got to be kidding me, Josh! Do you know how much heartache and pain you could've saved if you had just told me?"

A lot.

I could have saved everyone a lot of heartache, stress, and pain, but it wasn't my place.

Elizabeth shakes her head in disbelief. "I can't believe you, Josh. Nick is your best friend. He was hurting and—"

"He asked me not to say anything!"

"I trusted you with so many things, Josh. My parents, my scars, my love, my virginity…And you? You kept a secret that was tearing my family apart. The only family I had left. Nick and Nina could've been together that whole time without all of the Brina bullshit getting in the way. You knew that and you still chose not to say anything. You could've prevented all of that if you had just told me!"

"Shoulda, coulda, woulda, Sugar. That's not what this is about."

"You're right." Elizabeth takes a step back, arms crossed tightly over her chest. She chews on the inside of her cheek. "This is about you not trusting me."

"You don't trust me, either."

"How can I?" She all but yells, and it reopens the hole in my chest that had started to mend. "You continue to prove over and over and over again that you're not trustworthy."

"Five months," I hiss. "And then you *never* have to worry about it again."

Tears brim her eyes, and she tries to swallow them back, but they refuse to retreat. One breaks the surface, sliding down her cheek.

"Elizabeth?" Selena calls from downstairs. The silence that follows is almost eerie as we hold one another's burning stare.

She closes her eyes, swallowing down the tears. "Yeah?" The word is still wobbly and teary when she finally speaks.

"Could use your help down here!"

"Just a second." Elizabeth meets my stare again. Her bottom lip quivers, but she bites down, trying to hide it.

"Just go," I interrupt her when she starts to say something. "Wouldn't want to keep them waiting."

She swallows back the words she had intended and wipes her eyes before pushing past me to save the day for her friends, like always. When she's gone, the realization of what just happened rushes over me. The realization that I just fucked it all up again. There is no going back. There are no more second chances. The adrenaline courses through me, and I need to let it out. Before I can even think about it, my fist connects with the wall, cracking the drywall, and pain radiates in my knuckles.

Fuck.

The car ride back to Jupiter Beach is nice, long, and awkward. We haven't spoken since the hallway. I've gone through a million different ways how to apologize, but none of them seem good enough. None of them feel right because this time it's going to take a lot more than "I'm sorry" to fix it. No one knows how Georgie found out. My best guess is Elizabeth was right. Noah finally had enough and told her. I know I shouldn't have jumped to conclusions, but what else was I supposed to think?

Anything.

Literally anything.

Pulling into her driveway, there's a truck parked in front of the garage, and it's not hard to guess who it is. Elizabeth mumbles something under her breath before expelling a sigh, and I almost say something, but I swallow the words and get out of the car with a small scoff.

Elizabeth meets me at the trunk. "Josh—"

"You know, I was trying to find a way to apologize." I refuse to look at her, pulling her bags out of the car. "To say that I'm sorry because I was wrong, and I shouldn't have accused you. Whether you told Gigi or not, it doesn't matter. I don't care. I was going to apologize, ask you to dinner, but..." I glance toward the house, then back to her. "I see you already have plans."

"Josh, I didn't—"

"Lizzie!" His voice echoes around us. Every time he calls

her that, it makes me cringe. Why has she not corrected him? "Finally!"

We're still locked in a silent battle as he tromps down the steps toward us.

"I was starting to think you weren't coming home." Ryan laughs before turning to me. "Hey man, good to see you again. Thanks for giving her a lift."

"Sure." My lips curve into a tight smile before turning to Ryan. "No problem."

"I got us a reso at Jo's tonight," Ryan tells her, picking up her bags and heading back up the steps. When she doesn't follow him, he calls her, "Lizzie, you coming?"

Elizabeth stands in front of me like she's waiting for me to say something, but what else is there to say? She's made her choice.

"Y-yeah," she stammers. She walks away with the man she said she wasn't seeing anymore. The man she said she didn't see a future with.

Climbing into the driver's seat, I wait, like I always do, and watch to make sure she gets inside. When they make it to the front door, Ryan swings it open and steps inside, still talking, but she glances down the stairs one more time. When our eyes meet, there's still a sense of waiting in them, and it tugs at me. The same pull on my heart from the beach, pleading with me to get out of the damn car, walk up to her, and never let her go. But the moment ends when she finally rips her gaze from mine, following his orders to come inside.

I stand there a moment longer. One part of me is screaming to march up those stairs, open the door, and remind her who she belongs with. The other part hopes that by some miracle she will walk back outside, accept my apology, and tell me she still loves me.

The doorway remains motionless.

Neither part of me wins the fight as I climb back into my

car and back out of the driveway. Driving down the main drag of Jupiter Beach, I can't help but wonder if she knew Ryan was going to be here when we arrived. Before he interrupted us, it almost sounded like she was going to say she didn't know, but she didn't seem all that surprised either.

I can't say I'm that surprised. I didn't do myself any favors with how I acted this morning. I ran her straight back into his arms when I refused to believe her or apologize for how I acted. She deserves better than that. Deserves someone who isn't going to push her away, someone who can admit when they're wrong and isn't going to be afraid to tell her how they feel. Maybe Ryan doesn't know she hates roses and maybe he calls her by the nickname she despises, but I guarantee he can offer her things like time and attention.

He can give her everything I couldn't.

The Winchester Times
September 13, 2013
3:30 PM

Written by: Hannah Clemmons

Son Found Guilty in Deaths of Parents, Attempted Murder of Sister

Three hundred and sixty-four days after the murder of Thomas and Ethel Cain, a jury found their son, Nathanial Cain, guilty on all counts. Two counts of murder in the first degree, two counts of voluntary manslaughter, one count of attempted manslaughter, one count of arson, one count of tampering with evidence, and one count of obstruction of justice. Jurors deliberated for about two hours before convicting him.

"Justice was done today," said prosecutor Anna McCreery after the verdict. "We don't care who your family is or how much money you have or think you have. It doesn't matter what your name is, if you do wrong—if you murder someone—justice will be done."

Cain was accused of murdering his parents before turning the knife on his younger sister on the evening of September 14, 2012. Once a straight-A student, star basketball player, rugby player, and loving son, Nate fell into a dark spiral after moving to New York for college. A family friend, who has requested to remain anonymous said, "He turned away from his studies in business and finance, discovering the allure of the dark side of the city."
Nate began skipping classes, skipping practices and eventually was kicked off the basketball team, and put on academic probation. He was kicked out of the dorms his freshman year because of a fire-related

incident. However, he vehemently denied being part of the incident.

When asked whether Cain's involvement in the incident was ever confirmed, our anonymous source recalled Ethel Cain commenting on the rumor before her death. "She just said, 'boys will be boys' and tried to convince us it wasn't like that," they said. "A month later, Nathanial Cain dropped off the face of the Earth for at least a month or so after that. No one heard from him until he returned home, looking back to the same Nate the whole town had known before he went off to college."

Two months after his return to Winchester, Nate was arrested in Thailand for alleged possession and trafficking of drugs. Specifically, Cannabis which is still considered illegal, both medically and recreationally, in the country. He spent two days in a Thai prison before making contact with his family. Although, the charges were eventually dropped and Cain returned to the United States immediately, our source says when Nate landed in New York, his father was waiting for him, and "all but tossed [Nate] on the plane home."
Thomas moved his son back into the family home and gave him a job at Cain Real Estate, the major real estate company based in the Carolinas. But this time, Nate wasn't turning a new leaf, he was causing problems at home and work and wreaking havoc in the community.

Days before the murders, Nate was arrested by authorities in Charlotte for trafficking drugs. This time, Thomas refused to bail him out and told Nate he was being cut out of the will until he could learn how to grow up.

Two days later, Thomas and Ethel Cain were found dead in their home, with their daughter in critical condition at a nearby hospital. Elizabeth Cain underwent multiple surgeries and a medically induced coma before she woke up a week later.

After a two-week search for Nathanial Cain, authorities located him hiding out at a friend's house in upstate New York. Extradited to Hamilton County, Nathanial was indicted on the murder charges.
"He has never said anything to authorities since his arrest, maintaining a silent disposition even during the trial," said Ryder Coates, WPD Chief of Police. "Some believed putting his sister on the stand would elicit some kind of response, but [Cain] remained stone-faced the entire time."
The jury deliberated for about two hours Friday morning before they came back with a verdict just before lunchtime.

Court reconvened at 2:45 P.M., and the foreperson read out the verdict… Guilty on all counts. Cain didn't flinch as his fate was sealed.
The judge, someone who had known the family by way of living in the same town, offered him words of wisdom, but they fell on deaf ears before Cain was led out of the courtroom.

Cain faces a life sentence for each murder conviction and up to 122 years for the other charges. According to another source close to the family, Cain's remaining family requested prosecutors not seek the death penalty.

thirty-seven

THEN

September 2022

TODAY IS THE TENTH anniversary of the attack on the Cain family. The past two years, she'd been able to look ahead to celebrating our wedding anniversary the week following, but this year that doesn't seem to be as easy. I had planned on taking the day off work, spending the day with her, doing whatever she wanted—even if it meant spending the whole day in bed until we had to leave for the party. I wouldn't be opposed. Honestly, it sounded pretty good. I can't remember the last time we stayed in bed, cuddled together, making love, watching movies, and eating a bunch of junk. But she told me to go to work because she already had plans. She and Nina would be prepping for the celebration of life party Elizabeth had planned, and the best way for me to help her was by going to work.

I didn't want to leave her this morning, but she had practically pushed me out the door and promised she'd call if they needed anything.

The party was nice. It was lavish, and everything was the best of the best, as expected when you have the name Villa attached to something. Throughout the night, guests swapped their favorite stories about Thomas and Ethel Cain, eliciting a laugh or a smile or a tear from whoever was listening. I loved it. I felt like I was really getting to know her parents in a way I hadn't been able to before. Elizabeth has shared stories over the years but still held a lot about her parents close to her chest. Not that I blame her; I would probably do the same.

As the night wore on, I noticed the weight in her smile. The more she tried to hide it, the more noticeable it became. No one else seemed to notice, or they pretended not to, as they dragged her from one end of the room to the next, salivating at the chance for conversation. Finally, I stepped in and announced we had to be going because of an early morning tomorrow. Did we have an early morning? Well, she didn't, but they didn't need to know that. Besides, Nick and Nina had left about twenty minutes ago, so it wasn't like Elizabeth was waiting around for her sister. Those two have always tried to sync their arrivals and departures to make sure they never have to worry about being without some kind of escape from the droning conversations that happen at things like this. When Elizabeth didn't fight me, I knew I had made the right call.

Upon getting home, she disappeared into the bedroom without a word...That was about an hour ago.

Pouring a glass of wine, I pad my way into our bedroom and find her soaking in the oversized tub. Only a few bubbles remain, stationary on top of the shoulder-deep water. Her face is red, whether it's actually from crying or from the heat of the water, I'm not sure, but the tear tracks down her cheeks aren't hard to miss.

Elizabeth looks up at me when I set the glass down in the corner next to the book she had anticipated reading, but cracked open. Sitting on the floor next to the tub, I rest my arms on the edge and meet her glazed brown orbs.

"You okay?" I ask.

She takes a shaky breath, reaching for the wine glass and downing a heavy sip. Biting on the inside of her cheek, she says, "I went to see my brother earlier."

I should've known, I just wish she had let me come along. This isn't the first time she's gone to see Nate; she's tried multiple times over the years, but he never wanted to meet with her. Refused, actually. It's been a while since her last attempt, though. The last time I can think of was a few months before the wedding.

"He uh…he talked to me."

I can physically feel my eyes widen and my jaw fall to the floor. "What did he say?"

Elizabeth swirls the red wine in her glass, her eyes filling with more tears, one of them slipping down her cheek and falling into the water with a quiet *plop*. She sniffles.

"Sugar," I say, wiping another tear that falls down her cheek. "What did he say?"

"I told him I forgive him." She looks up to the ceiling, a tearful smile on her face.

That's the reason she has continued to try to see him. She wanted Nate to know that despite it all, she still loved him and forgave him. Did I agree with it? No. Did I understand it? Certainly not. But I know that I'll never be able to understand something I haven't been through.

"And he told me he was sorry he didn't finish the job."

The words leave me stunned.

Sorry he didn't finish the job.

Who the fuck says that? A psychopath, that's who.

My heart aches for the woman in front of me. She covers her mouth when a sob escapes her lips, but more follow, and she's no longer able to contain them. Without thinking, I just step into the tub and wrap myself around her. She has a death grip on my arms, holding on for dear life, and I pull her tighter against my chest as her sobs fill the space around us.

<h1 style="text-align:center">thirty-eight</h1>

NOW

THE FRONT DOOR OPENS and closes, followed by a chorus of heeled footsteps through the foyer, around the fireplace, and into the living room. Nina appears and she looks *pissed.* She steps in front of the TV, blocking the football game.

Nick called me earlier, saying Nina was supposed to be handling some DV Designs business late, he was on baby duty if I wanted to come over for Monday Night Football and steaks. After the weekend I'd just had, I wasn't sure I wanted to be around anyone, but it was better than going home to an empty house.

Nina's glare doesn't waver, her eyes glued to me. "Are you fucking dense?"

When I glance at my cousin, he shakes his head, brows raised. "Don't look at me."

Shit.

"I cannot believe you!" Nina hisses, trying to keep her voice down. "I didn't think either of you could do something dumber than you already have…But you did!"

"Nin, I—"

"What kind of sick game are you playing, Josh?"

"It's not a game!"

"Then why in the hell did you go this weekend? Do you not understand how—"

"I had to, Nina."

"You should've said no!" Her voice echoes through the house. Nick jumps to check the baby monitor, but Elena remains blissfully unaware, asleep in her crib. Nina pinches the bridge of her nose, trying to recenter herself.

"I couldn't, Nina." My head falls in my hands. "I didn't have a choice."

"There's *always* a choice."

"Dee," Nick finally interrupts. "He's telling the truth."

"And what do you know about it?" Her words are sharp against her husband. "Oh...You knew." When I look up, her fury has turned on her husband, but Nick doesn't back down. "You knew he was going this weekend."

"Now, look—"

"Don't you 'now look,' me. You knew, and you didn't tell me? Are you fuc—"

"She invoked the *Last Hoorah Clause,*" I say, cutting her off, and she whips her head toward me again. "It was part of the arrangement."

"Oh, right." Nina chuckles but forgets to add the humor to it. "The arranged fucking marriage. How could I forget?"

She starts to say something else but stops. Pressing her lips into a hard line, she shakes her head and storms out the back door. Her footsteps retreat down the steps and further into the backyard.

After a moment, Nick pats my back in a way that should be comforting, but it's not. He starts to stand, to go after her, but I stop him. "No, this is on me. I need to do this."

"Might want to take a glass of wine as a peace offering," he says before I reach the door.

Nina sits in one of the chairs surrounding the fire pit, her hands dug deep in her pockets, her gaze locked on the flames. I approach with caution, knowing better than to poke the bear too early. Setting the whiskey glass (I decided this was a whiskey kind of conversation, not wine) next to her, I fall into the chair one away from her, leaving some buffer room. She doesn't say anything. Doesn't even move to take the glass as we sit in silence. My leg bounces uncontrollably and my stomach twists in different knots, making the steak from dinner find its way back up into my throat. It's all too much. This is far worse than if she would just yell at me. The cold shoulder reminds me so much of her father, I feel like I'm back in his office after he discovered the truth.

We never used to be this way. Things used to be easy and fun, but since she discovered the truth, Nina and I have barely spoken. I think she's been avoiding me. Avoiding confronting the truth about things, avoiding the hurt she must feel. I think she's taking the whole thing harder than anyone because she was the hardest to fool.

"Please don't," she stops me when I attempt conversation.

"Nin—"

"Josh. Don't. I can't do this with you."

"Can't or won't?" I ask finally earning her stare. "You have never been one to hold your tongue, Nina. Why are you doing it now?"

Nina doesn't say anything, staring down into the flames.

"Look, you have every right to be mad at me—at us, but especially me. I lied to you…a lot. I betrayed your trust and took advantage of your family. But the one thing I can honestly say I never lied about is my love for Elizabeth. I hoped it wouldn't come to this. We wouldn't have to tell you guys anything because she and I could make it work, but…clearly, that didn't happen. And, this weekend, I thought—"

Nina scoffs, meeting my gaze again, the fire dancing across her face. "You thought you could go this weekend and win her back, is that it?"

"I don't know, Nina. I don't—"

"You were just doing what you had to because of the contract, right? You were playing your part." She shakes her head. "The problem is, you played it too well, Josh."

"I wasn't playing a part."

"You were *always* playing a part." Nina looks away again, this time letting the hurt cross her features. "You both were. It wasn't just you."

"Nin—"

"I just…I don't understand. Either you want a divorce, or you don't, but you can't have it both ways."

"I don't."

The confession hangs between us for a brief moment.

"I don't want a divorce," I say again. This is the first time I've admitted it out loud, and it hurts worse than I thought. "But, I don't deserve her, Nina. I don't deserve to be here, to be living the life I have had for the past ten years. I know that. I've always known that."

"What are you talking about?" Nina's stare is intense. "Josh, why would you say that? You've worked your ass off. You—"

"None of that matters anymore. She's with Ryan."

"Elizabeth is not with Ryan. They broke up."

A dry chuckle, I shake my head. "She was last night. He was there when I dropped her off from Palm Valley."

Nina doesn't say anything, turning back toward the fire. She bites down on her cheek, thinking, and absentmindedly takes hold of the whiskey glass I set beside her. The amber liquid splashes up and down the walls as she twirls the bottom rip against the armrest. "I don't understand," she says, more to herself than me. Her chest rises and falls with a breath before she sits forward, planting her feet on the cement pavers. Her stare locks on me when she says, "You asked me why I haven't said anything. The truth is, I wanted you two to figure this out on your own. And I thought you would. I never thought we would get to where we are now. When she told me the truth about all of this, I was hurt and I was angry. I felt betrayed, by both of you, but then I realized how I felt didn't matter. And I firmly believed that regardless of *why* you got together you'd figure it out because you love each other. You always have."

"We didn't always get along."

"But you stepped up that night at the ball…And you weren't standing where I was. It was pretty obvious. I always thought there was something there, you guys were just too stubborn to realize it." Nina reaches out to squeeze my hand. "Josh, I begged her not to file those papers. To talk to you. I thought I had convinced her, but then she filed anyway. She was so set on it. And then she met Ryan at one of our networking events and—"

"You introduced them?" I can't hide the surprise in my voice.

Nina shrugs. "Inadvertently. And when I tried to warn her about what an asshole he is, it only pushed her further into his radius."

"Were they together at your wedding?"

"No, as far as I know. But truthfully, I don't know. I didn't even know they were together until last month."

"What do you mean?" I ask.

"I have spent the last year trying to convince her to make it work with you and the whole time…she was talking to him. The night you showed up at her house in Jupiter, she called me earlier that day to tell me the truth about Ryan. She thought things were finally getting serious after a year of secretly seeing each other." Nina scoffs, shaking her head. "Josh, I don't know what the truth is anymore. I thought Ryan went with her this weekend, but the next thing I know, I'm seeing a photo of *you* with them, not him. And when I called her, she told me everything, including the part where she told you she wanted you and then you left her—"

"What was I supposed to do Nina? He was there!"

Her brow lifts at my outburst.

I take a deep breath trying to recollect my thoughts. "He was there and she walked away from me to be with him."

Nina bites on her bottom lip before swallowing the rest of the whiskey. "You say you don't want this divorce, Josh, but you're not fighting to stop it either." Without waiting for a response, she stands from her chair and leaves.

I don't watch her walk away, instead I stare into the dying flames of the fire. Scrubbing a hand down my face, I question if she's right. This isn't the first time someone has said that... Alex said the same thing at Thanksgiving.

And I think they might be right...I *haven't* done anything to stop this divorce from happening. Not really. I've been too scared to face the possibility that even if I tell Elizabeth how I feel, she will still turn me down.

Not anymore.

I'm going to do just that, right now.

When I walk back inside, the current conversation between Nick and Nina halts. I can tell by the look on Nina's face she has been rehashing our conversation outside with her husband. Stepping up to the island, I rap my fist on the marble countertop and suck my lips between my teeth before I clear my throat. "I'm...gonna drive down to Jupiter."

Dear Josh —

I hope this letter finds you well. It's been a long time, like a long time, and a lot has changed since you got in the car and drove off with your friends. Do you even remember me? Spring break 2010, Daytona. Coconut Joe's. After all this time, you would think those memories would have faded, but I still think about them often.

It's hard not to.

And I wonder if you do, too.

There's something that was left unsaid all those years ago, and we need to talk about it.

Viv Coffee Co
Wichita, KS

July 18th, 2024 @ 11am

Juliet Sinclaire

thirty-nine

THEN

July 2024

"I DIDN'T THINK YOU'D be back until tomorrow."

Over my shoulder, I see Elizabeth paused mid-step in the entryway to the kitchen, her computer in her arms. I dig through the refrigerator a little while longer before settling on a container with leftover lasagna.

"Get a lot of work done?"

I grunt a response, popping the lid off on all sides of the container and sticking it in the microwave.

"It must have been pretty important to make such a quick trip for one little meeting."

"Yeah, well, you know how Max is." I sigh and scrub a hand down my face. Stifling a yawn, I cross my arms and lean back against the counter. This might be the most we've talked in three weeks, outside of dinner for Nick's birthday last month.

Elizabeth gently rests her laptop on the counter, chewing on her bottom lip, her finger tracing a circle on the countertop. "Did Max go with you?"

"Yeah, he and Jack tagged along."

Her features fall as if she had just dropped the curtain,

revealing the person behind the mask. "Do you think I'm that stupid, Josh?"

"What do you mean?"

"You *know* what I mean."

And boy do I. Swallowing the lump that has formed in my throat, I can't find words.

"You didn't go to some work thing; you went to Wichita to meet *her*."

She doesn't know that for sure. Who am I kidding? Of course, she does. There's no use trying to deny it.

"You went when I asked you not to."

"I wasn't trying to hurt you, Elizabeth." That much was true. I had told her I was going to Nashville to meet with a client about a new collaboration opportunity, but that was far from the truth. Okay, maybe not far from…We did have a Nashville client and Max and Jack did go meet with them. But I told them I had to take a raincheck for personal reasons. "I only wanted to see what was so important that she had to send me a letter asking to meet her. It's been almost fifteen years!"

"You weren't trying to hurt me, but you went to meet up with the girl you called, and I quote, 'the one who got away.'"

Got me there.

But that was a long time ago when Elizabeth and I were still getting to know each other. We were talking about former lovers, and back then, I won't lie, I used to wonder what would have happened if Juliet and I had tried to make it work. And maybe, just maybe, I considered the thought again when the letter showed up, but only because Elizabeth and I were broken up, and she was sticking to her guns that we were done for good this time.

About a month ago, we had a big fight that ended with Elizabeth throwing her ring on the counter and walking out. Normally, I would have gone after her, but that night I let her walk away without putting up a fight. When she came home,

I was asleep on the couch. I had fallen asleep on the couch waiting for her to come back home, and her footsteps pulled me from the light sleep I was in. Keeping my eyes closed, I waited to see if she would call me to bed, but she didn't. She stood there for a moment longer and I swear I heard a small sniffle before her footsteps retreated down the hallway. I thought about going after her, but against my better judgment, I didn't.

She had gotten mad because she wanted me to go to Napa to celebrate the opening of a new winery or tasting room or something, I can't even remember. But I couldn't get the time off work. There's a rumor of a new promotion becoming available and...I want it.

Do I think I'll get it? No, but I think I can take over for the person who will get the real promotion, so in a way, it's still a promotion, just smaller. Elizabeth didn't understand why I wanted the job. I didn't need the money. But that wasn't the point.

I think a different issue we're facing is knowing the clock on our relationship is ticking, and fast. We have a choice to make: it's less than a year until our required time is up, and we can file for separation without any repercussions, or we can choose to stay together.

Neither one of us knew what the other one was going to do. Instead of being adults and just talking about it, we let our emotions get the best of us, and it turned into something ten times worse. And instead of trying to fix it, I guess you could say I've let the wound fester. If that letter showing up two weeks ago was like rubbing salt in the wound, actually getting on a plane and going to Wichita was dumping the whole damn jar in.

Two weeks ago, a letter arrived addressed to *Mr. Josh Davis* with only a return address and no name from Wichita, Kansas. Elizabeth had initially left it on the counter for me to open when I got home, but then her curiosity got the best of her, and she opened it anyway. Inside, she found a letter from Juliet Sinclaire, the girl I had met during spring break 2010 in Daytona. Juliet wanted to talk but didn't say what she wanted to talk about. Instead, she ended her letter with a time and place to meet.

When I got home that night to find it ripped open, it pissed me off. Who was she to going through my mail?

"You're not going," Elizabeth said, and that pissed me off even more. "Why would you go, Josh? You don't even know this woman! What if she wants money from you? You are married into a pretty well-known family, in case you've forgotten."

"Like you'd ever let me forget it." The words tumbled out before I even realized what I had said. But it was too late to take them back, and it's not like they were a lie. I've lost count of the number of times she has reminded me of the expectations of being related to not only the Villas but also a Cain. "We've barely spoken to each other for the last month. You don't get to pick and choose when you want me, Elizabeth. I am not some toy you can just toss to the side when you're tired of it."

Ultimately, though, I did tell her I wouldn't go after sleeping on it. She was right, I didn't know what Juliet wanted, didn't know her intentions, and it wasn't hard to find out who my family was.

But then...I did it anyway.

I went to Wichita under the guise of a work trip and went to the cafe Juliet named in the letter at the time she listed. I sat there for six hours. *Six.* But she never showed.

"Elizabeth." I sigh, rubbing my eyes. "It wasn't like that."

"You know what, I really don't care." Elizabeth simply shrugs and walks away, and I almost let her. I almost let her walk away without the fight because I was exhausted after the quick turnaround from Wichita, and I didn't want to fight about this. I'd rather go to bed, let the dust settle, and talk about it tomorrow. I think we both know holding off won't make the conversation any different. We have to do this—to have this conversation, and finally face the elephant in our relationship.

"You don't get to just walk away. We need to talk about this."

But she doesn't stop. Elizabeth continues down the hall toward the guest room she's been occupying for the last month. I'm finally able to catch her, taking hold of her wrist, preventing her from closing the door and locking herself away in her room. "What is there to talk about, Josh? You've made it pretty fucking clear the only thing standing in your way is me and our fucking predicament, which by the way, is *your* fault. We wouldn't be in this if *you* hadn't—"

"My fault?" My voice carries down the hall. "You're the one who didn't want to wait for her inheritance like some spoiled brat. How asinine is that? You act like you're some sweet, innocent angel, but you are far from it, Sugar."

Elizabeth takes a shaky breath, looking away from me.

"You pretend to be this perfect, wholesome girl, but you're nothing more than a snake in the grass."

Regret started to seep into every part of me with every word. My stomach churns as the words fall from my lips, and I hate myself for not stopping them. Sure, part of me meant what I said…She has always put on a show for other people and kept up appearances, but never to the detriment of others. Despite her reserved and hardened exterior, Elizabeth is one of the most kind and loyal people I've ever know.

Her head whips to meet my gaze again, her voice deadly, "Fuck you, Josh."

I take a deep breath, trying to settle the increasing beat of my heart, the adrenaline that has reached every end of me with nowhere to go. I can feel my hands begin to waver, my chest aches, and a black hole has formed in my stomach.

"All I've done the last six and a half years is support you, stand by your side. Love you. Even when we—"

"You don't love me."

Elizabeth gasps at my words. "I don't love you?"

"You've been waiting to leave since we said I do. Hell, from the moment we signed that damn contract."

She doesn't deny it, her gaze unwavering on the other side of the hallway.

"Time's almost up, Sugar; I was just preparing myself for the inevitable."

I hate to admit it, but I knew this day would come. I just never thought it would come so fast. Never thought I'd feel so attached to her. Never thought I'd fall in love with her. Fall in love with someone who would never fully be mine.

"The inevitable." Elizabeth scoffs and wets her lips. She takes a ragged breath and her brown eyes meet my gaze again, but she doesn't look like the same woman who had been standing in front of me moments ago. She reminds me of the eighteen-year-old girl who sat across the table ten years ago and agreed to this arrangement for a set amount of time. "You're right. This was always the plan. No use pretending there is anything between us anymore."

I swallow the lump in my throat, and the pit in my stomach begins to swallow me whole. This is what I wanted, though, isn't it? I just wanted her to be honest and stop pretending. Stop pretending we didn't know this was coming.

"You want her, Josh? Fine. But I'm not giving you a damn dime, so you'll just—"

"So, you're going to make us both suffer because you don't want to cough up chump change?"

Elizabeth's face falls, but her eyes are still set ablaze. "Go fuck yourself, Josh."

The bedroom door slams between us. I raise my fist to knock. I don't want that to be the last thing we say to each other tonight, but my hand falls to my side. I need to let her cool down. Hell, I need to cool down. We shouldn't talk in this frame of mind. It will only make things worse. I thought we'd be able to fix things, even after she said we were done for good after that last fight, but now...I'm not so sure. We've had our fair share of arguments before, but something about this one feels different. Final.

And why wouldn't it be?

That's what we wanted...right?

forty

NOW

THUNDER ROARS ABOVE ME less than a second after a strike of jagged white light stretches across the sky. About an hour outside of Charleston, I drove straight into a thick blanket of rain. Driving down the main stretch of Jupiter Beach, the rain comes down harder, pounding onto the roof of my Bronco, and it doesn't let up as I turn down her street.

The clock reads 11:58 p.m. I can only assume she's already in bed, but I couldn't wait. Pulling into her driveway, her house lit up like a damn Christmas tree, and not just because of the Christmas lights. All of the lights in the house are on, and that damn truck is in the driveway again. Through the sheet of rain, I can make out two figures on the front porch. Maybe I shouldn't do this if he's here...

No, I have to do this. I have to try.

There is nothing I can do to fend off the rain, so I make a mad dash for the porch. They have yet to realize I'm even here. They probably couldn't hear me pull in over the pounding rain or their raised voices. Ryan yells something I can't quite make out over the booming thunder above me, but as I walk up the steps to the porch, I can finally hear what he's saying.

"No one is ever going to want you. I mean, just *look* at you. Your family didn't want you. Your husband didn't want you. You're going to end up all alone in this big ol' house. You're just damaged goods! You—"

"I advise you to choose your next words very carefully when talking about my wife."

Both of their heated gazes turn in my direction. She softens slightly when she realizes it's me. I take the final two steps onto the porch, soaked from the rain, and my clothes have become like a second skin. I attempt to wipe my glasses, but it does little good. Pushing them back up my face, I keep my sights on Ryan, but he doesn't back down. He stands his ground despite the slight question in his eyes.

"Your wife?" Ryan questions, looking between me and Elizabeth, then laughs. "Wow. So, that's why Nina was so weird about you showing up. *You're* the ex-husband."

"Not yet."

"Don't tell me you're having second thoughts. Trust me, my guy, you're making the right choice. Sign those papers and run. Because this one—"

My fist connects with his jaw, sending him stumbling back a few paces. Ryan chuckles dryly before he charges, and I'm not able to move fast enough without slipping on the puddle beneath me. He tackles me, a clean shoulder-to-gut hit sending me flying into the porch rail, forcing the air from my lungs. Taking advantage, Ryan pulls me up by the collar of my jacket and punches me in the gut, and then the side, but I block my face and manage to lift my knee into his groin. When he stumbles back, I shove him into the side of the house and kick his stomach. He lets out a sharp breath, clutching his sides. I swing on his head once and then slide my arm around his thick neck, grabbing my wrist with my right hand, but despite the pain, Ryan is quick. He hurls his weight forward and steps to the left, falling to the porch across my body, and we break apart. Ryan scrambles to his feet as I pull myself up, but before either of us can move toward the other, Elizabeth steps between us.

"Stop it, both of you!" She glares at us both before narrowing her eyes at Ryan. "I'm not going to ask you again. Get off my property."

"You want her?" He asks me, ignoring her. "Fine. She's a lousy lay anyway."

Before I can hurl myself at him again, Elizabeth stops me and yells at him to leave *now*. Ryan laughs and walks backward down the steps through the rain to his truck, nursing his face. The sound of tires skidding across wet pavement echoes through the night air.

When he's finally gone, Elizabeth turns back to me. Her eyes roam across my face before she lets out a heavy sigh. "Come inside. I'll help clean you up."

forty-one

THEN

July 2024

IT'S BEEN A LITTLE over a week since our fight about Wichita. Thursday night was the first time I'd seen my wife since she slammed the guest room door in my face and told me to go fuck myself last Friday. Did I deserve it? Probably. That didn't make it sting any less. I had hoped we could have at least talked about what happened, but I get the feeling that won't happen any time soon.

On Thursday night, we'd had dinner at Mom and Dad's because Michaela came home for the first time in almost two years. When I got home from work that day, Elizabeth stood in the kitchen, flipping through the mail. That's how I knew she was still alive inside that room. Every day, I'd bring her mail in from the box and set it on the counter; the next day, it would be gone. "We need to be there at six-thirty," she'd said, passing a few envelopes my way and leaving without a second glance.

She'd kept herself preoccupied this weekend between that dinner and today, Sunday. She wasn't home, and I'm not sure where she went, but I woke up Friday morning to an empty house, and it stayed that way until eight o'clock this morning when I heard the garage door open. She had no choice but to come back today because we're hosting Uncle Jim and Dad's birthday party. The family has no idea Elizabeth and I are on the outs, so we have no choice but to pretend to be happy with one another.

"You need anything?" I ask, walking into the kitchen.

Elizabeth busies herself, setting out the food for the party. Normally, she'd make everything herself, but today, she chose to have it catered by The Gathering Place, a local restaurant in Winchester, citing a busy schedule. Whether that was true or not, I don't know, but it was an excuse no one in the family would question. Neither Dad nor Uncle Jim seemed to mind the change, but they still requested I make a few burgers—just in case. They were simple men who didn't always like all that "fancy shit at these restaurants nowadays." At least that's what Dad said a few years ago.

Without the need to prepare the rest of the meal, I felt like a useless lump most of the day. I was used to running around like a headless chicken, putting the finishing touches on things and completing her last-minute requests, but there was none of that today, and it felt...wrong.

"Nope," Elizabeth says without looking.

This is awkward. We've had our fair share of needing to put on a brave face in front of the family, but I think this might be the hardest time yet.

I should apologize. Start paving the road toward a more friendly cohabitation for the rest of our marriage. Stepping up to the island, I try to start the conversation, but I'm interrupted.

"It smells amazing in here," Nina says, walking in from the foyer hall, dressed more for a board meeting than a casual family birthday party: high-waisted navy-blue dress pants, a cream satin camisole, a tan blazer, and leopard print heels. "I'm so glad you went with GP; I've been craving the lamb meatballs."

She swoons over the food Elizabeth has already set out and gingerly lifts the lid on another container, searching for said meatballs.

I can almost guarantee Nina and Elizabeth kept the restaurant in business for the first two years it was open. They used to go there for two meals a day sometimes—especially Nina, whose office is only a few blocks away.

"Damn, dressed to impress, Nin?" Elizabeth pokes fun at her outfit.

"I just got done with a client. Sue me." Nina's gaze finally finds me across the kitchen, and the corners of her mouth lift slightly before she diverts her attention to the food on the counter. "Anything I can do?"

I don't even get a hello or a hug?

"No, I don't—Shit! They didn't give me the potatoes." Elizabeth groans and searches for the receipt. "I don't have time to go and get them, can you—"

"I got it," I say, and for the first time all day, Elizabeth looks at me.

Reaching for the receipt in her hand, I let my fingers graze hers. I'm surprised when she doesn't pull away from my touch, but her fingers remain in the same place under my hold. "You guys can finish up around here. I'll just be in the way."

Elizabeth sighs before relenting and dropping her hold on the receipt.

I lean in to kiss her cheek gently, and I'm even more surprised when she doesn't pull away, but she can't. Nina would know something was up if she did that...unless Nina already *knows*.

It's not like her to not at least say "Hi, Bub!" when she walks in, but today, I barely got any kind of acknowledgment.

Shit...she knows. She has to know.

"I'll be back," I whisper, but Elizabeth has already turned

back to working on the food presentation. Nina doesn't say anything as I stuff the receipt into my pocket and leave. They're waiting for me to leave so they can talk about it, and before I can even shut the garage door, I hear Elizabeth start venting to her sister.

"Thank God," I say, pulling into the driveway behind a black Escalade.

I wasn't sure Finn would show up; he was in a weird mood yesterday when I ran into him, but I'm glad he did. His weird demeanor probably had more to do with Oliver and that project he is making Finn work on—or it was just Oliver in general. That seems more likely. Finn's adoptive father always had a way of getting under Finn's skin like no one else could.

I grab the brown paper bag with two extra-large tubs of potatoes from the front seat and another brown bag with a bottle of wine—Elizabeth's favorite. The restaurant had added it to the pile as an apology. Instead of going straight inside, I walk to the front door where Finn's black Escalade now occupies the circle in front of the steps. Michaela stands with her arms crossed tight across her chest and her lips pulled back in a scowl.

"Why the long face, Shortcake? Not happy to see me?" Finn asks, and while I may not be able to see it, I can imagine the biggest smirk on his face. He loves taunting my sister, and she makes it too easy. When she could just walk away, she stands there and feeds into his shit, only making it worse. At this point, I don't know if they will ever grow out of it, this back and forth has been going on for almost thirteen years, maybe longer.

"I thought that was you!" I clamp down on his shoulder, disrupting their stare-off, and my sister's glare turns on me. "Glad you could make it."

"What is he doing here?" Michaela hisses.

God, she is such a drama queen.

"Oh, c'mon, *Shortcake*," Finn coos, and Michaela's lip twitches. She *hates* it when he calls her that. "Don't be like that. I know you missed me."

"Don't call me *that!*" Michaela swats away his hand when he outstretches it to ruffle her hair. She has always hated his nickname for her, but it stemmed from her difference in height compared to the rest of us. I don't think she's grown an inch since her freshman year of high school, stuck at five-foot-two for as long as I can remember. Even Nina stands a few inches taller than her without heels. Unfortunately for her, my sister did not inherit the Davis height genes, so the nickname stuck.

Michaela turns back to me, repeating herself. "What is he doing here?"

"We ran into each other in town yesterday," I say with a simple shrug.

I don't know why she is having such a cow about this—it's not like this is the first time Finn has been to a family function. And whether she likes it or not, it won't be the last.

"I invited him because Mom and Dad will want to see him before he jets off again."

Finn has been out galivanting a little more than usual lately. It's been hard to keep up with where exactly he's been, so when I saw him it felt like fate. My sister could deal with her emotions for a day because while she may not be excited to see him, everyone else would be.

"I'm going to be sticking around for a while," Finn says, opening the back of his Cadillac and reaching inside. He pulls out a decent-sized box covered in wrapping paper with the poop emoji on it. He nods with a smirk when I laugh at his choice of paper, and I notice Michaela roll her eyes. She thinks we're children, both of us. But hey, Dad will get a kick out of it, and that's all that matters.

"You're sticking around? What did Mommy and Daddy cut off your allowance?" Michaela quips.

Oh boy, here we go.

"From those split ends and your outfit, I'd say Nina did, too," Finn quips.

Damn, that was good. But I can't let them start now. Dad and Uncle Jim will be here any minute and I already have to juggle myself and Elizabeth today. I don't feel like playing referee in a Finn-Michaela verbal match.

"Alright, you two, enough," I say, stepping between them. "Can't we agree to get along for one day?"

"Easier said than done, Joshy-boy," Finn says, lugging the poop emoji gift box up the steps.

Michaela glares at him, and I won't lie, I'm a little scared she's going to trip him on the way by, but she doesn't. That's a win, right? Right.

"For Dad and Uncle Jim, can you *please* not start any shit today?" I ask, earning an offended glance from her. On cue, two more cars pull into the driveway, parking behind Finn's Cadillac. The birthday boys have finally arrived. "Just behave for one day. That's all I ask," I beg before turning to greet them.

"The party has arrived!" Dad says, stepping out of the car. He rushes to the passenger side to open the door and help Mom step out—it's a small gesture, but something he has always done for her. Growing up, I told myself I wanted to do the same for my wife one day, but Elizabeth doesn't always like to let me, especially when we're in the middle of a tiff.

"We were starting to think you got lost." I laugh, hugging my parents and then Uncle Jim.

"Your father decided this morning was a good time to trim the trees around the house." Mom shoots Dad a glare, but he only shrugs. That's just how Dad is, we all know it.

"Heard anything from Nick?" Uncle Jim asks.

"I haven't, but we can ask Nina if she knows anything. I'm sure he's almost here." I smile at my uncle, but I know it's not convincing.

Nick was supposed to be home yesterday, but his return flight has been pushed back about five times since he landed in California on Monday. He's been getting pulled all over the place since taking a job with Villa Inc. last year, becoming one of the principal architects at the firm under the Villa umbrella. I don't think I've seen him in almost a month—since his birthday last month. He was home last weekend for about two days before he had to leave again, and I didn't want to interrupt the little time he and Nina got together, so I didn't even try to contact him.

The new job keeps him busy by sending him around the country mostly to clean up messes and offer insight to their newly acquired companies. Occasionally he serves as a consultant to other firms, helping them find solutions for any problems they're encountering on their current projects. I don't know that it's exactly what he envisioned for his career, but it allows him more flexibility and the opportunity to be closer to his wife—considering she's co-owner of the whole operation. Under Nina and Kai (mostly Nina), Villa Inc. has become three times the size while Ric was still running it, officially becoming the world's largest investment company as of February. Nina had taken on a larger role when her brother took a step back to be a dad three years ago. And she never stopped, even after Kai returned. I think Kai preferred it that way. His sister was far more like their dad than he was and she enjoyed the job more than Kai did. When Ric passed, I was surprised he initially left the company to Kai, but I wasn't surprised when Nina ended up taking over.

I think it's starting to wear down on Nick and Nina— the distance—because he has been traveling with her a little more than normal lately. When he mentioned that a few weeks ago, I wasn't sure how that worked with his job, but I guess it doesn't matter when you're married to the big boss. I was happy they were making it work. I couldn't do what they do, that's for damn sure.

With the way Nick's schedule has been continuously pushed on this trip, I have a feeling he won't make it today, but I don't want to be the one to break Uncle Jim's heart. I know he'd been looking forward to seeing his son. I'll let Nina do that…

"Well, c'mon. Everyone else is here, and food should be about ready. I have to throw the burgers on the grill." I usher them up the steps and into the house, shooting my sister another warning glare as I pass by.

Walking inside, Elizabeth greets us in the foyer with open arms and a warm smile. She embraces my parents and Uncle Jim before coaxing them further inside with the promise of food. Before she can follow, I grab her hand before she can run away and spend the rest of the day up Nina's ass to avoid me.

"Something I can help you with?" Elizabeth asks, taking a step back, but doesn't try to pull out of my grasp yet.

"Does Nina know?" I ask.

"I don't know what you're talking about."

"Don't play coy, Sugar. Does Nina *know?*"

Elizabeth scoffs, running her tongue across her teeth, and steps into me. She removes her hand from my grasp, draping her arms around my shoulders and leaning close. She whispers, "She doesn't know anything she doesn't need to know." Elizabeth pulls back to look up at me sweetly, but her eyes tell a different story. "Now, give me a kiss. Everyone's watching."

forty-two

NOW

BEAR IS GOING BALLISTIC from a crate somewhere deeper in the house. Elizabeth disappears to the left, and I slip my shoes off, leaving them outside on the porch before stepping over the threshold. I'm still soaked from the storm outside. I close the front door quietly and take two steps inside the foyer, the sound of paws against hardwood fills the air. Bear rounds the corner and barrels straight down the main hall toward me, zeroed in. The softest hum reverberates in his chest, ready to sound the alarm, until he catches my scent and immediately begins to lick my hand, nudging it with his large head.

"Hiya, bud," I exhale, glad that he still likes me. I would not want to be on the other side of that dog.

I rub behind his ears, scratching his head and offering him small words of praise. When I look up, Elizabeth leans against the wall, watching for a brief moment until our eyes meet. She takes a deep breath and disappears down the hallway, swinging left again.

"Am I supposed to follow her?" I ask the dog, but his only response is a happy pant before trotting off behind her.

The main hallway spills into a living room centered around a fireplace; a TV hangs from the wall above the fire, playing *The Family Stone,* one of her favorite Christmas movies full of drama, romance, and Christmas spirit, right behind a movie of quite the opposite: *Miracle on 34th Street.* Accordion-style French doors line the back wall that opens up to the screened porch. To the far left end of the living space is an eat-in dining area featuring a large built-in banquette with a huge round table underneath a modern-looking, rounded crystal chandelier. Turning the corner, I find her in the kitchen, washing her hands in the farmhouse sink, but what catches my eye is the color of the island cabinets. It's the same color as the Savannah townhouse kitchen.

"Go sit," she orders, motioning toward the doorway on her left. Through the threshold, there's a butler's pantry fitted with a wet bar and a stainless steel double-door fridge. Who needs that much fridge space? I don't have long to ponder the question before she ushers me forward into the dining room to sit in one of the chairs and opens up a first-aid kit.

Elizabeth works quietly, avoiding any eye contact, as she uses a wet washcloth to clean my injuries. I'm mostly battered and bruised; the only real damage is a busted lip and a cut on my brow, but she takes her time. Using the cloth to wipe away any blood, she makes sure the cuts are clean before she applies a butterfly bandage. Bear watches from his bed in the corner, quiet and content.

When she's satisfied, Elizabeth closes up the kit and walks back through the kitchen disappearing around the corner. She returns moments later and wraps some ice in a towel. Taking the icepack, I offer her a grateful smile, but she ignores it, returning to the kitchen. Bear watches her walk away before glancing back at me, then at her. After a moment, I swear the dog rolls his eyes before settling back into his bed and going to sleep. Can dogs even roll their eyes?

Through the doorway, I watch her busy herself in the kitchen, cleaning up a nonexistent mess. I know I'm going to have to make the first move. Otherwise, we'll be doing the most awkward two-step all night. I lean against the doorway, holding the ice pack to my brow. "Wanna talk about it?"

"No," she says. But I don't say anything. We've had this conversation before and if I just give her a minute, she'll crack. She always does.

I watch her hand wipe invisible crumbs into her other awaiting one at the edge of the wood block island counter before dusting them into the sink. She tidies up the four miniature potted plants on the windowsill behind the sink. And then she runs her hand under a stream of warm water before rinsing out the bowl of the sink. When she's satisfied, she turns off the water and reaches for the towel to dry her hands, and just like clockwork...

"I told him to leave."

"At midnight?" I ask. "That's a bit harsh, don't ya think?"

"Yesterday," she says. "I told him to leave *yesterday*, not long after you did, actually. And when I refused to answer the phone and then blocked him, he showed up at my door. And when I still told him to leave...Well, you heard him."

"Oh."

"That's all you have to say?" Elizabeth finally turns to look at me. *"Oh?"*

What does she want me to say? I'm still trying to come to terms with the fact that I just got into a knock-down drag-out with her boyfriend...ex-boyfriend, sorry.

Elizabeth scoffs. "Unbelievable."

"What do you want me to say, Elizabeth?"

"I want you to acknowledge the fact that this is *your* fault!"

"My fault?"

"Yes!" She slams the kitchen towel on the counter. "Your fault."

I am still not following. How in the hell is what just happened with Ryan *my* fault?

"Josh, I can't move on when every time you're around, you act like everything is okay. Like *you're* okay. Like this isn't hurting you as much as it's fucking killing me."

Her words catch me off guard. What does she mean, I act like I'm okay? I am far from fucking okay. Most days, I can't keep my head above water. Ever since the rest of the family found out the truth, I can feel them slowly slipping away from me because, at the end of the day, she's going to be the one they choose. Not me.

Carefully, I meet her by the island, but she moves away when I get too close.

"I am not okay, Elizabeth," I whisper, but she doesn't say anything. "I don't want this. I don't want any of this. I want you. I don't want to wake up another day without you next to me. I don't want to come home, and you're not there. The house is empty, it's cold, it's not *home* without you...I don't want to know that you're with some asshole who doesn't love you like I do. Because I fucking love you. I do. I love you, I'm in love with you, and I always have been."

"Juliet—"

"Isn't you." I shut down her fears before she can voice them. "Yes, I thought I loved her once, and maybe I did, but she's not you."

"Then why did you go to Wichita when I asked you not to?" Her voice raises, and it ignites a spark in me.

"Because I was scared."

I start to match her volume but stop myself. I know better, I can't fight fire with fire, we'll only get burned.

Taking a deep breath, I say, "I didn't know what you wanted. I didn't know what was going to happen. Time was ticking by faster than a fucking freight train, we were in a bad spot, and I thought...I don't know what I thought. I just knew we were a time bomb waiting to explode. So, I did something about it. I guess I thought I was just preparing for what was coming sooner rather than later."

"Why didn't you just ask me?"

"I didn't know what to say."

"Say you love me, Josh!" Her hand comes down on the marbled countertop at the far end of the kitchen. "Say you want to be with me. Say anything! Anything would have been better than the silence of the last year."

"We were barely speaking to each other, Liz. The most conversation we had outside of family functions was the day you opened that damn letter."

"You're the one who pushed me away, Josh. You were so worried about work and Max and getting ahead…You let us slip to the wayside again. And when I brought it up, you acted like I was being unreasonable."

"You wanted me to drop everything and go on a vacation, Elizabeth. Or run off to New York because Nick and Nina were there. Or California to see Lola. Or to—"

"Because I thought it would make things better! Give us a chance to reconnect."

"But you didn't even *ask* me." I scoff. "You just assumed I could drop everything and go, but I can't do that, Elizabeth. I have a job, one that doesn't allow me to just run around the country."

We'd had this fight many times over the years. Every time I was overly busy at work, she would get mad. She didn't like it when I had to stay late or work overtime or miss certain things because duty called. I was married to her, not my job, she would say.

She didn't understand it—the constant need to prove myself. The constant tug-of-war I have felt inside, trying to be who she wanted me to be but also who I felt that I needed to be. I had to prove I was more than just some opportunist. I didn't want to sit back and reap the rewards of a life I wouldn't have if it hadn't been for one wrong decision back in college. I wasn't worthy of any of this, but I had been doing my damnedest to try and be.

"We were both wrong, okay?" I sigh. "That doesn't change the fact that I fucked up. I assumed you were going to walk away because that's what you kept saying…You moved into the guest room for fucksake!"

"And you went to meet up with your 'one true love.'"

I never called her that, but even if I had, it wasn't the truth.

"I've already told you, Elizabeth. Juliet never showed up that day," I say, reaching out for her hand.

"Doesn't matter," Elizabeth hisses, ripping her hand from mine. "You still went. You went and you lied about it. That's not love, Josh."

"You're right," I admit.

She looks taken aback. Guess that makes two times now that I've told her she was right.

"But all I can do is ask for your forgiveness. I can't take it back, but if you give me the chance, I will do everything I can to make it up to you."

Elizabeth stares at her shoes, arms crossed tightly over her chest as she leans back against the counter. She closes her eyes and looks up at the ceiling, her voice meek when she says, "You weren't even here on the anniversary."

No, not our anniversary, but the anniversary of her parents' death.

"You never came." She scoffs sadly.

"Yes, I did." I waste no time taking her hands in mine and stepping into her line of vision. "I was here. I drove down that afternoon after going back and forth about whether or not to come in the first place. I didn't think you'd want to see me, but I came anyway. And I guess you weren't home because you didn't answer the door. So, I sat out right out there on your porch for hours…I wanted to be here when you got home. I wanted to be here for you because I know that it's still the hardest day of every year for you." I cup the side of her face in my hands and wipe a stray tear that falls from her brown eyes. "So, I waited, but you never came home. And when I thought about leaving, I waited some more. I don't even know what time it was, but it was late when I left."

Her eyes well with more tears, and she tries to avoid my stare, but I won't let her. I want to look her in the eye when I tell her exactly how I feel.

"I'm sorry, Elizabeth. I'm so sorry for everything. For lying, for not telling you how I felt—how I feel—for not sticking around…I was trying to protect myself, and in doing so, I've hurt you…the one thing I never wanted to do. I thought—" A heavy sigh. "I thought this was what you wanted, to finally be done with *this*. To be done with me. We were barely speaking, I never saw you, we were living two different lives—"

"Whose fault was that?"

"It wasn't just me, Elizabeth."

What's that old saying? It takes two to tango. Yeah, that's the one. This relationship was never going to work if only one of us was fighting for it.

"I didn't feel like a priority to you," she whispers.

"And I was wrong for that. Work got the best of me, and everything else got the leftovers. You got the leftovers." I grip her chin between my fingers and stare into her eyes. "I am so sorry. I love you, Sugar. I'm *in* love with you. I have been since that day you called and begged me to help you decorate the house when you should've been studying. Hell, I think I loved you before that, I just didn't know it…and every day I've spent apart from you has been one too many. I don't want to be away from you for one more minute. I will quit my job and move to Jupiter if that's what it takes. I don't care as long as I'm with you. Because as long as I'm alive…I am yours and you are mine. I love you, Elizabeth Davis."

Tears flood her eyes and I wait for her to say something—anything—but she doesn't. She gnaws on the inside of her cheek, and the longer we stand here, the more time begins to still and anxiety fills my heart.

"Now would be a good time to say it back," I whisper.

Tears escape the corners of her eyes, but she presses up on her tiptoes and kisses me. "I love you too, Joshua Davis."

forty-three

THEN

August 2024

"SO, HOW WAS MY sister?"

I still can't believe Nina put Michaela on Finn's project. Was she trying to start World War III? The thought of them working alone in such close quarters made me want to duck and cover even from seven hundred miles away in South Carolina. Michaela called me after Nina told her she'd be helping Finn with his newest project to complain, and Finn did the same. They both spent at least twenty minutes each going on and on about how the other was going to ruin their life. They were equally insufferable drama queens that night.

Finn's eyes widen a little at my question. "W-what do you mean?"

"On Sheffield House." I laugh. What did he think I meant? "You were practically ready to throw in the towel when Nina told you Mic was taking over."

Nina put Michaela on the project because she needed to get some space to handle other projects, and Michaela needed a chance to prove herself. She hasn't exactly been employee of the month recently.

303

"Oh." A breath of relief. "Yeah, she was fine, I guess. Annoying, but I didn't expect any less. She did have the idea for Coney Island, though, so I guess something good did come out of it."

"Careful," I drawl. "Someone might think you're starting to like her or something."

His head whips around to meet my gaze, his eyes blown wide. If I didn't know any better I'd say he was nervous. He wipes his palms on the thighs of his jeans and adjusts in his seat. "She was helpful. What else do you want me to say?"

"Relax, man." I laugh, taking a tug of my water. "I'm just making sure she didn't screw around. I know how important this is for you."

Sheffield House was Finn's pet project that his father had forced on him. After one too many bailouts, Oliver told Finn he needed to get his shit together and fast. He gave his son three months to form a board-approved business. You'd think that was easy, but Finn had been struggling, so he went to the one person he knew could help him: Davina Villa.

Nina helped him form the idea for Sheffield House—a nonprofit organization that would help other foster kids—like Finn. When he told me about the idea, I felt like a proud father watching his son grow up. This was the moment we had all been waiting for, the moment Finnley Sheffield finally took hold of his future and did something with it.

"Did you only invite me over to interrogate me about your little sister?" Finn snaps.

"Hey, I have the inside scoop at my disposal, why not take advantage of it?"

I guess you could say I've always been an informed brother. My sister and I have been close from the moment my parents brought her home from the hospital. I'd do anything for her and vice versa. It killed me not to tell her the truth about me and Elizabeth, but I knew she'd never be able to keep that secret. The whole damn town would know before I'd even finished a sentence.

Growing up, Michaela had always hung around me and my friends, even if the others didn't want her to. Nick and Finn were the only ones who didn't give me much shit about it at first. Don't get me wrong, there were plenty of times it was a downer having her in the way of our teenage fun, but eventually, everyone got used to her being there. The others saw her as one of our own, adopting her as their little sister, except one—Finn. They were always at odds, in a constant state of bickering, picking fights, and talking shit to each other.

"Nina doesn't tell me shit," I say. "Girl code and all that."

"She's ratted Michaela out a time or two."

"Sure, but only when it's really bad. Besides, Mic usually tells on herself. You know she can't keep a secret to save her life."

"No shit." Finn rolls his eyes. Poor guy, my sister's big mouth is why he spent his junior year of high school at a boarding school instead of at home. And it wasn't one of the fun kind. "That little shit has never been able to keep her mouth shut."

"The way you guys still hate each other blows my mind. You'd think you were the brother instead of me."

"Dude, don't say that." Finn's face turns a ghostly white, and he looks like he might throw up.

"I'm serious!"

Finn shakes the thought from his mind. God, did they really hate each other that much? This has been going on for so long, maybe it's time for an intervention.

"Where's Ellie?" Finn asks, attempting to change the subject.

Shit.

Shit, shit, shit...I was hoping he wouldn't notice, but it's hard not to when he's used to her being around. Normally, Elizabeth would have greeted him with a hot breakfast and coffee, but when he arrived this morning, there was coffee but no breakfast, and no Elizabeth. I should've known this was coming.

"Oh, I think she had a meeting down in Charleston," I say, picking at the label on my water bottle.

"What does that mean, you 'think?'"

"She's been down there a lot more recently—lots of shoots for some family or something. She should be home any time now." I turn away from his curious stare, looking through the fridge for something new to drink, and then turn to my phone.

"Josh, why is our—Oh, Finn!" Elizabeth stands in the doorway from the mudroom, looking like a kid caught sneaking in. What is she doing here? She isn't supposed to be back until Monday for our meeting with the lawyer who laid out the contract years ago. I don't know for sure but I think she wants to go over every detail of what breaking off the arrangement early entails. "Finn, what are you doing here?"

"It's Oliver's birthday weekend," I say.

We stand on opposite ends of the kitchen, locked in a silent battle as Finn looks between us, sensing the tension, I'm sure. Elizabeth sets her purse in the empty place next to Finn but doesn't let go. Her movements are stiff and unsure. Her fingers twist around the strap.

"I told you he was coming over this weekend."

Elizabeth turns to him. "That's right, I'm so sorry. My weeks are starting to blur together more than I realized. How is Oliver?"

"Oh, you know...Oliver." Finn chuckles and she huffs a small laugh, but her smile doesn't quite reach her eyes. "Will you make it on Sunday?"

"Sunday?" She asks in genuine confusion before turning to look at me.

"The Coney Island event for the thing he's been working on," I answer with a little more annoyance than is probably necessary, but having to cover for her is starting to get old.

"Shit." Elizabeth sighs, her shoulders falling. "Finn, I'm sorry. I don't think I'll make it. I have to be in Asheville for a shoot tomorrow and then Charleston on Monday for—"

"Don't forget our appointment on Monday."

Elizabeth's glare whips toward me, but I'm not going to let her forget this appointment. She's the one who was adamant we needed to sit down and talk with him. "I'm sorry, Finn." She sighs. "Things are just extra crazy right now."

"No sweat, Ellie." Finn wraps his arm around her shoulders and gives them a gentle squeeze. "As long as you make it to the big party next month. You gotta take a break and celebrate occasionally."

Another sad smile. "I promise."

"Don't hold your breath," I mumble.

Elizabeth glares at me again before excusing herself. She claims she had to pick up the dry cleaning because she needs one of the shirts for tomorrow. Finn's eyes travel to the closet door outside the kitchen, where a plastic garment bag hangs filled with freshly pressed shirts. She doesn't waste time grabbing her purse and running out the door.

When she's gone, Finn turns to me, and without hesitation, he asks, "Dude, what was that?"

Pulling two beers from the fridge, I ignore his question.

"She didn't even tell you goodbye. Elizabeth never leaves without telling someone goodbye, let alone her own husband. She didn't even kiss you!"

I shrug. "Sure, she did."

His eyes look like they're about to jump out of his skull. We both know for a fact she did not tell me goodbye *or* kiss me. "Josh—"

"Finn," I snap. "Just drop it. Okay?"

NOW

THE RECEPTIONIST OFFERS US a tight smile when I follow Elizabeth into the Winchester office of DV Designs. I haven't been here much in the last few years. After Michaela moved to New York and Nina started spending more time opening other offices across the country, there wasn't anything here for me. It's crazy to think that only six years ago, I dragged Nick through the door to drop off some pies to Michaela and introduced him to Nina. Who would've imagined life would turn out the way it has? Nina taking him on a once-in-a-lifetime vacation? Sure. Them falling in love and having known each other longer than anyone knew? That wasn't on the bingo card.

"She's a little tense," the brunette behind the desk says.

Great. That's *just* what we need walking into this conversation.

Elizabeth takes a deep breath and smiles at the receptionist before pushing down the hallway toward Nina's office.

"Good luck," the girl says to me before turning back to the ringing phone, but her words do little to comfort me. If anything, they make me more nervous.

From the hallway, I can see Nina pace the length of her office. I'm surprised there isn't a wear stripe on the rug beneath her feet. Her footsteps falter when she catches sight of me through the door. Elizabeth sits with her back to the door in one of the blue velvet chairs in front of the desk. Nina looks between us as I walk into her office and I can hear the person on the other end of the phone calling her name.

"I have to call you back."

She hangs up without waiting for a response and looks between us once more before shaking her head with a scoff. She closes the office door but still doesn't say anything, and right now, the silence is worse than whatever she's about to say. She sits on the edge of her desk, directly in front of us, crossing her arms. "Does someone want to tell me what in the hell is going on?"

Isn't it obvious?

"We've decided to stay together," I say, beating Elizabeth to it.

"Just like that?" Her sharp green eyes bore into ours. "You're just going to call off the divorce and...what? Go back to your pretend marriage and act like none of this ever happened? Act like you didn't cause problems within the family."

Her words are met with silence. It's not that we hadn't realized any of this, but nothing can be done about it now.

Nina mumbles something in Italian, pinching the bridge of her nose. She takes a deep breath before crossing her arms. "Maybe you two are fine going back to pretend, but the rest of us now have to live with the consequences."

"We understand that, Nina," Elizabeth says.

"Davvero?" She hisses the simple word, leaning forward in the slightest, challenging us. *Do you?*

"We never meant for it to be like this," I push back.

"That doesn't change the fact that your secrets have

changed things. The family—"

"Will be just fine!" Elizabeth yells with a harsh breath. "The family will be fine, Nina. If anything, it's going to save everyone from a bunch of awkward family dinners and lonely holidays."

Elizabeth shakes her head. "I know that I hurt you by lying, but can you honestly say you would've accepted us the same way had you known?"

Nina doesn't say anything. She doesn't have to—her avoidant stare says it all.

"There were real reasons we kept this to ourselves, and as much as Brina pisses me off, she knew what was best when it came to handling this."

"So, all of this just to get your inheritance." I can see the way Nina's words hurt Elizabeth, the same words Ric had used six years ago, but unfortunately, it doesn't make them any less true. When Nina turns to me, she chews on her bottom lip, thinking. "But the question I still have is what did *you* get?"

I swallow hard, and my tongue sneaks out to wet my lips. Do I tell her the truth? What's one more thing to add to the fire, right?

How my sister has managed to keep her mouth shut about this, I don't know. She is the worst secret keeper in the world. Nick and Nina still don't know the real reason, and maybe I didn't tell them because I feared how they would view me if they knew the truth. It was hard enough seeing Michaela's reaction. Knowing I had let her down because I'm not the person she always thought I was. It's definitely the reason I haven't come clean to Dad. Seeing that same look of disappointment on his face would kill me.

"You got something out of it," Nina pushes. "You aren't going to enter an arranged marriage for free."

I look at Elizabeth. Her shoulders rise and fall with a sigh. "Nina, it doesn't—"

"I was about to be expelled from Chadwick," I confess,

holding Elizabeth's gaze.

"You were part of it, weren't you?" Nina asks, and when I finally look at her, I can see the disappointment I feared sinking in her features. "The Theta Pi hazing."

I nod and my gaze falls to the floor. "I didn't...I didn't *do* it, but I was there. I was the one who took him to the hospital."

"*Cazzo*," Nina mumbles. *Fuck.*

"My mom...That's why I came home. I went to her first and told her everything, but she told me not to tell anyone. She was looking for a way to keep me out of it. Your mom—"

Nina raises her hand to stop me. She doesn't care. She doesn't want to know. It's not like knowing is going to change anything.

"So what's your plan, huh?" She massages the crease in her brow. "Where do you go from here? The rest of the family will be rightfully confused when you show up on Christmas Day *together.*"

Elizabeth and I share a glance before looking back at Nina.

"Please tell me that you've discussed this. You can't just waltz in there and act like the past seven months didn't happen."

So maybe we haven't completely thought this through...I guess we were riding the wave of getting back together.

Nina scoffs. "Did you two talk about *anything?* Did you discuss the issues in your relationship that led to this or did you just apologize and act like it was sunshine and rainbows again?"

"We know it's not, but Nina—"

"You guys cannot just go back to normal. You will never make this work if—"

"Nina," Elizabeth cuts her off. "I love you very much, but right now, I need you not to be Davina Villa, matriarch of the family. I need you to be Nina, my sister."

Nina looks up to the ceiling, her hands gripping the edge

of her desk, like she's asking God himself for strength to deal with this. "You want me to be your sister?" With a slight scoff, she meets Elizabeth's gaze again. "If you want me to be your sister then I'm going to step outside and give you two the chance to have a conversation." She looks at me and adds, "The real conversation you should've had a long time ago, but didn't."

Without waiting for a response, Nina snatches her phone off the desk, mumbling something in Italian as she walks out.

"She's right." Elizabeth sighs after a moment.

As much as I hate to agree with her, Nina is right. We didn't have the full conversation that should've been had. Sure, we talked about work and Juliet, how that was the straw that broke the camel's back, but there was so much left to say.

"Josh—"

"I—"

"No," Elizabeth stops me. "Let me say this." She takes a deep breath and stares down into her hands folded on her lap, twirling her thumbs as she chooses the next words. "I-I should've been honest with you from the start about Ryan. I don't know why I kept it a secret. I guess…I was scared because that would have made it more real. I didn't even tell Nina until last month. She introduced us last year by accident, and when she found out he had asked me on a date, she warned me not to pursue it. Not only because he was a dick, but because I was still in love with you." She meets my gaze and a small smile tugs at the right corner of her lips. "When she found out… Well, let's just say she wasn't happy. I'd hidden it for over a year."

"Was he there when I told you about Michaela and Finn?"

Elizabeth nods but refuses to look at me. "We were just talking, getting to know each other."

"Elizabeth, we slept together at Nick and Nina's wedding!"

"I know, Josh. I know! And I should've never let that

happen. I should've stopped it, but…I missed you. I missed us. Being with you at the wedding really clouded my judgment and I took advantage of it. I took advantage of you."

"Did you sleep with him?" I ask. I don't know if I want the answer, but if we're going to put everything on the table…

"No."

"You were together for over a year and never slept together?"

Elizabeth chews on her bottom lip. "I couldn't do it, Josh. We started to…last month, but I couldn't do it. Despite what had been going on between you and me, I felt like I was cheating. Before that, nothing with Ryan felt real, it felt like we were playing house…but when the moment came, I couldn't do it. He got pissed and broke up with me."

"That's why you took me last weekend."

"Honestly, I was always going to invoke the clause. Can you imagine if I had taken Ryan to meet the girls? Georgie would eat him up."

"I don't know, I think motherhood has softened her."

Elizabeth rolls her eyes.

"I'm sorry for accusing you of telling her about Noah wanting a divorce," I say.

"As if I didn't accuse you of worse things."

"Elizabeth, I pushed you away time and time again. And I lied to you. I don't blame you for thinking the worst. But the truth is…" I sigh, staring down at my hands.

I don't know how to say this, to admit what we both already know but have refused to ever voice to one another.

"I buried myself in work because I know I'm not…I'm not worthy of this, of you. I haven't earned this life. It was given to me because of a stupid decision I made in college. I was a scared kid who didn't know any better and I took the easy way out. I'm not William or Ryan or these other guys who can give you the life you deserve, I'm not—"

"I'm going to stop you right there."

I hadn't even noticed she had stood from her chair until her delicate touch gripped my chin, forcing me to look at her.

"I love you, Josh, because you're not them. You are the most kind and gentle man I've ever known. You have the biggest heart and the way you care for your family, your friends…me. They've never loved me the way you do. You say you don't deserve me? I don't deserve you. I've spent the past ten years waiting for you to wake up and realize this isn't the life you wanted. You'd been forced into it because of some unexpected circumstances, none of which were *your* fault."

"Theta—"

"Wasn't your fault, Josh. Imagine if you hadn't been there. Imagine what would have happened then." Elizabeth takes my hands in hers. "That boy would have died, I guarantee it. You saved his life, Josh. Whether anyone else knows it or not, I know it. You know it. Hell, everyone there knows it. Despite whatever story was told to scrub your name out of it, whatever legal action Brina threatened to keep them quiet, everyone there that night knows it would have been so much worse if it wasn't for you. But regardless of why this happened, I'm happy it did because it means I have you."

I swallow the lump in my throat, trying to contain the blur in my eyes.

"Josh, you don't have to earn this." Elizabeth motions to the world around us. "Or me or my love or the love of our family. That's given to you, freely. My inheritance isn't just mine, it's ours, to build our life together." She pulls my gaze to hers. "I love you, Josh. You don't have to continue to prove yourself to anyone, including me. You've already done that. You don't have to try and exonerate yourself for something you didn't do. I wish you would've told me you felt this way…I could've put your worries to rest and maybe we could've avoided all of this."

"I was scared that my mom would be right."

"What are you talking about?" Elizabeth's gaze narrows.

"Every time I tried to talk to Mom about things…she'd tell me to stop whining and be grateful for what I had…before it was gone. Before *you* were gone. Enjoy it all while it lasted because one day it would disappear."

"Josh—"

"She used to remind me I couldn't mess this up because losing you meant losing everything. And she was right… Elizabeth, you are my everything. I could lose everything else and be okay, but losing you…I'd never recover from that."

When I meet her gaze, her eyes are full of unshed tears.

Elizabeth clears her throat. "I wish you had told me. We could've faced this together. You didn't have to be alone, Josh. You were always there for me when I needed you most, but you didn't let me do the same."

"I'm sorry."

"I love you, Josh. And, I'm not going anywhere," she says. "I'm yours." Elizabeth pulls my mouth to hers but she stops just before they touch. "And you're mine."

forty-five

THEN

October 2024

"I DON'T HAVE TIME for this. I have too much going on and don't have the patience for a fight with you today," Elizabeth answers the phone.

I called her earlier, but she didn't answer, so I called Nick instead. When I hung up with my cousin, I dialed her number again because she was the *only* person I wanted to talk to about what just happened.

"Hello?" She calls from the other end when I don't say anything. "Josh," she sighs. "I don't have time for games, I—"

"My sister is fucking my best friend."

"Excuse me?" Elizabeth laughs. "I could almost swear you just said Michaela is sleeping with—"

"Finn, yep."

"How do you—"

"I just walked in on them." I scrub my hand down my face, falling onto one of the benches in the courtyard a few blocks from Finn's condo building.

The last thing I had expected when I knocked on the door of my best friend's condo was for my little sister to answer the door half-naked this morning. She wasn't supposed to be there. She was supposed to be at her condo a few miles north with her *husband*, where I'd be meeting her in a few hours for lunch. That was the whole reason I had stayed in New York an extra day. I had work meetings at the beginning of the week to solidify a contract renewal and I was going to leave last night, but Michaela begged me to go to lunch with her today. There was something she just *had* to tell me. Never in my wildest dreams would I have imagined it would be that she's sleeping with Finn.

I shake out my hand, which still aches from the blow I landed on Finn's face not even an hour ago. After Michaela answered the door, I couldn't control myself. I felt hurt, betrayed, and downright furious. My sister was a married woman, what in the hell was Finn thinking? What was she thinking?

Don't get me wrong, I'm not exactly David's biggest fan, but I'd never condone *this*. I lashed out, punching my best friend, and he took it because despite how wrong I was for doing it, he knew he was wrong, too.

"Can you honestly say you're surprised?" Elizabeth asks.

"You're not?"

"No," she says with a small laugh. I can almost see her shaking her head as a smile tugs on the corner of her mouth. "Not at all, actually. Makes a lot of sense when you think about it."

That's what Nick said, too. Am I really the only one surprised by this whole thing? I can't be. Surely, Mom and Dad will be, too. Shit, Mom and Dad…Do they know about this? What am I saying? Of course they don't.

I can hear her shuffling around in the background and then whispering to someone else. Who in the hell is she with? It's a Wednesday morning. "Look, I have to go." Elizabeth sighs. "But Josh, don't be too hard on her, okay? Your sister doesn't need judgment right now; she needs support."

"I wish you were here." The words tumble out before I can stop them, and maybe I should regret it, but I don't. It's true. I wish she was here because she would know what to do and what to say in these situations. Maybe I wouldn't have punched my best friend if she had been there. Maybe I wouldn't have accused my sister of cheating on her husband. Maybe I would've taken a step back and looked at the bigger picture.

"I uh...I have to go. Just think about what I said, okay? And Josh...Don't be too hard on your sister. If anyone can understand where she's coming from right now, I think it might be you." She doesn't wait for me to reply before hanging up.

"Well, you're dressed, that's a good sign," I say when my sister opens the door of her condo.

I knocked a few minutes before two o'clock—when I was supposed to be here to talk about what in the hell was going on—and I could tell it pissed her off. Honestly, I expected her not to show at all after what happened this morning. I figured she would hide out at Finn's and ignore me, but since she's here I guess that's a positive, right? She can't be that mad at me about it.

"Oh, don't give me that look, Michaela. I'm not the one in the wrong here." I know Elizabeth said to try to be understanding, but that look my sister is giving me right now is making it very hard to do that.

"I forgot who I was talking to: Saint Josh."

I roll my eyes. I cannot stand when she calls me that. That's just as bad, if not worse than when Elizabeth's friends call us Mr. and Mrs. Perfect. "Don't be so dramatic, MJ."

"You're the one who threw punches this morning!"

"I'm not going to apologize! I came to see if my *best friend* wanted to grab breakfast before I met you, and what did I find? You. My *sister*, half-naked, answering the damn door of his apartment. Don't you think you should have asked me if it was okay to fuck my best friend first?"

"I'm an adult, Josh. I don't need your permission to sleep with someone, and that includes your best friend."

She thinks she's an adult? I scoff. She has no fucking idea what being an adult looks like.

"How long has this been going on?" I ask.

"That's none of your business."

"Not my business?" I scoff. "You don't think I have a right to know when you're fucking around on your husband with one of my friends?"

"Okay, first of all, I'm not fucking around on anyone." Michaela shakes her head in disbelief, but I think it's a reasonable question to ask. Last I knew, she was happily married to David Reid. No one has told me any different. "And second, it's not your business. We weren't ready to tell you because of shit like this! Because of how you reacted this morning."

"How could you do this to David? And with him!"

Don't get me wrong, Finn is my best friend, but I know what he's like. I grew up with the guy; he isn't exactly a knight in shining armor.

"You're not listening to a damn word I say! David and I are *not* together. We haven't been together for months now."

My brow furrows together as her words sink in. They're not...together? Meeting her gaze from across the living room, her shoulders rise and fall with a heavy sigh.

"David asked me for a divorce in Italy."

"Italy—that was practically five months ago, Michaela!"

"I'm aware of when it was, Josh." She rolls her eyes and wraps her cardigan tighter around her. Her arms crossed tightly as she chews on her bottom lip, suddenly finding her socked feet very interesting.

"Why didn't you tell me?" I wish she had come to me about this, I could've helped her deal with that asshole so she wasn't alone. I don't understand why she would confide in Finn instead of me. I know that I've been a little out of touch with things recently, but if my sister needed something...I would've been there for her.

"I don't know." Michaela shrugs, and I can see the tears building behind her eyes. One breaks the surface, falling down her cheek, but she wipes it away with the end of her sleeve. "I guess a part of me thought I could fix it...Because if I could fix it, I wouldn't have to tell anyone. It would be like it never happened, but..."

"Sleeping with Finn wasn't going to fix anything."

The opposite, actually.

"Finn was an accident," she whispers and falls onto the couch with her head in her hands. "I never meant for it to happen. God, Josh. It wasn't supposed to happen, but working with him...I got to know him, I-I saw this different person, and I—"

"Do not say you're falling in love with him."

I don't think I can handle another revelation today.

Michaela swallows the words she is about to utter, and when she meets my stare, I can see the chipping of the wall she's been hiding behind for months. Hell, maybe longer.

She's hurt by what happened this morning, but so am I. And it's going to take time before we can get back to ourselves again. I need time to process, time to get used to the idea of them being together...The thought of my friend and my little sister being together brings up thoughts I never want to have. I mean, this is someone who I used to trade sex stories with. How am I supposed to look at him the same? But then I think about what Elizabeth said before she hung up the phone. I need to be more understanding, toward both my sister and Finn, but especially my sister. If anyone can semi-understand what she's been going through…it's me.

"No," she laughs softly.

She's lying. I know she's lying. I can see it in the way her eyes light up just thinking about Finn. I could see it this morning after I punched him, in the way she ran to him and protected him. My little sister has fallen in love with my best friend.

"But I think I could."

"I don't like it, Michaela. I don't like it one bit." I cross my arms over my chest. "But if he makes you happy—"

"He does," my sister interrupts.

"Then I guess that's all that matters."

forty-six

NOW

"SO, YOU'RE LIKE TOGETHER together, right?" Michaela asks, leaning over the kitchen island in their New York penthouse.

Finn had opened the door mid-conversation earlier when we arrived at their condo, but his words faltered as soon as he saw us. I wasn't alone and I hadn't told him Elizabeth was coming with me. We hadn't told anyone. Finn did a double take and rubbed his eyes with his fists before reopening them and a wide grin split his face.

"Took you long enough," he said, ushering us inside.

When my sister walked out of the living room to see what was taking him so long, her blue eyes grew to the size of dinner plates, moving from me to Elizabeth to my hand on her lower back and back to me.

"C'mon, Shortcake," Finn chuckled, pushing her back into the living room despite her protests.

Now, my sister has me cornered in the kitchen, where she can ask me anything. She has been chomping at the bit to ask me every question that came to mind from the moment we arrived. She passes her glass of wine between her hands, letting it skate across a small portion of the marble before catching it and sending it back, but her eyes never leave mine. I'm waiting for it to skate right past her waiting hand and fly off the edge splattering the cabinets with white wine. But, she catches it every time. "Like, no-more-divorce together."

"Yes, MJ."

"Like, moving-back-in togeth—"

"Yes, Michaela," I groan. "In all the ways you can think of, we are back together. No more divorce, no more separate lives, no more arranged marriage. This is the real deal."

"Thank God." She sighs, a breath of relief. "I was worried how this was gonna go with you two awkwardly being around each other every time the family got together."

"Glad to know that's the only reason you wanted us to get back together." I roll my eyes and she shoves one of the cookies she and Elizabeth made earlier into her mouth. She tries to say something, but the cookie jumbles her words, and I take the opportunity to escape while I have the chance.

"Merry Christmas." The words whisper across my skin before Elizabeth's lips ghost over mine in a gentle kiss. She gasps when I kiss her back, nipping her bottom lip. "I thought you were asleep."

"I was, but then you got up," I say, stretching my arms across the head of the bed, feeling my shoulders pop with instant relief.

"I'm sorry, but I couldn't go back to sleep. I tried."

Behind the blackout curtains that cover the windows, the city still looks dark. What time is it?

"Well, it's…" I look up at the clock. "Six o'clock. Elizabeth, it's fucking six in the morning, why are we awake?"

She offers a sheepish smile. "I'm just excited! It's our first Christmas back together, and Elena's first Christmas ever, we get to meet Alex's new girlfriend, *and* Finn is proposing to your sister. There's so much to be excited about!"

While all that is true, I think she's most excited about the proposal. Elizabeth has been bouncing off the walls since I told her Finn asked me and Nick for permission to marry my sister last night before dinner.

"You're adorable, y'know that?" I match her smile, pulling her mouth to mine.

Elizabeth places her hand on my bare chest. The gesture sends a soothing wave through my system. I can't get enough of her touch. Her lips linger on mine, soft and sweet, before she pulls back only enough to say, "I love you, Joshua Davis."

"And I love you, Sugar."

"Show me," she pleads, her words lighting a fire under my skin.

I claim her lips again and wrap my arms around her waist, rolling her beneath me. I nibble her bottom lip, coaxing her mouth open, and my tongue sweeps over hers.

My mouth slides down her jaw to her ear, pulling the lobe between my teeth. Elizabeth shivers under my touch when my teeth graze the skin of the sensitive spot on her neck, and goosebumps rise across her golden skin, hardening her nipples through the white fabric of her nightgown.

I swoop down to take one of the raised peaks into my mouth through the cloth, my hand massaging her other breast, earning a low moan from her, and her back arches off the mattress to meet my touch. I nip gently at the left nipple before doing the same to the other. Gathering the end of her nightgown in my hands, I shove it up her body and over her head but leave it to rest over her eyes, creating a makeshift blindfold. Bending down, I take the hardened mound in my mouth again, sucking, nipping, licking it, enjoying the feel of her on my tongue as she squirms beneath me.

"Josh." She gasps when I ghost my fingers between her legs.

"Stay still, Sugar. Keep those hands up for me, okay?"

She nods fervently as I move my mouth down her body, leaving open-mouthed kisses in my wake and nipping at the soft skin of her abdomen just above her underwear. Sliding them down her legs, I push one finger inside her, and she purrs.

"Baby," she whines as I push another finger inside her, and she moves her hips against my touch, wanting more.

"Stay still, Sugar," I remind her before sucking her clit between my lips, and she practically leaps off the bed, her back bowing.

My name escapes her lips, but this time, it's an urgent demand for satisfaction. She's done playing, and while normally, I find my satisfaction in continuing to toy with her... not today. I don't want to hold off a second longer, either.

Pulling the white fabric from her eyes, I lift it over her head, and she brings my mouth down to hers. Pushing my pajama bottoms off my thighs, I settle between her legs. Arousal hums through my veins, as I grasp my erection and fit the head of my cock to her entrance. I rub it up and down her folds, over her clit, and back before slowly pushing inside her until my hips meet hers. Pulling my shirt over my head, I toss it on the floor, planting my hands on either side of her head and capturing her lips in a demanding kiss. She hooks her ankles around my back, moving with me, countering my thrusts.

She kisses a line down my jaw to my ear, the same path I had taken on her earlier. She nibbles playfully at the lobe before tracing the shell of my ear with her tongue. My nerves are on fucking fire, going haywire with every swipe of her tongue on my burning skin. "You like that, huh?" she murmurs when I moan in response.

My body begins to lose control, taking over my need and instinct to find release. "I'm close, baby," I grit out. "Want you to come on my dick."

Wrapping her arms around my neck, she lifts her body to mine, bringing us impossibly closer. With each thrust, my cock sinks deeper into her, and her nails dig further into the skin of my shoulders. "I love you," she breathes in my ear, and I almost lose my resolve, coming right then and there.

Speeding up my thrusts, I feel her walls clench around me and feel the start of her orgasm. Parting from her, I stare down into her dark brown eyes and utter, "I love you, Elizabeth. So much."

Euphoria is the only way I know how to describe the feeling that comes over me. Pure euphoria and adrenaline course through my veins as I drive into her through my orgasm and hers.

We lie motionless for a long time after that until she breathes out a deep sigh of contentment and kisses the side of my face. I slide my hand down her side and squeeze her hip affectionately before rolling onto my side next to her. Pushing a strand of honey-golden hair from her eyes, I kiss her and return the smile she offers against my lips.

"I could get used to this," she whispers.

"Is that a promise?"

"Hey Leia, I think I see another present?" Kai says, pointing toward the tree. Ophelia skips back to the tree to inspect it. She has been playing "elf" all morning—handing out gifts, and she was positive she had given them all out. But, sure enough, there's one more: a small box stuck between the faux snow-covered branches, wrapped in red and white striped paper with a white bow on top.

Ophelia carefully removes it from its hiding place and turns over the gift tag. Her eyes read over the words twice before she says, "It's for Uncle Finn."

"Who is it from?" Michaela leans forward, intrigued by the mystery gift. Nick and I share a knowing look because we have been waiting for this since last night.

We had gone to Nick and Nina's Plaza penthouse last night for dinner, and within the first ten minutes of our arrival, Nick ushered me and Finn into his office. It wasn't unusual for the guys to sneak away when we all got together, but I knew this was more than our normal shoot-the-shit session. "Care to explain what is going on?" he said, closing the door to his office.

"I don't know what you mean," I said, sitting in one of the leather chairs in front of his desk.

"Don't play dumb, Josh." Finn scoffed. "You guys were a stone's throw away from the courthouse steps, now you're showing up on my doorstep together."

"You act like Nina didn't tell you." I looked at Nick, but he only shrugged.

"Dee just said you guys would both be at Christmas. She didn't say it would be *together*, so imagine my surprise when Finn over here texts me that you both showed up last night."

"Narc," I said to Finn, who only laughed. "I love her. I've always loved her, and I...I can't imagine my life without her. Unfortunately, it took almost losing her for me to pull my head out of my ass."

"We've all been there." Finn clapped me on the back.

And wasn't that the truth—each of us in that room had almost lost the woman we loved once, but by some miracle, we had pulled our heads out of our asses and told them how we felt.

"And on that topic...I have something to ask you guys," Finn said, and I had a feeling I already knew what it was. It was only a matter of time before this came up. Honestly, I was surprised it took this long. "I want to ask Michaela to marry me tomorrow at Christmas."

"Did you ask Dad?" I asked.

"Last week."

"Well, you got my vote," Nick said before they both turned to me.

If you had told me last year that my best friend and sister would be getting engaged, I would have called you a liar. But now, I can't imagine them with anyone else, even if it's still a little weird to see them that way. "You've always been like my brother, why not make it official?"

Now on Christmas morning, Finn catches Nick and me staring before he grins. "It says it's from the Davis boys."

Michaela's gaze snaps from Finn to me, to Nick, to Dad, and back to Finn. He continues undoing the bow wrapped intricately around the box. From the way my sister bounces with anticipation, he's moving too slowly, she wants to know what's in the box *right now*.

"Actually," Finn stops and hands the box to my sister. "You open it."

"But it says it's for you."

"Something tells me it's more for you than me."

Michaela narrows her gaze, slowly taking the box from his hands and untying the bow the rest of the way. Undoing the striped paper, she finds it's just a plain box. "What is this?"

Finn rolls his eyes and motions for her to *open* the box. Elizabeth squeezes my thigh as the rest of us watch in anticipation. She curls her bottom lip inward, biting down as she waits for Michaela to stop toying around and open the damn box. I press a kiss to her temple and watch as Michaela finally reveals the gift: a black velvet box. The waterworks start before she even opens the damn thing.

Ever so slowly, Finn drops from his spot on the couch onto one knee in front of her. "Michaela, I—"

"Yes!" She interrupts him, kissing him.

"You didn't even let him ask!" Mom shouts from behind her camera, which she had pulled out moments before.

"I don't care. Yes. That's my answer. Always yes."

forty-seven

NOW

A FEW HOURS LATER, a knock at the front door echoes down the hallway into the foyer, halting my conversation with Nick, Alex, and Lara, his new girlfriend (sorry, just his *friend* who's a girl). We exchange glances, unsure who that could be because anyone who was invited is already here. Another knock sounds as Finn appears from the kitchen to answer it.

"Sorry to bother you, Mr. Sheffield," I hear a gruff voice say. As Nick and I inch down the hall, I see Scott, head of building security, over Finn's shoulder. "We have a small problem."

"Is it Greta down the hall again?" Michaela asks from behind me and joins Finn at the door.

"Her name is Gladys." Finn sighs, pinching the bridge of his nose. This war my sister has going on with the neighbor is getting out of hand. Michaela swears up and down that the feud isn't her fault, that Gladys is just a crotchety old woman with a vendetta against her for some unknown reason. I'm not sure I believe that, but Finn doesn't seem to know the real reason, either.

"No." Scott chuckles. "It's not Mrs. Perry."

"What's going on, Scott?" Finn asks, trying to move the conversation along.

"There's a girl here asking for Mr. Davis." Scott beckons someone forward from down the hall. There's a slight delay before another security guard escorts a young girl down the hall. "Do any of you recognize her?"

Upon first glance, I swear I've met her before, but that's impossible. She can't be more than fourteen or fifteen years old. Her brown eyes meet mine, and there's a tug of familiarity between us. Do we know each other? I don't think so, but she looks so familiar.

"Is everything okay?" Nina suddenly appears.

"Everything's fine, Dee," Nick says, trying to usher her back to the living room.

"Why do you look so concerned, Scott?" She blatantly ignores her husband, stepping closer to the door.

"Not concerned, ma'am. Just curious if anyone knows this young lady."

"What's going on?" I hear Kai ask when he and Eileen join us. Looks like we're moving the party to the foyer. Moments later, Ophelia runs down the hallway, chased by Elizabeth, and the little girl runs straight into the legs of her father.

Elizabeth looks around, noticing the obvious tension in the room. Her eyes roam over each of us before landing on the girl standing in the doorway. Security still holds back the young brunette, waiting for someone to tell them what to do. "Everything okay?" she asks me in a hushed tone, but I shrug. Right now, I know about as much as she does.

"Michaela," Nina says and places a hand on my sister's arm. "Can you take Leia? Keep her busy."

Michaela huffs. I know she's annoyed that Nina wants *her* to take care of the kids. She wants to be in on the conversation, but she does she's told. She takes Ophelia by the hand and leads her toward the kitchen with a promise of ice cream, much to the dismay of her mother. That kid has already had enough candy and cookies to power a freight train. The last thing she needed was more sugar. I feel sorry for Kai and Eileen when they have to deal with her later.

Nina turns back to security when they're gone. "Explain now."

"Go ahead and tell them what you told us," Scott instructs the girl. The girl swallows hard, her eyes roaming over the group of strangers before her. When they land on me, she looks down at her shoes. "Don't be shy, go ahead."

"Hey, sweetie." Nina steps forward, placing a gentle hand on the girl's shoulder. "You're okay. We just want to know what you're looking for."

"My dad," the girl whispers, and I barely hear her over the sound of the music.

"And who's your dad?"

Her eyes shoot up to mine. "Josh Davis."

The world slows down. What did she just say? Did she just say *my* name? She can't be serious. This has to be some kind of joke. A sick one, but a joke nonetheless.

"Take her upstairs to the office." Nina directs Eileen. "Now, before the others see her."

"Is this some Godfather shit?" the young girl asks.

Nick chuckles. "No...Well, kind of."

Eileen shoots him a glare before wrapping her arm around the girl's shoulders. "C'mon, I'll show you the way."

She doesn't budge, instead, she looks at me for some kind of approval—her brown eyes wide with fear.

I don't know why I say it, but I offer her an encouraging smile and say, "It's okay. We'll be right there."

Eileen leads her away from the scene, security following closely behind.

"Can't we ever just have a normal holiday?" Kai asks.

"Where would the fun be in that?" Finn chuckles, walking

down the hallway toward the stairs.

I know it was meant to be a joke, but if someone walked in, they probably would think this is a scene from your favorite mobster show—*Godfather, Goodfellas, Scarface, Once Upon a Time in America*...take your pick. Eileen sits on the far edge of the couch, and Kai stands nearby, his arms crossed over his chest, leaning against the wall. Nick sits on the other end of the sofa. He keeps a close eye on his wife, who sits in the black leather armchair across the coffee table from the girl. Finn and I stand off to the side near the window while Elizabeth stands near the door. Occasionally, her eyes meet mine, and she offers a small smile, but the hesitation in brown her eyes doesn't go unnoticed.

We just figured our shit out, and now *this* happens. What. The. Fuck? Isn't that how life works, though? Out of the frying pan and into the fire.

Scott stands in the doorway, just in case. The young girl stares back at us from her place on the pristine white suede couch between Nick and Eileen. She sticks out like a sore thumb, dressed in high-waisted jeans and a white tank top with a green checkered flannel, especially compared to the rest of us who are dressed for the holiday. Her long brown hair ghosts across her back, landing just below her shoulder blades, and she switches between sitting on her hands and playing with a stray piece that hangs over her shoulder.

"What's your name, sweetie?" Nina asks. Her velvety voice wraps around the room like a warm blanket. If there's one thing Nina knows how to do, it's put you at ease in a stressful situation…Well, when she wants to. Again, one of those superpowers that comes from years of training at the hands of someone like Brina Villa.

"Brie," the girl says.

"Okay, Brie." Nina's reddish-brown lips pull into a soft smile. "What makes you think Josh is your dad?" Her green eyes pierce through me briefly as Brie begins to dig into her bag, and I notice Scott flinch, but Nina shakes her head at him, never taking her focus off the girl. Brie slides a piece of paper and an envelope across the table, and Nina examines them. The paper looks like some kind of official document, but I can't quite make out what it is from this angle. She looks over her shoulder at me. "Do you know a Juliet Sinclaire?"

Juliet Sinclaire.

Holy shit.

My eyes raise to meet Elizabeth, her features set in stone, waiting for my reply. This cannot be happening. We just got over this shit.

"How old are you?" I ask, turning back to Brie.

"I just turned fifteen." Brie chews on her bottom lip.

"Shit." I sigh, pinching the bridge of my nose. If Brie was born in December fifteen years ago, that would make it 2010. That would mean Juliet had to get pregnant in November, October, September…June…May…March. And that's when… Shit.

The timing adds up perfectly. I don't need to see the paper in Nina's hands, I know what it is. It's a birth certificate.

A fucking birth certificate with my name on it.

"That mean something?" Kai asks me.

I nod. "I met Juliet on spring break in Daytona almost sixteen years ago. We uh—we spent the week together, and you can guess what happened."

"Dammit, Josh," Finn mumbles. I glare at him. He's one to

talk. He had his own fling that week.

"Why now?" Kai steps away from the wall. "Why are you showing up now? And where is your mother, shouldn't she be with you?"

Brie shrugs. "I just found out. She's never told me much. I didn't know you were some old, rich guy."

"Far from." I chuckle.

"We'll need to do a paternity test," Nina says to no one in particular, continuing to stare at the birth certificate. Her eyes linger on the envelope for a moment before she looks up at me. Do I even want to know what that is? "Your name on a piece of paper doesn't mean anything."

"But the timing—"

"Still isn't solid evidence. She could've been with more than you that week."

While that's a fair statement, considering the circumstances, I know it isn't true, but I don't want to cause a fight in front of everyone—especially Brie—so I nod in understanding.

Elizabeth's stoic features chip away at the filling in the pit in my stomach that had been closed just over a week ago. She's trying to digest what's going on, what this means for us...She rips her gaze away from the carpet to look at Nina, a silent exchange passing between them.

I hate when they do that because it usually means I'm not going to like what comes next.

Nina sighs and tears away from her sister. "We'll get it figured out, but for now, we have a holiday to finish celebrating."

"I'm sure you're hungry too, huh?" Eileen asks Brie, and the teenager offers a small smile. "C'mon, let's get you something to eat. I think there's a few of the mini tree pizzas left."

"Mini tree pizzas?" Brie questions, following Eileen toward the door.

"Joshua Davis," Nina hisses when the office door closes behind them. *"Che cazzo sta succedendo?"* I don't know what that means, but I can take one guess, and it's not good.

I don't think I've ever seen Nina look this pissed. Her green eyes burn with such intensity, but the control she has over her emotions right now is incredible. She's ready to strangle me after everything that has already happened and now this…her patience is running ice thin. Nick touches her hand trying to calm her, but she pulls it from his grasp. Shit.

"I have no idea. I don't—"

"Well, you better get one." Her words drip with venom. "Fast."

Brie looks around the guest room in amazement, letting her duffel bag fall from her shoulder onto the green velvet ottoman at the foot of the bed. Michaela told me to put her in the guest room at the end of the hall, next to Mom and Dad. The room wasn't exactly ready for a guest, but we weren't expecting anyone else. There were a few boxes in the corner that Michaela still needed to go through from the move, and the dresser was covered in random shit: a few books, some design samples, and random knickknacks. Brie's right hand fingers the cream duvet, and she chews on the thumbnail of her left. Her head moves in sync with her eyes taking in every inch of the space—the floor-to-ceiling windows that overlook the city below us, the fireplace behind a plate of glass, the California King that takes up most of the back wall, the ensuite bathroom, and the walk-in closet. Finally, she looks at me. "I feel like I'm going to break something if I breathe the wrong way. It's so…perfect."

"Don't say that too loud. Michaela hates the fact someone is going to be in here, and it hasn't been prepped." I chuckle.

Eileen had introduced Brie to the rest of the family and when I finally came downstairs to rejoin them, Mom had already pulled Brie into her clutches. She led her around the kitchen filling her plate with a little bit of everything leftover from Christmas dinner. No one said anything, not even Michaela—I had a sneaky suspicion Finn warned her against it—and tiptoeing around the subject made it all the more awkward. Honestly, I kind of wish they had just come out and said whatever was on their mind, like ripping off a band-aid. It might sting a little at first, but at least you get it over with.

"Make yourself comfortable, Brie," I say, watching her continue to take in her new surroundings like she had been all evening. She had the same look of wonder and awe that I'd seen cross my family's face multiple times since we'd joined the Villa clan.

"But not too comfortable."

I pull my lips between my teeth, shoving my hands into my pockets as I rock back on my heels. What am I supposed to say? I don't even know how long this is going to last. I need to get in touch with Juliet and figure out what all of this means. Am I supposed to start taking Brie on weekends? Are we going to be splitting custody? Or does she still want sole custody? Will I have to pay child support?

"It's okay. I get it," Brie sighs. "Some random girl crashes your family Christmas and—"

"I don't want you to get the wrong idea of me, Brie, but you have to understand this is weird for me. I had no idea your mother got pregnant. I haven't spoken to her in years. Had I known—"

"What, you would've done the noble thing and taken responsibility? Maybe even married her to uphold her reputation? This isn't the old days; you don't have to do that shit anymore."

"Language."

"Like you've never heard it before?" She rolls her eyes.

Oh God, is this what it's like to deal with a teenager?

"That's not the point," I say. "You're fifteen, you shouldn't—"

"Exactly. I'm old enough to use words like that." Brie stops me when I try to fight her on it further. "Oh, trust me." Brie scoffs. "I've said *way* worse."

I take a deep breath but let it go. I'm not here to fight with her. I'm here to try and figure out what is going on, and the best way to do that is to get ahold of Juliet. "When you get a minute, can you give me your mother's number?"

"Why?" I don't miss the way Brie's eyes light up.

"I want to speak with her about all of this. There are a lot of things we need to figure out. The sooner I can get ahold of her, the sooner we can figure out how long you'll be staying."

And the sooner I can put any doubts Elizabeth may have behind us.

Walking into the bedroom is like déjà vu. Elizabeth sits on the ottoman against the floor-to-ceiling window overlooking the East side of Manhattan. She has shed her clothes from the day and changed into a white nightgown that looks delicious against her tanned skin.

"A kid, Josh?" Elizabeth asks before I can say anything. She turns from the window, her lips set into a straight line. I've been dreading this conversation since Brie uttered my name at the front door. "How are we supposed to—"

"I didn't know!" I sigh, falling onto the edge of the bed, and rub my eyes.

"Awesome, this is just fan-freaking-tastic."

"Sugar, you can't be mad at me for something I didn't even know about until a few hours ago."

"Is this what she wanted to tell you?" She asks, but I don't have an answer. The truth is, I don't know what she wanted to tell me last year, but I can only assume it had something to do with this. Why didn't she show up to the cafe last July? "Josh," Elizabeth says quietly, drawing my gaze to her. "I'm not going to get mad, okay? But, you have to tell me the truth. What happened when you went to Wichita?"

Is she implying that I lied about not seeing Juliet last year?

"Elizabeth, I haven't seen Juliet since twenty-ten. I told you, she never showed up last year. I swear to you—"

"She knew our address, for godsakes. How would she get that unless—"

"I don't know!" I dig my fingers into my hair, standing from the bed and tugging on the strands. "I don't know. And I know that's not a good enough answer, but it's the truth. I have no idea how she found our address or how Brie found Michaela's. The whole thing makes no sense."

"I will not be made a fool of, Joshua Davis." Elizabeth takes a deep breath, her hands clenching the edge of the ottoman. "This has to be what she wanted to tell you. This is *why* she wrote that letter. She wants to—"

"Elizabeth, stop."

I cross the room and kneel in front of her. Taking her hands in mine, I try to gain her attention. "Look at me," I beg, but she still refuses. I grip her chin finally turning her gaze toward mine. "It's all going to be okay, Sugar. We'll figure it out."

"What if Brie *is* your daughter?"

"Then we find a way to deal with it. Together." A sigh of relief escapes me when Elizabeth slumps forward resting her forehead on my shoulder. I tighten my arms around her, kissing her temple. "I love you."

"You better."

forty-seven

THEN

October 2024

HAVE YOU EVER BEEN to a wedding with your soon-to-be ex-wife, but nobody *knows* she's your soon-to-be ex-wife? No? Well, I don't recommend it.

Thankfully, we have both been too preoccupied with wedding hoopla to see much of each other, but at the end of the day, when everyone goes to bed, we're left to deal with one another in the close quarters of the hotel room. We can't have separate rooms, that would raise brows. I don't think we've spoken a word to each other away from the others… No, scratch that. She huffed out a *goody* from the passenger seat of my Bronco when I quoted the trip from our house in Winchester to the Alderidge Estate at a little over two hours.

But tonight at the reception, I have found it hard to differentiate between what is real and what isn't. I haven't heard her laugh in months, but she giggles and clings to my arm as we sit in conversation with other party guests. And when she drags me to the dance floor, I feel a high like never before…

Holding her in my arms, dancing beneath the starry sky…

it feels like a dream. I cradle her hand in mine between our beating hearts and sway to the gentle beat of a country ballad about falling in love. Her brown eyes tell a different story than her actions the rest of the weekend, and without saying it, I'm sure she feels that tug between us, too. When the song ends, I can't fight the urge to swoop down and kiss her.

She doesn't retreat like I thought she would, and it's not just because everyone is watching. Her right hand threads through the hair at my nape and pulls my mouth back to hers when I pull away—only to be interrupted when a cough sounds behind us. We turn to see none other than the bride.

"Mind if I steal your...husband for a moment?" Nina asks with a hesitant smile, looking between the two of us.

She knows the truth; I know she does. The subtle hints she has been dropping all weekend tell me she knows. It's a weird feeling knowing that someone knows something about you, but on the off chance you're wrong about it, you don't want to say anything. I mean, imagine *that* conversation.

"Shouldn't you be off doing married woman things?" I chuckle, but she doesn't reciprocate it.

"Everything okay, Nin?" Elizabeth asks, our hands still intertwined between us. I give her hand a gentle squeeze, which she reciprocates.

"Fine. I might suggest you find your way to the hotel though. Before Finn leaves," Nina says, looking over her shoulder when Nick calls to her. He stands at the edge of the dance floor with a pair of older gentlemen I think he said were from the Villa Inc. board.

"What do you mean?" Elizabeth asks.

"Just try to catch him before he's gone." Nina ignores Elizabeth, directing her demand at me before she finally meets her husband and their guests.

Elizabeth and I share a questioning glance. Why is it so important I catch him before he leaves? I just spoke to Finn not even an hour ago. I caught up with him before he left the reception. He mentioned he wasn't going to make it to brunch tomorrow, something about needing to get back to the city for some Sheffield House plans. That didn't seem out of the ordinary. Since the launch, he's been inundated with all things Sheffield House. So, why was Nina so adamant I needed to catch up to him?

When we get back to the hotel, I practically run straight into the man I'm supposed to be looking for. Heeding Nina's warning, I suggest we have one more drink before he leaves for the airport. He's about to decline the invite, but I insist and push him toward the hotel bar. It doesn't take long for the floodgates to open, and he lets it slip that my sister has decided to go back to what should have been her soon-to-be ex-husband, David.

"What the fuck do you mean, she's going back to David?" I hiss. "You guys just started dating! I thought everything was—"

"We haven't spoken since the launch gala. Tonight was the first time I've seen her. " Finn scoffs, staring into the amber liquid in his glass. There's a sadness in his voice I've never heard before. "Found out about Oliver and his little wager, said I wasn't honest with her about my intentions."

"Finn—"

"No, Josh. It's okay." He sighs, downing the rest of his drink. "Probably for the best, anyway." He slaps a fifty on the bar and claps me on the back, heaving his bag on his shoulder and walking out of the hotel.

"What was that about?" Elizabeth asks when I walk back into our hotel room.

I sit on the ottoman at the foot of the bed, still trying to comprehend what my best friend just told me. How can my sister do this? Why would she do this? I need to talk to Michaela. To try and knock some fucking sense into her.

Elizabeth calls my name from the bathroom doorway. Her blonde hair has been unleashed from the mess of rubber bands and bobby pins that held it together earlier, brushing against her shoulders. I miss the longer length she used to keep, but this new length accentuates her facial features better. Either way, she's fucking beautiful. The most beautiful woman on the damn planet, and she's all mine…

Or she was.

It won't be long before I've lost her for good and there's not a damn thing I can do about it.

Elizabeth says something else, but I can't hear her over the thoughts running through my head or the pounding of blood in my ears.

What happens next occurs so quickly that I don't realize I've crossed the room and reached the threshold until I feel my lips on hers. She doesn't resist; she doesn't even seem surprised. She meets my kiss with her own, gripping the front of my shirt to pull me close.

God forgive me, I know this is going to make things worse between us, but I'm going to devour her tonight if she allows. I may never be allowed to be with her again, to *show* her how much I love her…I need to grasp the opportunity while it's right in front of me.

"Josh," she whispers, pulling back just enough to put a small gap between us, but she has yet to let go of my shirt.

"Do you want me to stop?"

She takes in a soft breath but doesn't reply.

"Sugar." I plant my left hand against the doorframe and grip her chin to lift her gaze to mine. Her body presses forward involuntarily as her tongue pokes out to wet her lips. "What do you want?"

Her brown eyes darken.

"We can stop right now," I say.

"Is that what *you* want?" Elizabeth asks, her fingers toying with the hem of my dress pants.

"Not even close, Sugar." The pads of my fingers skate along her jaw, pulling her mouth back to mine, but I don't let our lips touch. She gasps when I nip at her bottom lip. "Tell me you want this, Elizabeth. That you want me."

Her brows pinch together, eyes roaming my face before she whispers, "I *need* you, Josh."

Her words send the blood rushing to my cock. Elizabeth closes the gap between us and I can taste the wine on her tongue. Her fingertips take their time as if rememorizing every crevice and ridge as they slide up my chest, gliding around the sides of my neck and interlocking at the base of my skull.

Keeping one hand braced against the wall, my other tugs at the messy blonde waves. I move from her mouth to her jaw, working my way down the column of her throat. I nip at her collarbone, sucking the sweet skin between my teeth, soothing the bite with my tongue. Repeating the process until the beginnings of a mark form. Her head falls back against the wall, pressing her chest flush against mine, and I can feel her nipples through the fabric of the burgundy-colored dress.

I can't wait to rip the damn thing off, but not yet...Patience is a virtue and if this is truly the last opportunity I have to show this woman my love for her, I'm going to take my time.

Kissing her again, I nudge her legs apart with my foot, and lift my thigh to meet her center. She moans against my mouth when my leg presses against her clit, and she grinds against me, chasing after her release. The sleeves of her dress begin to fall down the slopes of her shoulders, exposing the swell of her breasts.

"Good baby," I whisper, pulling away from her mouth to watch. Wet arousal begins to cover my leg and just knowing the effect this is having on her makes me grow harder. Her head falls back, eyes screwed shut and she rubs against me, growing needier by the second, as I grind into her. "Eyes on me, Sugar." I grasp her chin, forcing her brown eyes to meet mine. "Do you want to come?"

She whines, her nails digging into the white shirt that covers my shoulders.

I pull her mouth back to mine in a searing kiss and press my thigh a little further into her clit, until my name falls off her lips and her orgasm rips through her. Her hands clutch my shirt as I work her through the release, watching her come undone in the palms of my hands. And it's fucking breathtaking.

She takes a few steadying breaths, but I don't wait for her to catch her breath, lifting her off her feet and slinging her legs over my hips, pinning her against the wall. I kiss and lick the delicate skin of her neck, pulling the top of her dress completely off her arms to expose her chest. Her nipples are like perfect little peaks. I cup one of her breasts in my hand, massaging the doughy flesh and pinching the sensitive bud. When I press my mouth to hers again, there's nothing calculated about the way I kiss her. It's frantic and messy, but she meets me with the same amount of passion, and I fucking love it.

"Josh," she pleads, grinding her pussy over my throbbing erection.

"Let's see how wet you are for me," I say, using my hips to pin her to the wall. I pull her dress up, bunching the fabric around her waist. Pushing the material of her underwear out of the way, I run my finger up her slit and hum in satisfaction. "Fuck, Sugar. You're drenched."

Her head falls back against the wall when I slip one finger inside her, using my thumb to circle her clit.

"Shit," she exhales when I pull my finger from her and slip it into my mouth, moaning at the taste of her.

I carry her to the bed, dropping her on her back, my mouth still latched to her, sucking the delicate skin behind her ear. Her fingers grab for the buttons on my shirt, undoing them as I kiss down the column of her throat. Soft hands rake down my chest, finally opening the white dress shirt.

Elizabeth presses her lips to my throat, planting soft kisses on my skin, before she pulls my mouth back to hers. "Please fuck me, Josh," she begs, and something swells inside my chest.

Fear? Regret? Need? Love? A combination of all four? I don't know how to describe it, but it makes my chest tighten. What are we doing? We shouldn't be doing this. We've been separated for months, living separate lives unbeknownst to everyone else. When we wake up tomorrow, we won't go back to Josh and Elizabeth, we'll still be Josh *and* Elizabeth. We'll go back to our new lives, apart from one another...

"Baby," Elizabeth whispers, gripping my chin to bring my gaze back to her. "Don't. Don't think about it. Tonight, it's you and me. Okay?"

My tongue pokes out to wet my lips, and I slowly begin to meet her nod with my own, but not without seeing the saddened look in her warm chocolate eyes. I don't miss the tears that collect in the corners of her eyes as she brushes her fingers along the side of my face, offering me a soft smile.

"I want *you*, Josh. I've always wanted you."

"Then kiss me, Sugar."

And she does, soft and leisurely, nails raking through my hair.

I cup her face as we take our time. This kiss isn't like the others, it's not frantic or messy. Our mouths mold together, tongues tangling in a dance as we relish in the moment. And there isn't a damn question in my mind about whether this is real. I know it is...was.

We shrug out of our clothes, letting them fall to the floor without caring where they land.

"Come here," I urge when I crawl back onto the bed, wrapping my arm around her waist and pulling her to straddle me.

Her palms brace against my chest, rocking her hips against mine, and my cock hardens. She leans down to kiss me and I cradle her neck, exchanging a few wet kisses. My fingers dig into the flesh of her hips when she lifts, rubbing against my length.

It's been too long since I had her last, and the anticipation is fucking brutal.

Centering my cock, Elizabeth's head falls back as soon as the tip rubs against her entrance. I waste no time, gripping her hips and pushing into her with a shared gasp.

"You okay, Sugar?" I ask, and she nods fervently, lowering herself further until she is fully seated on me. "You're so tight, my god," I hiss.

She begins to rock her hips slowly, taking her time, and I let her set the pace. Her head falls back again and the view is fucking spectacular. She's perfect. The same emotion from earlier builds in my chest again, but I refuse to let it boil over. Not right now. Right now I'm going to enjoy the view and enjoy the last little bit of time I have with this magnificent woman.

"Right here, baby." Elizabeth brings my attention back to her.

"I'm with you, Sugar," I say, bringing her lips down to mine. She gasps when I flex my hips into her, taking control. Her tits rub against my chest as she clutches the comforter on either side of my head, the soft moans of pleasure spilling from her lips spurring me on. Sounds of wet skin fill the room. Warm breaths and wet kisses pepper the side of my face and neck as I thrust into her. She whispers small words of love and praise against my ear, and I realize this isn't just one last hoorah before we hit the road. This is so much more than that, but that nagging feeling is back and I know this won't last. It was never meant to.

"Josh," she cries when my thumb finds her clit. It doesn't take long for her to fall over the edge, her pussy gripping me as her mouth falls open in ecstasy. And I fall with her, giving myself to her one last time.

We lay like that for a while, catching our breath and letting the high last for as long as possible. After a few more moments, Elizabeth kisses me and rolls to her side. I pull her into my side and kiss the crown of her head.

"You wanna talk about it?" She asks, letting her arms drape across my waist. "What Finn said, I mean."

I take a deep breath, drawing invisible circles against the skin of her shoulder. "My sister is going back to David."

"Michaela." She sighs.

"Don't know what happened, but she told Finn tonight at the reception when he tried to talk to her...Something happened at the gala and she's been avoiding him since."

Elizabeth huffs out another breath, burying herself into my side. "Don't be too hard on her, Josh."

"Easier said than done, Sugar." I kiss the top of her head again and pull her close, inhaling her scent as it's mixed with mine. Before I know it, soft snores fall from her lips and the sound makes me smile. "Goodnight, baby."

forty-nine

THEN

October 2024

"HAS ANYONE SEEN FINN?" Dean asks the next morning. Stuffing a cheese Danish in his mouth, he plops down in a seat next to Michaela across the table. "I gotta talk to him about Christmas."

"I haven't seen him since the bouquet toss," Alex says, massaging his temples from behind a pair of sunglasses. Elizabeth gave him some Tylenol earlier, but it doesn't seem to be helping. Poor kid, I can't imagine it's much fun watching your brother remarry his wife not long after your girlfriend rejects your marriage proposal. Truth be told, I'm not that surprised. Anna was nice, but she didn't seem like the one he'd eventually settle down with. Alex needed someone to match his energy—someone who could be a proper young lady when she needed to be but could let her hair down and be a goofball too. Anna leaned heavily on the proper young lady, all the time.

Without looking up from my plate, I say, "Finn left last night."

"What the hell for? We're supposed to hang out today."

350

Dean rolls his eyes before zeroing in on Raeanne who walks into the restaurant. He follows her every move, even motions for her to sit next to him, but she completely ignores him. If what Finn said is true, he went traipsing through the garden last night with another girl, and I get the feeling Rae has had enough of his antics with the way she seems to be actively avoiding him. She goes as far as to sit at the opposite end of the table.

"Had some family shit to take care of."

"Oh!" Romy—Nina's cousin from Italy—appears with a mimosa in hand. A smirk pulls on her bright red lips as her boyfriend, Enzo, pulls out the chair next to Alex for her. "Michaela, you're here? I didn't think we'd see you this morning."

"And, why's that?" My sister rolls her eyes. I don't understand Michaela's dislike of Romy, she seems sweet.

"Well, when you disappeared with Finn last night, I figured you'd be a little indisposed this morning." Romy tries to stifle a giggle, hiding behind her hand.

The fork in my hand clatters on the plate at her words, silencing conversation around the table. Glancing up, I glare at my sister before pushing back from the table without a word.

Shoving open the door to the patio of the restaurant, I take a deep breath and let out a frustrated sigh. How can my sister sit there and act like everything is fine? Has she even told Mom and Dad what she is doing—or is she hiding it from them, too? First, she hides the fact she's getting divorced. Then forgets to mention she is dating my best friend, who she has supposedly hated all this time. And now, she can't even tell us that she's going back to her husband. I have to find out from the man she was dating not even two weeks ago…What is with her and these secrets?

The patio door opens again and I already know who it is. "Don't," I say as she opens her mouth to say something. I don't want to hear whatever excuse she's about to spew. "Don't fucking start your bullshit, Michaela."

"My bullshit?" She scoffs. "You're the one acting like a child stomping away from the table like that."

"Unbelievable," I say, my tongue running over the back of my front teeth. "You're like a toddler who can't decide which toy she wants, so you take them all until you're tired of them."

Tears form in her blue eyes, avoiding my stare. I guess she's not feeling so confident now, huh?

"I didn't mean for any of this to happen, Josh. I thought I was over David. I thought we were done. We *were* done, but then—"

"Forgive me if I don't give a fuck, Michaela Jane." A half chuckle spills from my lips.

She stands there acting like she's sorry for what she's doing. What she's done. When in reality, she couldn't give two shits about anyone but herself and not how this affects me. *Finn.* I mean, how this affects Finn.

"You know, I thought Finn would be the one to hurt you, but turns out you're the one who ended up breaking his heart."

"Broke his—I broke his heart? Josh, do you hear yourself? A month ago, you were pissed at the thought of us dating! Now you're defending him?"

"I'm tired of your shit. Don't fucking bring David around because I don't want anything to do with him or your 'marriage.'"

"He's my husband, Josh! That has to count for something. If anyone should understand that, it's you. You and Elizabeth—"

"What makes you think this time will be any different?"

I don't need to ask the question because I already know the answer. It won't be different. David is a controlling asshole, but no one ever wanted to talk about it before. Everyone was okay with sweeping the truth under the rug because Michaela pretended to be happy. She has always pretended not to notice what an asshole he is and how he hates our family. Not anymore. I'm done pretending not to notice the way he treats her like an accessory instead of a human being—instead of his wife.

"You're choosing *him* over me?" Michaela cries.

This isn't me choosing Finn over her. This is me choosing my sister. Supporting her the best way I can because I refuse to watch as she hurts herself.

"I'm your sister! Does that mean nothing to you?" She scoffs when I don't respond. "So, I'm back to the annoying kid sister you left behind, while you *once again* choose your friends over me. You don't want to include me in your shit, but you feel *just* guilty enough to let me stand on the sidelines and watch. Watch as you live your perfect life with your perfect friends, your perfect house, your perfect job, and your own perfect marriage."

If she only knew.

"And I'm expected to be the good little girl who is seen and not heard—that's what you want, right?"

Well, she is right, but I'm not the one who wants her to be that way. She's having this conversation with the *wrong* person. My sister needs to have this conversation with her husband.

"You didn't answer the question, Michaela," I say. "What's going to be different?"

Michaela's shoulders slump and she refuses to look at me, staring off into the distant mountains. She bites down on her bottom lip, eyes beginning to glaze over. "He's my husband."

"Y'know." I scoff. "Finn was wrong when he said you were *acting* stupid."

"Fuck you, Josh. I'm not—"

"Hey, can you two wrap it up?" Elizabeth says, stepping out the door. "Nick and Nina just got here."

"We're done," I say. If my sister wants to run back to David with her tail between her legs that's her problem, not mine.

Nothing I say is going to change her mind. She has to figure this out on her own.

"You okay?" Elizabeth asks, touching my arm when I reach the door.

"She's being fucking stupid," I say, shaking my head.

Elizabeth motions inside. "I got this, okay? Just make sure they stay preoccupied and don't let them know what's going on."

"I think you underestimate Nina's spidey senses."

Elizabeth rolls her eyes and leans in to place a soft peck on my cheek. "Just try to cool off a little. She needs her big brother, not another dad."

"Thank you," I say, keeping my eyes on the road. The car ride home hasn't been as silent as the one to the wedding. That's a good sign, right? We've at least had small conversations here and there, nothing groundbreaking, but that's...progress. "For talking to Michaela earlier."

"Josh." Elizabeth sighs. "I know you're just worried about her, but you realize you're being a little hypocritical, right?"

"Hypocritical?" I scoff. "Elizabeth, she's been lying to everyone!"

"So have we." Elizabeth laughs. "Josh, we haven't been the most honest with everyone either. Getting mad at her for not telling you what's been going on, kind of makes you a—"

"Hypocrite." I sigh.

"Look, I get it, but you have to look at it from her perspective. She sees everyone around her with these long-term relationships. You, your parents, Nick and Nina...I'm not surprised she tried to hide it."

"I don't understand why she's going back to David. Finn—"

"Loves her. Finn is completely in love with your sister. And that's why he's letting her do this. Why he's letting her go. He wants her to be happy, and if she thinks this is the thing that will make her happy...then he will let her go."

I get the feeling we're not talking about just Michaela anymore.

When I glance to my right, Elizabeth is no longer looking at me, her gaze locked on laced fingers in her lap. We shouldn't have done what we did last night, we both know that, but I don't regret it. Even if she does, I can't bring myself to regret making love to her one more time before I have to let her go. With my eyes back on the road, I reach my hand across the console and take both of hers in mine, squeezing gently. I swear I feel a wet drop land on my skin before she slides her left hand into mine, covering them with her other one.

The rest of the car ride is quiet, our hands intertwined on her lap, and when we pull into the driveway an hour later, neither makes the first move to get out.

"I bought a house," Elizabeth whispers after a few minutes. The words chip away at what's left of my heart. She bought a house...by herself. "In Jupiter Beach."

What does she want me to say? Don't go?

Nothing I can say will change her mind. This is what's going to make her happy. And who am I to stand in the way of her happiness? I've been doing that for the past nine years. It's time for her to get what she wants without me getting in her way.

Elizabeth leans across the center console and ghosts her lips over my cheek. "Goodbye, Josh."

fifty

THE HUM OF THE crowded diner is better than the deafening silence of the taxi ride. My legs feel almost confined underneath the table. My chest tightens every so often, and I need to take a deep breath, but it never feels deep enough to free the grip on my lungs. I'm still trying to figure out what I'm supposed to do with a teenager who quite literally just walked into my life. When I woke up yesterday morning, I expected to enjoy Christmas with my wife and family as we did our best to get back into the swing of things. There was zero cause for excitement. But now…Well, nothing could have prepared me for this.

Brie looks around the restaurant with the occasional glance in my direction, but never enough to make full eye contact. I'm surprised she isn't staring into her phone. Isn't that what most teenagers do? Instead, it sits facedown on the table but not too far from her, and she sits on her hands. Most of her pent-up energy is being released through the shaking of her leg. How do I know? Because it's vibrating the entire table. Occasionally, it will stop, only to pick up after just a few seconds.

"So..."

"Here we go, folks," the waitress interrupts right on time, dropping a plate in front of me. Steak and eggs. She drops a stack of pancakes in front of Brie, who starts digging into the food like she hasn't eaten in days. The same way she did last night when Mom helped her put together a plate of food.

"Hungry?" I raise an eyebrow, and she freezes. Her brown eyes lift from the plate as she swallows the bite she had just taken. "If you like those, you should try Tessa's cake down at Honeybee's. Best ones in all of South Carolina."

"Sorry. I haven't eaten much, being on the bus and all."

"You rode the bus by yourself?"

Brie shrugs, stabbing a loose piece of pancake. "It's not as bad as it sounds."

"Brie." I sigh and shove my plate away. "I have to ask, how did you find me? Your mother and I haven't exactly kept in touch the last fifteen years."

Instead of answering, she takes a large gulp of coffee. Black with exactly two sugars. I had been opposed to letting her order a coffee—what fifteen-year-old needs coffee?—but I didn't put up much of a fight.

"How did you find me?" I ask again.

"It's not hard when you're related to people like the Villas."

That's fair. I have always done my best to remain as low-profile as possible, and Nina does a great job at keeping her private life private, but there will always be a certain level of publicity when it comes to the Villas. How could there not be when you own the largest investment firm in the world? Ric's death was a tragedy on a global scale. There were family, friends, and business partners from all over the world at his funeral. And then there's my sister...She does not maintain a low profile online. Neither does Finn, come to think of it.

She pops the pancake in her mouth. "And I found the letter

you wrote Mom."

Right.

The letter I wrote back to Juliet last year.

I almost forgot about that. The one I sent to the return address with a simple *I'll be there.* What else was I supposed to say? I wonder if that is the envelope Brie handed Nina with the birth certificate last night.

"Does your mother know you're here?"

"Of course." Brie scoffs. "What, do you think I just ran away from home and didn't tell her where I was going?"

"Well, I didn't, but now I'm starting to wonder."

"Yes, she knows where I am." Brie rolls her eyes with so much exaggeration I'm surprised they don't fall out of her head onto the black and white tiled floor.

"Why didn't she call me first? Or send a message. Anything to let me know this was happening."

Brie shrugs, taking another bite. "Guess she wanted to surprise you."

Juliet was pretty spontaneous and free-spirited, but I would think she might call about something like this. Warn me that she's been hiding a daughter for the last fifteen years, and *Oh, by the way, I'm sending her up to New York to meet you.*

"You guys don't trust me," Brie says. It's less of a question and more of a statement.

Can you blame us?

"It's not that we don't trust you," I say, trying to think of the right way to phrase it. "We just don't know you."

"You don't know that I'm telling the truth."

"That too." I can't lie to her. Scratch that, I won't lie to her. "I'm not trying to say you're a liar or that your mom is, but—"

"I get it, *Mr. Davis.* I mean, I did kind of spring this on you."

"You don't have to call me that."

"What would you prefer?" Brie raises a curious eyebrow, and I find myself tongue-tied. I don't have an answer, but Mr.

Davis seems way too formal.

"Let's just stick with Josh for now."

"Sure, *Josh.*" She offers a tight smile before taking another sip of coffee.

"Now that we have you alone," Michaela says, falling on the couch next to Finn.

When I try to get up and make my escape, she pushes me back into the chair. I have no one to save me from this impending interrogation. It's just the three of us here. Dad has been gone all day with Uncle Jim—they're seeing a concert or something—and Mom took Brie shopping as soon as we got back from breakfast. Brie showed up with a duffle bag filled with only a few days worth of clothes and a backpack filled to the brim with books. She assured me she didn't need any more clothes (that's what a washing machine was for). But until I can get ahold of Juliet, I need to make sure she has whatever she needs. And I'm more than happy to let Mom take the lead on shopping. I wouldn't have the slightest idea where to start. I was surprised when Elizabeth decided to tag along, but she'd probably have a better idea of what a teenager would like over Mom. Glancing at the clock, I still have two hours before I need to leave, but I could find something to do to pass the time. This is New York; there's always something to do. Before I can put my plan into action Michaela starts with, "How are you feeling?"

"About?" I ask.

"Don't be coy, Josh."

"I'm not discussing this with you, MJ." I roll my eyes, and suddenly, a glass of the amber liquid on the bar shelf in the corner looks pretty good.

No. Alcohol isn't going to help this situation. It's only going to make me more annoyed with my sister.

"Josh—"

"You were in on this?" I ask Finn, and he shrugs.

"Listen, man, you've been through the ringer the past few months. We just want to make sure you're okay." Finn adjusts his position, stretching his arm behind Michaela on the back of the couch, his fingers ghosting across the exposed skin just beneath the sleeve of her shirt.

The sun reflects off the diamond on her finger when Michaela takes a sip of her hot chocolate. "Yeah, c'mon, spill. You gotta know something about her or her mom."

"I don't know anything."

Why is that so hard to believe?

My sister mumbles something that sounds like "liar" behind her mug.

"I am fine, okay? Everything is fine. We're going to get it all straightened out, I mean, we don't even know if—"

"Oh, trust me." Finn stops me. "There is *no* denying it. She has your eyes."

"Your nose, too," Michaela adds. "What does her mom look like?"

"She was cute from what I remember," Finn says.

"You met her?" If Michaela's head whipped around any faster, it might have twisted all the way around.

"Spring break twenty-ten was a good time." Finn smirks, raising a knowing brow toward me, and I roll my eyes. My sister smacks his chest, and Finn chuckles, kissing her temple. "I can think of something a lot more fun, though." He winks at her, and I have to resist the urge to gag.

"Well, as fun as this hasn't been," I say, clapping my hands down on the tops of my thighs and standing from the chair. "I have to go. Nina has requested our presence at her office."

"It's the day after Christmas," Michaela protests.

"You know who we're talking about, right?"

She rolls her eyes. "Well, bring back some pizza when you come home."

"Just order it, MJ," I say over my shoulder, walking into the kitchen as she says something about wanting it from the place near Columbus Circle. "I'm going to Corporate, not DV."

"Oh good, then grab—" I don't hear the rest of her request, picking up my pace to the door.

I have no idea what to expect walking into Villa Inc. The office is empty, as one would expect the day after Christmas, and it will stay that way until January 5th of next year, minus the occasional visit from the woman who called me here today. The woman never stops, I swear.

Turning the corner to walk down the hallway leading to the offices that belong to Nina and Kai, I see Mom step out of the restroom. She straightens out her dress and almost begins her way back down the hallway, but catches sight of me first.

"Oh, there you are, Joshua," she huffs. "I was beginning to wonder if you'd make it at all."

"I was helping Michaela with something. Lost track of time." The truth was, I started walking and somehow ended up by the Empire State Building. When I realized I needed to get back down to the Financial District, traffic was a shitshow. But she didn't need to know that.

"So, you don't tell your mother anything anymore?"

"What's that supposed to mean?"

"Well, first you don't tell me that you and Elizabeth have decided to stay together, and then I find out from *Eileen,* of all people, that you have a daughter."

Why did she say Eileen's name like that? Eileen has been nothing but nice to her.

"I suppose I should be happy because you and Elizabeth haven't been very gracious in the grandchildren department, have you? I'll take what I can get." Mom shakes her head. "Not sure how I'm going to explain this back home, though."

"Tell those busybodies to mind their own damn business."

"Watch your mouth, Josh. I am still your mother."

"And you've been a disappointing one at that," Elizabeth says, interrupting our conversation as she walks down the hallway.

"What's the supposed to mean?" Mom scoffs.

"I know all about your conversations with Josh over the past ten years." Elizabeth loops her arm through mine when she reaches us, squeezing my hand gently. "Telling him that he's not good enough, not worthy of me or this life. I would have expected something like that from Brina, but never you, Jenny."

"You two may not like the way I've handled things, but without me *and* Brina, this little union would've never happened."

"I think we would've figured it out eventually."

While I'd like to agree with my wife, I don't know if I can. Before this arrangement, neither of us had ever looked at each other as anything more than an annoyance that came with being within the radius of Nina and Michaela. But I suppose stranger things have happened, and if something is meant to be, it will always find a way...Right?

"Does Brina know you've decided to stay together?" Mom

asks, straightening her shoulders. "I'm sure she'd love to know."

"I couldn't care less what that bitch thinks." Elizabeth practically laughs. "She single-handedly almost dismantled the only family I have left. She can rot alone in that SoHo apartment for all I care."

"Shame." Mom glances at me, then Elizabeth, and back at me. "Don't mess it up this time, Josh." She turns on her heel and walks down the hallway to Nina's office.

"I know I shouldn't have said anything, but…I came looking for you when you weren't here yet, and—"

"Thank you," I say, halting her explanation. Elizabeth smiles, standing on her tiptoes to kiss me, and drags me down the hall to our awaiting doom.

Walking into the office, Brie is showing off a long sleeve lavender-colored sequin dress that looks like it won't even cover her ass. There are multiple shopping bags at her feet from the shopping haul and I'm scared to see what else lies in those bags. Nina sits behind her desk and only seems half-interested in the display Brie has been putting on, meeting my stare from the doorway. I doubt she's happy I was late, and even later now with my altercation with Mom.

"Where's the rest of it?" I ask, motioning toward the dress. Nina raises a brow before she glances at Elizabeth.

"It's a lot longer than it looks," Brie defends, stuffing the dress back into the bag.

"Come along, Brie," Mom says. "We best leave them to their business."

"Yes, ma'am."

"I told you, call me Grandma."

Brie tries to hide her giggle. "Yes, *Grandma*."

The corners of Brie's lips pull back slightly when she passes by me, but she doesn't say any more until they're outside the office, and then they burst into a fit of giggles. The whole interaction makes me sick to my stomach thinking back to what Mom said in the hallway.

When their voices fade down the hall, Nina motions for me to close the door, and a new fire ignites in my nervous system.

Fuck, we are so fucked.

Being across from a disappointed Nina is almost worse than being across from a disappointed Ric. Being here reminds me of the day he called us to his office because he discovered the truth about our marriage. Ric was angry, rightfully so, I suppose. He had opened his home and his family, to me and my family. And weeks before we were supposed to walk down the aisle, he found out it was all a farce.

That was one of the hardest conversations I've ever had, but it almost feels worse letting Nina down.

Nina motions with her eyes for me to sit in the chair, but I lean over the back of it instead. I can't sit, I'm too full of nerves.

Elizabeth doesn't waste any more time, sitting in the other chair. "What is this about, Nin?"

"I want to have someone do some digging."

What does that mean?

Nina looks between us before settling on Elizabeth. "We know next to nothing about this girl. For all we know, she could be some scam artist."

"You can't be serious," I say, but her face doesn't falter. "Nina, she's not a scam artist. She's a kid!"

"Who can easily be manipulated." Her piercing gaze sets on me now. "When was the last time you saw this Juliet person?"

I'd like to say it hasn't been fifteen years, but that isn't the truth. While I may have "heard" from her, I haven't seen her since I left her in the parking lot of that motel. I sigh, looking down at my folded hands over the edge of the chair. "I haven't seen her since Daytona."

"You're part of this family, Josh," Nina says. "And with that comes situations like this. When things like this happen, actions have to be taken. Whether you like it or not."

There's a knock at the door, and my stomach sinks. Who the fuck is that? Nina glances at the door and back at us. With a tight smile, she pushes from the desk to answer the door. It feels like five years as she walks around the desk, crossing the room. There's a click of her heel against the floor with each step until she grips the handle and takes her sweet time swinging the door open. An older gentleman stands on the other side. He removes his hat briefly and nods toward her, stepping inside.

"Josh, Elizabeth, this is Ed Brown, private investigator," Nina introduces us, and Ed tips his hat toward us. "He's gonna help with your little...problem."

fifty-one

NOW

"HAVE YOU SPOKEN TO her mom yet?" Nick takes a sip of his beer.

It's been three days since we met Ed Brown in Nina's office, and he has yet to turn up with any information. He's a gruff man with a medium build and a bald head that he hides underneath a black fedora. His pressed three-piece suit looked tailor-made, with a Christmas tie and leather shoes. If you saw him on the side of the street, you wouldn't think twice; he looked like your normal businessman, but something told me he was anything but. Ed told us it could take up to a week before he could provide us with any information, depending on how well Juliet covered her tracks. The way he said it made it sound like we were looking for some master criminal.

"I tried to call her the other night and then again last night," I sigh. "But she didn't answer."

"That's a little suspicious, right? I mean, it's almost been a week. Tomorrow is New Year's Eve, for godsake."

I shrug. "A little, but Brie says she's hard to get ahold of—something about her job."

Nick taps the neck of his beer bottle, sorting through the thoughts running through his mind. "Suspicious."

"What's suspicious?" Alex asks, joining us in the loft.

We flew home two days ago, and today, everyone descended on the Jupiter Beach house. It was good to be back, but I don't think anyone was more excited than Bear. As soon as Elizabeth unlocked the door the other night, he ran inside, curled up on his bed in the living room, and went to sleep. Nina had stayed in New York with Elena—she and Kai had some work to get done this week before some big meeting at the beginning of the year—but Finn and Michaela had come with us. They planned to stay through the new year. Alex and Lara, too. Nick was supposed to fly back to New York tomorrow night so he could be with his girls going into the new year.

"Josh hasn't been able to get ahold of Brie's mother," Nick says.

"Dude, it's been like a week since she showed up."

"That's what I said." Nick points at his brother but looks at me. "See, I'm not the only one who thinks so! The whole thing is suspicious."

"Well, what do you want me to do about it?" I ask, looking between them. I can't throw Brie out on the street. She's a fifteen-year-old girl.

"How do you know this girl isn't some psychopath?" Alex takes a tug on his beer and grabs a handful of stale popcorn from the bowl on the table.

"What does she have to gain? It's not like *I'm* the one married to Nina."

"No, but you're related, and it's not like Elizabeth is too far off," Nick says, and it makes me think of the comment Brie made when I asked how she found me.

It's not hard when you're related to people like the Villas.

Shit. Maybe they were on to something.

"Look, we're not saying that's what she is, but you have to

consider all the options," Alex adds. "Where is she anyway?"

"Mom and Dad took her to lunch." My parents had just come down for the day, arriving late last night so Mom could make breakfast this morning before they took Brie into town and then head home before it got too late. Didn't even ask if Michaela or I wanted to join them...I guess this is how it's going to be from now on. Their focus has shifted from me and Michaela to their granddaughter...if she really is their granddaughter.

"What do they think about all this?" Nick asks.

"A little suspicious, but they seem into it. It's not like they have any other grandchildren or signs of getting them anytime soon."

They had been getting along well since Brie showed up, but I could sense some hesitation on Dad's part. While Mom had been excited to have someone else to spoil, Dad kept a polite distance.

"Michaela and Finn might—"

"Be serious, Alex." I stop him. "They aren't jumping on the kid boat anytime soon. They just got engaged."

At least that's what I'm telling myself.

A silence falls between us, the only sounds from the football game projected on the screen. Buccs versus the Panthers. The third story has a loft that Elizabeth had turned into a movie room fitted with a large screen, a projector, and surround sound. When Alex saw it, he salivated at the idea of watching football games up here.

"You gotta get ahold of this girl's mother," Nick says after a minute. He stares blankly at the screen, his thumb tracing the rim of the beer bottle. "You have to find out what's going on. You don't want to be caught off guard."

"I don't think Juliet would do something like this just for shits and giggles." I scratch at the label on my bottle. "She was nice—"

"Not enough to keep in touch, though," Alex quips. "Don't get ahead of yourself, dude. You don't even know for sure if she's your daughter."

Nick takes a sip of beer and says, "Yeah, Juliet was chill, but—"

"You know her?" Alex seems confused.

"I was there." Nick shrugs before a smirk tugs on his lips probably thinking about his own memories of that week. "Spring break twenty-ten was a good ol' time."

"Do you potentially have a daughter out there we need to look into?"

"Shut the fuck up, Alex." Nick's smirk falls, and he rolls his eyes, but I can't hold back my laugh. "You, too."

"You have to admit, it was kind of funny." I still chuckle.

"There you boys are!" Dad walks into the movie area.

I expect to see Brie following behind, but she doesn't.

"Brie is with Elizabeth," Dad says, noticing my confusion. "She whisked her away as soon as we arrived, something about books."

The thought of them bonding makes my heart feel a little lighter. If she is my daughter, at least I know they can get along…Right?

"Y'know Bub, I think she's a lovely girl, but there seems to be some hesitation when it comes to talking about her home life." Dad lifts his hat and runs a hand through his hair before replacing it. "You noticed that?"

Yes. Anytime I bring up home, Brie tries changing the subject almost immediately.

"Have you had any more luck getting ahold of her mother?" Dad asks.

"No, she still hasn't answered."

Dad hums in response but doesn't say anything. I know what he's thinking; I need to do something more than just sit around and wait for Juliet to answer the phone. But what am I supposed to do? Call the police? Brie doesn't seem concerned about her mother's lack of communication. In fact, to her, it seems to be perfectly normal. Not to mention, we have a private investigator looking into Juliet, Brie, and the entire Sinclaire family. If there is anything suspicious going on, I have no doubt Ed Brown is going to find it.

"Well, your Mom and I are 'bout to head out. Got a long drive ahead of us. You'll let me know when you hear something, wont'cha?" Dad asks, and I nod.

Things have still been a little off between me and Dad, or maybe it's just me. There are times when I feel like he wants to ask me about what happened, but he holds back. He nods toward my cousins and heads for the door when I call after him.

"Can we talk for a second?"

The walk outside is quiet. Even as I step out the front door, it's hard to know where to begin. I follow Dad down the steps toward the driveway, taking each step one at a time until I reach solid ground and he is already halfway to the car. Elizabeth and I are supposed to go back to Winchester next week to discuss our options with the house. We've considered keeping it, but don't see a reason to. Jupiter Beach welcomes a fresh start all the way around.

With his back to me, Dad opens the back seat and asks, "What's on your mind, Son?"

It's hard to find the right words, but the best ones I come up with are: "Are we okay?"

No answer. His movements inside the backseat of the car have paused, and after a brief moment that feels like a lifetime, he sighs. It's a long, hard sigh. The kind of sigh that signals you're not about to like the answer on the other side of it. A sigh is not the answer I was looking for. When he straightens, he turns to face me—his gaze narrowed, his lips pursed slightly—and he rests his arm over the door pane, tapping his fingers on the black exterior. "Josh—"

"I'm sorry."

"I know that, but this whole thing has been…difficult. I feel like I don't even know you or Elizabeth, not really. Hell, I feel like I don't even know my own wife."

"Wait, you know? I thought she didn't tell you."

"I have two ears to hear, son."

Now, it's my turn to sigh. "I'm sorry, Dad."

"What in God's name would make either of you think going to Brina Villa for an arranged marriage was a good idea?"

My tongue swipes across my teeth before I suck my bottom lip between them. He knows the truth, but not the *whole* truth. Do I tell him?

"I've asked your mother a hundred times, but she just tells me not to worry about it. Says it's none of my concern because it was handled, but that's the problem. I don't know *what* was handled, and it makes me feel like I don't know my own damn family!"

My heart jumps out of my chest when his hand pounds down on the roof of the sedan. My blood is going a million miles a minute, the adrenaline pounding through me.

"Does your sister know?" He chuckles when I don't answer. "Wow, so I'm the only one who—"

"MJ didn't know before. She just found out."

"So, you can tell your sister, but not me?"

"I didn't want to disappoint you anymore than I already have. I don't want you to hate me."

Dad pinches the bridge of his nose and takes a deep breath. "Josh, there's nothing that could make me hate you."

"I don't know—"

"Josh." He grips my shoulders. "You're my son, and I love you. There is nothing in this world that could make me hate you. Disappointed? Sure. That's to be expected. But never hate."

Tears well in my dad's eyes, and they make mine burn with unshed tears. Dad isn't a very emotional person. He's always been the more reserved type. He keeps to himself and lets Mom handle most things, but when he does let that guard down and show his feelings...it hits you harder.

"Josh?" Elizabeth calls from the side porch off the mudroom. "Oh," I hear her say, sensing the tension. "Never mind."

"What is it, Sugar?" I call over my shoulder.

"Nothing that can't wait." She smiles softly and waves at Dad. "Jenny should be out in just a second, Pat."

"Thank you, Elizabeth," Dad says, offering her a small nod before she goes inside. When she closes the door, he turns back to me. "Despite everything that has happened, I'm glad the two of you managed to make this work. She's good for you. And I think you've been good for her too."

"I love her."

"I know you do. I just hope this thing with Brie doesn't mess things up again. I don't know if the family can handle another round of Josh versus Elizabeth."

I laugh softly.

"You really didn't know about her?" Dad asks.

"No idea."

"Well." He sighs. "She seems to have a good head on her shoulders. You just need to get ahold of her mother and figure this whole thing out." Dad's hand clamps down on my shoulder and squeezes. "I'm proud of you, Josh. Whatever happened all those years ago…you came out better for it. And when you're ready to talk about it, I'll be here."

The tears well in my eyes again and my stomach is in knots. I want to tell him, but…I don't want to see the disappointment on his face when he finds out what I did.

"Dad…I don't want to keep secrets anymore," I say, swallowing the lump in my throat. "Do you remember the Theta Pi hazing?"

"Sure, that kid who almost died your senior year. But you weren't there. You were home the night of the—" His words fall off as the realization hits him. "Oh, Josh."

"It wasn't me. I didn't hurt anyone, but I was…there. I was the one who took him to the hospital."

"You took him to the hospital?" Dad asks. "Why didn't you just tell the police that?"

"I was scared." I shrug. "The school was talking about expulsion and I was already supposed to graduate late because—"

"I don't understand how you decided an arranged marriage was the answer."

"I went to Mom for help and she went to—"

"Brina." Dad shakes his head, stuffing his hands in his pockets. He sighs, looking back at me. "All of this drama for what? You did the right thing, Josh! You helped that kid and made sure he lived. Had you just come to me, we could've hired a lawyer to take care of it. You didn't need to go into an arranged marriage."

"I didn't want to cause you any extra stress," I say, folding my arms.

He puts his hands on my shoulders, looking me square in the eye. "That wasn't your burden to bear and I'm sorry you felt like you had to. That's not your job, son."

"I know that now, but I don't regret it." A small smile tugs on the corner of my mouth. "Because I got Elizabeth out of it."

Dad sighs and pulls me into a bone-crushing hug—the kind of hug that heals your spirit a little and helps put you back together after years of quick fixes. Before we part, he says, "I'm proud of you, Josh. You're a good kid, this doesn't change that. I love you, son."

fifty-two

NOW

"JOSH!" JUSTIN BARLOW'S VOICE rings through the phone. "How was your holiday?"

"It was…eventful."

How else could I describe the events that had transpired?

I find Elizabeth and Lara, preparing dinner in the kitchen while Michaela sits on the counter with a glass of wine. They giggled at whatever my sister said before I walked in. I kiss Elizabeth's cheek and swat her ass, earning my own giggle as I walk by. Stepping through the pantry to the dining room, I close the double doors for more privacy. I haven't told Elizabeth about this yet. I wanted to find out if this was even a possibility before getting anyone else's hopes up.

"Do I even want to know?" Justin asks.

"Probably not. What about you? Did you get a chance to get out to Washington to see your mom?"

"Unfortunately, no, things have been…eventful."

"Seems to be the trend lately," I say. "Do I want to know?"

"Probably not," he says, and we both chuckle.

I check in on Justin a few times a year. He went to Chadwick and was part of Theta Pi until it was dismantled. Justin Barlow used to go by Justin Henderson but changed his name in late 2016 after he transferred schools.

Justin Henderson is the reason I was put into an arranged marriage. Justin Henderson is the boy who was beaten so severely by a sophomore during initiation in the fall of 2015 that he had to be taken to the hospital. He doesn't know I was there that night. He doesn't remember most of it and he doesn't remember I'm the one who took him to the hospital. After the hazing incident, he tried to return to Chadwick, but it was too hard—mentally and socially—so he moved back to Washington State for a while to let the dust settle. He's originally from Washington and lived there until his parents divorced when he was barely a year old. He stayed there with his mom for a while, but she struggled to care for him and eventually sent him to live in Florida with his dad.

A few years ago, he moved back East, landing a job in Charleston.

"You still interested in a job in Charleston?" Justin asks.

"You have something?"

"Well, not my company, but I've been hearing rumors that one of the hospitals is gonna be looking for a marketing director soon."

"You're kidding."

"Nope, guess the VP is retiring, so the director spot is about to open up."

"Holy shit." I brace myself on the back of the dining chair. This almost seems too good to be true.

"You want me to throw your name in the pot? My source tells me there aren't many options right now, so I think you have a pretty good chance. Not to mention, you're not a far transfer."

"I'm actually in Jupiter now."

"Even better! Send me your resumé again, and I'll get it

over to 'em. Can't promise you'll hear anything right away since tomorrow is New Year's Eve, but—"

"No, yeah, I get it. I appreciate it, man. You have no idea."

Before we hang up, Justin suggests catching up over lunch in the next week. Dropping my phone to the table, I can't hold back a smile.

"Holy shit." The words tumble out again.

"Who was that?" Elizabeth asks, slipping through the double doors.

"You remember Justin? Well, I asked him a few weeks ago if he knew of any jobs in the area."

With a lift at the corner of her mouth, she drapes her arms over my shoulders, locking her fingers behind my neck.

"I didn't want to tell you in case things went…south, but he just called with an opportunity." I plant my hands on her hips, pulling her flush against me.

"Josh, are you sure you want this? To move. We can go back home. We can—"

Gripping her hips, I lift her onto the table and tilt her chin up to stare into the eyes of my beautiful brown-eyed girl. "I want you." I kiss her, and she smiles against me. "Home is wherever you are, Sugar. Whether that's here or Winchester or Antarctica, I don't care. As long as I'm with you, I'm home."

Elizabeth pulls my mouth down on hers with the collar of my polo. Cupping her cheeks, I ply her mouth open and delve further into her, swallowing her moans. Her fingers slip underneath my shirt, cool against my heated skin.

"Sugar," I warn against her mouth.

I'm two seconds away from laying her out on this table and fucking her. Honestly, the idea of doing it right here where we could get caught by the others who are less than fifty feet away is exhilarating. But the last thing I need is for Brie to come down the stairs and scar for life before we even get to know each other.

Elizabeth giggles and pulls her hands from under my shirt.

"Tease," I mumble.

"What's the job?" she asks, wiping the corner of her mouth, but it does little good. Her lipstick is smeared which means I have it on my face. That's not going to be obvious whatsoever.

"Director at a hospital."

"Josh, that's amazing!" She kisses me again.

"It is, but it means a lot more work. I already increased my load when I took over Warren's position."

"The difference is you'll have a bigger team to back you up. You're not alone."

She's right. While I've never been busier since my promotion, I have more help and I'd have even more in this new position. With the power to delegate things and pass projects down to my team, I can handle the bigger things. Being a director is the same thing I'm already doing...just on a much bigger scale. I can do that.

"You can do this, Josh," Elizabeth says, touching my cheeks. "If you want to, that is."

"I don't even know if I'll *get* the job."

"You'll get the job."

"Elizabeth." I sigh. Not even five minutes ago, the thought of a new job felt like a sign from above, but now it feels like I'm taking two steps backward. My commitment to work has proven to be one of our downfalls, why would I want to take on an even bigger role than before? "We just...We're barely two weeks into starting over, and now I'm going to jump into something that was one of our biggest issues before?"

"We can do this, Josh. I know we can."

Her confidence is reassuring, but there is still a hint of hesitation in the back of my mind.

"And if it becomes too much, we'll handle it." Elizabeth shrugs. She makes it sound so simple, but I guess it is, isn't it? "I called Liam, by the way."

My heart stops. She called Liam. Her attorney. Why did she call her attorney?

"I asked him to file a motion to dismiss the divorce petition."

My heart jumps. Of course that's why she called him. What was I thinking?

"That's okay, right?"

"Yes!" My outburst catches her off guard.

I hadn't even realized I hadn't said anything. Of course, that was okay—it was more than okay. She didn't even need to ask. Truthfully, I hadn't even thought about it, but I guess telling our attorneys we no longer needed their services was a pretty important step. "I mean...yeah, of course."

"Are you guys decent?" my sister asks. Looking over my shoulder, I see her sticking her head through the double doors with her eyes covered.

"Yes, MJ." Elizabeth laughs, stepping down from the table.

Michaela lets out a breath and uncovers her eyes. "Well, if you two are done canoodling in here, the rest of us would like to eat while the food is hot."

"Go tell the boys to wash up, then," Elizabeth directs her, and Michaela scurries away. Elizabeth turns back to me, standing on her tiptoes to press a quick peck on my lips. "Will you tell Brie dinner is ready?"

"Anything for you, Sug." I smile and kiss her one more time before heading up the stairs.

We made an appointment to have a paternity test done at the end of next week, and in just a few short days, we will have confirmation whether or not Brie is my daughter. I don't know how I'm supposed to feel about that. Part of me is relieved, but part of me is extremely anxious. What if the results come back positive? Then, I'll have a daughter I am now responsible for, and I have to decide how she fits into this new phase of my life. But the bigger question is, what if the results come back negative?

Either way, I have to get ahold of Juliet, and hopefully Ed Brown can help me with that if Brie can't. Does he work on holidays? I'd imagine so—Nina called him the day after Christmas, after all. One thing that's been on my mind: when we finally learn the truth, what do I say to Juliet when we speak for the first time in over fifteen years?

Stepping up to the third floor, Brie walks out of the bedroom, and I have to do a double take. For a moment, I swear I'm looking at Juliet with her skin and angel face—big brown eyes and a small button nose. She even has the same dimple on her right cheek. If it weren't for Brie's brunette hair, I'd swear it *was* Juliet.

"Everything okay?" she asks, breaking the spell.

"F-fine." I clear my throat and stuff my hands in my pockets. "Dinner is ready."

She nods and walks past me to the stairs but pauses a few steps down. "Josh, I—"

My brow quirks in response when she doesn't continue.

"I um—I talked to my mom a few minutes ago." Her words come out more confident with each word. "You were on the phone, though, so she told me not to bother you."

"Brie!"

"I'm sorry! When I told her you were on the phone, she told me not to disturb you."

"Call her back," I demand, crossing my arms over my chest. "Right now."

"She can't answer, but…you can call tomorrow. Yeah! She said that she'll be available tomorrow."

I sigh and rub the crease of my forehead—the beginning stages of a headache building between my eyes. "Brie, I need to speak with your mother. I don't care if I'm on the phone or working or whatever excuse you come up with to not interrupt me…Just do it. Do you understand?"

fifty-three

NOW

"I APOLOGIZE FOR THE late call," Ed Brown says from across the table at Millers All Day. My stomach plummeted when I saw his name stretched across my screen last night. He had called to set up a meeting for this morning—answering my earlier question about whether or not he worked on holidays. Was New Year's Eve technically a holiday, though?

He was already here when we arrived, sipping on a cup of coffee that had just been refilled by Holly, the same server from the last time we were here. She offered him something to eat, but he politely declined as we slid into the booth, my eyes drawn to the folder in the middle of the table. He waited to begin until after we had placed our order with Holly, both of us only ordering a coffee. I'm not sure we could stomach anything more right now.

My eyes shift between him and the manila folder beneath his hands. He's found something. That much is reassuring, but whatever is in that folder is about to change our lives forever, and that scares the shit out of me.

"I know it's the holiday, but I didn't think you'd want to

wait." He clears his throat and pulls the folder toward him. "Do you recognize this man?"

He sets a photo face-up on the table, and I have to do a double-take.

"Isn't that...Justin?" Elizabeth asks, picking up the photo to get a better look. Showing it to me, there isn't a doubt in my mind that it is Justin.

"So, you do know him?" Ed confirms.

"We went to college together," I say. "Well, for a while, he transferred after—"

"After a hazing incident in which he ended up in the hospital." The older man takes a sip of coffee, his sharp stare locked on me the whole time. "Yes, I'm aware." Ed pulls a packet from the folder. "Mrs. Villa's lawyer did a great job covering up the fact that you were involved in the incident, but I'm a lot more thorough than most."

Before me, a copy of the contract Elizabeth and I signed ten years ago. How in the hell did he get that? Looking up from the contract, I meet his blank stare.

"What does that have to do with any of this?" I hiss, shoving the papers back toward him. "I thought you were supposed to be looking for Juliet, not digging into *our* past."

"Justin is Juliet's brother." He says it so simply, so plainly, my brain almost doesn't register the words. Did he just say Justin is Juliet's *brother?* How did I not know that?

"You've got to be kidding me." Elizabeth scoffs, turning to glare at me.

"I had no idea!" I defend myself. "I didn't—Justin has never told me he had a sister."

"They weren't very close, from the intel I've gathered," Ed says, pulling out another photo. A family stands in front of a large two-story house—a boy, maybe three or four, stands next to a girl, maybe six or seven, in front of their parents. There's a cluster of palm trees in the corner, a bush with pink flowers near the front door, and shrubs lining the front under the windowsill. "They share a father but not much else."

"But he's from Washington—"

"His father had been married previously—before a small stint with Justin's mother in Washington—and returned to his previous wife in Florida, Juliet's mother."

"Their last names—"

"Justin was given his mother's last name, not his father's. There's some discrepancy whether it is his father or not, but that's not my business," Ed says over his coffe mug. "So for all intents and purposes of this investigation, he is Justin's father."

Elizabeth fingers the family photo, gliding across the face of the young girl, before she looks up at Ed. "And where is Juliet now?"

"Juliet is dead."

The coffee mug falls from my hands, flooding the table with brown liquid, and the restaurant falls into a hushed silence. All eyes are on us, and Holly rushes over with towels to stop the spread. Ed rescues the folder from drowning in the scolding liquid, and luckily, none had spilled over the edge, burning anyone's lap. I offer Holly an apologetic smile, but she brushes me off. "Happens all the time. I'll get you another one."

Elizabeth waits until she returns with the fresh coffee to continue. "What do you mean she's *dead?*"

"Unfortunately, she passed away last year. Cancer," Ed says, pulling an obituary from the folder and laying it on the table. The top of it reads *The Wichita Tribune*, a local newspaper in Wichita. I had picked one up while I sat in the cafe, waiting for her to show up last year. There's a photo next to the write-up—it looks like her but doesn't at the same time.

Juliet Sinclaire-Donovan, born September 16, 1991, passed away July 17, 2024, it reads. She died the day before we were supposed to meet.

"She moved around quite a bit after college, went by

different names, got involved in some pretty bad stuff...She went to rehab in twenty-nineteen."

"Rehab?" Elizabeth asks.

"Drugs—mostly cocaine and cannabis. Got arrested a few times for possession and once for trafficking."

"And where was Brie during all of this?" I ask, finally looking up from the photo.

"The girl was placed in the care of Juliet's parents until she was released from rehab and cleared by the court at the beginning of twenty-twenty."

"Why wouldn't they bring her to me? I'm her father. Why wouldn't—"

"Are you?" Ed asks, his brow practically touching his hairline. My mouth falls open but closes almost immediately. The truth is, I don't know for certain, but something tells me I already know the answer. "Have you done a paternity test already?"

"No," Elizabeth answers.

"Do you know how many Joshua Davises there are in the world? I imagine starting a search for you was the last thing on the mind of those in charge of placing her somewhere. Placing her with Juliet's parents was much easier than looking for you."

"So, if Juliet is...dead," Elizabeth says, tapping the obituary. "Are we housing a runaway right now?"

"There hasn't been a BOLO issued, but I can't say how long before there is one. Sources tell me she's supposed to be back in Wichita at her best friend's house. She's been living with her uncle since her mother died—"

"Not her grandparents?" I ask.

"Grandfather passed away in twenty-two, Grandmother passed away earlier this year, and the girl was placed in the care of Justin."

"The letter." I scoff, meeting Elizabeth's stare. "She must have known her time was limited; it's why she wanted to meet."

"So, what now?" Elizabeth asks, not even acknowledging what I said.

"I suggest confronting the girl. And then, I'd get in touch with Justin. Last thing you want is a runaway on your hands."

Brie giggles as Finn taunts my sister about her poor cookie-decorating skills.

"For a designer, you're not very good at this," he continues as Elizabeth and I walk through the front door.

Elizabeth walks up the stairs without a word. The ride home was quiet, both of us processing everything we had just learned. I glance up the steps when I hear the bedroom door slam shut before peering into the dining room, where Michaela flips off her fiancé and stuffs the snowman cookie she had been decorating in his mouth to shut him up. As much as I want to get this conversation with Brie over with, I need to talk to Elizabeth first.

I find her in the bathroom, gripping the edge of the vanity. I wrap my arms around her waist, pull her body flush against mine, and kiss the back of her neck. She takes a deep breath and turns in my arms, clutching my sweater and burying her face in my chest. Before I know it, I can feel warm tears soaking through the material, and her body racks with a sob. Tightening my grip on her, I kiss the crown of her head and rub small circles on her back. This response surprises me. From her reaction at the restaurant, I thought she was mad, not upset.

When Elizabeth pulls away, she wipes under her eyes and

sniffles. "She barely got her mother back before..."

She can't get the words out, and suddenly, I realize why she's so upset. Elizabeth understands the grief Brie must be dealing with better than anyone.

"I know, Sugar," I say gently, pulling her back into my grasp when tears begin to burn my own eyes. I can't imagine what it must have been like to lose your mother so young, only to get her back and have her savagely ripped away again.

"What if the test says you're not her father?"

"I don't know," I whisper.

Elizabeth takes a small step back, and I wipe away a tear that has trailed down her cheek. She does the same for me and reaches up to press a quick peck to my lips.

"Will you do this with me?" I ask, studying her hands before I look up to meet her gaze. "Please, I-I need you there."

Brie looks small, sitting on the couch across from me, with her hands stuffed under her thighs and her sock-covered feet barely scraping the floor of the back porch. Elizabeth joins us with three mugs of hot cocoa—Mom's recipe, Elizabeth is the only person I know who can make it almost as good as Mom. She hands one to each of us before sitting next to me. She sits on her feet and offers me a smile before taking a sip of the cocoa and motioning toward Brie with her eyes.

"Brie...is there anything you want to tell us?" I ask.

She traces the rim of her mug and shuffles her feet in front of her, chewing on the inside of her lip before meeting my stare. She clears her throat, sitting up a little straighter as she pulls her feet under her. "Like what?"

"We know." I sigh. "About your mother."

Her eyes grow ten times in size, and she looks between us. "I don't—I don't know what you—"

"Brie." Elizabeth stops her gently. Setting her mug on the table, she makes her way over to the other couch and takes one of Brie's hands in hers. With a soft smile, Elizabeth says, "I am so sorry, truly."

Brie's eyes begin to fill with water, and she swallows hard, trying to keep the tears at bay.

"I, um…I lost both of my parents when I was young, too." Elizabeth rolls up the left sleeve of her sweater and turns over her wrist, tracing the worn scar that trails up her arm. "I was a little older than you were. My brother attacked us, and unfortunately, my parents didn't make it, so I know what it's like to grow up without my momma, too."

Elizabeth reaches up and wipes a few tears that fall down Brie's cheeks. "Does your Uncle Justin know you're here?"

Brie averts her gaze down to the mug in her lap. I'm guessing that would be a no.

"He thinks you're at your friend's house, right?" Elizabeth continues and Brie meets her gaze before offering a slow nod. Elizabeth glances at me, and a sad smile graces her lips. "We should probably tell him where you are, don't you think?"

"Probably," Brie whispers.

"We're not mad," I say, meeting both of their gazes. "But I wish you had been honest with us."

Her bottom lip trembles, looking between us. "I'm sorry."

Elizabeth wraps her arms around the young girl, and I join them, wrapping my arms around both of them, sandwiching Brie between us. My wife offers a tearful smile atop Brie's head, and I return the gesture. I didn't think it was possible, but I've fallen more in love with this woman in the last few moments. She handled this entire situation with grace and compassion, while I hadn't the slightest idea where to begin. I can only thank God that she and I reconciled before this happened because I don't think I would've been able to handle this on my own.

fifty-four

THEN

May 2025

"WHERE'S ELLIE?" FINN ASKS when I hand him a fresh beer. I had invited Finn, Nick, and Alex over for a pre-Memorial Day BBQ since everyone was going to be in town at the same time, and I hadn't seen much of Finn since New Year's. After everything that happened between him and Michaela, he's kept his distance. He spent Thanksgiving with us but joined the Monroes at their cabin for Christmas. In doing so, he got a free ticket to the Dean and Raeanne showdown. Twenty years of sexual tension and hidden feelings came to a head and ended with Rae leaving without even saying goodbye. I liked them together, but Dean refused to tell her the truth, scared she might reject him—look how that turned out. "And I thought I had problems," Finn joked when he told me about it on New Year's Eve in Los Angeles. He's kept his distance from all of us since.

Elizabeth and I spent the new year apart—I was in Los Angeles, and she was in New York with Nina.

"She's back in Charleston," I say, running a hand through my hair.

It's longer than I normally keep it, but I've been so busy I haven't even thought about getting it cut. Michaela said it was starting to look like a sophisticated mullet before she left for Europe. While she meant it as a jab, I kind of liked it.

My sister had been here long enough to drop off a few suitcases and make sure there was enough room for her shit that would be delivered by movers the next week. Michaela had finally left David, for good this time. The fact she even went back to that asshole in the first place blows my mind, but I'm just glad she realized the mistake she made. I almost didn't answer when she called to say she was leaving and needed a place to stay while she figured things out. A day later, I got a call that she was going on a sabbatical...in Europe.

So now, all of her shit is packed away in one of the guest rooms, waiting for her to return. And what am I going to tell her when she gets back and realizes Elizabeth hasn't been home in months? I have no fucking clue.

"Been gone a lot, hasn't she?" Finn pushes and tries to hide the questioning glance he shares with Nick across the fire pit.

Nick knowingly raises his eyebrows, taking a drink of his beer instead of offering a verbal response. He doesn't *know* anything, but he suspects it. The only person I'm sure of who knows something is Nina, and maybe Kai, but Nina has kept this from her husband (unsurprisingly).

"Everything okay with you guys?"

"Sure, why wouldn't it be?" I shrug, taking a long drag of my beer.

Lie. Everything is far from fine.

The sound of the doorbell echoes outside, and at first, no one moves. When it sounds again, I finally get up to answer it with a long sigh. Who in the hell could that be?

Padding through the house, I open the front door to find a young kid standing on the stoop dressed in a suit and tie, holding a manila envelope in his hands. "Is this the home of

Michaela Reed?" He asks peering over my shoulder.

"As of now," I say, and he just stares at me. Rolling my eyes, I repeat myself, but this time in the way he wants.

"Is she home?"

"That depends who's asking."

"I'm Luke, a courier for—"

"You new?" I've met almost everyone who works at the law firm handling my sister's divorce, but not this guy. "I'm Josh, her brother. I'll take the paperwork; she's still out of the country."

"Oh, well, I don't know if—"

"Luke, if you like your job, hand me those documents because my sister is getting *very* impatient about it," I say. His eyes widen, and he almost throws the envelope at me. "You can tell Elias and Jason you gave them to me. You'll be fine."

Luke skitters away to his car without looking back, climbing into the beat-up Toyota just as another car pulls into the driveway. This one is much nicer—a sleek, black BMW—and the afternoon sun reflects off the shiny body. It parks directly in front of the steps, and the driver climbs out. She slides her sunglasses on top of her fiery red hair and reaches inside the car to pull out a manilla envelope.

"Can I help you?"

"I'm looking for Joshua Davis," she says without a smile.

"What for?"

The woman steps around the car, dressed in skin-tight jeans and a black blazer. "Got some paperwork for him." She lifts the envelopes in the air.

"I'm Josh."

"Oh good." Redhead smiles and walks up the steps. "You just need to sign that you got them."

She peels away a document stuck to the manila envelope and hands it over with a pen.

By signing my name, it feels like I'm already signing the

divorce papers. Handing back my signature, she pushes the envelopes into my hands with a grim smile, turning on her heel and skipping down the stairs. I think about ripping it open just to see what it looks like, but I also think about throwing it straight in the garbage. I've been waiting for it to show up since Wednesday—exactly five and a half years from our wedding day.

Oh, but you thought it was six and a half years…

Well, according to Line Eight of our terms, if we decided not to stay together, the required year separation under South Carolina law *would* count towards the final year.

Walking back to the backyard, I hide my envelope behind Michaela's and hold them up for the others to see. "Divorce papers finally came. Signed, sealed, delivered."

Don't think I don't notice the way Finn's eyes turn into giant saucers at my words. He's confused; I haven't told him anything about what's going on.

"Whose divorce papers?" Finn's voice breaks, treading carefully through unknown waters.

"My sister's." I rip open the envelope and pull the documents out to make sure everything is here. "We've been waiting for these. David and his attorney have been dragging their feet."

David and his attorney have been taking their sweet time getting everything finalized, delaying the process until they couldn't anymore. And why? David was already back together with what's-her-face (Karina, or something?); the tabloids caught them sneaking around, and it cost him a few points in the polls. Call me crazy, but I think he'll still pull out the win.

My best friend's eyes light up, looking around the group. "Wait, Michaela left him?"

"About two months ago," Nick says. "She's been Eat, Pray, Loving it all over Europe since."

I toss the envelope onto the table between me and Finn, and the other envelope displays itself beneath it. When I scramble to hide it, I notice the item that falls out of Michaela's envelope—her locket. The same one Finn helped me pick out for her eighteenth birthday present.

"Is that her locket?" Finn reaches for it, but I grab it first.

"Yeah, David has been holding it hostage since she left," I say.

Sunlight reflects off the silver heart dangling from the small chain. I hate that she's been without it for so long, Michaela has worn this thing every day since she got it. Normally, I would have asked Nick for help picking out a gift; he was far better with that sort of thing, but he was dealing with Aunt Evie's death, and I didn't want to bother him. So, I went to Finn, and we swore never to tell Michaela otherwise she'd throw it straight in the garbage. That was before she fell in love with him. "His campaign manager made her take it off because it didn't go with the aesthetic they were creating for the wife of the future congressman."

"I wondered where it was the night of the Valentine's Day dinner," Finn says, and all heads turn toward him. I'm pretty sure I just gave myself whiplash. Did he just say they saw each other on Valentine's Day?

"What Valentine's Day dinner?" Alex asks.

"Oh, we were at the same event and ran into each other."

"And you're just now telling me this?" My voice raises slightly. How could he not tell me about this? Why didn't Mic tell me?

"Nothing happened." Finn shrugs as if it's no big deal. "I don't think we said two words to each other. David made sure of that."

"Did Nina know about this?" I ask Nick.

"Don't think so." Nick shrugs. " She and MJ have only started talking again after she left him." Nick chuckles, seeing Finn's face, a big ol' *what the fuck* displayed front and center. "David didn't want her involved with Nina. Told her that our family is plain and Nina was holding her back."

"He's such an ass," Alex mumbles under his breath.

"Here's to never seeing that asshole again." I lift my beer in the air between us, and they join me in cheering. After a long sip of my beer, I stand from my chair to call my sister and tell her the good news.

I make my way to my office and she answers just before her voicemail picks up. She is relieved to find out she no longer has the looming David cloud over her. It even makes her more excited to come home in a few days, but then she starts to fill me in on the gossip in the vineyard, and I stop listening. My focus returns to the other envelope on my desk—inside, my own fate. My fingers toy with the edges, I consider opening it to see what all it says, but I stuff it into the top drawer of my desk instead.

"Please tell me he sent the locket," Michaela begs.

"He did."

She breathes a sigh of relief. "Can you mail it to me?"

"Mail it to you? Are you insane, MJ?."

Absolutely not. I am not overnighting her locket to *Italy*. Michaela's final stop on her European getaway was the vineyard owned by Romy's boyfriend, Enzo, in Estranei. Do you know how much that would cost? Not to mention, it probably wouldn't make it before she left to come home anyway.

"You're going to be home in a few days! You can get it then."

"Bub, come on!" Michaela whines.

"No." I slam my desk drawer closed. "It will never make it in time. You've waited this long, a few more days won't hurt you."

fifty-five

NOW

"HOW IS BRIE DOING?" Elizabeth asks when I find her in my office at our Winchester home. There are three sealed moving boxes near the door and another one at her feet, filled almost to the brim with things from the shelves along the back wall. The movers come in two hours to load everything up and drive it down to Jupiter. My office is the last thing that needs to be packed. We put the house on the market at the end of January and received a full offer two days later. We signed our part of the paperwork this morning, and the sale is scheduled to close in two days, on February 25th, Michaela's birthday. My sister and Finn are coming into town tomorrow so we can celebrate and they plan on scoping out a potential wedding venue. Why she has gone straight to St. Patrick's Cathedral in New York, I'll never understand. That's where they're going to end up anyway.

"She's asking when we'll be home so she can come by," I say, putting together two more boxes that can be used to pack up my desk and the remainder of the shelves. "She wants to plan out her room."

Since we took Brie home the day after Ed Brown presented all of the information he had gathered about Juliet, she has been staying there until we could get things straightened out. Justin had been extremely surprised to see not only his niece but me standing at his front door on New Year's Day.

The hour-long drive from Jupiter to Justin's home on the furthest end of Mount Pleasant started normally; everyone was in decent spirits, but as we got closer, the mood shifted little by little until it plummeted the moment we pulled into the driveway of the brick home. We sat in complete silence for two whole minutes before Brie met my gaze in the rearview and, with a whole-body sigh, opened the car door. I couldn't sleep the night before, tossing and turning with constant thoughts of everything going on. Contemplating the whys and the what-ifs and the how-comes. Too many unanswered questions, and I wasn't sure Justin could or would tell me the truth.

I extended my hand toward Elizabeth as she rounded the front of my Bronco, and we followed the sidewalk around the front of the brick house to the steps that led up to the porch where Brie was greeting her uncle. I could hear him fretting over her. Confused. "You're supposed to be at Cali's until—Is that…Josh, is that you?" Justin stepped around his niece as Elizabeth and I reached the porch. "What are you doing here? I thought we were gonna meet next week."

"That's not why I'm here," I said, offering a tight-lipped smile, glancing from him to Brie and back.

He looked between us…once, twice, three times before asking, "Am I missing something?"

"I think it's best if we go inside," Elizabeth suggested.

"Wait, did you come together?" Justin turned to Brie, but she had suddenly found her boots way more interesting. "What in the hell are you doing with them, Brie? You're supposed to be in Wichita! I bought the ticket myself, I-I don't understand.

How do you even know them?"

"Well, I was hoping you could shed some light on that," I said, and Justin's glare turned to me. "I'm—I'm her father."

"Her fath—Oh my god." Justin scoffed, rubbing the scruff under his chin. "You're *him.*"

"Him?" Elizabeth asked.

"The guy Juliet never got over."

I glanced at my wife, but she kept her stare trained on him, face pulled into a thin line. I imagined that wasn't exactly what she wanted to hear, but did it matter now? Juliet was dead, and even if she wasn't…I only wanted Elizabeth.

"Jules said she heard that he'd ended up married to some rich bitch—"

"Watch your mouth," I interrupted, taking a step forward, but Elizabeth placed a hand on my arm. Brie's eyes snapped up at her uncle's words and the threat in mine.

"—but I never guessed it was you two." Justin turned to look at Brie over his shoulder. "You never went back home, did you?" He scoffed when she didn't reply. "Go inside."

"Get your stuff together, Brie," I redirected her. "We're leaving."

"Do you have proof?"

"Justin, he is—"

But he cut Brie off. "Until we have a test proving you *are* her father, she stays with me. You might think you were special, but Juliet had a way of making people feel that way. You were just one of several."

Elizabeth squeezed my hand, pulling the words right out of my mouth. When I met Brie's eyes over his shoulder, my stomach sank. I didn't want to leave her, but he was right. I didn't have any proof—solid proof—that she was my daughter. I had no right to take her with me.

"It's okay, Brie. We'll get it figured out." I tried to comfort myself as much as her.

"We have an appointment downtown for a test on Monday," Elizabeth said.

"Great, we'll see you there. You can go now," Justin said, trying to usher us off the porch, but Elizabeth wasn't done. She wasn't leaving until he promised to bring Brie to the appointment. After a few more tries, he agreed to be there.

Justin and Brie were already at the office when Elizabeth and I arrived at the test center Monday morning. Elizabeth invited Brie to join her for a quick coffee and I took the opportunity to have a long overdue conversation. It wasn't a conversation I was looking forward to, but in the spirit of coming clean about everything else, I knew I had to.

"She really liked you," he said before I could. "Juliet, I mean."

"Hate to break it to you, but I liked her too."

"She came home from that spring break telling her mom all about the guy she'd met. How she thought she had fallen in love. Of course, Dad popped that bubble and told her to keep her head out of the clouds. Then she found out she was pregnant...Dad didn't want her to keep the baby, but Jules refused to give it up." Justin chewed on the corner of his mouth, his eyes glazed over thinking back on the memory. He shook his head with a light scoff, turning toward me. "I don't know why she never called you. I was too young to understand all of that, but I think it had something to do with Dad. He was so against her keeping the baby, but she was eighteen, there was nothin' he could do."

"I wish she had found a way to get in touch with me. I would've been there for her."

"As much as she liked you, I think she was scared you'd only stick around because of the baby...not her." He rubs at some invisible dirt on his hands. "Jules and I were never that close growing up, not until I was older and she was...sober. Her husband, Tom, was an asshole, but he helped her get clean. Helped her get her life back before..."

I didn't have to look at him to know tears had formed in his eyes, I could hear it in the thickness of his voice. Justin cleared his throat, trying to rid it of the emotion, but it was still there when he spoke again.

"Juliet wanted to tell Brie's father before it all happened, and I never knew if she got ahold of you. When they put Brie with Mom and Dad after she passed, I figured she never did or you rejected her. Either way, when you showed up the other night…I don't know, I felt like the last bit of my sister was about to be ripped away from me."

"I'm sorry, Justin." It seemed like the only thing to say. "Truly, I am. There won't be a day that I won't be sorry for the time I've missed, but I'm just glad I can be here now."

"I think you did okay for yourself." He motioned down the hall where Elizabeth and Brie walked toward us. "Brie loves her. It's been Elizabeth this…Elizabeth that…I'm like 'Hey, nice to see you too.'"

I couldn't hold back my smile, watching my wife and daughter laugh together. A strong bond had already formed between them, one that ran deeper than a simple parent-child relationship. They both understood the pain of such a devasting loss that the rest of us couldn't.

"I'm sorry for how I acted the other day." Justin sighed. "And I'm sorry for calling Elizabeth a 'rich bitch.' That was uncalled for."

"Thank you, but I think that apology belongs to someone else."

We sat there silently until we both attempted to start the conversation again. There was still one more thing I needed to say, to come clean about…Part of the reason I had kept in touch with him all of these years. We both waited for the other to continue, until finally I conceded. Taking a deep breath, I said, "There's something else that I feel I need to apologize for."

"What's that?"

"Chadwick."

Justin sat up a little straighter in his seat.

"I know you don't remember much from that night, but...I'm the one who took you to the hospital."

Justin looked at me like I had two heads. "But you weren't there."

"That's the story." I nodded. "I wasn't there for what happened to you, but I was there afterward. And while the rest of those idiots stood around freaking out, I loaded you up and drove you down to Mercy Hospital."

Before anything more could be said, a nurse stepped out of the door leading to the back. "Davis and Sinclaire."

"Moment of truth," I whispered, standing from my chair. Wiping the sweat on my hands on my jeans, I followed Brie through the door to the point of no return.

A week later, we had a result confirming what, I think, we all already knew...Brie was my daughter.

But since then, we've had to jump through hoops to get custody transferred to me and Elizabeth. You'd think it was easy to get custody of your own child, especially when you have a test and documents to prove it, but it's not. It wasn't until we proved that we were fit parents to the court that they granted us custody—that was last Friday. Brie will be moving from Justin's house in Mount Pleasant to Jupiter with us at the end of this week. Justin didn't say much following my admission; truthfully he hasn't said much to me ever since. Whenever we're in the same room, he keeps things cordial and respectful, but still far from the way we used to be. I can only hope that with time we'll be able to get back there...for Brie's sake.

"She was just there two weeks ago." Elizabeth laughs, taping up the box at her feet.

"That was for paint. Now she wants to get the dimensions so she can make sure the new bedroom set will fit."

"I thought you said you measured it out already."

"I thought she did."

Elizabeth leans her head against the back of my desk chair with a groan. "You two would give Nina a coronary."

"Guess it's a good thing Brina arranged a marriage to you, then." I lean over the back of the chair to kiss her. "Want some help with this? Might go faster with two people."

"You do the shelves, I'll do the desk?"

"Aye, aye, Captain." I salute her, earning an eye roll before she rips open the top desk drawer, and the first thing she notices is the manilla envelope stuffed on top.

"What's this?" Elizabeth pulls it out, turning it over to see the name of my attorney stamped on the front. "Is this...You never opened this?"

"Didn't see the need to. I knew what it was."

"Josh," she sighs, slipping her finger underneath the seal to free the flap.

"What? It's not like anything is surprising about a divorce petition. Why would I want to—" My words falter when she pulls out a white envelope stuck inside of the manilla one. "What is *that?*"

Elizabeth stares down at the envelope in her hands, running her fingers over it before looking up at me. Her eyes are wet with unshed tears, and I drop the book in my hands, crossing the room to her. "I wrote this for you and asked my attorney to give it to you...Actually, I asked him to give it to you *before* anything was filed, but I guess he missed that part. When I thought you didn't respond, I told him to go ahead and file."

"What's it say?"

"Read it." She shoves the envelope into my hands with a small smile.

Dear Josh,

I miss you...

I wish I could find a way to fix this, but I don't know how. Whenever I think about calling you or coming home, I am reminded you don't want this.

I wish you could've seen your face when you read that letter. It was like she was standing in the room, and suddenly, I realized I never truly had all of your heart.

I think that hurt the most. I suppose it's my fault, though...

There were a lot of times I still held you at arm's length. I never fully let you in, and the few times I did, I got scared and pushed you away again. Losing my parents. Losing my brother. Feeling like a burden to the Villas, and never being totally accepted into their family...it was all too much.

And I made a promise to myself when Brina brought up the idea of this whole thing that I would never let myself go through that pain again. I wasn't going to let you in. I wasn't going to fall for you. I didn't even want to be friends with you because I didn't want to risk losing you in any way shape or form. Serve my time and enjoy my freedom at the end of my sentence.

But then...you were there.

September 13, 2016, the night before the fourth anniversary of my parents' death. When I woke up, you were there and I didn't have to ask why. I thought you wouldn't show up because of how I left things at home.

It had been what...almost two weeks, I

think? I stopped talking to Brody that night after I left your condo. I never told you that. Talking to him didn't feel right. And I fucking <u>hated</u> that.

I hated that I felt like I couldn't do what I wanted just because of some piece of paper saying we were together.

I was allowed to talk to other people. I was allowed to date other people. But it felt wrong. It felt like even though we weren't in a real relationship, I was cheating on you. And the worst part? When I went back to Nina's that night, I couldn't even tell her the truth. I had to make up some lie about why we got into a fight. I had no one I could talk to.

Then, I woke up, and you were there...

At that moment, I knew I was in trouble. I knew I was going to fall in love with you. I was going to let you in and it was going to shatter my heart.

I fell in love with you on November 1, 2018.

The night I called and begged you to come down to Savannah and decorate with me. You told me I should be studying but got in the car and drove down anyway. You were exhausted after a long day of work but did it anyway. You even called off work the next day. No one but Nina had done anything like that for me before and I got butterflies when you said you'd be there in a few hours...That had never happened before. They danced around my stomach all night until you arrived. Seeing you quelled them and I couldn't resist jumping into your arms when you walked in the door. It felt right in the moment. And the sense of peace you brought me... Even though I was scared to admit it, I knew I was in love with you.

I think I was in love with you before, but that's when I realized it.

A week later, you were back down to pick me up for Thanksgiving break, and you proposed. I still think about that night sometimes. You picked the perfect setting and I don't think you realized it. That night, I gave myself wholly to you and when I woke up the next morning, I was fucking terrified. I had done what I promised myself I'd never do and what scared me most was that I didn't regret it.

Over the years, there was still a part of me that was trying to protect myself from the inevitable. There was always that small voice in the back of my mind telling me you were only there because you _had_ to be. You were just waiting until you could leave without repercussions. I know it was wrong, but that's why I still kept you at a distance. I should've talked to you, told you how I was feeling...

We probably could've avoided all of this mess.

I thought about it, but then that letter showed up...

Juliet Sinclaire — "the one who got away."

Your eyes lit up in a way I hadn't seen in a long time when you saw her name on that paper. And then, when you called to tell me Max wanted you to go on a work trip, I knew what was happening. Even though you said you wouldn't, you went to Wichita. You went to meet her. Your curiosity got the best of you and the final piece of my heart cracked.

It hurt. A lot. Knowing you would run to her like that.

I guess it was my fault, though. We'd

had that fight...One thing led to another, and then I was moving into the guest room. It wasn't supposed to be like that... but you let me go without putting up a real fight. You let me move out. You let me walk away. And then you ran to her like a fly to honey.

That's how I knew it was the end.

I'm sorry, Josh. I'm sorry for not letting my guard down. I'm sorry for not letting you in. I'm sorry for not being honest with you. Because I wish I had been.

I don't want this. I don't want to lose you.

But if you truly want this to be the end of us, I'll be okay. I'll understand because I know this was never what either of us wanted in the first place. We were thrown together by circumstance and we shouldn't expect anything from each other. So, if this is what you want, I'll sign the papers, and you can finally have a chance with Juliet.

I can't promise I'll be happy about it or that I'll want to be around you for a little while, but I'll understand.

You're mine, and I'm yours... until we sign the papers.

Elizabeth Davis

fifty-six

Elizabeth

TWO AND HALF YEARS LATER
April 2028

I'M PREGNANT. SURPRISE! I haven't told Josh. I haven't told anyone because I just found out last night. We've been trying for six months now and have been unsuccessful up until this point. Michaela called two nights ago to tell me *she* is pregnant—nine weeks along—and that's what made me take a test. I hadn't even realized it, but I was almost three weeks late. We've had so much going on—moving into the new house, Brie's spring art show, Pat and Jenny moving down to Jupiter, and cheerleading practices and competitions—I hadn't even thought about it.

I should've known something was going on when I got extra emotional when Brie introduced us to her teacher a week ago. Josh and I walked into the art show at Jupiter Beach High and Brie dragged us across the library to her art teacher. When she made her introductions, she referred to me as her "momma." And standing there in the middle of the school library, tears welled in my eyes. I couldn't stop them as they flowed down my cheeks. I don't consider myself a particularly emotional person, so that should've been my first sign.

Over the past two years, Brie and I have gotten closer, bonding over our love of art and cheerleading, two things she was able to pursue further by returning to school. Brie had been homeschooled after she moved in with Juliet and her husband, Tom Donovan. He had two other kids from a previous marriage who were homeschooled, and they decided Brie should be too. And she hated it. Hated the limited interaction with her friends and the lack of true stimulation you can only get from in-person learning. When Brie moved in with me and Josh, she begged to return to real school for her final two years of high school. She has integrated into the family as if she's always been here. Even Justin stops by now and then—he even joined us for Christmas last year. It took a little time, but he and Josh have finally managed to work through their differences. I wouldn't say they're completely back to normal, but they're getting there.

"Brie!" I scold as she stuffs a bunny cookie in her mouth.

"Wha'? I meth i' up!" She defends herself with her mouth full and laughs at how ridiculous she sounds. She licks some white icing from the side of her hand before taking a large gulp of water. "I messed it up! I couldn't just leave it there."

"If you keep eating them, you're going to have to make even more."

Half of the ten-foot marble island of our new home is littered with undecorated spring-themed sugar cookies—daisies, roses, tulips, bumblebees, butterflies, and bunnies. There's a bake sale happening tomorrow to raise money for the cheerleading squad. Jenny had offered her help, but I declined, telling her Brie and I were more than capable of baking and decorating a few cookies.

Mending things with Jenny has taken some time and a handful of hard conversations. I've made it abundantly clear that I don't appreciate the things she has said to Josh over the years. Not only because it was part of what drove the wedge between us, but also because what kind of mother says those things to her son? It reminded me so much of Brina, and I refused to put up with Brina 2.0. Even though things are better, they're not great. Jenny is still on probation with Josh. He keeps his mom at arm's length and I'm not sure if they'll ever be able to go back to normal—whatever that truly looked like for them. His relationship with Pat, on the other hand, has only gotten better. Now that they've moved down to Jupiter, he and Josh spend most Sundays watching football and grilling burgers.

Don't get me wrong, while Josh's sense of self-worth has gotten better, there are still times he falls back into old habits. Times the imposter syndrome sneaks its way into his mind, making him feel like he doesn't belong. Like he's not worthy of this life we've built. But we're working on it, and I'll continue to remind him that he's worthy of this, of us, every day if I have to. Sometimes, I catch him re-reading the letter I wrote him before the divorce, the one my lawyer never delivered on time. It serves as a quiet reminder that no matter what thoughts run through his head, I'll always choose him.

"I love you," was the first thing Josh said when he finished reading the letter that day in his office. And that's the first thing I say when I catch him reading it now.

The sound of the oven going off reminds me of the current task at hand, and you know what? I'm starting to regret not taking Jenny up on that offer to help with the cookies...Not only are we making them for Brie's contribution, but she told me this morning we're helping her best friend Blake, too.

Blake Evans was another transfer student who started at JBHS a year before Brie, and they became fast friends when Brie tried out for the cheer squad. They reminded me a lot of me and Nina, Blake taking Brie under her wing and showing her the ropes of Jupiter Beach High.

"Is Dad coming back today?" Brie asks, her tongue poking

out of the corner of her mouth as she tries to line the edges of another bunny.

Josh has been gone since last Thursday for Alex's bachelor party. The whole group of guys had gone out to Nick and Nina's house in Haven, Colorado—Alex, Nick, Josh, Finn, Elijah, Jeremy, Kai, Dean, and Alex's friend, Cole. It was sure to be a wild time, especially when Josh told me they were going to have a phone-free weekend. Cole had planned the whole thing, but Alex's one request was no phones. It was sweet when you think about it. He just wanted to spend some uninterrupted time with some of his favorite people. I think that's why none of the significant others fought the idea, but I have a sneaky suspicion that Kai, Nick, and Jeremy have been making secret phone calls to the kids.

"They should be back tomorrow," I say, and when I look up from my bumblebee, she has another cookie in her mouth. "Brooke Parker Sinclaire-Davis, are you eating the cookies again?"

"It was calling to me!" Brie giggles.

I roll my eyes, returning to the next cookie in front of me, a tulip this time. "Shouldn't Blake be here by now?"

"ETA is ten minutes," Brie says, checking her phone.

Blake was bringing more ingredients for another batch of cookies and icing since they both waited until the last minute to decide what they were going to bring to the sale and I didn't have enough ingredients for both of them. And in true Blake fashion, she was running fifteen late—it's a little something we like to call *Blake Time.*

"That girl is slower than molasses in January."

Brie smirks. "Your southern is showing."

I glare at her before tossing a pinch of edible glitter across the island and she does the same. Before we know it, the whole thing is covered in different shades of edible glitter.

"I hope everyone likes their cookies a little sparkly," Brie says, and we both erupt in laughter.

The fun is cut short when my phone rings from the other side of the kitchen. It's probably just Michaela; she had her ten-week doctor's appointment today. I'll call her back later after we finish these damn cookies. It starts ringing again immediately after it ends, and my stomach drops. Something is wrong and Brie's gaze on the phone tells me she's thinking the same.

Picking up my phone, the name on the screen only confirms my fear. The guys aren't supposed to have their phones until tomorrow afternoon when they leave. Josh's name across the screen only lessens my worry a small amount. His call means something is wrong, but at least I know whatever it is…it's not him.

"I thought you guys were phone-free this weekend," I say, trying to maintain a smile, knowing I have an audience.

Brie continues to ice the cookies, but I can tell she's not paying much attention to what she's doing. She's trying to listen in on my conversation without being too obvious, but she's doing a poor job at it. She curses under her breath when she drops a large dollop of orange icing on a yellow bumblebee.

I'm about to tell Josh I have to go when his words catch me off guard. I can barely get the words out to ask him to repeat himself. How is this even possible? They were supposed to stick together. How could they let this happen? I have so many questions, but the only thing I can manage is: "What do you— what do you mean he's *missing?*"

fifty-seven

Unknown

AN OVERWHELMING BLAST OF antiseptic fills my lungs with the first breath I register. Antiseptic, bleach, and the slightest tang of metal. I can almost taste it on my tongue. Fuck, my tongue feels like sandpaper against the roof of my mouth.

Why can't I see anything? No matter how hard I try, my eyes won't open. A door closes in the distance. A few loud dings echo through the air. Muffled voices sound, but I can't make out what they're saying. I force my lids to blink, one, two, three times until finally, the weights fall off, and the lids peel back to reveal a blinding white light.

What the hell?

I try to shield my eyes, but my left arm feels like a ton of bricks. My right is easier to manage. It releases from its binding, and I rub my eyes until they adjust to reveal a... hospital room.

I'm in a hospital.

Why am I in a hospital?

I have to get out of here. I have to—

"Oh!" a shrill voice sends a jolt through my head, and the dull pain that had been sitting in my left temple cracks my skull in two.

The voice belongs to an older woman, a nurse, dressed in blue scrubs with yellow ducks on them. Her blonde hair has been pulled into a tight bun on top of her head, and her eyes are hidden behind round glasses. She's standing in the doorway with bright eyes and a wide smile.

"You're awake! Good, I'll get the doctor. He'll be so glad to hear this."

Great, maybe he can tell me why I'm here.

The nurse returns seconds later with a grey plastic pitcher and a white styrofoam cup filled to the brim with ice.

"I was startin' to think you'd never wake up," she says, pouring water into the cup and opening the bendy straw, stabbing it through the ice. She holds it up to my mouth. "Drink, sweetie, it'll help your throat. You've been out a few days. Guarantee your throat's as raw as sandpaper."

Her name tag dangles from a daisy clip off the pocket of her scrubs—*Janet*, it reads. She radiates the same type of energy you'd expect your grandma to have. There are crows feet in the corners of her eyes and a smile that drags down around the sides of her lips. As she holds the cup to my mouth, I can see a jagged line on the outside of her thumb extending through her wrist to her arm.

"T-thank y-you," I rasp out, barely able to hear myself.

"Take it easy, darlin'. Don't want to strain yourself."

"Good morning, Sunshine!"

My stomach twists in knots when an older man walks into the room. He's dressed professionally, with a white lab coat over his clothes, *Doctor Sanders, M.D.* embroidered on the left side. His stark white hair is perfectly styled with a small swoop over his forehead, a white mustache rests atop his upper lip, and his striking blue eyes pierce right through me. He reminds me of Dick Van Dyke in *Diagnosis: Murder.*

"Glad to see you're still with us. How are we feeling?" Doctor Sanders swoops down with his stethoscope, placing the cool metal against my chest. He moves it around my chest and then my back, and instinctively, I take a few deep breaths. "You sound great," he says, straightening himself and wrapping the listening device around the back of his neck.

I take another sip of water, and the liquid feels great against the rawness of my throat. "W-what happened?"

"Well." Doctor Sanders starts and pulls the stool up next to the bed. He crosses one foot over his knee and leans back against the thin air. "I was kind of hoping you could tell me."

"What do you mean?"

"Ol' Bill Wyatt, his boy, and Mr. Blackwood found you wandering out in the woods 'bout two days or so ago. You were in pretty bad shape, son. Two bruised ribs, a sprained ankle, and a pretty bad hit to the ol' noggin. Looked like you'd been out there a while, you were severely dehydrated and chilled to the bone. Honestly, don't know how you were still up and movin' when they found you."

"I don't—I don't remember anything."

Doctor Sanders shares a look with Janet. I don't like that look. "You remember your name?"

"It's...It's..."

I swear, I know my own fucking name.

How could I forget my name? It's...it's right on the tip of my tongue! Ready to roll off the edge so I can tell him who the fuck I am and go the fuck home. *Home.* Where is home? Why can't I remember *anything?*

My fists ball at my sides, gripping the cream knit blanket covering my legs, grasping for anything. "It's..."

"Take it easy, son," Doctor Sanders says. "It's alright. We'll get this whole thing straightened out."

This time, he doesn't hide the concern etched in his

features—the way his brow creases, his lips pull into a thin line, his eyes expressing a new level of pity—when he looks at the nurse.

"Just give me a few minutes, I'm gonna make a few calls."

Before the door closes behind them, I can hear them talking in hushed tones, trying to figure out what they're going to do. I can't decipher what they're saying, but I know it's not looking good. Having an amnesiac loony toon show up in their town was probably the last thing on their list of wants.

A gaping hole forms in my stomach, slowly sucking me inside of it. How could I forget who I am? What the hell happened to me and why was I wandering in the woods? Was I alone? Of course, I was alone. Sanders would've said if they found someone with me here in…

Wait. Where the hell am I?

He said I was wandering in the woods…that really narrows it down. There are a million different areas in the continental United States where there are woods.

After what feels like hours, the door clicks open again. This time, Doctor Sanders is followed by two other men. One of them is an older man dressed in blue jeans and a button-up with a cowboy hat resting on his head. The other is a police officer. He's a tall, aging, dark-skinned man with thinning gray hair. His white button-up looks freshly pressed, with two patches on either arm and a thin black tie clipped to the middle of his shirt by a gold tie-clip. The patch on his right sleeve reads *Bezer Police Department.* That's when I notice a whiteboard behind his head: *Bezer General.* Janet's name badge says the same thing, and so does Doctor Sanders'.

Bezer.

Where the fuck is Bezer?

"What's your name, son?" the officer asks and takes a step forward.

"I already told the doc, I don't know."

"Just give it another go for me."

I sigh. "It's…"

A million names go through my mind, but not a single one hits home. I rub my eyes, trying to connect the dots, searching for anything that will tell me who I am, but I get nothing.

"Alright, take it easy," the officer says, patting my shoulder. "I'm Officer Sloan. I'm the officer who responded when Bill and Joe found you the other day. Do you remember anything?"

I shake my head.

"I thought you said it wasn't that bad." Officer Sloan hisses toward Sanders.

"I said we couldn't be sure until he woke up," Sanders says, defending himself. "There's no way to tell what the body will do to protect itself. He's obviously been through something, that much was apparent from his injuries."

Officer Sloan sighs, rubbing the crease of his brow before he meets my eyes again.

"Where am I?" I ask.

Finally, the other man steps forward, clearing his throat. "Bezer. Bezer, Colorado."

Colorado? What the hell am I doing in Colorado?

The four of them look down at me, then at each other, a hint of pity etched in their features. They don't know what to do with me. They don't know who I am or what I'm doing here, but neither do I. They said I've been here for two days, but how long was I out in the wilderness before that? Isn't there anyone looking for me? Don't I have a family trying to find me? Or maybe I'm just a drifter—alone in the world with nothing to call my own—with no one to care if I find my way home or not.

"Welcome to the City of Refuge, son."

Thank you!

Did you enjoy *Terms & Conditions*? Please consider leaving a review on Amazon, Goodreads, etc!

Interested in more from Jensen Parker? Scan the code below to sign up for the newsletter

WHAT'S NEXT?

The *Strangers* Series will continue with an amnesia, lost identity romance. And it's up to you to figure out who it is (don't worry you'll get it...eventually).

acknowledgments

This book has been nothing short of a rollercoaster from start to finish. This wasn't even supposed to be a book. Josh and Elizabeth were supposed to live happily ever after post Until Now, but so many of you reached out begging for their story. And as I picked up Strictly Business last year, I found something new in their story—a source of unknown tension that wasn't supposed to exist. The further I got into Michaela's story, the more I understood Josh's severe reaction to his sister's secrets. He was dealing with his own (and not well, might I add).

Terms & Conditions couldn't have come at a better time. This past year has been full of change, love, loss, and self-identity in my own life. Writing this book was therapeutic in a lot of ways, as writing can be in general. Writing has always been one of my biggest forms of therapy, and sometimes I don't think it gets enough credit. But this time…it's getting all of the credit.

If you have found yourself in a similar position, I hope this book was able to help you, even if only a little bit. We've all lost something or dealt with the struggles of feeling unworthy, but we don't always deal with it the way we should. We don't allow ourselves to grieve or go through the emotions, bottling them until they explode and we're left with an even bigger mess. This book is for those of us who like to work through things quietly, but still need a little help now and then…

You are not alone. Remember that.

First, I need to thank the Lord. He blessed me with the gift of stringing 26 letters together to make an over 108k word book, and then do it again and again...

Second, my husband. I know this past year has been a learning curve, but there isn't anyone else in this world I'd want to do it with. I love you to the moon and back.

Third, my mom. Her help with the baby doesn't go unappreciated, even when they FaceTime me one million times when I'm out of the house.

My editor, Sophie. Bless you. Her feedback and attention to detail have helped me develop my craft tenfold and push myself to be a better writer.

My incredible alpha readers, Ashley and Alexandra, they guys helped me so much through this journey, offering suggestions and ideas that would make the experience of this book that much better. They listened to my rants and rambles, helped me pick this thing apart, and gave me thoughtful insight. Get ready because Book Four is a JOURNEY.

There are so many people who have shown support through my writing journey, I can't even begin to name all of you, but I appreciate and love you all.

And finally, to the one I lost last year. I'm proud of you and I wish you nothing but the best. Thank you for so many years of laughter, I'll miss that always. Things might look different now, but I will always love you.

That's all for now. Until we **begin again**...

Jensen

Jensen Parker is a wife, mother, and contemporary romance author. Her hobbies include coffee, wine, travel, and books. A former retail store manager and real estate professional, but her heart has always belonged to writing. She recently moved back to her home state of Indiana with her husband, daughter, and their zoo. When she isn't writing, you'll find her reading, playing with her daughter, cooking new recipes from scratch, or planning a vacation.

For sneak peeks, giveaways, and more... Sign up for Jensen's newsletter! https://www.jensenparker.com/subscribe

Follow her on social media!

Instagram : instagram.com/jensenparkerauthor

Facebook : facebook.com/jparkerauthor

Threads : threads.net/@jensenparkerauthor

Twitter : twitter.com/jensenpauthor

Goodreads : goodreads.com/jensenparkerauthor

Amazon : amazon.com/author/jensenparkerauthor

TikTok : tiktok.com/@jensenparkerauthor

"I urge you to live a life worthy of the calling you have received. Be completely humble and gentle; be patient, bearing with one another in love."

- Ephesians 4:1-2

#MadeforMore

REFERENCES

Merriam-Webster Dictionary, "terms," accessed on January 13, 2025. https://www.merriam-webster.com/dictionary/terms

Merriam-Webster Dictionary, "conditions," accessed on January 13, 2025. https://www.merriam-webster.com/dictionary/conditions

Merriam-Webster Dictionary, "marriage," accessed on January 13, 2025. https://www.merriam-webster.com/dictionary/marriage

Dictionary.com, "marriage," accessed on January 13, 2025. https://www.dictionary.com/browse/marriage